Ford Madox Ford's original name was Ford Madox Hueffer. He was born in 1873 of a family prominent in the artistic world of the day. At nineteen he published his first book, a fairy story; by the time he was twenty-two he had written four novels; and in 1898 he began several years of fruitful collaboration with Joseph Conrad. He went on to edit the *English Review* and to write a cycle of successful historical novels, but it was not until 1915 that he created a truly major work, *The Good Soldier*. After serving on active duty in World War I, he settled in France and later in America. As editor of the *transatlantic review,* he published such writers as Joyce and Hemingway while he himself was producing his masterpiece *Parade's End,* consisting of *Some Do Not . . .* (1924), *No More Parades* (1925), *A Man Could Stand Up—* (1926), and *Last Post* (1928), a tetralogy not to be published in a single edition until after his death. Though he continued to write voluminously, his subsequent work was of markedly inferior quality, with the exception of his autobiographical *It Was the Nightingale.* He spent his last years in obscurity, teaching at Olivet College in Michigan, and it was while on vacation from this post that he died in France in 1939.

PARADE'S END

VOLUME TWO

A Man Could Stand Up—
Last Post

FORD MADOX FORD

With an Afterword by
Arthur Mizener

A SIGNET CLASSIC

Published by
THE NEW AMERICAN LIBRARY

"A MAN COULD STAND UP—" COPYRIGHT 1926 BY ALBERT & CHARLES
BONI, INC.
"LAST POST" COPYRIGHT 1928 BY ALBERT & CHARLES BONI, INC.
AFTERWORD COPYRIGHT © 1964 BY THE NEW AMERICAN LIBRARY OF
WORLD LITERATURE, INC.

Published as a SIGNET CLASSIC
by arrangement with Alfred A. Knopf, Inc.,
who have authorized this softcover edition.
A hardcover edition of the text is available
from Alfred A. Knopf, Inc.

First Printing, November, 1964

SIGNET TRADEMARK REG. U.S. PAT. OFF. AND FOREIGN COUNTRIES
REGISTERED TRADEMARK—MARCA REGISTRADA
HECHO EN CHICAGO, U.S.A.

Signet Classics are published by
The New American Library of World Literature, Inc.
501 Madison Avenue, New York, New York 10022

PRINTED IN THE UNITED STATES OF AMERICA

CONTENTS

A Man Could Stand Up—

PART ONE

I ～

SLOWLY, amidst intolerable noises from, on the one hand, the street and, on the other, from the large and voluminously echoing playground, the depths of the telephone began, for Valentine, to assume an aspect that years ago it had used to have—of being a part of the supernatural paraphernalia of inscrutable Destiny.

The telephone, for some ingeniously torturing reason, was in a corner of the great schoolroom without any protection, and, called imperatively, at a moment of considerable suspense, out of the asphalt playground, where, under her command, ranks of girls had stood electrically only just within the margin of control, Valentine with the receiver at her ear was plunged immediately into incomprehensible news uttered by a voice that she seemed half to remember. Right in the middle of a sentence it hit her:

". . . that he ought presumably to be under control, which you mightn't like!"; after that the noise burst out again and rendered the voice inaudible.

It occurred to her that probably at that minute the whole population of the world needed to be under control; she knew she herself did. But she had no male relative that the verdict could apply to in especial. Her brother? But he was on a mine-sweeper. In dock at the moment. And now . . . safe for good! There was also an aged great-uncle that she had never seen. Dean of somewhere . . . Hereford? Exeter? . . . Somewhere . . . Had she just said *safe?* She was shaken with joy!

She said into the mouthpiece:

"Valentine Wannop speaking. . . . Physical instructress at this school, you know!"

She had to present an appearance of sanity . . . a sane voice at the very least!

The tantalizingly half-remembered voice in the telephone now got in some more incomprehensibilities. It came as if from caverns, and as if with exasperated rapidity it exaggerated its S's with an effect of spitting vehemence.

"His brother's-s-s got pneumonia, so his mistress-s-s even is unavailable to look after . . ."

The voice disappeared; then it emerged again with:

"They're said to be friends now!"

It was drowned then for a long period in a sea of shrill girls' voices from the playground, in an ocean of factory-hooters' ululations, amongst innumerable explosions that trod upon one another's heels. From where on earth did they get explosives, the population of squalid suburban streets amidst which the school lay? For the matter of that, where did they get the spirits to make such an appalling row? Pretty drab people! Inhabiting liver-coloured boxes. Not on the face of it an imperial race.

The sibilating voice in the telephone went on spitting out spitefully that the porter said he had no furniture at all, that he did not appear to recognize the porter. . . . Improbable-sounding pieces of information half extinguished by the external sounds but uttered in a voice that seemed to mean to give pain by what it said.

Nevertheless it was impossible not to take it gaily. The thing, out there, miles and miles away, must have been signed —a few minutes ago. She imagined along an immense line sullen and disgruntled cannon sounding for a last time.

"I haven't," Valentine Wannop shouted into the mouthpiece, "the least idea of what you want or who you are."

She got back a title. . . . Lady someone or other. . . . It might have been Blastus. She imagined that one of the lady governeresses of the school must be wanting to order something in the way of school sports organized to celebrate the auspicious day. A lady governeress or other was always wanting something done by the school to celebrate something. No doubt the head, who was not wanting in a sense of humour—not *absolutely* wanting!—had turned this lady of title on to Valentine Wannop after having listened with patience to her for half an hour. The head had certainly sent out to where in the playground they all had stood

breathless, to tell Valentine Wannop that there was someone
on the telephone that she—Miss Wanostrocht, the said head
—thought that she, Miss Wannop, ought to listen to. . . .
Then: Miss Wanostrocht must have been able to distinguish
what had been said by the now indistinguishable lady of
title. But of course that had been ten minutes ago. . . .
Before the maroons or the sirens, whichever it had been,
had sounded. . . . "The porter said he had no furniture at
all. . . . He did not appear to recognize the porter. . . .
Ought presumably to be under control!" Valentine's mind
thus recapitulated the information that she had from Lady
(provisionally) Blastus. She imagined now that the lady must
be concerned for the superannuated drill-sergeant the school
had had before it had acquired her, Valentine, as physical
instructor. She figured to herself the venerable, mumbling
gentleman, with several ribbons on a black commissionaire's
tunic. In an alms-house, probably. Placed there by the governors of the school. Had pawned his furniture, no doubt. . . .

Intense heat possessed Valentine Wannop. She imagined,
indeed, her eyes flashing. Was this the moment?

She didn't even know whether what they had let off had
been maroons or aircraft-guns or sirens. It had happened—
the noise, whatever it was—whilst she had been coming
through the underground passage from the playground to
the schoolroom to answer this wicked telephone. So she had
not heard the sound. She had missed the sound for which
the ears of a world had waited for years, for a generation.
For an eternity. No sound. When she had left the playground, there had been dead silence. All waiting: girls rubbing one ankle with the other rubber sole. . . .

Then . . . For the rest of her life she was never to be
able to remember the greatest stab of joy that had ever
been known by waiting millions. There would be no one but
she who would not be able to remember that. . . . Probably
a stirring of the heart that was like a stab; probably a catch-
ing of the breath that was like an inhalation of flame! . . .
It was over now; they were by now in a situation, a condition, something that would affect certain things in certain
ways. . . .

She remembered that the putative ex-drill-sergeant had a
brother who had pneumonia and thus an unavailable mistress. . . .

She was about to say to herself:

"That's just my luck!" when she remembered good-
humouredly that her luck was not like that at all. On the

whole she had had good luck—ups and downs. A good deal
of anxiety at one time—but who hadn't had! But good
health, a mother with good health, a brother safe . . . Anxieties, yes! But nothing that had gone so very wrong. . . .

This, then, was an exceptional stroke of bad luck! Might
it be no omen—to the effect that things in future *would* go
wrong: to the effect that she would miss other universal experiences. Never marry, say; or never know the joy of child-
bearing: if it was a joy! Perhaps it was; perhaps it wasn't.
One said one thing, one another. At any rate, might it not
be an omen that she would miss some universal and necessary experience! . . . Never see Carcassonne, the French
said. . . . Perhaps she would never see the Mediterranean.
You could not be a proper man if you had never seen the
Mediterranean: the sea of Tibullus, of the Anthologists, of
Sappho, even. . . . Blue: incredibly blue!

People would be able to travel now. It was incredible!
Incredible! Incredible! But you *could*. Next week you would
be able to! You could call a taxi! And go to Charing Cross!
And have a porter! A whole porter! . . . The wings, the
wings of a dove: then would I flee away, flee away and
eat pomegranates beside an infinite wash-tub of Reckitt's
blue. Incredible, but you *could!*

She felt eighteen again. Cocky! She said, using the good,
metallic, Cockney bottoms of her lungs that she had used
for shouting back at interrupters at suffrage meetings before
. . . before this . . . she shouted blatantly into the telephone:

"I say, whoever you are! I suppose they have *done* it;
did they announce it in your parts by maroons or sirens?"
She repeated it three times; she did not care for Lady Blastus
or Lady Blast Anybody Else. She was going to leave that
old school and eat pomegranates in the shadow of the rock
where Penelope, wife of Ulysses, did her washing. With lashings of blue in the water! Was all your underlinen bluish in
those parts owing to the colour of the sea? She could! She
could! She *could!* Go with her mother and brother and all
to where you could eat . . . oh, new potatoes! In December,
the sea being blue . . . *What songs the Sirens sang and
whether* . . .

She was not going to show respect for any Lady Anything
ever again. She had had to hitherto, independent young
woman of means though she were, so as not to damage the
school and Miss Wanostrocht with the governeresses. Now
. . . She was never going to show respect for anyone ever

again. She had been through the mill: the whole world had been through the mill! No more respect!

As she might have expected, she got it in the neck immediately afterwards—for overcockiness!

The hissing, bitter voice from the telephone enunciated the one address she did not want to hear:

"Lincolnss-s-s . . . sInn!"

Sin! . . . Like the Devil!

It hurt.

The cruel voice said:

"I'm s-s-peaking from there!"

Valentine said courageously:

"Well, it's a great day. I suppose you're bothered by the cheering, like me. I can't hear what you want. I don't care. Let 'em cheer!"

She felt like that. She should not have.

The voice said:

"You remember your Carlyle . . ."

It was exactly what she did not want to hear. With the receiver hard at her ear, she looked round at the great schoolroom—the hall, made to let a thousand girls sit silent while the head made the speeches that were the note of the school. Repressive! . . . The place was like a Nonconformist chapel, high, bare walls with Gothic windows running up to a pitch-pine varnished roof. Repression, the note of the place; the place, the very place not to be in to-day. . . . You *ought* to be in the streets, hitting policemen's helmets with bladders. This was Cockney London: that was how Cockney London expressed itself. Hit policemen innocuously because policemen were stiff, embarrassed at these tributes of affection, swayed in rejoicing mobs over whose heads they looked remotely, like poplar-trees jostled by vulgarer vegetables!

But she was there, being reminded of the dyspepsia of Thomas Carlyle!

"*Oh!*" she exclaimed into the instrument. "You're Edith Ethel!" Edith Ethel Duchemin, now of course Lady Macmaster! But you weren't used to thinking of her as Lady Somebody.

The last person in the world: the very last! Because long ago she had made up her mind that it was all over between herself and Edith Ethel. She certainly could not make any advance to the ennobled personage who vindictively disapproved of all things made—with a black thought in a black shade, as you might say. Of all things that were not being immediately useful to Edith Ethel!

And, aesthetically draped and meagre, she had sets of quotations for appropriate occasions. Rossetti for love; Browning for optimism—not frequent, that; Walter Savage Landor to show acquaintance with more esoteric prose. And the unfailing quotation from Carlyle for damping off Saturnalia, for New Year's Day, Te Deums, victories, anniversaries, celebrations . . . It was coming over the wire now, that quotation:

". . . And then I remembered that it was the birthday of their Redeemer!"

How well Valentine knew it: how often with spiteful conceit had not Edith Ethel intoned that. A passage from the diary of the Sage of Chelsea, who lived near the barracks.

"To-day," the quotation ran, "I saw that the soldiers by the public-house at the corner were more than usually drunk. And then I remembered that it was the birthday of their Redeemer!"

How superior of the Sage of Chelsea not to remember till then that that had been Christmas Day! Edith Ethel, too, was trying to show how superior she was. She wanted to prove that until she, Valentine Wannop, had reminded her, Lady Macmaster, that that day had about it something of the popularly festival, she, Lady Mac, had been unaware of the fact. Really quite unaware, you know. She lived in her rapt seclusion along with Sir Vincent—the critic, you know: their eyes fixed on the higher things, they disregarded maroons and had really a quite remarkable collection by now of first editions, official-titled friends and At Homes to their credit.

Yet Valentine remembered that once she had sat at the feet of the darkly mysterious Edith Ethel Duchemin—where had *that* all gone?—and had sympathized with her marital martyrdoms, her impressive taste in furniture, her large rooms and her spiritual adulteries. So she said good-humouredly to the instrument:

"Aren't you just the same, Edith Ethel? And what can I do for you?"

The good-natured patronage in her tone astonished her, and she was astonished, too, at the ease with which she spoke. Then she realized that the noises had been going away: silence was falling: the cries receded. They were going towards a cumulation at a distance. The girls' voices in the playground no longer existed: the head must have let them go. Naturally, too, the local population wasn't going to go on letting off crackers in side-streets. . . . She was alone: cloistered with the utterly improbable!

Lady Macmaster had sought her out and here was she, Valentine Wannop, patronizing Lady Macmaster! Why? What could Lady Macmaster want her to do? She *couldn't* —but of course she jolly well could!—be thinking of being unfaithful to Macmaster and be wanting her, Valentine Wannop, to play the innocent, the virginal gooseberry or disciple. Or alibi. Whatever it was. Goose was the most appropriate word. . . . Obviously Macmaster was the sort of person to whom any Lady Macmaster would want—would have—to be unfaithful. A little, dark-bearded, drooping, deprecatory fellow. A typical critic! All critics' wives were probably unfaithful to them. They lacked the creative gift. What did you call it? A word unfit for a young lady to use!

Her mind ran about in this unbridled, Cockney schoolgirl's vein. There was no stopping it. It was in honour of the DAY! She was temporarily inhibited from bashing policemen on the head, so she was mentally disrespectful to constituted authority—to Sir Vincent Macmaster, principal secretary to H.M. Department of Statistics, author of "Walter Savage Landor, a Critical Monograph," and of twenty-two other critical monographs in the Eminent Bores' Series. . . . *Such* books! And she was being disrespectful and patronizing to Lady Macmaster, Egeria to innumerable Scottish Men of Letters! No more respect! Was that to be a lasting effect of the cataclysm that had involved the world? The *late* cataclysm! Thank God, since ten minutes ago they could call it the late cataclysm!

She was positively tittering in front of the telephone, from which Lady Macmaster's voice was now coming in earnest, cajoling tones—as if she knew that Valentine was not paying very much attention—saying:

"Valentine! *Val*entine! *Valentine!*"

Valentine said negligently:

"I'm listening!"

She wasn't really. She was really reflecting on whether there had not been more sense in the Mistresses' Conference that that morning, solemnly, had taken place in the head's private room. Undoubtedly what the mistresses with the head at their head had feared was that if they, headmistresses, mistresses, masters, pastors—by whom I was made, et cetera! —should cease to be respected because Saturnalia broke out on the sounding of a maroon, the whole world would go to pieces! An awful thought! The girls no longer sitting silent in the Nonconformist hall while the head addressed repressive speeches to them. . . .

She had addressed a speech containing the phrase "the Credit of a Great Public School" in that hall only last afternoon, in which, fair thin woman, square-elbowed, with a little of sunlight really still in her coiled fair hair, she had seriously requested the girls not again to repeat the manifestations of joy of the day before. The day before, there had been a false alarm and the school—horribly!—had sung:

> "Hang Kaiser Bill from the hoar apple-tree
> And Glory Glory Glory till it's tea-time!"

The head, now, making her speech, was certain that she had now before her a chastened school, a school that anyhow felt foolish because the rumour of the day before had turned out to be a canard. So she impressed on the girls the nature of the joy they ought to feel: a joy repressed that should send them silent home. Blood was to cease to be shed: a fitting cause for home-joy—as it were, a home-lesson. But there was to be no triumph. The very fact that you ceased hostilities precluded triumph. . . .

Valentine, to her surprise, had found herself wondering when you *might* feel triumph? . . . You couldn't whilst you were still contending: you must not when you had won! Then when? The head told the girls that it was their province as the future mothers of England—nay, of reunited Europe!—to—well, in fact, to go on with their home-lessons and not run about the streets with effigies of the Great Defeated! She put it that it was their function to shed further light of womanly culture—that there, Thank Heaven, they had never been allowed to forget!—athwart a reillumined Continent. . . . As if you could light up now there was no fear of submarines or raids!

And Valentine wondered why, for a mutinous moment, she had wanted to feel triumph . . . had wanted *someone* to feel triumph. Well, he . . . they . . . had wanted it so much. Couldn't they have it just for a moment—for the space of one Benkollerdy! Even if it were wrong? Or vulgar? Something human, someone had once said, is dearer than a wilderness of decalogues!

But at the Mistresses' Conference that morning, Valentine had realized that what was really frightening them was the other note. A quite definite fear. If, at this parting of the

ways, at this crack across the table of History, the School—
the World, the future mothers of Europe—got out of hand,
would they ever come back? The Authorities—Authority all
over the world—was afraid of that; more afraid of that
than of any other thing. Wasn't it a possibility that there was
to be no more Respect? None for constituted Authority and
consecrated Experience?

And listening to the fears of those care-worn, faded, ill-
nourished gentlewomen, Valentine Wannop had found herself speculating.

"No more respect . . . For the Equator! For the Metric
System. For Sir Walter Scott! Or George Washington! Or
Abraham Lincoln! Or the Seventh Commandment!!!!!!"

And she had a blushing vision of fair, shy, square-elbowed
Miss Wanostrocht—the head!—succumbing to some specious-
tongued beguiler! . . . That was where the shoe really pinched!
You had to keep them—the girls, the populace, everybody!
—in hand now, for once you let go there was no knowing
where They, like waters parted from the seas, mightn't carry
You. Goodness knew! You might arrive anywhere—at county
families taking to trade, gentlefolk selling for profit! All the
unthinkable sorts of things!

And with a little inward smirk of pleasure Valentine realized that that conference was deciding that the girls were
to be kept in the playground that morning—at Physical
Jerks. She hadn't ever put up with *much* in the way of
patronage from the rather untidy-haired bookish branch of
the establishment. Still, accomplished classicist as she once
had been, she had had to acknowledge that the bookish
branch of a school was what you might call the Senior Service. She was there only to oblige—because her distinguished
father had insisted on paying minute attention to her physique, which was vital and admirable. She had been there,
for some time past, only to oblige—war work and all that—
but still she had always kept her place and had never hitherto
raised her voice at a Mistresses' Conference. So it was
indeed the World Turned Upside Down—already!—when
Miss Wanostrocht hopefully, from behind her desk, decorated
with two pale pink carnations, said:

"The idea is, Miss Wannop, that they should be kept—
that you should keep them, please—as nearly as possible—
isn't it called?—at attention until the—eh—noises . . . announce the . . . well, *you* know. Then we suppose they will
have to give, say, three cheers. And then perhaps you could
get them—in an orderly way—back to their classrooms. . . ."

Valentine felt that she was by no means certain that she
could. It was not really practicable to keep every one of
six hundred aligned girls under your eye. Still, she was ready
to have a shot. She was ready to concede that it might not
be altogether—oh, expedient!—to turn six hundred girls
stark mad with excitement into the streets already filled with
populations that would no doubt be also stark mad with
excitement. You had better keep them in if you could. She
would have a shot. And she was pleased. She felt fit: amazingly fit! Fit to do the quarter in . . . oh, in any time! And
to give a clump on the jaw to any large, troublesome Jewish
type of maiden—or Anglo-Teutonic—who should try to
break ranks. Which was more than the head or any one of
the other worried and underfed ones could do. She was
pleased that they recognized it. Still, she was also generous,
and recognizing that the world ought not really to be turned
upside down, at any rate until the maroons went, she said:

"Of course I will have a shot at it. But it would be a
reinforcement, in the way of keeping order, if the head—
you, Miss Wanostrocht—and one or two others of the mistresses would be strolling about. In relays, of course; not all
of the staff all the morning.. . ."

That had been two and a half hours or so ago: before
the world changed, the conference having taken place at
eight-thirty. Now here she was, after having kept those girls
pretty exhaustingly jumping about for most of the interven-
ing time—here she was treating with disrespect obviously
constituted Authority. For whom *ought* you to respect if
not the wife of the head of a department, with a title, a
country place and most highly attended Thursday afternoons?

She was not really listening to the telephone, because Edith
Ethel was telling her about the condition of Sir Vincent: so
overworked, poor man, over Statistics that a nervous break-
down was imminently to be expected. Worried over money,
too. Those dreadful taxes for this iniquitous affair . . .

Valentine took leisure to wonder why—why in the world!
—Miss Wanostrocht, who must know at the least the burden
of Edith Ethel's story, had sent for her to hear this farrago?
Miss Wanostrocht must know: she had obviously been talked
to by Edith Ethel for long enough to form a judgement. Then
the matter must be of importance. Urgent, even, since the
keeping of discipline in the playground was of such utter
importance to Miss Wanostrocht: a crucial point in the history of the school and the mothers of Europe.

But to whom, then, could Lady Macmaster's communication be of life-and-death importance? To her, Valentine Wannop? It could not be: there were no events of importance that could affect her life outside the playground, her mother safe at home and her brother safe on a mine-sweeper in Pembroke Dock. . . .

Then . . . of importance to Lady Macmaster herself? But how? What could she do for Lady Macmaster? Was she wanted to teach Sir Vincent to perform physical exercises so that he might avoid his nervous break-down and, in excess of physical health, get the mortgage taken off his country place, which she gathered was proving an overwhelming burden on account of iniquitous taxes, the result of a war that ought never to have been waged?

It was absurd to think that she could be wanted for that! An absurd business. . . . There she was, bursting with health, strength, good humour, perfectly *full* of beans—there she was, ready in the cause of order to give Leah Heldenstamm, the large girl, no end of a clump on the side of the jaw or, alternatively, for the sake of all the beanfeastishnesses in the world to assist in the amiable discomfiture of the police. There she was in a sort of Nonconformist cloister. Nunlike! Positively nunlike! At the parting of the ways of the universe!

She whistled slightly to herself.

"By Jove," she exclaimed coolly, "I hope it does not mean an omen that I'm to be—oh, nunlike—for the rest of my career in the reconstructed world!"

She began for a moment seriously to take stock of her position—of her whole position in life. It had certainly been hitherto rather nunlike. She was twenty-threeish: rising twenty-four. As fit as a fiddle; as clean as a whistle. Five foot four in her gym shoes. And no one had ever wanted to marry her. No doubt that was because she was so clean and fit. No one even had ever tried to seduce her. That was *certainly* because she was so clean-run. She didn't obviously offer—what was it the fellow called it?—promise of pneumatic bliss to the gentlemen with sergeant-majors' horseshoe moustaches and gurglish voices! She never would. Then perhaps she would never marry. And never be seduced!

Nunlike! She would have to stand at an attitude of attention beside a telephone all her life, in an empty schoolroom with the world shouting from the playground. Or not even shouting from the playground any more. Gone to Piccadilly!

. . . But, hang it all, she wanted some fun! Now!

For years now she had been—oh, yes, nunlike!—looking

after the lungs and limbs of the girls of the adenoidy, Non-conformistish—really undenominational or so little Established as made no difference!—Great Public Girls' School. She had had to worry about impossible but not repulsive little Cockney creatures' breathing when they had their arms extended. . . . You *mustn't* breathe rhythmically with your movements. No. No. *No!* . . . *Don't* breathe out with the first movement and in with the second! Breathe naturally! Look at me! . . . She breathed perfectly!

Well, for years that! War work for a b——y pro-German. Or pacifist. Yes, that too she had been for years. She hadn't liked being it because it was the attitude of the superior and she did not like being superior. Like Edith Ethel!

But now! Wasn't it manifest? She could put her hand whole-heartedly into the hand of any Tom, Dick or Harry. And wish him luck! Whole-heartedly! Luck for himself and for his enterprise. She came back: into the fold: into the Nation even. She could open her mouth! She could let out the good little Cockney yelps that were her birthright. She could be free, independent!

Even her dear, blessed, muddle-headed, tremendously eminent mother by now had a depressed-looking secretary. She, Valentine Wannop, didn't have to sit up all night typing after all day enjoining perfection of breathing in the playground. . . . By Jove, they could go all, brother, mother in untidy black and mauve, secretary in untidy black without mauve, and she, Valentine, out of her imitation Girl Scout's uniform and in—oh, white muslin or Harris tweeds—and with Cockney yawps discuss the cooking under the stone-pines of Amalfi. By the Mediterranean. . . . No one, then, would be able to say that she had never seen the sea of Penelope, the Mother of the Gracchi, Delia, Lesbia, Nausicaa, Sappho. . . .

"*Saepe te in somnis vidi!*"

She said:

"Good . . . *God!*"

Not in the least with a Cockney intonation but like a good Tory English gentleman confronted by an unspeakable proposition. Well, it was an unspeakable proposition. For the voice from the telephone had been saying to her inattention, rather crawlingly, after no end of details as to the financial position of the house of Macmaster:

"So I thought, my dear Val, in remembrance of old times, that . . . If, in short, I were the means of bringing you together again . . . For I believe you have not been corresponding. . . . You might in return . . . You can see for yourself that at this moment the sum would be absolutely *crushing*. . . ."

2 ~

TEN MINUTES later she was putting to Miss Wanostrocht, firmly if without ferocity, the question:

"Look here, head, what did that woman say to you? I don't like her; I don't approve of her and I didn't really listen to her. But I want to hear!"

Miss Wanostrocht, who had been taking her thin, black cloth coat from its peg behind the highly varnished pitch-pine door of her own private cell, flushed, hung up her garment again and turned from the door. She stood, thin, a little rigid, a little flushed, faded and a little, as it were, at bay.

"You must remember," she began, "that I am a school-mistress." She pressed, with a gesture she constantly had, the noticeably golden plait of her dun-coloured hair with the palm of her thin left hand. None of the gentlewomen of that school had had quite enough to eat—for years now. "It's," she continued, "an instinct to accept any means of knowledge. I like you so much, Valentine—if in private you'll let me call you that. And it seemed to me that if you were in . . ."

"In what?" Valentine asked. "Danger? . . . Trouble?"

"You understand," Miss Wanostrocht replied, "that . . . person seemed as anxious to communicate to me facts about yourself as to give you—that was her ostensible reason for ringing you up—news about a . . . another person. With whom you once had . . . relations. And who has reappeared."

"Ah," Valentine heard herself exclaim. "He has reappeared, has he? I gathered as much." She was glad to be able to keep herself under control to that extent.

Perhaps she did not have to trouble. She could not say that she felt changed from what she had been—just before ten minutes ago—by the reappearance of a man she hoped she had put out of her mind. A man who had "insulted" her. In one way or the other he had insulted her!

But probably all her circumstances had changed. Before Edith Ethel had uttered her impossible sentence in that in-strument, her complete prospects had consisted of no more than the family picnic, under fig-trees, beside an unusually blue sea—and the prospect had seemed as near—as near as kiss your finger! Mother in black and purple; mother's secre-

tary in black without adornments. Brother? Oh, a romantic
figure; slight, muscular, in white flannels with a Leghorn hat
and—well, why *not* be romantic over one's brother—with a
broad scarlet sash. One foot on shore and one . . . in a
light skiff that gently bobbed in the lapping tide. Nice boy;
nice little brother. Lately employed nautically, so up to managing a light skiff. They were going to-morrow . . . but why
not that very afternoon by the 4:20?

> "They'd got the ships, they'd got the men,
> They'd got the money too!"

Thank goodness they'd got the money!

The ships, Charing Cross to Vallambrosa, would no doubt
run in a fortnight. The men—the porters—would also be
released. You can't travel in any comfort with mother, mother's secretary and brother—with your whole world and its
baggage—without lots of porters. . . . Talk about rationed
butter! What was that to trying to get on without porters?

Once having begun it, her mind went on singing the old
eighteen-fiftyish or -seventyish, martial, British, anti-Russian
patriotic song that one of her little friends had unearthed
lately—to prove the historic ferocity of his countrymen:

> "We've fought the Bear before,
> And so we will again!
> The Russians shall not have Constantino . . ."

She exclaimed suddenly: *"Oh!"*

She had been about to say: "Oh, *hell!*" but the sudden
recollection that the war had been over a quarter of an
hour made her leave it at *"Oh!"* You would have to drop
war-time phraseology! You became again a Young Lady.
Peace, too, has its Defence of the Realm Acts. Nevertheless,
she had been thinking of the man who had once insulted her
as the Bear, whom she would have to fight again! But with
warm generosity she said:

"It's a shame to call him the Bear!" Nevertheless he was
—the man who was said to have "reappeared"—with his
problems and all, something devouring. . . . Overwhelming,
with rolling grey shoulders that with their intolerable problems pushed you and your own problems out of the
road. . . .

She had been thinking all that whilst still in the school

hall, before she had gone to see the head: immediately after Edith Ethel, Lady Macmaster, had uttered the *intolerable* sentence.

She had gone on thinking there for a long time. . . . Ten minutes!

She formulated for herself summarily the first item of a period of nasty worries of a time she flattered herself she had nearly forgotten. Years ago Edith Ethel out of a clear sky had accused her of having had a child by that man. But she hardly thought of him as a man. She thought of him as a ponderous, grey, intellectual mass who now, presumably, was mooning, obviously dotty, since he did not recognize the porter, behind the closed shutters of an empty house in Lincoln's Inn. . . . Nothing less, I assure you! She had never been in that house, but she figured him, with cracks of light coming between the shutters, looking back over his shoulder at you in the doorway, grey, super-ursine. . . . Ready to envelope you in suffocating bothers!

She wondered how long it had been since the egregious Edith Ethel had made that assertion . . . with, naturally, every appearance of indignation for the sake of the man's Wife, with whom, equally naturally, Edith Ethel had "sided." (Now she was trying to "bring you together again. . . ." The Wife presumably did not go to Edith Ethel's tea-parties often enough, or was too brilliantly conspicuous when there. Probably the latter!) How many years ago? Two? Not so much! Eighteen months, then? Surely more! . . . Surely, surely more! . . . When you thought of time in those days, your mind wavered impotently like eyes tired by reading too small print. . . . He went out surely in the autumn of . . . No, it had been the first time he went that he went in the autumn. It was her brother's friend, Ted, that went in '16. Or the other . . . Malachi. So many goings-out and returnings: and goings-out and perhaps not returning. Or only in bits: the nose gone . . . or both eyes. Or—or, hell! oh, hell! and she clenched her fists, her nails into her palms—no mind!

You'd think it must be that from what Edith Ethel had said. He hadn't recognized the porter: he was reported to have no furniture. Then . . . She remembered. . . .

She was then—ten minutes before she interviewed Miss Wanostrocht, ten seconds after she had been blown out of the mouth of the telephone—sitting on a varnished pitch-pine bench that had black iron, clamped legs against the plaster wall, Nonconformishistically distempered in torpedo-grey; and she had thought all that in ten seconds. . . . But that had been *really* how it had been!

The minute Edith Ethel had finished saying the words: "The sum would be absolutely *crushing*. . . ." Valentine had realized that she had been talking about a debt owed by her miserable husband to the one human being she, Valentine, could not bear to think about. It had naturally at the same moment flashed upon her that Edith Ethel had been giving her his news: He was in new troubles: broken down, broken up, broke to the wide . . . Anything in the world but broken in . . . But broken . . . And alone. . . . And calling for her!

She could not afford—she could not bear!—to recall even his name or to so much as bring up before her mind, into which, nevertheless, they were continually forcing themselves, his grey-blond face; his clumsy, square, reliable feet; his humpish bulk; his calculatedly wooden expression; his perfectly overwhelming, but authentic, omniscience. . . . His masculinity. His . . . his Frightfulness!

Now, through Edith Ethel—you would have thought that even *he* would have found someone more appropriate—he was calling to her again to enter into the suffocating web of his imbroglios. Not even Edith Ethel would have dared to speak to her again of him without his having taken the first step. . . .

It was unthinkable; it was intolerable; and it had been as if she had been lifted off her feet and deposited on that bench against the wall by the mere sound of the offer. . . . What was the offer?

"I thought that you might, if I were the means of bringing you together . . ." She might . . . what?

Intercede with that man, that grey mass, not to enforce the pecuniary claim that it had against Sir Vincent Macmaster. No doubt she and . . . the grey mass! . . . would then be allowed the Macmaster drawing-room to . . . to discuss the ethics of the day in! Just like that!

She was still breathless; the telephone continued to quack. She wished it would stop, but she felt too weak to get up and hang the receiver on its hook. She wished it would stop; it gave her the feeling that a strand of Edith Ethel's hair, say, was penetrating nauseously to her torpedo-grey cloister. Something like that!

The grey mass never would enforce its pecuniary claim. . . . Those people had sponged mercilessly on him for years and years without ever knowing the kind of object upon which they sponged. It made them the more pitiful. For it *was* pitiful to clamour to be allowed to become a pimp in order to evade debts that would never be reclaimed. . . .

Now, in the empty rooms at Lincoln's Inn—for that was probably what it came to!—that man was a grey ball of mist; a grey bear rolling tenebrously about an empty room with closed shutters. A grey problem! Calling to *her!*

A hell of a lot—beg pardon, she meant a remarkably great deal!—to have thought of in ten seconds! Eleven by now, probably. Later she realized that that was what thought was. In ten minutes, after large, impassive arms had carried you away from a telephone and deposited you on a clamped bench against a wall of the peculiar coldness of torpedo-grey distempered plaster, the sort of thing rejoiced in by Great Public (Girls') Schools . . . in those ten minutes you found you thought out more than in two years. Or it was not as long ago as that.

Perhaps that was not astonishing. If you had not thought about, say, washable distemper for two years and then thought about it for ten minutes, you could think a hell of a lot about it in those ten minutes. Probably all there was to think. Still, of course, washable distemper was not like the poor—always with you. At least it always was in those cloisters, but not spiritually. On the other hand, you always *were* with yourself!

But perhaps you were not always with yourself spiritually; you went on explaining how to breathe without thinking of how the life you were leading was influencing your . . . what? Immortal soul? Aura? Personality? . . . Something!

Well, for two years. . . . oh, *call* it two years, for goodness' sake, and get it over! . . . she must have been in . . . well, call *that* a "state of suspended animation" and get that over too! A sort of what they called inhibition. She had been inhibiting—*pro*hibiting—herself from thinking about herself. Well, hadn't she been right? What had a b——y pro-German to think about in an embattled, engrossed, clamouring nation: especially when she had not much liked her brother-pros! A solitary state, only to be dissolved by . . . maroons! In suspension!

But . . . Be conscientious with yourself, my good girl! *When that telephone blew you out of its mouth you knew really that for two years you had been avoiding wondering whether you had not been insulted!* Avoiding wondering that. And nothing else! No other qualified thing!

She had, of course, been, not in suspension, but in suspense.

Because, if he made a sign—"I understand," Edith Ethel had said, "that you have not been in correspondence" . . . or had it been "in communication" that she had said? . . . Well, they hadn't been either. . . .

Anyhow, if that grey Problem, that ravelled ball of grey knitting-worsted, had made a sign, she would have known that she had not been insulted. Or was there any sense in that?

Was it really true that if a male and female of the same species were alone in a room together and the male didn't . . . then it was an insult? That was an idea that did not exist in a girl's head without someone to put it there, but once it had been put there it became a luminous veracity! It had been put into her, Valentine Wannop's, head, naturally by Edith Ethel, who equally naturally said that she did not believe it, but that it was a tenet of . . . oh, the man's wife! Of the idle, surpassing-the-Lily-and-Solomon-too, surprisingly svelte, tall, clean-run creature who forever on the shiny paper of illustrated journals advanced towards you with improbable strides along the railings of the Row, laughing, in company with the Honourable Somebody, second son of Lord Someone-or-other. . . . Edith Ethel was more refined. She had a title, whereas the other hadn't, but she was pensive. She showed you that she had read Walter Savage Landor, and had only very lately given up wearing opaque amber beads, as affected by the later Pre-Raphaelites. She was practically never in the illustrated papers, but she held more refined views. She held that there were some men who were not like that—and those, all of them, were the men to whom Edith Ethel accorded the *entrée* to her Afternoons. She was their Egeria! A refining influence!

The Husband of the Wife then? Once he had been allowed in Edith Ethel's drawing-room: now he wasn't! . . . Must have deteriorated!

She said to herself sharply, in her "No nonsense, there" mood:

"Chuck it. You're in love with a married man who's a Society wife, and you're upset because the Titled Lady has put into your head the idea that you might 'come together again.' After ten years!"

But immediately she protested:

"No. NO. No! It isn't that. It's all right, the habit of putting things incisively, but it's misleading to put things too crudely."

What was the coming together that was offered her? Nothing, on the face of it, but being dragged again into that man's intolerable worries as unfortunate machinists are dragged into wheels by belts—and all the flesh torn off their bones! Upon her word, that had been her first thought. She was afraid, afraid, afraid! She suddenly appreciated the advantages of nunlike seclusion. Besides, she wanted to be bashing policemen with bladders in celebration of Eleven Eleven!

That fellow—he had no furniture; he did not appear to recognize the hall porter. . . . Dotty. Dotty and too morally deteriorated to be admitted to drawing-room of titled lady, the frequenters of which could be trusted not to make love to you on insufficient provocation if left alone with you. . . .

Her generous mind reacted painfully.

"Oh, that's not *fair!*" she said.

There were all sorts of sides to the unfairness. Before this war, and, of course, before he had lent all his money to Vincent Macmaster, that—that grey grizzly had been perfectly fit for the country-parsonage drawing-room of Edith Ethel Duchemin: he had been welcomed there with effusion. . . . After the war and when his money was—presumably exhausted, and his mind exhausted, for he had no furniture and did not know the porter . . . After the war, then, and when his money was exhausted, he was not fit for the Salon of Lady Macmaster—the only Lady to have a Salon in London.

It was what you called kicking down your ladder!

Obviously it had to be done. There were such a lot of these bothering war heroes that if you let them all into your Salon it would cease to be a Salon, particularly if you were under obligations to them! . . . That was already a pressing national problem: it was going to become an overwhelming one now—in twenty minutes' time, after those maroons. The impoverished war heroes would all be coming back. Innumerable. You would have to tell your parlour-maid that you weren't at home to . . . about seven million!

But wait a minute. . . . Where did they just stand?

He . . . But she could not go on calling him just HE like a schoolgirl of eighteen, thinking of her favourite actor. . . in the purity of her young thoughts. What was she to call him? She had never—even when they had known each other —called him anything other than Mr. So and So. . . . She could not bring herself to let her mental lips frame his name. . . . She had never used anything but his surname to this grey thing, familiar object of her mother's study, seen frequently at tea-parties. . . . Once she had been out with it for a whole night in a dog-cart! Think of that! . . . And

they had spouted Tibullus one to another in moonlit mist.
And she had certainly wanted it to kiss her—in the moonlit
mists a practically, a really completely, strange bear!

It couldn't be done, of course, but she remembered still
how she had shivered. . . . Ph . . . Ph . . . Ph. . . Shivering.
She shivered.

Afterwards they had been run into by the car of General
Lord Edward Campion, V.C., P.G. Heaven knows what!
Godfather of the man's Society wife, then taking the waters
in Germany. . . . Or perhaps not *her* godfather. The man's
rather; but her especial champion, in shining armour. In
these days they had worn broad red stripes down the out-
sides of their trousers, generals. What a change! *How* significant of the times!

That had been in 1912. . . . Say the first of July; she
could not remember exactly. Summer weather, anyhow, before haymaking or just about. The grass had been long in
Hoggs's Forty Acre when they had walked through it discuss-
ing Woman's Suffrage. She had brushed the seed-tops of the
heavy grass with her hands as they walked. . . . Say the
1/7/12.

Now it was Eleven Eleven. . . What? Oh, Eighteen, of
course!

Six years ago! What changes in the world! What cataclysms!
What revolutions! . . . She heard all the newspapers, all the
halfpenny paper journalists in creation crying in chorus!

But hang it: it was true! If, six years ago, she had kissed
the . . . the greyish lacuna of her mind, then sitting beside
her on the dog-cart seat, it would have been the larkish freak
of a schoolgirl: if she did it to-day—as per invitation presumably of Lady Macmaster, bringing them together, for,
of course, it could not be performed from a distance or
without correspondence— No, communication! . . . If, then,
she did it to-day . . . to-day . . . to-day—the Eleven Eleven!—
Oh, what a day to-day would be. . . . Not her sentiments,
those; quotation from Christina, sister of Lady Macmaster's
favourite poet. . . . Or, perhaps, since she had had a title
she would have found poets more . . . more chic! The poet
who was killed at Gallipoli . . . Gerald Osborne, was it?
Couldn't remember the name!

But for six years, then, she had been a member of that
. . . triangle. You couldn't call it a *ménage à trois*, even
if you didn't know French. They hadn't lived together! . . .
They had d——d near died together when the general's car
hit their dog-cart! D——d near! (You *must* not use those

war-time idioms. *Do* break yourself of it! Remember the maroons!)

An oafish thing to do! To take a schoolgirl, just . . . oh, just past the age of consent, out all night in a dog-cart and then get yourself run into by the car of the V.C., P.G., champion-in-red-trouser-stripe of your legitimate! You'd think any man who *was* a man would have avoided that!

Most men knew enough to know that the Woman Pays . . . the schoolgirl too!

But they get it both ways. . . . Look here: when Edith Ethel Duchemin, then, just—or perhaps not quite—Lady Macmaster! At any rate, her husband was dead and she had just married that miserable little . . . (Mustn't use that word!) She, Valentine Wannop, had been the only witness of the marriage—as of the previous, discreet, but so praiseworthy adultery! . . . When, then, Edith Ethel had . . . It must have been on the very day of the knighthood, because Edith Ethel made it an excuse not to ask her to the resultant party. . . . Edith Ethel had accused her of having had a baby by . . . oh, Mr. So and So. . . . And heaven was her, Valentine Wannop's, witness that although Mr. So and So was her mother's constant adviser, she, Valentine Wannop, was still in such a state of acquaintance with him that she still called him by his surname. . . . When Lady Macmaster, spitting like the South American beast of burden called a llama, had accused her of having had a baby by her mother's adviser —to her natural astonishment, but, of course, it had been the result of the dog-cart and the motor and the general, and the general's sister, Lady Pauline Something—or perhaps it was Claudine? Yes, Lady Claudine!—who had been in the car, and the Society wife, who was always striding along the railings of the Row . . . When she had been so accused out of the blue, her first thought—and, confound it, her enduring thought!—had not been concern for her own reputation but for *his*. . . .

That was the *quality* of his entanglements, their very essence. He got into appalling messes, unending and unravellable—no, she meant un-unravellable!—messes, and other people suffered for him whilst he mooned on—into more messes! The general charging the dog-cart was symbolical of him. He was perfectly on his right side and all, but it was like him to be in a dog-cart when flagitious automobiles carrying generals were running amuck! Then . . . the Woman Paid! . . . She really did, in this case. It had been her mother's horse they had been driving, and although they had got

damages out of the general, the costs were twice that. . . .
And her, Valentine's, reputation had suffered from being in
a dog-cart at dawn, alone with a man. . . . It made no odds
that he had—or was it hadn't?—"insulted" her in any way
all through that—oh, that delicious, delirious night. . . . She
had to be said to have a baby by him, and then she had
to be dreadfully worried about *his* poor old reputation. . . .
Of course it *would* have been pretty rotten of him—she so
young and innocent, daughter of so preposterously eminent,
if so impoverished, a man, his father's best friend and all.
"He hadn't oughter'er done it!" He hadn't really oughter. . . .
She heard them all saying it, still!

Well, he hadn't! . . . But she?

That magic night. It was just before dawn, the mists nearly up to their necks as they drove, the sky going pale in a
sort of twilight. And one immense star! She remembered
only one immense star, though, historically, there had been
also a dilapidated sort of moon. But the star was *her* best
boy—what her waggon was hitched on to. . . . And they had
been quoting—quarrelling over, she remembered—

> "Flebis et arsuro me, Delia, lecto
>   Tristibus et . . ."

She exclaimed suddenly:

> "Twilight and evening star
>   And one clear call for me
> And may there be no moaning at the bar
>   When I . . ."

She said:

"Oh, but you *oughtn't* to, my dear! That's *Tennyson!*"
Tennyson, with a difference!

She said:

"All the same, that would have been an inexperienced
schoolgirl's prank. . . . But if I let him kiss me now, I should
be . . ." She would be a, what was it . . . a fornicatress?
. . . *trix!* Fornicatrix is preferable! Very preferable. Then
why not adultrix? You couldn't: you had to be a "cold-
blooded adultress!" or morality was not avenged.

Oh, but surely not cold-blooded! . . . Deliberate, then! . . .
That wasn't, either, the word for the process. Of osculation!
. . . Comic things, words, as applied to states of feelings!
But if she went now to Lincoln's Inn and the Problem

held out its arms . . . That would be "deliberate." It would
be asking for it in the fullest sense of the term.

She said to herself quickly:

"This way madness lies!" And then:

"What an imbecile thing to say!"

She had had an Affair with a man, she made her mind
say to her, two years ago. That was all right. There could
not be a, say, a schoolmistress rising twenty-four or twenty-
five in the world who hadn't had *some* affair, even if it
were no more than a gentleman in a tea-shop who every
afternoon for a week had gazed at her disrespectfully over a
slice of plum-cake. . . . And then disappeared. . . . But you
had to have had at least a might-have-been or you couldn't
go on being a schoolmistress or a girl in a ministry or a
dactylographer of respectability. You packed *that* away in the
bottom of your mind, and on Sunday mornings before the
perfectly insufficient Sunday dinner, you took it out and built
castles in Spain in which you were a castanetted heroine
turning on wonderful hips, but casting behind you inflam-
ing glances. . . . Something like that!

Well, she had had an affair with this honest, simple creature! So good! So unspeakably GOOD. . . . Like the late
Albert, prince consort! The very helpless, immobile sort of
creature that she ought not to have tempted. It had been like
shooting tame pigeons! Because he had had a Society wife
always in the illustrated papers whilst he sat at home and
evolved Statistics or came to tea with her dear, tremendous,
distracted mother, whom he helped to get her articles accurate. So a woman tempted him and he did . . . No; he didn't
quite eat!

But why? . . . Because he was GOOD?

Very likely!

Or was it—that was the intolerable thought that she shut
up within her along with the material for castles in the air!
—was it because he had been really indifferent?

They had revolved round each other at tea-parties—or
rather he had revolved around her, because at Edith Ethel's
affairs she always sat, a fixed starlet, behind the tea-urn and
dispensed cups. But he would moon round the room, looking at the backs of books, occasionally laying down the law
to some guest, and always drifting in the end to her side,
where he would say a trifle or two. . . . And the beautiful
—the quite excruciatingly beautiful—wife striding along the
Row with the second son of the Earl of Someone at her
side. . . . Asking for it. . . .

So it had been from the 1/7/12, say, to the 4/8/14!

After that things had become more rubbled—mixed up with alarums. Excursions on his part to unapproved places. And trouble. He was quite damnably in trouble. With his Superiors; with, so unnecessarily, Hun projectiles, wire, mud; over money, politics; mooning on without a good word from anyone. . . . Unravellable muddles that never got unravelled but that somehow got you caught up in them. . . .

Because he needed her moral support! When, during the late Hostilities, he hadn't been out there, he had drifted to the tea-table much earlier of an afternoon and stayed beside it much longer: till after everyone else had gone and they could go and sit on the tall fender, side by side, and argue. . . about the rights and wrongs of the war!

Because she was the only soul in the world with whom he could talk. . . . They had the same sort of good, bread-and-butter brains; without much of the romantic. . . . No doubt a touch . . . in him. Otherwise he would not have always been in these muddles. He gave all he possessed to anyone who asked for it. That was all right. But that those who sponged on him should also involve him in intolerable messes. . . . That was not proper. One ought to defend oneself against that!

Because . . . if you do not defend yourself against that, look how you let in your nearest and dearest—those who have to sympathize with you in your confounded troubles whilst you moon on, giving away more and more and getting into more troubles! In this case it was she who was his Nearest and Dearest. . . . Or had been!

At that her nerves suddenly got the better of her and her mind went mad. . . . Supposing that that fellow, from whom she had not heard for two years, *hadn't* now communicated with her. . . . Like an ass, she had taken it for granted that he had *asked* Lady . . . Blast her! . . . to "bring them together again"! She had imagined that even Edith Ethel would not have had the cheek to ring her up if he hadn't asked her to!

But she had nothing to go on. . . . Feeble, oversexed ass that she was, she had let her mind jump at once to the conclusion, the moment the mere mention of him seemed implied—jump to the conclusion that he was asking her again to come and be his mistress. . . . Or nurse him through his present muddle till he should be fit to. . . .

Mind, she did not say that she would have succumbed. But if she had not jumped at the idea that it was he, really, speaking through Edith Ethel, she would never have permitted her mind to dwell on . . . on his blasted, complacent perfections!

Because she had taken it for granted that if he had had her rung up, he would not have been monkeying with other girls during the two years he hadn't written to her. . . . Ah, but hadn't he?

Look here! *Was* it reasonable? Here was a fellow who had all but . . . all BUT . . . "taken advantage of her" one night just before going out to France, say, two years ago. . . . And not another word from him after that! . . . It was all very well to say that he was portentous, looming, luminous, loony: John Peel with his coat so grey, the English Country Gentleman *pur sang* and then some; saintly; Godlike, Jesus Christ-like. . . . He was all that. But you don't seduce, as near as can be, a young woman and then go off to Hell, leaving her, God knows, in Hell, and not so much as send her, in two years, a picture postcard with MIZPAH on it. You don't. You don't!

Or if you do, you have to have your character revised. You have to have it taken for granted that you were only monkeying with her and that you've been monkeying ever since with Waacs in Rouen or some other base. . . .

Of course, if you ring your young woman up when you come back . . . or have her rung up by a titled lady . . . That might restore you in the eyes of the world, or at least in the eyes of the young woman if she was a bit of a softie. . . .

But *had* he? *Had* he? It was absurd to think that Edith Ethel hadn't had the face to do it unasked! To save three thousand, two hundred pounds, not to mention interest— which was what Vincent owed *him!*—Edith Ethel with the sweetest possible smile would beg the pillows off a whole hospital ward full of dying. . . . She was quite right. She had to save her man. You go to any depths of ignominy to save your man.

But that did not help her, Valentine Wannop!

She sprang off the bench; she clenched her nails into her palms; she stamped her thin-soled shoes into the coke-brise floor that was singularly unresilient. She exclaimed:

"Damn it all, he didn't ask her to ring me up. He didn't ask her to. He didn't ask her to!" still stamping about.

She marched straight at the telephone, that was by now uttering long, tinny, nightjar's calls and, with one snap,

pulled the receiver right off the twisted, green-blue cord.
. . . Broke it! With incidental satisfaction.

Then she said:

"Steady the Buffs!" not out of repentance for having damaged School Property, but because she was accustomed to
call her thoughts the Buffs because of their practical, un-
romantic charater as a rule. . . . A fine regiment, the Buffs!

Of course, if she had not broken the telephone she could
have rung up Edith Ethel and have asked her whether he
had or hadn't asked to . . . to be brought together again. . . .
It was like her, Valentine Wannop, to smash the only means
of resolving a torturing doubt. . . .

It wasn't, really, in the least like her. *She* was practical
enough: none of the "under-the-ban-of-fatality" business about
her. She had smashed the telephone because it had been like
smashing a connexion with Edith Ethel, or because she hated
tinny nightjars, or because she had smashed it. For nothing
in the world, for nothing, nothing, nothing in the world would
she ever ring up Edith Ethel and ask her:

"Did *he* put you up to ringing me up?"

That would be to let Edith Ethel come between their
intimacy.

A subconscious volition was directing her feet towards
the great doors at the end of the hall, varnished, pitch-pine
doors of Gothic architecture, economically decorated as if
with straps and tin-lids of Brunswick-blacked cast iron.

She said:

"Of course, if it's his wife who has removed his furniture,
that would be a reason for his wanting to get into communication. They would have split. . . . But he does not hold
with a man divorcing a woman, and she won't divorce."

As she went through the sticky postern—all that wood-
work seemed sticky on account of its varnish!—beside the
great doors, she said:

"Who cares!"

The great thing was . . . but she could not formulate
what the great thing was. You had to settle the preliminaries.

3 ~

SHE SAID eventually to Miss Wanostrocht, who had sat down
at her table behind two pink carnations:

"I didn't consciously want to bother you, but a spirit in

my feet has led me who knows how . . . That's Shelley,
isn't it?"

And indeed a quite unconscious but shrewd mind had
pointed out to her whilst still in the school hall, and even
before she had broken the telephone, that Miss Wanostrocht
very probably would be able to tell her what she wanted to
know and that if she didn't hurry she might miss her, since
the head would probably go now the girls were gone. So she
had hurried through gauntish corridors whose Decorated
Gothic windows positively had bits of pink glass here and
there interspersed in their lattices. Nevertheless a nearly de-
serted, darkish, locker-lined dressing-room being a short cut,
she had paused in it before the figure of a clumsyish girl,
freckled, in black and, on a stool, desultorily lacing a dull
black boot, an ankle on her knee. She felt an impulse to say:
"Good-bye, Pettigul!" She didn't know why.

The clumsy, fifteenish, bumpy-faced girl was a symbol of
that place—healthyish, but not overhealthy; honestish but
with no craving for intellectual honesty; big-boned in unexpected places . . . and uncomelily blubbering, so that her
face appeared dirtyish. . . . It was, in fact, all "ishes" about
that institution. They were all healthyish, honestish, clumsyish,
twelve-to-eighteenish and big-boned in unexpected places
because of the late insufficient feeding. . . . Emotionalish, too;
apt to blubber rather than to go into hysterics.

Instead of saying good-bye to the girl she said:

"Here!" and roughly, since she was exhibiting too much
leg, pulled down the girl's shortish skirt and set to work to
lace the unyielding boot on the unyielding shin-bone. . . .
After a period of youthful bloom, which would certainly
come and as certainly go, this girl would, normally, find
herself one of the mothers of Europe, marriage being due to
the period of youthful bloom. . . . Normally, that is to say,
according to a normality that that day might restore. Of
course, it mightn't!

A tepid drop of moisture fell on Valentine's right knuckle.

"My cousin Bob was killed the day before yesterday," the
girl's voice said above her head. Valentine bent her head
still lower over the boot with the patience that, in educational
establishments, you must, if you want to be business-like
and shrewd, acquire and display in face of unusual mental
vagaries. . . . This girl had never had a cousin Bob, or
anything else. Pettigul and her two sisters, Pettiguls Two
and Three, were all in that institution at extremely reduced
rates precisely because they had not got, apart from their

widowed mother, a discoverable relative. The father, a half-pay major, had been killed early in the war. All the mistresses had had to hand in reports on the moral qualities of the Pettiguls, so all the mistresses had this information.

"He gave me his puppy to keep for him before he went out," the girl said. "It doesn't seem just!"

Valentine, straightening herself, said:

"I should wash my face, if I were you, before I went out. Or you might get yourself taken for a German!" She pulled the girl's clumsyish blouse straight on her shoulders.

"Try," she added, "to imagine that you've got someone just come back! It's just as easy and it will make you look more attractive!"

Scurrying along the corridors, she said to herself:

"Heaven help me, does it make *me* look more attractive?"

She caught the head, as she had anticipated, just on the point of going to her home in Fulham, an unattractive suburb but near a bishop's palace nevertheless. It seemed somehow appropriate. The lady was episcopally minded but experienced in the vicissitudes of suburban children: very astonishing, some of them, unless you took them very much in the lump.

Miss Head had stood behind her table for the first three questions and answers, in an attitude of someone who is a little at bay, but she had sat down just before Valentine had quoted her Shelley at her, and she had now the air of one who is ready to make a night of it. Valentine continued to stand.

"This," Miss Wanostrocht said very gently, "is a day on which one might . . . take steps . . . that might influence one's whole life."

"That's," Valentine answered, "exactly why I've come to you. I want to know what that woman said to you so as to know where I stand before I take a step."

The head said:

"I had to let the girls go. I don't mind saying that you are very valuable to me. The governors—I had an express from Lord Boulnois—ordered them to be given a holiday to-morrow. It's very inconsistent. But that makes it all the . . ."

She stopped. Valentine said to herself:

"By Jove, I don't know anything about men; but how little I know about women. What's she getting at?"

She added:

"She's nervous. She must be wanting to say something she thinks I won't like!"

She said chivalrously:

"I don't believe anybody could have kept those girls in to-day. It's a thing one has no experience of. There's never been a day like this before."

Out there in Piccadilly there would be seething mobs shoulder to shoulder: she had never seen the Nelson column stand out of a solid mass. They might roast oxen whole in the Strand: Whitechapel would be seething, enamelled-iron advertisements looking down on millions of bowler hats. All sordid and immense London stretched out under her gaze. She felt herself *of* London as the grouse feels itself of the heather, and there she was in an emptied suburb looking at two pink carnations. Dyed, probably: offering of Lord Boulnois to Miss Wanostrocht! You never saw a natural-grown carnation that shade!

She said:

"I'd be glad to know what that woman—Lady Macmaster —told you."

Miss Wanostrocht looked down at her hands. She had the little-fingers hooked together, the hands back to back; it was a demoded gesture. . . . Girton of 1897, Valentine thought. Indulged in by the thoughtfully blond. . . . Fair girl graduates, the sympathetic comic papers of those days had called them. It pointed to a long sitting. Well, she, Valentine, was not going to brusque the issue! . . . French-derived expression, that. But how would you put it otherwise?

Miss Wanostrocht said:

"I sat at the feet of your father!"

"You see!" Valentine said to herself. "But she must, then, have gone to Oxford, not Newnham!" She could not remember whether there had been women's colleges at Oxford as early as 1895 or 1897. There must have been.

"The greatest teacher . . . The greatest influence in the world," Miss Wanostrocht said.

It was queer, Valentine thought: This woman had known all about her—at any rate all about her distinguished descent—all the time she, Valentine, had been physical instructress at that Great Public School (Girls'). Yet, except for an invariable courtesy such as she imagined generals might show to non-commissioned officers, Miss Wanostrocht had hitherto taken no more notice of her than she might have taken of a superior parlour-maid. On the other hand, she had let Valentine arrange her physical training exactly as she liked: without any interference.

"We used to hear," Miss Wanostrocht said, "how he spoke Latin with you and your brother from the day of your births. . . . He used to be regarded as eccentric, but how *right!* . . . Miss Hall says that you are the most remarkable Latinist she has ever so much as imagined."

"It's not true," Valentine said, "I can't *think* in Latin. You cannot be a real Latinist unless you do that. He did, of course."

"It was the last thing you would think of him as doing," the head answered with a pale gleam of youth. "He was such a thorough man of the world. So awake!"

"We ought to be a queer lot, my brother and I," Valentine said. "With such a father . . . and mother of course!"

Miss Wanostrocht said:

"Oh . . . your *mother* . . ."

And immediately Valentine conjured up the little, adoring female clique of Miss Wanostrocht's youth, all spying on her father and mother in their walks under the Oxford Sunday trees, the father so jaunty and awake, the mother so trailing, large, generous, unobservant. And all the little clique saying: "If only he had *us* to look after him. . . ." She said with a little malice:

"You don't read my mother's novels, I suppose. . . . It was she who did all my father's writing for him. He couldn't write; he was too impatient!"

Miss Wanostrocht exclaimed:

"Oh, you *shouldn't* say that!" with almost the pain of someone defending her own personal reputation.

"I don't see why I shouldn't," Valentine said. "He was the first person to say it about himself."

"He shouldn't have said it either," Miss Wanostrocht answered with a sort of soft unction. "He should have taken care more of his own reputation for the sake of his Work!"

Valentine considered this thin, ecstatic spinster with ironic curiosity.

"Of course, if you've sat . . . if you're still sitting at father's feet as much as all that," she conceded, "it gives you a certain right to be careful about his reputation. . . . All the same, I wish you would tell me what that person said on the phone!"

The bust of Miss Wanostrocht moved with a sudden eagerness further towards the edge of her table.

"It's precisely because of that," she said, "that I want to speak to you first . . . that I want you to consider . . ."

Valentine said:

"Because of my father's reputation. . . . Look here, did that person—Lady Macmaster!—speak to you as if you were me? Our names are near enough to make it possible."

"You're," Miss Wanostrocht said, "as one might say, the fine fruit of the product of his views on the education of women. And if you . . . It's been such a satisfaction to me to observe in you such a . . . a sound, instructed head on such a . . . oh, you know, sane body. . . . And then . . . An earning capacity. A commercial value. Your father, of course, never minced words. . . ." She added:

"I'm bound to say that my interview with Lady Macmaster . . . who surely isn't a lady of whom you could say that you disapprove. I've read her husband's work. It surely— you'd say, wouldn't you?—conserves some of the ancient fire."

"He," Valentine said, "hasn't a word of Latin to his tail. He makes his quotations out, if he uses them, by means of school-cribs. . . . I know his methods of work, you know."

It occurred to Valentine to think that if Edith Ethel really *had* at first taken Miss Wanostrocht for herself, there might pretty obviously be some cause for Miss Wanostrocht's concern for her father's reputation as an intimate trainer of young women. She figured Edith Ethel suddenly bursting into a description of the circumstances of that man who was without furniture and did not appear to recognize the porter. The relations she might have described as having existed between her and him might well worry the head of a Great Public School for Middle Class Girls. She had no doubt been described as having had a baby. A disagreeable and outraged current invaded her feelings. . . .

It was suddenly obscured by a recrudescence of the thought that had come to her only incidentally in the hall. It rushed over her with extraordinary vividness now, like a wave of warm liquid. . . . If it *had* really been that fellow's wife who had removed his furniture, what *was* there to keep them apart? He couldn't have pawned or sold or burnt his furniture whilst he had been with the British Expeditionary Force in the Low Countries! He couldn't have without extraordinary difficulty! Then . . . What *should* keep them apart? . . . Middle Class Morality? A pretty gory carnival that had been for the last four years! Was this, then, Lent, pressing hard on the heels of Saturnalia? Not so hard as that, surely! So that if one hurried . . . What on earth did she want, unknown to herself?

She heard herself saying, almost with a sob, so that she was evidently in a state of emotion:

"Look here: I disapprove of this whole thing: of what my father has brought me to! Those people . . . The brilliant Victorians talked all the time through their hats. They evolved a theory from anywhere and then went brilliantly mad over it. Perfectly recklessly. . . . Have you noticed Pettigul One? . . . Hasn't it occurred to you that you *can't* carry on violent physical jerks and mental work side by side? I ought not to be in this school and I ought not to be what I am!"

At Miss Wanostrocht's perturbed expression, she said to herself:

"What on earth am I saying all this for? You'd think I was trying to cut loose from this school! Am I?"

Nevertheless her voice was going on:

"There's too much oxygenation of the lungs here. It's unnatural. It affects the brain, deleteriously. Pettigul One is an example of it. She's earnest with me and earnest with her books. Now she's gone dotty. Most of them it only stupefies."

It was incredible to her that the mere imagination that that fellow's wife had left him should make her spout out like this—for all the world like her father spouting out one of his ingenious theories! . . . It had really occurred to her once or twice to think that you could not run a dual physical and mental existence without some risk. The military physical developments of the last four years had been responsible for a real exaggeration of physical values. She was aware that in that institution, for the last four years, she had been regarded as supplementing if not as actually replacing both the doctor and the priest. . . But from that to evolving a complete theory that the Pettigul's lie was the product of an overoxygenated brain was going pretty far. . . .

Still, she was prevented from taking part in national rejoicings; pretty certainly Edith Ethel had been talking scandal about her to Miss Wanostrocht. She had the right to take it out in some sort of exaggerated declamation!

"It appears," Miss Wanostrocht said, "for we can't now go into the question of the whole curriculum of the school, though I am inclined to agree with you. What, by the bye, is the matter with Pettigul One? I thought her rather a solid sort of girl. But it appears that the wife of a friend . . . perhaps it's only a former friend of yours, is in a nursing home."

Valentine exclaimed:

"Oh, he . . . But that's too ghastly!"

"It appears," Miss Wanostrocht said, "to be rather a mess." She added: "That appears to be the only expression to use."

For Valentine, that piece of news threw a blinding light upon herself. She was overwhelmingly appalled because that woman was in a nursing home. Because in that case it would not be sporting to go and see the husband!

Miss Wanostrocht went on:

"Lady Macmaster was anxious for your advice. . . . It appears that the only other person that could look after the interests of . . . of your friend: his brother . . ."

Valentine missed something out of that sentence. Miss Wanostrocht talked too fluently. If people wanted you to appreciate items of sledge-hammering news, they should not use long sentences. They should say:

"He's mad and penniless. His brother's dying: his wife's just been operated on." Like that! Then you could take it in, even if your mind was rioting about like a cat in a barrel.

"The brother's . . . female companion," Miss Wanostrocht was wandering on, "though it appears that she would have been willing, is therefore not available. . . . The theory is that he—he himself, your friend—has been considerably unhinged by his experiences in the war. Then . . . Who in your opinion should take the responsibility of looking after his interests?"

Valentine heard herself say:

"Me!"

She added:

"Him! Looking after him. I don't know that he has any . . . interests!"

He didn't appear to have any furniture, so how could he have the other things? She wished Miss Wanostrocht would leave off using the word "appear." It was irritating. . . . and infectious. Could the lady not make a direct statement? But then, no one ever made clear statements, and this no doubt appeared to that anaemic spinster a singularly tenebrous affair.

As for clear statements. . . . If there had ever been any in precisely this tenebrous mess, she, Valentine, would know how she stood with that man's wife. For it was part of the preposterous way in which she herself and all her friends behaved that they never made clear staements—except for Edith Ethel, who had the nature of a female costermonger and could not tell the truth, though she could be clear enough.

But even Edith Ethel had never hitherto said anything about the way the wife in this case treated the husband. She had given Valentine very clearly to understand that she "sided" with the wife—but she had never gone as far as to say that the wife was a good wife. If she—Valentine—could only know that.

Miss Wanostrocht was asking:

"When you say 'me,' do you mean that you would propose to look after that man yourself? I trust not."

. . . Because, obviously, if she were a good wife, she, Valentine, couldn't butt in . . . not generously. As her father's and still more her mother's daughter. . . . On the face of it you would say that a wife who was always striding along the palings of the Row, or the paths of other resorts of the fashionable, could not be a good—a domestic—wife for a statistician. On the other hand, he was a pretty smart man, governing class, county family and the rest of it—so he might like his wife to figure in Society: he might even exact it. He was quite capable of that. Why, for all she knew, the wife might be a retiring, shy person whom he thrust out into the hard world. It was not likely: but it was as possible as anything else.

Miss Wanostrocht was asking:

"Aren't there institutions . . . military sanatoria. . . . for cases precisely like that of this Captain Tietjens? It appears to be the war that has broken him down, not merely evil living."

"It's precisely," Valentine said, "because of that that one should want . . . shouldn't one. . . Because it's because of the war . . ."

The sentence would not finish itself.

Miss Wanostrocht said:

"I thought . . . It has been represented to me . . . that you were a pacifist. Of an extreme type!"

It had given Valentine a turn—like the breaking out of sweat in a case of fever—to hear the name, coldly: "Captain Tietjens," for it was like a release. She had been irrationally determined that hers should not be the first tongue to utter that name.

And apparently from her tone Miss Wanostrocht was prepared to detest that Captian Tietjens. Perhaps she detested him already.

She was beginning to say:

"If one is an extreme pacifist because one cannot bear to think of the sufferings of men, isn't that a precise reason why one should wish that a poor devil, all broken up? . . ."

But Miss Wanostrocht had begun one of her own long sentences. Their voices went on together, like trains dragging along ballast—disagreeably. Miss Wanostrocht's organ, however, won out with the words:

". . . behaved very badly indeed."

Valentine said hotly:

"You ought not to believe anything of the sort—on the strength of anything said by a woman like Lady Macmaster."

Miss Wanostrocht appeared to have been brought to a complete stop: she leaned forward in her chair; her mouth was a little open. And Valentine said "Thank goodness!" to herself.

She had to have a moment to herself to digest what had the air of being new evidence of the baseness of Edith Ethel; she felt herself to be infuriated in regions of her own being that she hardly knew. That seemed to her to be a littleness in herself. She had not thought that she had been as little as that. It ought not to matter what people said of you. She was perfectly accustomed to think of Edith Ethel as telling whole crowds of people very bad things about her, Valentine Wannop. But there was about this a recklessness that was hardly believable. To tell an unknown person, encountered by chance on the telephone, derogatory facts about a third party who might be expected to come to the telephone herself in a minute or two—and, not only that—who must in all probability hear what had been said very soon after, from the first listener . . . That was surely a recklessness of evil-speaking that almost outpassed sanity. . . . Or else it betrayed a contempt for her, Valentine Wannop, and what she could do in the way of reprisals that was extremely hard to bear!

She said suddenly to Miss Wanostrocht:

"Look here! Are you speaking to me as a friend to my father's daughter or as a head mistress to a physical instructor?"

A certain amount of blood came into the lady's pinkish features. She had certainly been ruffled when Valentine had permitted her voice to sound so long alongside her own, for although Valentine knew next to nothing about the head's likes or dislikes, she had once or twice before seen her evince marked distaste on being interrupted in one of her formal sentences.

Miss Wanostrocht said with a certain coldness:

"I'm speaking at present . . . I'm allowing myself the

liberty—as a much older woman—in the capacity of a friend
of your father. I have been, in short, trying to recall to you
all that you owe to yourself as being an example of his training!"

Involuntarily Valentine's lips formed themselves for a low
whistle of incredulity. She said to herself:

"By Jove! I am in the middle of a nasty affair. . . . This
is a sort of professional cross-examination."

"I am in a way glad," the lady was now continuing, "that
you take that line. . . . I mean of defending Mrs. Tietjens
with such heat against Lady Macmaster. Lady Macmaster
appears to dislike Mrs. Tietjens, but I am bound to say that
she appears to be in the right of it. I mean of her dislike.
Lady Macmaster is a serious personality, and even on her
public record Mrs. Tietjens appears to be very much the
reverse. No doubt you wish to be loyal to your . . . friends,
but . . ."

"We appear," Valentine said, "to be getting into an extraordinary muddle."

She added:

"I haven't, as you seem to think, been defending Mrs.
Tietjens. I would have. I would at any time. I have always
thought of her as beautiful and kind. But I heard you say the
words: *'has been behaving very badly,'* and I thought you
meant that Captain Tietjens had. I denied it. If you meant
that his wife has, I deny it too. She's an admirable wife . . .
and mother . . . that sort of thing, for all I know. . . ."

She said to herself:

"Now why do I say that? What's Hecuba to me?" and
then:

"It's to defend *his* honour, of course. . . . I'm trying to
present Captain Tietjens as English Country Gentleman complete with admirably arranged establishment, stables, kennels,
spouse, offspring . . . That's a queer thing to want to do!"

Miss Wanostrocht, who had breathed deeply, said now:

"I'm extremely glad to hear that. Lady Macmaster certainly said that Mrs. Tietjens was—let us say—at least a neglect-
ful wife. . . . Vain, you know; idle; overdressed. . . . All
that . . . And you appeared to defend Mrs. Tietjens."

"She's a smart woman in smart Society," Valentine said,
"but it's with her husband's concurrence. She has a right to
be. . . ."

"We shouldn't," Miss Wanostrocht said, "be in the extraordinary muddle to which you referred if you did not so
continually interrupt me. I was trying to say that, for you,

an inexperienced girl, brought up in a sheltered home, no pitfall could be more dangerous than a man with a wife who neglected her duties!"

Valentine said:

"You will have to excuse my interrupting you. It *is*, you know, rather more my funeral than yours."

Miss Wanostrocht said quickly:

"You can't say that. You don't know how ardently . . ."

Valentine said:

"Yes, yes. . . . Your *schwaerm* for my father's memory and all. . . . But my father couldn't bring it about that I should lead a sheltered life. . . . I'm about as experienced as any girl of the lower classes. . . . No doubt it was his doing, but don't make any mistakes."

She added:

"Still, it's I that's the corpse. You're conducting the inquest. So it's more fun for you."

Miss Wanostrocht had grown slightly pale: "I; if . . ." she stammered slightly, "by 'experience' you mean . . ."

"I don't," Valentine exclaimed, "and you have no right to infer that I do on the strength of a conversation you've had, but shouldn't have had, with one of the worst tongues in London. . . . I mean that my father left us so that I had to earn my and my mother's living as a servant for some months after his death. That was what his training came to. But I can look after myself. . . . In consequence . . ."

Miss Wanostrocht had thrown herself back in her chair.

"But . . ." she exclaimed: she had grown completely pale —like discoloured wax. "There was a subscription. . . . We . . ." She began again: "We knew that he hadn't . . ."

"You subscribed," Valentine said, "to purchase his library and presented it to his wife . . . who had nothing to eat but what my wages as a tweeny maid got for her." But before the pallor of the other lady she tried to add a touch of generosity: "Of course the subscribers wanted, very naturally, to preserve as much as they could of his personality. A man's books are very much himself. That was all right." She added: "All the same, I had that training: in a suburban basement. So you cannot teach me a great deal about the shady in life. I was in the family of a Middlesex county councillor. In Ealing."

Miss Wanostrocht said faintly:

"This is very dreadful!"

"It isn't really!" Valentine said. "I wasn't badly treated as tweeny maids go. It would have been better if the mistress

hadn't been a constant invalid and the cook constantly drunk.
. . . After that I did a little office work. For the suffragettes.
That was after old Mr. Tietjens came back from abroad and
gave mother some work on a paper he owned. We scrambled
along then, somehow. Old Mr. Tietjens was father's greatest
friend, so father's side, as you might say, turned up trumps
—if you like to think that to console you. . . ."

Miss Wanostrocht was bending her face down over her
table, presumably to hide a little of it from Valentine or to
avoid the girl's eyes.

Valentine went on:

"One knows all about the conflict between a man's private
duties and his public achievements. But with a very little less
of the flamboyant in his life my father might have left us
very much better off. It isn't what I *want*—to be a cross
between a sergeant in the army and an upper housemaid.
Any more than I wanted to be an under one."

Miss Wanostrocht uttered an "Oh!" of pain. She exclaimed
rapidly:

"It was your moral rather than your mere athletic influence
that made me so glad to have you here. . . . It was because
I felt that you did not set such a high value on the physical. . . ."

"Well, you aren't going to have me here much longer,"
Valentine said. "Not an instant more than I can in decency
help. I am going to . . ."

She said to herself:

"What on earth am I going to do? . . . What do I want?"

She wanted to lie in a hammock beside a blue, tideless
sea and think about Tibullus. . . . There was no nonsense
about her. She did not want to engage in intellectual pursuits herself. She had not the training. But she intended to
enjoy the more luxurious forms of the intellectual products of
others. . . . That appeared to be the moral of the day!

And looking rather minutely at Miss Wanostrocht's inclined face, she wondered if, in the history of the world,
there had ever been such another day. Had Miss Wanostrocht, for instance, ever known what it was to have a man
come back? Ah, but amid the tumult of a million other
men coming back! A collective impulse to slacken off! Immense! Softening!

Miss Wanostrocht had apparently loved her father. No
doubt in company with fifty damsels. Did they ever get a
collective kick out of that affair? It was even possible that
she had spoken as she had . . . *pour cause*. Warning her,

Valentine, against the deleterious effect of being connected with a man whose wife was unsatisfactory. . . . Because the fifty damsels had all, in duty bound, thought that her mother was an unsatisfactory wife for the brilliant, grey-black-haired Eminence with the figure of a stripling that her father had been. . . . They had probably thought that without the untidy figure of Mrs. Wannop as a weight upon him, he might have become . . . Well, with one of *them!* . . . Anything! Any sort of figure in the councils of the nation. Why not Prime Minister? For along with his pedagogic theories he had had political occupations. He had certainly had the friendship of Disraeli. He supplied—it was historic!—materials for eternally famous, meretricious speeches. He would have been head trainer of the empire's proconsuls if the other fellow, at Balliol, had not got in first. . . . As it was he had had to specialize in the education of women. Building up Primrose Dames. . . .

So Miss Wanostrocht warned her against the deleterious effect of neglected wives upon young, attached virgins! It probably *was* deleterious. Where would she, Valentine Wannop, have been by now if she had thought that Sylvia Tietjens was really a bad one?

Miss Wanostrocht said, as if with sudden anxiety:

"You are going to do what? You propose to do what?"

Valentine said:

"Obviously after your conversation with Edith Ethel you won't be so glad to have me here. My moral influence has not been brightened in aspect!" A wave of passionate resentment swept over her.

"Look here," she said; "if you think that I am prepared to . . ."

She stopped, however. "No," she said, "I am not going to introduce the housemaid note. But you will probably see that this is irritating." She added: "I would have the case of Pettigul One looked into, if I were you. It might become epidemic in a big school like this. And we've no means of knowing where we stand now-a-days!"

PART TWO

I ～

MONTHS AND months before, Christopher Tietjens had stood extremely wishing that his head were level with a particular splash of purposeless whitewash. Something behind his mind forced him to the conviction that if his head—and of course the rest of his trunk and lower limbs—were suspended by a process of levitation to that distance above the duckboard on which now his feet were, he would be in an inviolable sphere. These waves of conviction recurred continually: he was constantly glancing aside and upwards at that splash: it was in the shape of the comb of a healthy rooster; it gleamed, with five serrations, in the just-beginning light that shone along the thin, unroofed channel in the gravel slope. Wet half-light, just filtering, more visible there than in the surrounding desolation because the deep, narrow channel framed a section of just-illuminated rift in the watery eastwards!

Twice he had stood up on a rifleman's step enforced by a bully-beef case to look over—in the last few minutes. Each time, on stepping down again, he had been struck by that phenomenon: the light seen from the trench seemed, if not brighter, then more definite. So, from the bottom of a pit-shaft in broad day you can see the stars. The wind was light, but from the north-west. They had there the weariness of a beaten army: the weariness of having to begin always new days again. . . .

He glanced aside and upwards: that cockscomb of phosphorescence. . . . He felt waves of some X force propelling his temples towards it. He wondered if perhaps the night before he had not observed that that was a patch of rein-

forced concrete, therefore more resistant. He might of course
have observed that and then forgotten it. He hadn't! It was
therefore irrational.

If you are lying down under fire—flat under pretty smart
fire—and you have only a paper bag in front of your head
for cover, you feel immeasurably safer than you do without
it. You have a mind at rest. This must be the same thing.

It remained dark and quiet. It was forty-five minutes:
it became forty-four . . . forty-three . . . forty-two minutes
and thirty seconds before a crucial moment and the slate-
grey cases of miniature metal pineapples had not come from
the bothering place. . . . Who knew if there was anyone
in charge there?

Twice that night he had sent runners back. No results yet.
That bothering fellow might quite well have forgotten to
leave a substitute. That was not likely. A careful man. But
a man with a mania might forget. Still, it was not likely! . . .

Thoughts menaced him as clouds threaten the heads of
mountains, but for the moment they kept away. It was quiet;
the wet, cool air was agreeable. They had autumn mornings
that felt like that in Yorkshire. The wheels of his physique
moved smoothly; he was more free in the chest than he had
been for months.

A single immense cannon, at a tremendous distance, said
something. Something sulky. Aroused in its sleep and protesting. But it was not a signal to begin anything. Too heavy.
Firing at something at a tremendous distance. At Paris, maybe: or the North Pole: or the moon! They were capable of
that, those fellows!

It would be a tremendous piece of frightfulness to hit the
moon. Great gain in prestige. And useless. There was no
knowing what they would not be up to, as long as it was
stupid and useless. And, naturally, boring. . . . And it was a
mistake to be boring. One went on fighting to get rid of
those bores—as you would to get rid of a bore in a club.

It was more descriptive to call what had spoken a cannon than a gun—though it was not done in the best local
circles. It was all right to call 75's or the implements of the
horse artillery "guns"; they were mobile and toylike. But
those immense things were cannons, the sullen muzzles always
elevated. Sullen, like cathedral dignitaries or butlers. The
thickness of barrel compared to the bore appeared enormous
as they pointed at the moon, or Paris, or Nova Scotia.

Well, that cannon had not announced anything except itself! It was not the beginning of any barrage; our own fel-

lows were not pooping off to shut it up. It had just announced itself, saying protestingly, "CAN . . . NON," and its shell soaring away to an enormous height caught the reflection of the unrisen sun on its base. A shining disk, like a halo in flight. . . . Pretty! A pretty motive for a decoration, tiny pretty planes up on a blue sky amongst shiny, flying haloes! Dragon-flies amongst saints. . . . No, "with angels and arch-angels"! . . . Well, one had seen it!

Cannon. . . . Yes, that was the right thing to call them. Like the up-ended, rusted things that stuck up out of parades when one had been a child.

No, not the signal for a barrage! A good thing! One might as well say "Thank goodness," for the later they began the less long it lasted. . . . Less long it lasted was ugly alliteration. Sooner it was over was better. . . . No doubt half-past eight or at half-past eight to the stroke those boring fellows would let off their usual offering, probably plump, right on top of that spot. . . . As far as one could tell, three salvos of a dozen shells each at half-minute intervals between the salvos. Perhaps salvos was not the right word. Damn all artillery, anyhow!

Why did those fellows do it? Every morning at half-past eight; every afternoon at half-past two. Presumably just to show that they were still alive, and still boring. They were methodical. That was their secret. The secret of their bore-dom. Trying to kill them was like trying to shut up Liberals who would talk party politics in a non-political club . . . had to be done, though! Otherwise the world was no place for . . . oh, postprandial naps! . . . Simple philosophy of the contest! . . . Forty minutes! And he glanced aside and upwards at the phosphorescent cockscomb! Within his mind something said that if he were only suspended up there . . .

He stepped once more on to the rifle-step and on to the bully-beef case. He elevated his head cautiously: grey desola-tion sloped down and away. F-R-R-R-r-r-r! A gentle purring sound!

He was automatically back, on the duckboard, his break-fast hurting his chest. He said:

"By Jove! I got the fright of my life!" A laugh was called for: he managed it, his whole stomach shaking. And cold.

A head in a metal pudding-basin—a Suffolk type of blond head—pushed itself from a withdrawn curtain of sacking in the gravel wall beside him, at his back. A voice said with concern:

"There ain't no beastly snipers, is there, sir? I did 'ope there wouldn'n be henny beastly snipers 'ere. It gives such a beastly lot of extra trouble warning the men."

Tietjens said it was a beastly skylark that almost walked into his mouth. The acting sergeant-major said with enthusiasm that them 'ere skylarks could fair scare the guts out of you. He remembered a raid in the dark, crawling on 'is 'ands 'n knees wen 'e put 'is 'and on a skylark on its nest. Never left 'is nest till 'is 'and was on 'im! Then it went up and fair scared the wind out of 'im. Cor! Never would 'e fergit that!

With an air of carefully pulling parcels out of a carrier's cart he produced from the cavern behind the sacking two blinking assemblages of tubular khaki-clad limbs. They wavered to erectness, pink cheeses of faces yawning beside tall rifles and bayonets. The sergeant said:

"Keep yer 'eds down as you go along. You never knows!"

Tietjens told the lance-corporal of that party of two that his confounded gas-mask nozzle was broken. Hadn't he seen that for himself? The dismembered object bobbed on the man's chest. He was to go and borrow another from another man and see the other drew a new one at once.

Tietjens' eyes were drawn aside and upwards. His knees were still weak. If he were levitated to the level of that thing, he would not have to use his legs for support.

The elderly sergeant went on with enthusiasm about skylarks. Wonderful the trust they showed in hus 'uman beens! Never left ther nesteses till you trod on them, though hall 'ell was rockin' around them. . . . An appropriate skylark from above and before the parapet made its shrill and heartless noise heard. No doubt the skylark that Tietjens had frightened —that had frightened him.

There'd bin, the sergeant went on, still enthusiastically, pointing a hand in the direction of the noise, skylarks singin' on the mornin' of every straf'e'd ever bin in! Won'erful trust in 'umanity. Won'erful hinstinck set in the feathered breast by the Halmighty! For *oo* was goin' to 'it a skylark on a battle-field!

The solitary man drooped beside his long, bayonetted rifle that was muddied from stock to bayonet attachment. Tietjens said mildly that he thought the sergeant had got his natural history wrong. He must divide the males from the females. The females sat on the nest through obstinate attachment to their eggs; the males obstinately soared above the nests in order to pour out abuse at other male skylarks in the vicinity.

He said to himself that he must get the doctor to give him a bromide. A filthy state his nerves had got into unknown to himself. The agitation communicated to him by that bird was still turning his stomach round. . . .

"Gilbert White of Selbourne," he said to the sergeant, "called the behaviour of the female STORGE: a good word for it." But, as for trust in humanity, the sergeant might take it that larks never gave us a thought. We were part of the landscape and if what destroyed their nests whilst they sat on them was a bit of H.E. shell or the coulter of a plough it was all one to them.

The sergeant said to the rejoined lance-corporal, whose box now hung correctly on his muddied chest:

"Now it's Hay post you gotter wait at!" They were to go along the trench and wait where another trench ran into it and there was a great A in whitewash on a bit of corrugated iron that was half buried. "You can tell a great Hay from a bull's foot as well as another, can't you, corporal?" patiently.

Wen they Mills bombs come 'e was to send 'is man into Hay Cumpny dug-out fer a fatigue to bring 'em along 'ere, but Hay Cumpny could keep '*is* little lot fer 'isself.

An' if they Mills bombs did'n' come, the corporal'd better manufacture them on 'is own. An' not make no mistakes!

The lance-corporal said "Yes sargint, no sargint!" and the two went desultorily wavering along the duckboards, grey silhouettes against the wet bar of light, equilibrating themselves with hands on the walls of the trench.

"Ju 'ear what the orfcer said, corporal," the one said to the other. "Wottever'll 'e say next! Skylarks not trust 'uman beens in battles! Cor!" The other grunted and, mournfully, the voices died out.

The cockscomb-shaped splash became of overwhelming interest momentarily to Tietjens; at the same time, his mind began upon abstruse calculation of chances. Of his chances! A bad sign when the mind takes to doing that. Chances of direct hits by shells, by rifle bullets, by grenades, by fragments of shells or grenades. By any fragment of metal impinging on soft flesh. He was aware that he was going to be hit in the soft spot behind the collar-bone. He was conscious of that spot—the right-hand one; he felt none of the rest of his body. It is bad when the mind takes charge like that. A bromide was needed. The doctor must give him one. His mind felt pleasure at the thought of the M.O. A pleasant little fellow of the no-account order that knows his job. And carried liquor cheerfully. Confoundedly cheerfully!

He saw the doctor—plainly! It was one of the plainest things he could see of this whole show. . . . The doctor, a slight figure, vault on to the parapet, like a vaulting horse for height; stand up in the early-morning sun. . . . Blind to the world, but humming "Father O'Flynn." And stroll in the sunlight, a swagger-cane, of all things in the world, under his arm, right straight over to the German trench. . . . Then throw his cap down into that trench. And walk back! Delicately avoiding the strands in the cut apron of wire that he had to walk through!

The doctor said he had seen a Hun—probably an officer's batman—cleaning a top-boot with an apron over his knees. The Hun had shied a boot-brush at him and he had shied his cap at the Hun. The blinking Hun, he called him! No doubt the fellow had blinked!

No doubt you could do the unthinkable with impunity!

No manner of doubt: if you were blind drunk and all! . . . And however you strained, in an army you fell into routine. Of a quiet morning you do not expect drunken doctors strolling along your parapet. Besides, the German front lines were very thinly held. Amazingly! There might not have been a Hun with a gun within half a mile of that boot-black!

If he, Tietjens, stood in space, his head level with that cockscomb, he would be in an inviolable vacuum—as far as projectiles were concerned!

He was asking desultorily of the sergeant whether he often shocked the men by what he said and the sergeant was answering with blushes: Well, you do *say* things, sir! Not believing in skylarks now! If there was one thing the men believed, hit was in the hinstincks of them little creatures!

"So that," Tietjens said, "they look at me as a sort of an atheist."

He forced himself to look over the parapet again, climbing heavily to his place of observation. It was sheer impatience and purely culpable technically. But he was in command of the regiment, of an establishment of a thousand and eighteen men, or that used to be the establishment of a battalion, of a strength of three hundred and thirty-three. Say seventy-five per company. And two companies in command of second-lieutenants, one just out . . . The last four days . . . There ought to be, say, eighty pairs of eyes surveying what he was going to survey. If there were fifteen it was as much as there were! . . . Figures were clean and comforting things. The chance against being struck by a shell-fragment that day, if the Germans came in any force, was fourteen to one against. There were battalions worse off than they. The Sixth had only one-one-six left!

The tortured ground sloped down into mists. Say a quarter of a mile away. The German front lines were just shadows, like the corrugations of photographs of the moon: the paradoses of our own trenches two nights ago! The Germans did not seem to have troubled to chuck up much in the way of parapets. They didn't. They were coming on. Anyhow, they held their front lines always very sparsely. . . . Was that the phrase? Was it even English?

Above the shadows the mist behaved tortuously: mounting up into umbrella shapes. Like snow-covered umbrella pines.

Disagreeable to force the eye to examine that mist. His stomach turned over. . . . That was the sacks. A flat, slightly disordered pile of wet sacks, half right at two hundred yards. No doubt a shell had hit a G.S. waggon coming up with sacks for trenching. Or the bearers had bolted, chucking the sacks down. His eyes had fallen on that scattered pile four times already that morning. Each time his stomach had turned over. The resemblance to prostrate men was appalling. The enemy creeping up . . . Christ! Within two hundred yards. So his stomach said. Each time, in spite of the preparation.

Otherwise the ground had been so smashed that it was flat: went down into holes but did not rise up into mounds. That made it look gentle. It sloped down. To the untidiness. They appeared mostly to lie on their faces. Why? Presumably they were mostly Germans pushed back in the last counter-attack. Anyhow, you saw mostly the seats of their trousers. When you did not, how profound was their repose! You must phrase it a little like that—rhetorically. There was no other way to get the effect of that profoundness. Call it profundity!

It was different from sleep. Flatter. No doubt when the appalled soul left the weary body, the panting lungs . . . Well, you can't go on with a sentence like that. . . But you collapsed inwards. Like the dying pig they sold on trays in the street. Painter fellows doing battle-fields never got that *intimate* effect. Intimate to them there. Unknown to the corridors in Whitehall. . . . Probably because they—the painters —drew from living models or had ideas as to the human form. . . . But these were not limbs, muscles, torsi. . . .

Collections of tubular shapes in field-grey or mud-colour they
were. Chucked about by Almighty God! As if He had dropped
them from on high to make them flatten into the earth. . . .
Good gravel soil, that slope, and relatively dry. No dew to
speak of. The night had been covered. . . .

Dawn on the battle-field. . . . Damn it all, why sneer?
It *was* dawn on the battle-field. . . . The trouble was that
this battle was not over. By no means over. There would be
a hundred and eleven years, nine months and twenty-seven
days of it still. . . . No, you could not get the effect of that
endless monotony of effort by numbers. Nor yet by saying
"Endless monotony of effort." It was like bending down to
look into darkness of corridors under dark curtains. Under
clouds . . . Mist . . .

At that, with dreadful reluctance his eyes went back to
the spectral mists over the photographic shadows. He forced
himself to put his glasses on the mists. They mopped and
mowed, fantastically; grey, with black shadows; drooping
like the dishevelled veils of murdered bodies. They were engaged in fantastic and horrifying layings-out of corpses of
vast dimensions; in silence but in accord they performed unthinkable tasks. They were the Germans. This was fear. This
was the intimate fear of black, quiet nights, in dug-outs
where you heard the obscene suggestions of the miners' picks
below you: tranquil, engrossed. Infinitely threatening. . . .
But not FEAR.

It was, in effect, the desire for privacy. What he dreaded
at those normal times when fear visited him at lunch, whilst
seeing that the men got their baths or when writing, in a
trench, in support, a letter to his bank-manager, was finding
himself unhurt, surrounded by figures like the brothers of
the Misericordia, going unconcerned about their tasks, notic-
ing him hardly at all. . . . Whole hill-sides, whole stretches
of territory, alive with myriads of whitish-grey, long cagoules,
with slits for eye-holes. Occasionally one would look at him
through the eye-slits in the hoods. . . . The prisoner!

He would be the prisoner: liable to physical contacts—to
being handled and being questioned. An invasion of his privacy!

As a matter of fact, that wasn't so far out; not so dotty
as it sounded. If the Huns got him—as they precious near
had the night before last!—they would be—they had then
been—in gas-masks of various patterns. They must be short
of these things: but they looked, certainly, like goblin pigs
with sore eyes, the hood with the askew, blind-looking eye-

holes and the mouthpiece or the other nose attachment going down into a box, astonishingly like snouts! . . . Mopping and mowing—no doubt shouting through the masks!

They had appeared with startling suddenness and as if with a supernatural silence, beneath a din so overwhelming that you could not any longer bother to notice it. They were there, as it were, under a glass dome of silence that sheltered beneath that dark tumult, in the white illumination of Verey lights that went on. They were there, those of them that had already emerged from holes—astonishingly alert hooded figures with the long rifles that always looked rather amateurish—though, hell, they weren't. The hoods and the white light gave them the aspects of Canadian trappers in snow, made them no doubt look still more husky fellows as against our poor rats of Derby men. The heads of goblin pigs were emerging from shell-holes, from rifts in the torn earth, from old trenches . . . This ground had been fought over again and again. . . . Then the counter-attack had come through his, Tietjens', own crowd. One disorderly mob, as you might think, going through a disordered crowd that was damn glad to let them through, realizing slowly, in the midst of a general not knowing what was going to happen, that the fellows were reliefs. They shot past you clumsily in a darkness spangled with shafts of light coming from God knows where, and appeared going forward, whilst you at least had the satisfaction that, by order, you were going back. In an atmosphere of questioning. What was happening? What was going to happen? . . . What the bloody hell . . . what . . .

Tidy-sized shells began to drop among them, saying: "Wee . . . ee . . . ry. . . . Whack!" Some fellow showed Tietjens the way through an immense apron of wire that was beginning to fly about. He, Tietjens, was carrying a hell of a lot of paper folders and books. They ought to have evacuated an hour ago, or the Huns ought not to have got out of their holes for an hour. . . . But the colonel had been too . . . too exalted. Call it too exalted. He was not going to evacuate for a pack of . . . damn orders! . . . The fellow, McKechnie, had at last had to beg Tietjens to give the order. . . . Not that the order mattered. The men could not have held ten minutes longer. The ghostly Huns would have been in the trenches. But the company commanders knew that there was a divisional order to retire, and no doubt they had passed it on to their subalterns before getting killed. Still, that Bn. H.Q. should have given the order made it better even if there was no one to take it to the companies.

It turned a practical expulsion into an officially strategic retreat. . . . And damn good divisional staff work at that.
They had been fitted into beautiful, clean, new trenches, all
ready for them—like chessmen fitting into their boxes. Damn
good for a beaten army that was being forced off the face
of the earth. Into the English Channel. . . . What made
them stick it? What the devil made the men stick it? They
were unbelievable.

There was a stroking on his leg. A gentle, timid stroking!
Well, he *ought* to get down: it was setting a bad example.
The admirable trenches were perfectly efficiently fitted up
with spy-holes. For himself, he always disliked them. You
thought of a rifle bullet coming smack through them and
guided by the telescope into your right eye. Or perhaps you
would not have a telescope. Anyhow, you wouldn't know. . . .

There were still the three wheels, atilt, attached to slant-
ing axles: in a haze of disintegrated wire that, bedewed, made
profuse patterns like frost on a window. There was their
own apron—a perfect village!—of wire over which he
looked. Fairly intact. The Germans had put up some of their
own in front of the lost trenches, a quarter of a mile off:
over the reposing untidinesses. In between, there was a perfect maze: their own of the night before last. How the
deuce had it not been *all* mashed to pieces by the last Hun
barrage? Yet there were three frosty erections—like fairy
sheds—half-way between the two lines. And, suspended in
them, as there would have to be, three bundles of rags and
what appeared to be a very large, squashed crow. How the
devil had that fellow managed to get smashed into that shape?
It was improbable. There was also—suspended, too—a tall
melodramatic object, the head cast back to the sky. One
arm raised in the attitude of, say, a Walter Scott Highland
officer waving his men on. Waving a sword that wasn't there.
. . . That was what wire did for you. Supported you in
grotesque attitudes, even in death! The beastly stuff! The men
said that was Lieutenant Constantine. It might well be. The
night before last he, Tietjens, had looked round at all the
officers that were in H.Q. dug-out, come for a last-moment
conference. He had speculated on which of them would be
killed. Ghostly! Well, they had all been killed: and more on
to that. But his premonition hadn't run to thinking that
Constantine would get caught up in the wire. But perhaps
it was not Constantine. Probably they would never know. The
Huns would be where he stood by lunch-time. If the attack

of which brigade H.Q. had warned them came off. But it mightn't. . . .

As a final salute to the, on the whole, not thrilling landscape, he wetted his forefinger by inserting it in his mouth and held it in the air. It was comfortingly chilly on the exterior, towards his back. Light airs were going right in the other fellows' faces. It might be only the dawn wind. But if it stiffened a very little or even held, those blessed Württembergers would never that day get out of their trenches. They couldn't come without gas. They were probably pretty well weakened too. . . . You were not traditionally supposed to think much of Württembergers. Mild, dull creatures they were supposed to be. With funny hats. Good Lord! Traditions were going by the board!

He dropped down into the trench. The rather reddish soil with flakes of flint and little pinkish nodules of pebbles was a friendly thing to face closely.

That sergeant was saying:

"You hadn't ought to do it, sir. Give me the creeps." He added rather lachrymosely that they couldn't do without superior officers *alt*ogether. Odd creatures, these Derby N.C.O.s! They tried to get the tone of the old, time-serving N.C.O. They couldn't; all the same, you couldn't say they weren't creditable achievements.

Yes, it was friendly, the trench face. And singularly unbellicose. When you looked at it you hardly believed that it was part of this affair. . . . Friendly! You felt at peace looking at its flints and pebbles. Like being in the butts up above Groby on the moor, waiting for the grouse to come over. The soil was not of course like those butts which were built of turfs. . . .

He asked, not so much for information as to get the note of this fellow:

Why? What difference did it make whether there were senior officers or not? Anyone above eighteen would do, wouldn't they? They would keep on going on. It was a young man's war!

"It hasn't got that comfortable feeling, sir!" the sergeant expressed it. The young officers were very well for keeping you going through wire and barrages. But when you looked at them you didn't feel they knew so well what you were doing it for, if he might put it that way.

Tietjens said:

"Why? What are you doing it for?"

It wanted thirty-two minutes to the crucial moment. He said:

"Where are those bloody bombs?"

A trench cut in gravel wasn't, for all its friendly reddish-orange coloration, the ideal trench. Particularly against rifle-fire. There were rifts, presumably alongside flakes of flint that a rifle bullet would get along. Still, the chances against a hit by a rifle bullet were eighty thousand to one in a deep gravel trench like that. And he had had poor Jimmy Johns killed beside him by a bullet like that. So that gave him, say, 140,000 chances to one against. He wished his mind would not go on and on figuring. It did it whilst you weren't looking. As a well-trained dog will do when you tell it to stay in one part of a room and it prefers another. It prefers to do figuring. Creeps from the rug by the door to the hearth-rug, its eyes on your unconscious face. . . . That was what your mind was like. Like a dog!

The sergeant said:

"They do say the first consignment of bombs was 'it 'n smashed. Hin a gully; well be'ind the line. Another was coming down."

"Then you'd better whistle," Tietjens said. "Whistle for all you're worth."

The sergeant said:

"Fer a wind, sir? Keep the 'Uns beck, sir?"

Looking up at the whitewash cockscomb, Tietjens lectured the sergeant on gas. He always *had* said, and he said now, that the Germans had ruined themselves with their gas. . . .

He went on lecturing that sergeant on gas. . . .

He considered his mind: it was alarming him. All through the war he had had one dread—that a wound, the physical shock of a wound, would cause his mind to fail. He was going to be hit behind the collar-bone. He could feel the spot; not itching, but the blood pulsing just a little warmer. Just as you can become conscious of the end of your nose if you think about it!

The sergeant said that 'e wished 'e could *feel* the Germans 'ad ruined theirselves: they seemed to be drivin' us into the channel. Tietjens gave his reasons. They were driving us. But not fast enough. Not fast enough. It was a race between our disappearance and their endurance. They had been hung up yesterday by the wind: they were as like as not going to be held up to-day. . . . They were not going fast enough. They could not keep it up.

The sergeant said 'e wished, sir, you'd tell the men that.

That was what the men ought to be told: not the stuff that was hin Divisional Comic Cuts and the 'ome pipers. . . .

A key-bugle of singular sweetness—at least Tietjens supposed it to be a key-bugle, for he knew the identities of practically no wind-instruments; it was certainly not a cavalry bugle, for there were no cavalry and even no Army Service Corps at all near—a bugle, then, of astounding sweetness made some remarks to the cool, wet dawn. It induced an astonishingly melting mood. He remarked:

"Do you mean to say, then, that your men, sergeant, are really damned heroes? I suppose they are!"

He said "your men," instead of "our" or even "the" men because he had been till the day before yesterday merely the second-in-command—and was likely to be to-morrow again merely the perfectly inactive second-in-command of what was called a rag-time collection that was astonishingly a clique and mutely combined to regard him as an outsider. So he really regarded himself as rather a spectator, as if a railway passenger had taken charge of a locomotive whilst the engine-driver had gone to have a drink.

The sergeant flushed with pleasure. Hit was, he said, good to 'ave prise from Regular officers. Tietjens said that he was not a Regular. The sergeant stammered:

"*Hain't* you, sir, a ranker. The men all thinks you are a promoted ranker."

No, Tietjens said, he was not a promoted ranker. He added, after consideration, that he was a militiaman. The men would have, by the will of chance, to put up with his leadership for at least that day. They might as well feel as good about it as they could—as settled in their stomachs! It certainly made a difference that the men should feel assured about their officers: what exact difference there was no knowing. This crowd was not going to get any satisfaction out of being led by a "gentleman." They did not know what a gentleman was: a quite unfeudal crowd. Mostly Derby men. Small drapers, rate-collectors' clerks, gas-inspectors. There were even three music-hall performers, two scene-shifters and several milkmen.

It was another tradition that was gone. Still, they desired the companionship of elder, heavier men who had certain knowledges. A militiaman probably filled the bill! Well, he was that, officially!

He glanced aside and upwards at the whitewash cockscomb. He regarded it carefully. And with amusement. He knew what it was that had made his mind take the particular turn it had insisted on taking. . . . The picks going in the dark under the H.Q. dug-out in the Cassenoisette section. The men called it Crackerjack.

He had been all his life familiar with the idea of picks going in the dark, underground. There is no North Country man who is not. All through that country, if you awake at night you hear the sound, and always it appears supernatural. You know it is the miners, at the pit-face, hundreds and hundreds of feet down.

But just because it was familiar it was familiarly rather dreadful. Haunting. And the silence had come at a bad moment. After a perfect hell of noise, after so much of noise that he had been forced to ascend the slippery clay stairs of the dug-out. . . . And heaven knew, if there was one thing that on account of his heavy-breathing chest he loathed, it was slippery clay . . . he had been forced to pant up those slippery stairs. . . . His chest had been much worse then . . . two months ago!

Curiosity had forced him up. And no doubt FEAR. The large battle-fear, not the constant little haunting misgivings. God knew! Curiosity or fear. In terrific noise, noise like the rushing up of innumerable noises determined not to be late, whilst the earth rocks or bumps or quakes or protests, you cannot be very coherent about your thoughts. So it might have been cool curiosity or it might have been sheer panic at the thought of being buried alive in that dug-out, its mouth sealed up. Anyhow, he had gone up from the dug-out, where, in his capacity of second-in-command, detested as an interloper by his C.O., he had sat ignominiously in that idleness of the second-in-command that it is in the power of the C.O. to inflict. He was to sit there till the C.O. dropped dead: then, however much the C.O. might detest him, to step into his shoes. Nothing the C.O. could do could stop that. In the meantime, as long as the C.O. existed the second-in-command must be idle; he would be given nothing to do. For fear he got kudos!

Tietjens flattered himself that he cared nothing about kudos. He was still Tietjens of Groby: no man could give him anything, no man could take anything from him. He flattered himself that he in no way feared death, pain, dishonour, the after-death, feared very little disease—except for choking sensations! . . . But his colonel got in on him.

He had no disagreeable feelings, thinking of the colonel. A good boy, as boys go: perfectly warranted in hating his second-in-command. . . . There are positions like that! But the fellow got in on him. He shut him up in that reeling cellar. And, of course, you might lose control of your mind in a reeling cellar, where you cannot hear your thoughts. If you cannot hear your thoughts, how the hell are you going to tell what your thoughts are doing?

You couldn't hear. There was an orderly with fever or shell-shock or something—a rather favourite orderly of the orderly room—asleep on a pile of rugs. Earlier in the night orderly room had asked permission to dump the boy in there because he was making such a beastly row in his sleep that they could not hear themselves speak, and they had a lot of paper-work to do. They could not tell what had happened to the boy, whom they liked. The acting sergeant-major thought he must have got at some methylated spirits.

Immediately, that strafe had begun. The boy had lain, his face to the light of the lamp, on his pile of rugs—army blankets, that is to say. . . . A very blond boy's face, contorted in the strong light, shrieking—positively shrieking obscenities at the flame. But with his eyes shut. And two minutes after that strafe had begun, you could see his lips move; that was all.

Well, he, Tietjens, had gone up. Curiosity or fear? In the trench you could see nothing and noise rushed like black angels gone mad, solid noise that swept you off your feet. . . . Swept your brain off its feet. Something else took control of it. You became second-in-command of your own soul. Waiting for its C.O. to be squashed flat by the direct hit of a four-point-two before you got control again.

There was nothing to see; mad lights whirled over the black heavens. He moved along the mud of the trench. It amazed him to find that it was raining. In torrents. You imagined that the heavenly powers in decency suspended their activities at such moments. But there was positively lightning. They didn't! A Verey light or something extinguished *that:* not very efficient lightning, really. Just at that moment he fell on his nose at an angle of forty-five degrees against some squashed earth where, as he remembered, the parapet had been revetted. The trench had been squashed in. Level with the outside ground. A pair of boots emerged from the pile of mud. How the deuce did the fellow get into that position?

Broadside on to the hostilities in progress! . . . But, naturally, he had been running along the trench when that stuff buried him. Clean buried, anyhow. The obliging Verey light showed to Tietjens, just level with his left hand, a number of small smoking fragments. The white smoke ran level with the ground in a stiff breeze. Other little patches of smoke added themselves quickly. The Verey light went out. Things were coming over. Something hit his foot, the heel of his boot. Not unpleasantly, a smarting feeling, as if his sole had been slapped.

It suggested itself to him, under all the noise, that there being no parapet there . . . He got back into the trench towards the dug-out, skating in the sticky mud. The duckboards were completely sunk in it. In the whole affair it was the slippery mud he hated most. Again a Verey light obliged, but the trench being deep, there was nothing to see except the backside of a man. Tietjens said:

"If he's wounded . . . Even if he's dead, one ought to pull him down. . . . And get the Victoria Cross!"

The figure slid down into the trench. Speedily, with drill-movements, engrossed, it crammed two clips of cartridges into a rifle correctly held at the loading angle. In a rift of the noise, like a crack in the wall of a house, it remarked:

"Can't reload lying up there, sir. Mud gets into your magazine." He became again merely the sitting portion of a man, presenting to view the only part of him that was not caked with mud. The Verey light faded. Another reinforced the blinking effect. From just overhead.

Round the next traverse after the mouth of their dug-out, a rapt face of a tiny subaltern, gazing upwards at a Verey illumination, with an elbow on an inequality of the trench and the forearm pointing upwards, suggested—the rapt face suggested The Soul's Awakening! . . . In another rift in the sound the voice of the tiny subaltern stated that he had to economize the Verey cartridges. The battalion was very short. At the same time, it was difficult to time them so as to keep the lights going. . . . This seemed fantastic! The Huns were just coming over.

With the finger of his upward-pointing hand the tiny subaltern pulled the trigger of his upward-pointing pistol. A second later more brilliant illumination descended from above. The subaltern pointed the clumsy pistol to the ground in the considerable physical effort—for such a tiny person! —to reload the large implement. A very gallant child—name of Aranjuez. Maltese, or Portuguese, or Levantine—in origin.

The pointing of the pistol downwards revealed that he had practically coiled around his little feet a collection of tubular, dead, khaki limbs. It didn't need any rift in the sound to make you understand that his loader had been killed on him.

. . . By signs and removing his pistol from his grasp Tietjens made the subaltern—he was only two days out from England —understand that he had better go and get a drink and some bearers for the man, who might not be dead.

He was, however. When they removed him a little to make room for Tietjens' immensely larger boots, his arms just flopped in the mud, the tin hat that covered the face, to the sky. Like a clay figure, but a little less stiff. Not yet cold.

Tietjens became like a solitary statue of the Bard of Avon, the shelf for his elbow being rather low. Noise increased. The orchestra was bringing in *all* the brass, *all* the strings, *all* the wood-wind, *all* the percussion instruments. The performers threw about biscuit tins filled with horseshoes; they emptied sacks of coal on cracked gongs; they threw down forty-storey iron houses. It was comic to the extent that an operatic orchestra's crescendo is comic. Crescendo! . . . C r e s c e n d o ! C R R R R R E S C . . . The Hero *must* be coming! He didn't!

Still like Shakespeare contemplating the creation of, say, Cordelia, Tietjens leaned against his shelf. From time to time he pulled the trigger of the horse-pistol; from time to time he rested the butt on his ledge and rammed a charge home. When one jammed he took another. He found himself keeping up a fairly steady illumination.

The Hero arrived. Naturally, he was a Hun. He came over, all legs and arms going, like a catamount; struck the face of the parados; fell into the trench on the dead body, with his hands to his eyes; sprang up again and danced. With heavy deliberation Tietjens drew his great trench-knife rather than his revolver. Why? The butcher-instinct? Or trying to think himself with the Exmoor stag-hounds. The man's shoulders had come heavily on him as he had rebounded from the parados face. He felt outraged. Watching that performing Hun, he held the knife pointed and tried to think of the German for "Hands Up." He imagined it to be *Hoch die Haende!* He looked for a nice spot in the Hun's side.

His excursion into a foreign tongue proved supererogatory. The German threw his arms abroad, his—considerably mashed!—face to the sky.

Always dramatic, Cousin Fritz! Too dramatic, really.

He fell, crumpling, into his untidy boots. Nasty boots, all crumpled too, up the calves! But he didn't say *Hoch der Kaiser,* or *Deutschland uber alles,* or anything valedictory. Tietjens fired another light upwards and filled in another charge, then, down on his hams in the mud, he squatted over the German's head, the fingers of both hands under the head. He could feel the great groans thrill his fingers. He let go and felt tentatively for his brandy flask.

But there was a muddy group round the traverse end. The noise reduced itself to half. It was bearers for the corpse. And the absurdly wee Aranjuez and a new loader. . . . In those days they had not been so short of men! Shouts were coming along the trench. No doubt other Huns were in.

Noise reduced itself to a third. A bumpy diminuendo. Bumpy! Sacks of coal continued to fall down the stairs with a regular cadence; more irregularly, Bloody Mary, who was just behind the trench, or seemed like it, shook the whole house, as you might say, and there were other naval howitzers or something, somewhere.

Tietjens said to the bearers:

"Take the Hun first. He's alive. Our man's dead." He was quite remarkably dead. He hadn't, Tietjens had observed when he bent over the German, really got what you might call a head, though there was something in its place. What had done that?

Aranjuez, taking his place beside the trench face, said:

"Damn cool you were, sir. Damn cool. I never saw a knife drawn so slow!" They had watched the Hun do the *danse du ventre!* The poor beggar had had rifles and the young feller's revolver turned on him all the time. They would probably have shot him some more but for the fear of hitting Tietjens. Half a dozen Germans had jumped into that sector of trenches in various places. As mad as march hares! . . . That fellow had been shot through both eyes, a fact that seemed to fill the little Aranjuez with singular horror. He said he would go mad if he thought he would be blinded, because there was a girl in the tea-shop at Bailleul, and a fellow called Spofforth of the Wiltshires would get her if his, Aranjuez's, beauty was spoiled. He positively whimpered at the thought and then gave the information that this was considered to be a false alarm: he meant a feigned attack to draw off troops from somewhere else, where the real attempt was being made. There must be pretty good hell going on somewhere else, then.

It looked like that. For almost immediately all the guns had fallen silent except for one or two that bumped and grumped. . . . It had all been just for fun, then!

Well, they were damn near Bailleul now. They would be

driven past it in a day or two. On the way to the channel.
Aranjuez would have to hurry to see his girl. The little
devil! He had overdrawn his confounded little account over
his girl, and Tietjens had had to guarantee his overdraft—
which he could not afford to do. Now the little wretch would
probably overdraw still more—and Tietjens would have to
guarantee still more of an overdraft.

But that night, when Tietjens had gone down into the
black silence of his own particular branch of a cellar—they
really had been in wine-cellars at that date, cellars stretching for hundreds of yards under chalk with strata of clay,
which made the mud so particularly sticky and offensive—
he had found the sound of the pickaxes beneath his flea-bag
almost unbearable. They were probably our own men. Obviously they were our own men. But it had not made much
difference, for, of course, if they were there they would be
an attraction, and the Germans might just as well be below
them, countermining.

His nerves had been put in a bad way by that rotten
strafe—that had been just for fun. He knew his nerves
were in a bad way because he had a ghostly visit from 09
Evans, a fellow whose head had been smashed, as it were,
on his, Tietjens', own hands, just after Tietjens had refused
him home-leave to go and get killed by a prize-fighter who
had taken up with his, 09 Evans', wife. It was complicated,
but Tietjens wished that fellows who wished to fall on him
when they were stopping things would choose to stop things
with something else than their heads. That wretched Hun
dropping on his shoulder, when, by the laws of war, he
ought to have been running back to his own lines, had given
him, Tietjens, a jar that still shook his whole body. And, of
course, a shock. The fellow had looked something positively
Apocalyptic, his whitey-grey arms and legs spread abroad.
. . . And it had been an imbecile affair, with no basis of
real fighting. . . .

That thin surge of whitey-grey objects of whom not more
than a dozen had reached the line—Tietjens knew that, because, with a melodramatically drawn revolver and the fellows who would have been really better employed carrying
away the unfortunate Hun, who had had in consequence to
wait half an hour before being attended to—with those fellows loaded up with Mills bombs like people carrying pears,
he had dodged, revolver first, round half a dozen traverses,
and in quite enough of remains of gas to make his lungs
unpleasant. . . . Like a child playing a game of "I Spy!" Just

like that. . . . But only to come on several lots of Tommies standing round unfortunate objects who were either trembling with fear and wet and sweat, or panting with their nice little run. . . .

This surge, then, of whitey-grey objects, sacrificed for fun, was intended . . . was intended ulti . . . ultim . . . then . . .

A voice, just under his camp-bed, said:

"Bringt dem Hauptmann eine Kerze. . . ." As who should say: "Bring a candle for the captain. . . ." Just like that! A dream!

It hadn't been as considerable of a shock as you might have thought to a man just dozing off. Not really as bad as the falling dream: but quite as awakening. . . . His mind had resumed that sentence.

The handful of Germans who had reached the trench had been sacrificed for the stupid sort of fun called Strategy. Probably. Stupid! . . . It was, of course, just like German spooks to go mining by candlelight. Obsoletely Nibelungen-like. Dwarfs, probably! . . . They had sent over that thin waft of men under a blessed lot of barrage and stuff. . . . A lot! A *whole* lot! It had been really quite an artillery strafe. Ten thousand shells as like as not. Then, somewhere up the line they had probably made a demonstration in force. *Great* bodies of men, an immense surge. And twenty to thirty thousand shells. Very likely some miles of esplanade, as it were, with the sea battering against it. And only a demonstration in force. . . .

It could not be real fighting. They had not been ready for their spring advance.

It had been meant to impress somebody imbecile. . . . Somebody imbecile in Wallachia, or Sofia, or Asia Minor. Or Whitehall, very likely. Or the White House! . . . Perhaps they had killed a lot of Yankees—to make themselves transatlantically popular. There were no doubt, by then, whole American Army corps in the line somewhere. By then! Poor devils, coming so late into such an accentuated hell. Damnably accentuated. . . . The sound of even that little bit of fun had been portentously more awful than even quite a big show, say, in '15. It was better to have been in then and got used to it. . . . If it hadn't broken you, just by duration. . . .

Might be to impress anybody. . . . But who was going to be impressed? Of course, our legislators with the stewed-pear brains running about the ignoble corridors with coke-brise floors and mahogany doors . . . might be impressed.

. . . You must not rhyme! . . . Or, of course, our own
legislators might have been trying a nice little demonstration
in force, equally idiotic, somewhere else to impress someone
just as unlikely to be impressed. . . . This, then, would be
the answer! But no one ever would be impressed again. We
all had each other's measures. So it was just wearisome. . . .

It was remarkably quiet in that thick darkness. Down below, the picks continued their sinister confidences in each
other's ears. . . . It was really like that. Like children in
the corner of a schoolroom whispering nasty comments about
their masters, one to the other. . . . Girls, for choice. . . .
"Chop, chop, chop," a pick whispered. "Chop?" another asked
in an undertone. The first said "Chopchopchop." Then *"Chup."*
. . . And a silence of irregular duration. . . . Like what
happens when you listen to typewriting and the young woman
has to stop to put in another page. . . .

Nice young women with typewriters in Whitehall had
very likely taken from dictation, on hot-pressed, square
sheets with embossed royal arms, the plan for that very strafe.
. . . Because obviously it might have been dictated from
Whitehall almost as directly as from Unter den Linden. We
might have been making a demonstration in force on the
Dwolologda in order to get the Huns to make a counter-
demonstration in Flanders. Hoping poor old Puffles would
get it in the neck. For they were trying still to smash poor
old General Puffles and stop the single command. . . . They
might very well be hoping that our losses through the
counter-demonstration would be so heavy that the country
would cry out for the evacuation of the Western Front. . . .
If they could get half a million of us killed, perhaps the
country might . . . They, no doubt, thought it worth trying.
But it was wearisome: those fellows in Whitehall never
learned. Any more than Brother Boche. . . .

Nice to be in poor old Puffles' army. Nice but wearisome.
. . . Nice girls with typewriters in well-ventilated offices.
Did they still put paper cuffs on to keep their sleeves from
ink? He would ask Valen . . . Valen . . . It was warm and
still. . . . On such a night . . .

"Bringt dem Hauptmann eine Kerze!" A voice from under
his camp-bed! He imagined that the Hauptmann spook must
be myopic: short-sightedly examining a tamping-fuse. . . .
If they used tamping-fuses or if that was what they called
them in the army!

He could not see the face or the spectacles of the Haupt-

mann any more than he could see the faces of his men. Not
through his flea-bag and shins! They were packed in the
tunnel; whitish-grey, tubular agglomerations. . . . Large! Like
the maggots that are eaten by Australian natives. . . . Fear
possessed him!

He sat up in his flea-bag, dripping with icy sweat.

"By Jove, I'm for it!" he said. He imagined that his brain
was going: he was mad and seeing himself go mad. He
cast about in his mind for some subject about which to think
so that he could prove to himself that he had not gone mad.

2 ～

THE KEY-BUGLE remarked with singular distinctness to the
dawn:

I know a la   *fair*   *kind*   *dy*
              and
Was never face
         so   *mind*
       pleased my
         y

A sudden waft of pleasure at the seventeenth-century air
that the tones gave to the landscape went all over Tietjens.
. . . Herrick and Purcell! . . . Or it was perhaps a modern
imitation. Good enough. He asked:

"What the devil's that row, sergeant?"

The sergeant disappeared behind the muddied sacking curtain. There was a guard-room in there. The key-bugle said:

Fair   *kind.* . . .
    and
Fair   *Fair*   *Fair*
                      kind. . . .
    and . . .   *and* . . .   *and*

It might be two hundred yards off along the trenches.
Astonishing pleasure came to him from that seventeenth-
century air and the remembrance of those exact, quiet words.
. . . Or perhaps he had not got them right. Nevertheless,
they were exact and quiet. As efficient working beneath the
soul as the picks of miners in the dark.

The sergeant returned with the obvious information that it was 09 Griffiths practising on the cornet. Captain McKechnie 'ad promised to 'ear 'im after breakfast 'n' recommend 'im to the Divisional Follies to play at the concert to-night, if 'e likes 'im.

Tietjens said:

"Well, I hope Captain McKechnie likes him!"

He hoped McKechnie, with his mad eyes and his pestilential accent, would like that fellow. That fellow spread seventeenth-century atmosphere across the landscape over which the sun's rays were beginning to flood a yellow wash. Then, might the seventeenth century save the fellow's life for his good taste! For his life would probably be saved. He, Tietjens, would give him a pass back to division to get ready for the concert. So he would be out of the strafe. . . . Probably none of them would be alive after the strafe that brigade reported to be coming in. . . . Twenty-seven minutes, by now! Three hundred and twenty-eight fighting men against . . . say, a division. Any preposterous number . . . Well, the seventeenth century might as well save one man!

What had become of the seventeenth century? And Herbert and Donne and Crashaw and Vaughan, the silurist? . . . "Sweet day so cool, so calm, so bright, the bridal of the earth and sky! . . ." By Jove, it was that! . . . Old Campion, flashing like a popinjay in the scarlet and gilt of the major-general, had quoted that in the base camp, years ago. Or was it months? Or wasn't it: "But at my back I always hear Time's winged chariots hurrying near," that he had quoted?

Anyhow, not bad for an old general!

He wondered what had become of that elegant collection of light yellow, scarlet and gilt. . . . Somehow he always thought of Campion as in light yellow, rather than khaki, so much did he radiate light. . . . Campion and his, Tietjens', wife, radiating light together—she in a golden gown!

Campion was about due in these latitudes. It was astonishing that he had not turned up before. But poor old Puffles with his abominably weakened army had done too jolly well to be replaced. Even at the request of the minister who hated him. Good for him!

It occurred to him that if he . . . call it "stopped one" that day, Campion would probably marry his, Tietjens', widow. . . Sylvia in crape. With perhaps a little white about it!

The cornet—obviously it was not a key-bugle—remarked:

                  : *her pass   by . . .*
                          ing
  I did but view

and then stopped to reflect. After a moment it added med-
itatively:

              .her . . .
            .   .
And   .   .
    now   .   .
       I   .   .
    love   . *till*
              I die!

That would scarcely refer to Sylvia. . . . Still, perhaps in
crape, with a touch of white, passing by, very tall . . . Say,
in a seventeenth-century street . . .

   The only satisfactory age in England! . . . Yet what chance
had it to-day? Or, still more, to-morrow? In the sense that
the age of, say, Shakespeare had a chance. Or Pericles! Or
Augustus!

   Heaven knew, we did not want a preposterous drum-beating
such as the Elizabethans produced—and received. Like lions
at a fair. . . . But what chance had quiet fields, Anglican
sainthood, accuracy of thought, heavy-leaved, timbered
hedgerows, slowly creeping plough-lands moving up the
slopes? . . . Still, the land remains. . . .

   The land remains. . . . It remains! . . . At that same
moment the dawn was wetly revealing; over there in George
Herbert's parish . . . What was it called? . . . What the
devil was its name? Oh, hell! . . . Between Salisbury and
Wilton . . . The tiny church . . . But he refused to consider
the plough-lands, the heavy groves, the slow high road above
the church that the dawn was at that moment wetly revealing
—until he could remember that name. . . . He refused to
consider that, probably even to-day, that land ran to . . .
produced the stock of . . . Anglican sainthood. The quiet
thing!

   But until he could remember the name he would consider
nothing. . . .

   He said:

   "Are those damned Mills bombs coming?"

   The sergeant said:

   "In ten minutes they'll be 'ere, sir." Hay Cumpny had just
telephoned that they were coming in now.

It was almost a disappointment: in an hour or so, without bombs, they might all have been done with. As quiet as the seventeenth century: in heaven. . . . The beastly bombs would have to explode before that, now! They might, in consequence, survive. . . . Then what was he, Tietjens, going to do! Take orders! It was thinkable. . . .

He said:

"Those bloody imbeciles of Huns are coming over in an hour's time, brigade says. Get the beastly bombs served out, but keep enough in store to serve as an emergency ration if we should want to advance. . . . Say a third. For C and D companies. . . . Tell the adjutant I'm going along all the trenches and I want the assistant-adjutant, Mr. Aranjuez, and Orderly-Corporal Colley to come with me. . . . As soon as the bombs come for certain! . . . I don't want the men to think they've got to stop a Hun rush without bombs. . . . They're due to begin their barrage in fourteen minutes, but they won't really come over without a hell of a lot of preparation. . . . I don't know how brigade knows all this!"

The name "Bemerton" suddenly came on to his tongue. Yes, Bemerton, Bemerton, Bemerton was George Herbert's parsonage. Bemerton, outside Salisbury. . . . The cradle of the race as far as our race was worth thinking about. He imagined himself standing up on a little hill, a lean contemplative parson, looking at the land sloping down to Salisbury spire. A large, clumsily bound seventeenth-century testament, Greek, beneath his elbow. . . . Imagine standing up on a hill! It was the unthinkable thing there!

The sergeant was lamenting, a little wearily, that the Huns were coming.

"Hi did think them bleeding 'Uns, 'scuse me, sir, wasn' per'aps coming this morning. . . . Give us a rest an' a chance to clear up a bit. . . ." He had the tone of a resigned schoolboy saying that the head *might* have given the school a holiday on the Queen's birthday. But what the devil did that man think about his approaching dissolution?

That was the unanswerable question. He, Tietjens, had been asked several times what death was like. . . . Once, in a cattle-truck under a bridge, near a Red Cross Clearing Station, by a miserable fellow called Perowne. In the presence of the troublesome lunatic called McKechnie. You would have thought that even a movement-order officer would have managed to send up the line that triangle differently arranged. Perowne was known to have been his wife's lover; he, Tietjens, against his will, had been given the job, as second-in-

command of the battalion, that McKechnie wanted madly.
And indeed he had a right to it. They *ought* not to have
been sent up together.

But there they had been—Perowne broken down, princi-
pally at the thought that he was not going to see his, Tietjens', wife ever again in a golden gown. . . . Unless, perhaps,
with a golden harp on a cloud, for he looked at things like
that. . . . And, positively, as soon as that baggage-car—it
had been a baggage-car, not a cattle-truck!—had discharged
the deserter with escort and the three wounded Cochin-
Chinese plate-layers whom the French authorities had palmed
off on them . . . And where the devil had they all been
going? Obviously up into the line, and already pretty near
it: near division headquarters. But where? . . . God knew!
Or when? God knew too! . . . A fine-ish day with a scanty
remains of not quite melted snow in the cutting and the
robins singing in the coppice above. Say February. . . . Say
St. Valentine's Day: which, of course, would agitate Perowne
some more. . . . Well, positively as soon as the baggage-car
had discharged the wounded, who had groaned, and the
sheepish escort, who did not know whether they ought to be
civil to the deserter in the presence of the orfcers, and the
deserter, who kept on defiantly—or, if you like, broken-
heartedly, for there was no telling the difference—asking the
escort questions as to the nature of their girls, or volunteering
information as to the intimate behaviour of *his* . . . The
deserter a gipsyfied, black-eyed fellow with an immense jeer-
ing mouth; the escort a corporal and two Tommies, blond
and blushing East Kents, remarkably polished about the buttons and brass numerals, with beautifully neatly put on put-
tees: obviously Regulars, coming from behind the lines; the
Cochin-Chinese, with indistinguishable broad yellow faces,
brown poetic eyes, furred top-boots and blue-furred hoods
over their bandaged heads and swathed faces. Seated, leaning
back against the side of the box-truck and groaning now and
then and shivering all the time. . . .

Well, the moment they had been cleared out at the deputy
sub. R.T.O.s tin shed by the railway bridge, the fellow Perowne with his well-padded presence and his dark babu-Hin-
duish aspect had bubbled out with questions as to the hereafter
according to Tietjens and as to the nature of death; the
immediate process of dissolution: dying. . . . And in
between Perowne's questions McKechnie, with his unspeakable intonation and his dark eyes as mad as a cat's, had asked
Tietjens how he dared get himself appointed second-in-com-

mand of his, McKechnie's, own battalion. . . . "You're no soldier," he would burst out. "Do you think you are a b——y infantryman? You're a meal-sack, and what the devil's to become of *my* battalion. . . . Mine. . . . My battalion! *Our* battalion of pals!"

That had been in, presumably, February, and, presumably, it was now April. The way the dawn came up looked like April. . . . What did it matter? . . . That damned truck had stayed under that bridge for two hours and a half . . . in the process of the eternal waiting that is war. You hung about and you hung about, and you kicked your heels and you kicked your heels: waiting for Mills bombs to come, or for jam, or for generals, or for the tanks, or transport, or the clearance of the road ahead. You waited in offices under the eyes of somnolent orderlies, under fire on the banks of canals; you waited in hotels, dug-outs, tin sheds, ruined houses. There will be no man who survives of His Majesty's Armed Forces that shall not remember those eternal hours when time itself stayed still as the true image of bloody war! . . .

Well, in that case Providence seemed to have decreed a waiting just long enough to allow Tietjens to persuade the unhappy mortal called Perowne that death was not a very dreadful affair. . . . He had enough intellectual authority to persuade the fellow with his glued-down black hair that death supplied his own anaesthetics. That was the argument. On the approach of death all the faculties are so numbed that you feel neither pain nor apprehension. . . . He could still hear the heavy, authoritative words that, on that occasion, he had used.

The Providence of Perowne! For, when he was dug out after, next night having been buried in going up into the trenches, they said he had a smile like a young baby's on his face. He didn't have long to wait and died with a smile on his face . . . nothing having so much become him during the life as . . . well, a becoming smile! During life he had seemed a worried, fussing sort of chap.

Bully for Perowne. . . . But what about him, Tietjens? Was that the sort of thing that Providence ought to do to one? . . . That's TEMPTING GOD!

The sergeant beside him said:

"Then a man could stand hup on an 'ill. . . . You really mean to say, sir, that you think a man will be able to stand up on a bleedin' 'ill. . . ."

Presumably Tietjens had been putting heart into that acting temporary sergeant-major. He could not remember what he had been saying to the N.C.O. because his mind had been so deeply occupied with the image of Perowne. . . . He said:

"You're a Lincolnshire man, aren't you? You come from a Fen country. What do you want to stand up on a hill for?"

The man said:

"Ah, but you *do,* sir!"

He added:

"You want to stand up! Take a look around. . . ." He struggled for expression: "Like as if you wanted to breathe deep after bein' in a stoopin' posture for a long time!"

Tietjens said:

"Well, you can do that here. With discretion. I did it just now. . . ."

The man said:

"You, sir. . . You're a law hunto yourself!"

It was the most considerable shock that Tietjens received in the course of his military career. And the most considerable reward.

There were all these inscrutable beings: the Other Ranks, a brownish mass, spreading underground, like clay strata in the gravel, beneath all this waving country that the sun would soon be warming: they were in holes, in tunnels, behind sackcloth curtains, carrying on . . . carrying on some sort of life: conversing, breathing, desiring. But completely mysterious, in the mass. Now and then you got a glimpse of a passionate desire: "A man could stand up on a bleedin' 'ill!"; now and then you got—though you knew that they watched you eternally and knew the minutest gestures of your sleep —you got some sort of indication as to how they regarded you: "You are a law unto yourself!"

That must be hero-worship: an acting temporary regimental sergeant-major, without any real knowledge of his job, extemporizing, not so long ago a carrier in an eastern county of remarkable flatness, does not tell his acting commanding officer that he is a law unto himself without meaning it to be a flattering testimony: a certificate, as far as it went, of trustworthiness. . . .

They were now crawling out into the light of day . . . from behind the sacking: six files that he had last night transferred from C to D Coy., D having been reduced to forty-three rank and file. They shuffled out, an extraordinary Falstaff's battalion of muddy odd-come shorts; fell into some sort of alignment in the trench; shuffled an inch further this way, an inch further that; pushed up their chin-straps and

pulled them down; humped up their packs by hunching their
shoulders and jerking; adjusted their water bottles and fell
into some sort of immobility, their rifles, more or less aligned,
poked out before them. In that small company they were
men of all sorts of sizes, of all sorts of disparities and gro-
tesquenesses of physique. Two of them were music-hall co-
medians, and the whole lot looked as if they made up a
knock-about turn. . . . The Rag-Time Army: at its vocation:
living and breathing.

The sergeant called them to attention and they wavered
back and forward. The sergeant said:

"The commandin' officer's lookin' at you. FIX . . . B'ts!"

And, positively, a dwarf concealed under a puddin-basin
shuffled a foot-length and a half forward in the mud, protruded his rifle-muzzle between his bent knees, jerked his head
swiftly to strain his sight along the minute line. . . . It was
like a blurred fairy-tale! Why did that dwarf behave in a
smart and soldierly manner? Through despair? It wasn't
likely!

The men wavered like the edge of a field of tall grass
with the wind running along it; they felt round themselves
for their bayonet-handles, like women attempting difficult
feats with their skirts. . . . The dwarf cut his hand smartly
away to his side, as the saying is; the men pulled their rifles
up into line. Tietjens exclaimed:

"Stand at ease: stand easy," negligently enough, then he
burst out in uncontrollable irritation: "For *God's* sake, put
your beastly hats straight!" The men shuffled uneasily, this
being no order known to them, and Tietjens explained: "No,
this isn't drill. It's only that your hats all at sixes and sevens
give me the pip!" And the whispers of the men went down
the little line:

"You 'ear the orfcer. . . . Gives 'im the pip, we do! . . .
Goin' for a wawk in the pawk wiv our gels, we are. . . ."
They glanced nevertheless aside and upwards at each other's
tin-hat rims and said: "Shove 'im a shade forward, 'Orace. . . .
You tighten your martingale, 'Erb!" They were gaily rueful
and impenitently profane: they had had thirty-six hours of
let-off. A fellow louder-than-hummed:

  " 'As I wawk erlong ther Bor dee Berlong
   Wiv an indipendent air. . .'

"W'ere's me swegger-kine, you fellers!"

Tietjens addressed him:

"Did you ever hear Coborn sing that, Runt?" and Runt replied:

"Yes, sir. I was the hind legs of the elephant when he sung it in the Old Drury panto!" A little, dark, beady-eyed Cockney; his enormous mouth moved lip on lip as if he were chewing a pebble in pride at the reminiscence. The men's voices went on: " 'Ind legs 'f the elephink! . . . good ol' helefink. . . . I'll go 'n' see 'n elephink first thing I do in Blighty!"

Tietjens said:

"I'll give every man of you a ticket for Drury Lane next Boxing Day. We'll all be in London for the next Boxing Day. Or Berlin!"

They exclaimed polyphonically and low:

"Oo-er! Djee 'ear 'im? Djee 'ear the orfcer? The noo C.O.?"

A hidden man said:

"Mike it the old Shoreditch Empire, sir, 'n' we'll thenk you!"

Another:

"I never keered fer the Lane meself! Give me the old Balham for Boxing Day." The sergeant made the sounds for them to move off.

They shuffled off up the trench. An unseen man said:

"Better'n a bleedin' dipso!" Lips said "S-h-h-h!"

The sergeant shouted—with an astonishing, brutal panic:

"You shut your bleedin' mouth, you man, or I'll shove you in the b——y clink!" He looked nevertheless at Tietjens with calm satisfaction a second later.

"A good lot of chaps, sir," he said. "The best!" He was anxious to wipe out the remembrance of the last spoken word. "Give 'em the right sort of officers 'n' they'll beat the world!"

"Do you think it makes any difference to them what officers they have?" Tietjens asked. "Wouldn't it be all the same if they had just anyone?"

The sergeant said:

"No, sir. They bin frightened these last few days. Now they're better."

This was just exactly what Tietjens did not want to hear. He hardly knew why. Or he did. . . . He said:

"I should have thought these men knew their job so well —for this sort of thing—that they hardly needed orders. It cannot make much difference whether they receive orders or not."

The sergeant said:

"It *does* make a difference, sir," in a tone as near that of cold obstinacy as he dare attain to; the feeling of the approaching strafe was growing on them. It hung over them.

McKechnie stuck his head out from behind the sacking. The sacking had the lettering P X L in red and the word *Minn* in black. McKechnie's eyes were blazing maniacally. Jumping maniacally in his head. They always were jumping maniacally in his head. He was a tiring fellow. He was wearing not a tin hat, but an officer's helmet. The gilt dragon on it glittered. The sun was practically up, somewhere. As soon as its disk cleared the horizon, the Huns, according to brigade, were to begin sending over their wearisome stuff. In thirteen and a half minutes.

McKechnie gripped Tietjens by the arm, a familiarity that Tietjens detested. He hissed—he really hissed because he was trying to speak under his breath:

"Come past the next traverse. I want to speak to you."

In correctly prepared trenches, made according to order, as these had been to receive them in retreat, by a Regular battalion acting under the orders of the Royal Engineers, you go along a straight ditch of trench for some yards; then you find a square block of earth protruding inwards from the parapet round which you must walk; then you come to another straight piece, then to another traverse, and so on to the end of the line, the lengths and dimensions varying to suit the nature of the terrain or the character of the soil. These outjuttings were designed to prevent the lateral spreading of fragments of shell bursting in the trench, which would otherwise serve as a funnel, like the barrel of a gun, to direct those parts of missiles into men's bodies. It was also exciting—as Tietjens expected to be doing before the setting of the not quite risen sun—to crouch rapidly along past one of them, the heart moving very disagreeably, the revolver protruded well in advance, with half a dozen careless fellows with grenades of sorts just behind you. And you not knowing whether, crouching against the side that was just round the corner, you would or would not find a whitish, pallid, dangerous object that you would have no time to scrutinize closely.

Past the nearest of these McKechnie led Tietjens. He was portentous and agitated.

At the end of the next stretch of trench, leaning, as it were, against a buttress in an attitude of intense fatigue, was a mud-coloured, very thin, tall fellow; squatting dozing on his heels in the mud just beside that one's foot was another, a proper Glamorganshire man, of whom not many more than ten were left in the battalion. The standing man was leaning like that to look through a loop-hole that had been placed very close to the buttress of raw earth. He grunted something to his companion and continued looking intently. The other man grunted too.

McKechnie withdrew precipitately into the recessed pathway. The column of earth in their faces gave a sense of oppression. He said:

"Did you put that fellow up to saying that damnable thing? . . ." He repeated: "That perfectly damnable thing! Damnable!" Besides hating Tietjens, he was shocked, pained, femininely lachrymose. He gazed into Tietjens' eyes like a forsaken mistress fit to do a murder, with a sort of wistful incredulity of despair.

To that Tietjens was accustomed. For the last two months McKechnie whispering in the ear of the C.O. wherever battalion headquarters might happen to be, McKechnie with his arms spread abroad on the table and his chin nearly on the cloth that they had always managed to retain in spite of three precipitate moves, McKechnie with his mad eyes every now and then moving in the direction of Tietjens, had been almost the most familiar object of Tietjens' night landscapes. They wanted him gone so that McKechnie might once again become second-in-command of that body of pals. . . . That indeed was what they were . . . with the addition of a great deal too much of what they called 'ooch.

Tietjens obviously could not go. There was no way of managing it: he had been put there by old Campion, and there he must remain. So that by the agreeable irony of Providence there was Tietjens, who had wanted above all McKechnie's present relatively bucolic job, hated to hell by half a dozen quite decent if trying young squits—the pals—because Tietjens was in his, McKechnie's, desired position. It seemed to make it all the worse that they were all, with the exception of the commanding officer himself, of the little, dark, Cockney type and had the Cockney's voice, gesture and intonation, so that Tietjens felt himself like a blond Gulliver with hair very silver in patches, rising up amongst a lot of Lilliputian brown creatures. . . . Portentous and unreasonably noticeable.

A large cannon, nearer than the one that had lately spoken, but, as it were, with a larger but softer voice, remarked: "Phoh-h-h-h-h-h-h-h," the sound wandering round the landscape for a long while. After a time about four

coupled railway trains hurtled jovially amongst the clouds
and went a long way away—four in one. They were probably trying to impress the North Sea.

It might of course be the signal for the German barrage
to begin. Tietjens' heart stopped; his skin on the nape of the
neck began to prickle; his hands were cold. That was fear:
the BATTLE FEAR, experienced in strafes. He might not
again be able to hear himself think. Not ever. What did he
want of life? . . . Well, just not to lose his reason. One
would pray. Not that . . . Otherwise, perhaps a nice parsonage might do. It was just thinkable. A place in which
forever to work at the theory of waves. . . . But of course
it was not thinkable. . .

He was saying to McKechnie:

"You ought not to be here without a tin hat. You will
have to put a tin hat on if you mean to stop here. I can
give you four minutes if that is not the strafe beginning.
Who's been saying what?"

McKechnie said:

"I'm not stopping here. I'm going back, after I've given
you a piece of my mind, to the beastly job you have got
me defiled with."

Tietjens said:

"Well, you'll put on a tin hat to go there, please. And
don't ride your horse, if you've got it here, till after you're
a hundred yards at least down a communication trench."

McKechnie asked how Tietjens dared give him orders and
Tietjens said: Fine he would look with divisional transport
dead in his lines at five in the morning in a parade hat.
McKechnie with objurgations said that the transport officer
had the right to consult the C.O. of a battalion he supplied.
Tietjens said:

"I'm commanding here. You've not consulted me!"

It appeared to him queer that they should be behaving
like that when you could hear . . . oh, say, the wings of
the angel of death. . . . You can "almost hear the very
rustling of his wings" was the quotation. Good enough rhet-
oric. . . But of course that was how armed men would behave. . . . At all times!

He had been trying the old trick of the military, clipped
voice on the half-dotty subject. It had before then reduced
McKechnie to some sort of military behaviour.

It reduced him in this case to a maudlin state. He exclaimed with a sort of lachrymose agony:

"This is what it has come to with the old battalion . . .

the b——y, b——y, b——y old battalion of b——rs!" Each
imprecation was a sob. "How we worked at it. . . . And now
. . . *you've* got it!"

Tietjens said:

"Well, you were Vice-Chancellor's Latin Prize man once.
It's what we get reduced to." He added: "*Vos mellificatis
apes!*"

McKechnie said with gloomy contempt:

"You . . . You're no Latinist!"

By now Tietjens had counted two hundred and eighty since
the big cannon had said "Pho-o-o-o-h." Perhaps, then, it was
not the signal for the barrage to begin. . . . Had it been, it
would have begun before now; it would have come thumping along on the heels of the "Pho-o-o-h." His hands and
the nape of his neck were preparing to become normal.

Perhaps the strafe would not come at all that day. There
was the wind. If anything it was strengthening. Yesterday he
had suspected that the Germans hadn't got any tanks handy.
Perhaps the ugly, senseless armadilloes—and incapable at
that! underengined!—had all got stuck in the marshes in
front of G section. Perhaps the heavy artillery fire of ours
that had gone on most of yesterday had been meant to pound
the beastly things to pieces. Moving, they looked like slow
rats, their noses to the ground, snouting crumbs of garbage.
When they were still they looked merely pensive!

Perhaps the strafe would not come. He hoped it would
not. He did not want a strafe with himself in command of
the battalion. He did not know what to do: what he ought
to do by the book. He knew what he would do. He would
stroll about along those deep trenches. Stroll. With his hands
in his pockets. Like General Gordon in pictures. He would
say contemplative things as the time dragged on. . . . A
rather abominable sort of time, really. . . . But that would
introduce into the battalion a spirit of calm that it had
lately lacked . . . The night before last the C.O., with a
bottle in each hand, had hurled them both at Huns who
did not materialize for an hour and a half. Even the pals
had omitted to laugh. After that he, Tietjens, had taken
command. With lots of the orderly-room papers under both
arms. They had had to be in a hurry. At night. With men
suggesting pale-grey Canadian trappers coming out of holes!

He did not want to command in a strafe: or at any other
time! He hoped the unfortunate C.O. would get over his
trouble by the evening. . . . But he supposed that he, Tiet-

jens, would get through it all right if he had to. Like the
man who had never tried playing the violin!

McKechnie had suddenly become lachrymosely feminine:
like a woman pleading, large-eyed, for her lover; his eyes
explored Tietjens' face for signs of treachery: for signs that
what he said was not what he meant in his heart. He said:

"What are you going to do about Bill? Poor old Bill that
has sweated for his battalion as you never . . ." He began
again:

"Think of poor old Bill! You can't be *thinking* of doing
the dirty on him. . . . *No* man could be such a swine!"

It was curious how those circumstances brought out the
feminine that was in man. What was that ass of a German
professor's theory . . . formula? M^y *plus* W^x equals man? . . .
Well, if God hadn't invented woman, men would have had
to do so. In that sort of place. You grew sentimental. He,
Tietjens, was growing sentimental. He said:

"What does Terence say about him this morning?"

The nice thing to have said would have been:

"Of course, old man, I'll do all I can to keep it dark!"
Terence was the M.O.—the man who had chucked his cap
at the Hun orderly.

McKechnie said:

"That's the damnable thing! Terence is ratty with him. He
won't take a pill!"

Tietjens said:

"What's that? What's that?"

McKechnie wavered: his desire for comfort became overpowering.

He said:

"Look here! *Do* the decent thing! You know how poor
Bill has worked for us! Get Terence not to report him to
brigade!"

This was wearisome: but it had to be faced.

A very minute subaltern—Aranjuez—in a perfectly impossible tin hat peered round the side of the bank. Tietjens
sent him away for a moment. . . . These tin hats were
probably all right: but they were the curse of the army. They
bred distrust! How could you trust a man whose incapable
hat tumbled forward on his nose? Or another, with his hat
on the back of his head, giving him the air of a ruined
gambler! Or a fellow who had put on a soap-dish. To amuse
the children: not a serious proceeding. . . . The German
things were better—coming down over the nape of the neck
and rising over the brows. When you saw a Hun sideways

he looked something: a serious proposition. Full of ferocity. A Hun up against a Tommy looked like a Holbein *lansknecht* fighting a music-hall turn. It made you feel that you were indeed a rag-time army. Rubbed it in!

McKechnie was reporting that the C.O. had refused to take a pill ordered him by the M.O. Unfortunately the M.O. was ratty that morning—too much hooch overnight! So he said he should report the C.O. to brigade. Not as being unfit for further service, for he wasn't. But for refusing to take the pill. It was damnable. Because if Bill wouldn't take a pill, he wouldn't . . . The M.O. said that if he took a pill, and stayed in bed that day—without hooch of course! —he would be perfectly fit on the morrow. He had been like that often enough before. The C.O. had always been given the dose before as a drench. He swore he would not take it as a ball. Sheer contrariety!

Tietjens was accustomed to think of the C.O. as a lad—a good lad, but young. They were, all the same, much of an age, and, for the matter of that, because of his deeply lined forehead the colonel looked the older often enough. But when he was fit he was fine. He had a hooked nose, a forcible, grey moustache, like two badger-haired paint-brushes joined beneath the nose, pink skin as polished as the surface of a billiard-ball, a noticeably narrow but high forehead, an extremely piercing glance from rather colourless eyes; his hair was black and most polished in slight waves. He was a soldier.

He was, that is to say, the ranker. Of soldiering in the English sense—the real soldiering of peace-time, parades, social events, spit and polish, hard-worked summers, leisurely winters, India, the Bahamas, Cairo seasons and the rest—he only knew the outside, having looked at it from the barrack windows, the parade-ground and, luckily for him, from his colonel's house. He had been a most admirable batman to that colonel, had—in Simla—married the colonel memsahib's lady's maid, had been promoted to the orderly room, to the corporals' and sergeants' messes, had become a musketry colour-sergeant and, two months before the war, had been given a commission. He would have gained this before but for a slight—a very slight—tendency to overdrinking, which had given on occasion a similarly slight tone of insolence to his answers to field-officers. Elderly field-officers on parade are apt to make slight mistakes in their drill, giving the command to move to the right when technically, though troops are moving to the right, the command should be: "Move to the left!"; and the officer's left being the troops' right, on a field-day, after lunch, field-officers of a little rustiness are apt to grow confused. It then becomes the duty of warrant-officers present, if possible, to rectify, or if not, to accept the responsibility for the resultant commotion. On two occasions during his brilliant career, being slightly elated, this wartime C.O. had neglected this military duty, the result being subsequent orderly-room strafes which remained as black patches when he looked back on his past life and which constantly embittered his remembrances. Professional soldiers are like that.

In spite of an exceptionally fine service record, he remained bitter, and upon occasion he became unreasonable. Being what the men—and for the matter of that, the officers of the battalion too—called a b——y h——ll of a pusher, he had brought his battalion up to a great state of efficiency; he had earned a double string of ribbons and by pushing his battalion into extremely tight places, by volunteering it for difficult services which, even during trench warfare, did present themselves, and by extricating what remained of it with singular skill during the first battle of the Somme on an occasion—perhaps the most lamentable of the whole war—when an entire division commanded by a political rather than a military general had been wiped out, he had earned for his battalion a French decoration called a *Fourragère,* which is seldom given to other than French regiments. These exploits and the spirit which dictated them were perhaps less appreciated by the men under his command than was imagined by the C.O. and his bosom friend Captain McKechnie, who had loyally aided him, but they *did* justify the two in attaching to the battalion the sort of almost maudlin sentimentality that certain parents will bestow upon their children.

In spite, however, of the appreciation that his services had received, the C.O. remained embittered. He considered that, by this time, he ought at least to have been given a brigade, if not a division, and he considered that if that was not the case, it was largely due to the two black marks against him as well as to the fact of his low social origin. And when he had a little liquor taken, these obsessions exaggerated themselves very quickly to a degree that very nearly endangered his career. It was not that he soaked—but there were occasions during that period of warfare when the consumption of a certain amount of alcohol was a necessity if the human being were to keep on carrying on and through

rough places. Then happy was the man who carried his liquor well.

Unfortunately the C.O. was not one of these. Worn out by continual attention to papers—at which he was no great hand—and by fighting that would continue for days on end, he would fortify himself with whisky, and immediately his bitternesses would overwhelm his mentality, the aspect of the world would change and he would rail at his superiors in the army and sometimes would completely refuse to obey orders, as had been the occasion a few nights before, when he had refused to let his battalion take part in the concerted retreat of the army corps. Tietjens had had to see to this.

Now, exasperated by the after-effects of several days' great anxieties and alcoholisms, he was refusing to take a pill. This was a token of his contempt for his superiors, the outcome of his obsession of bitterness.

3 ~

AN ARMY—especially in peace-time!—is a very complex and nicely adjusted affair, and though active operations against an enemy force are apt to blunt nicenesses and upset compensations—as they might for a chronometer!—and although this of ours, according to its own computation, was only a rag-time aggregation, certain customs of times when this force was also Regular had an enormous power of survival.

It may seem a comic affair that a colonel commanding a regiment in the midst of the most breathless period of hostilities should refuse to take a pill. But the refusal, precisely like a grain of sand in the works of a chronometer, may cause the most singular perturbations. It was so in this case.

A sick officer of the very highest rank is the subordinate of his doctor the moment he puts himself into the M.O.'s hands: he must obey orders as if he were a Tommy. A colonel whole and in his senses may obviously order his M.O. to go here and there and to perform this or that duty; the moment he becomes sick, the fact that his body is the property of His Majesty the King comes forcibly into operation and the M.O. is the representative of the sovereign in so far as bodies are concerned. This is very reasonable and proper, because sick bodies are not only of no use to the King, but are enormously detrimental to the army that has to cart them about.

In the case that Tietjens had perforce to worry over, the

matter was very much complicated in the first place by the
fact of the great personal dislike that the C.O. had mani-
fested—though always with a sort of field-officer's monumental courtesy—towards himself, and then because Tietjens had
a very great respect for the abilities of the commanding
officer as commanding officer. His rag-time battalion of a
rag-time army was as nearly on the level of an impeccable
Regular battalion as such a unit with its constantly changing
personnel could possibly be. Nothing had much more impressed Tietjens in the course of even the whole war than
the demeanour of the soldier whom the other night he had
seen firing engrossedly into invisibility. The man had fired
with care, had come down to reload with exact drill movements—which are the quickest possible. He had muttered
some words which showed that his mind was entirely on his
job, like a mathematician engrossed in an abstruse calculation. He had climbed back on to the parapet, continued to
fire engrossedly into invisibility, had returned and reloaded
and had again climbed back. He might have been firing off a
tie at the butts!

It was a very great achievement to have got men to fire
at moments of such stress with such complete tranquillity.
For discipline works in two ways: In the first place, it enables
the soldier in action to get through his movements in the
shortest possible time; and then the engrossment in the exact
performance begets a great indifference to danger. When,
with various-sized pieces of metal flying all round you, you
go composedly through efficient bodily movements, you are
not only wrapped up in your task, but you have the knowledge that that exact performance is every minute decreasing
your personal danger. In addition, you have the feeling that
Providence ought to—and very frequently does—specially
protect you. It would not be right that a man exactly and
scrupulously performing his duty to his sovereign, his native
land and those it holds dear should not be protected by a
special Providence. And he is!

It is not only that that engrossed marksman might—and
very probably did—pick off an advancing enemy with every
second shot, and thus diminish his personal danger to that
extent, it is that the regular and as if mechanical falling
of comrades spreads disproportionate dismay in advancing
or halted troops. It is no doubt terrible to you to have large
numbers of your comrades instantaneously annihilated by the
explosion of some huge engine, but huge engines are blind
and thus accidental; a slow, regular picking off of the men

beside you is evidence that human terribleness that is not blind or accidental is cold-bloodedly and unshakably turning its attention to a spot very near you. It may very shortly turn its attention to yourself.

Of course, it is disagreeable when artillery is bracketing across your line: a shell falls a hundred yards in front of you, another a hundred yards behind you: the next will be half-way between, and you are half-way between. The waiting wrings your soul, but it does not induce panic or the desire to run—at any rate to nearly the same extent. Where, in any event, could you run to?

But from coldly and mechanically advancing and firing troops you *can* run. And the C.O. was accustomed to boast that on the several occasions when imitating the second battalion of the regiment he had been able to line his men up on tapes before letting them go in an attack and had insisted that they should advance at a very slow double indeed, and in exact alignment, his losses had been not only less than those of every other battalion in the division, but they had been almost farcically negligible. Faced with troops advancing remorselessly and with complete equanimity, the good Württembergers had fired so wildly and so high that you could hear their bullets overhead like a flock of wild geese at night. The effect of panic is to make men fire high. They pull too sharply on their triggers.

These boasts of their Old Man naturally reached the men: they would be uttered before warrant-officers and the orderly-room staff; and the men—than whom in this matter none are keener mathematicians—were quick to see that the losses of their battalion until lately, at any rate, had been remarkably smaller than those of other units engaged in the same places. So that hitherto, though the men had regarded their colonel with mixed feelings, he had certainly come out on top. That he was a b——y h——ll of a pusher did not elate them; they would have preferred to be reserved for less dangerous enterprises than those by which the battalion gained its remarkable prestige. On the other hand, though they were constantly being pushed into nasty scrapes, they lost less than units in quieter positions, and that pleased them. But they still asked themselves: "If the Old Man let us be quiet, shouldn't we lose proportionately still less? No one at all?"

That had been the position until very lately: until a week or so, or even a day or so, before.

But for more than a fortnight this army had been what amounted to on the run. It retreated with some personal

stubbornness and upon prepared positions, but these prepared
positions were taken with such great speed and method by
the enormous forces attacking it that hostilities had assumed
the aspect almost of a war of movement. For this these
troops were singularly ill-adapted, their training having been
almost purely that suited for the process of attrition known
as trench warfare. In fact, though good with bombs and even
with the bayonet, and though courageous and composed when
not in motion, these troops were singularly inept when it was
a matter of keeping in communication with the units on
either side of them, or even within their own unit, and they
had practically no experience in the use of the rifle when
in motion. To both these branches the enemy had devoted
untiring attention all through the period of relative inaction
of the winter that had now closed, and in both particulars
their troops though by now apparently inferior in *moral* were
remarkably superior. So it appeared to be merely a matter
of waiting for a period of easterly winds for this army to be
pushed into the North Sea. The easterly winds were needed
for the use of the gas, without which, in the idea of the
German leaders, it was impossible to attack.

The position, nevertheless, had been desperate and remained desperate, and standing there in the complete tranquillity and inaction of an April morning with a slight westerly
breeze, Tietjens realized that he was experiencing what
were the emotions of an army practically in flight. So at
least he saw it. The use of gas had always been extremely
disliked by the enemy's men, and its employment in cylinders
had long since been abandoned. But the German Higher
Staff persisted in preparing their attacks by dense screens of
gas put over by huge plasterings of shells. These screens the
enemy forces refused to enter if the wind blew in their
direction.

There had come in, then, the factor which caused him
himself to feel particular discomfort.

The fact that the battalion was remarkably ably commanded and unusually well disciplined had not, of course,
been overlooked by either brigade or division. And the brigade, too, happened to be admirable. Thus—these things did
happen even in the confused periods that preceded the final
breaking up of trench warfare—the brigade was selected to
occupy positions where the enemy divisions might be expected
to be hottest in attack, the battalion was selected to occupy
the hottest points in that hottest sector of the line. The
chickens of the C.O.'s efficiency had come home to roost.

It had been, as Tietjens felt all over his body, nearly more than flesh and blood could stand. Do what the C.O. had been able to do to husband his men, and do what discipline could do to aid in the process, the battalion was reduced to not more than a third of what would have been a reasonable strength for the position it had had to occupy—and to abandon. And it was small comfort to the men that the Wiltshires on their right and the Cheshires on their left were in far worse case. So the aspect of the Old Man as a b——y h——ll of a pusher became foremost in their considerations.

To a sensitive officer—and all good officers in this respect are sensitive—the psychology of the men makes itself felt in innumerable ways. He can afford to be blind to the feelings of his officers, for officers have to stand so much at the hands of their seniors before the rules of the service give them a chance to retaliate that it takes a really bad colonel to put his own mess in a bad way. As officer you *have* to jump to your C.O.'s orders, to applaud his sentiments, to smile at his lighter witticisms and to guffaw at those that are more gross. That is the service. With the Other Ranks it is different. A discreet warrant-officer will discreetly applaud his officer's eccentricities and good humours, as will a sergeant desirous of promotion; but the rank and file are under no such compulsion. As long as a man comes to attention when spoken to, that is all that can be expected of him. He is under no obligation to understand his officer's witticisms, so he can still less be expected to laugh at or to repeat them with gusto. He need not even come very smartly to attention. . . .

And for some days the rank and file of the battalion had gone dead, and the C.O. was aware that it had gone dead. Of the various types of field-officer upon whom he could have modelled himself as regards the men, he had chosen that of the genial, rubicund, slightly whiskyfied C.O. who finishes every sentence with the words: "Eh, what?" In him it was a perfectly cold-blooded game for the benefit of the senior non-commissioned officers and the Other Ranks, but it had gradually become automatic.

For some days now, this mannerism had refused to work. It was as if Napoleon the Great had suddenly found that the device of pinching the ear of a grenadier on parade had suddenly become ineffective. After the "Eh, what!" like a pistol-shot the man to whom it was addressed had not all but shuffled nor had any other men within earshot tittered and whispered to their pals. They had all remained just loutish. And it is a considerable test of courage to remain loutish under the Old Man's eyes!

All this the C.O. knew by the book, having been through it. And Tietjens knew that the C.O. knew it; and he half suspected that the C.O. knew that he, Tietjens, knew it. . . . And that the pals and the Other Ranks also knew: that, in fact, everyone knew that everyone knew. It was like a nightmare game of bridge with all hands exposed and all the players ready to snatch pistols from their hip pockets. . . .

And Tietjens, for his sins, now held the trump card and was in play!

It was a loathsome position. He loathed having to decide the fate of the C.O. as he loathed the prospect of having to restore the *moral* of the men—if they survived.

And he was faced now by the conviction that he could do it. If he hadn't felt himself get his hand in with that dozen of disreputable tramps, he would not have felt that he could do it. Then he must have used his moral authority with the doctor to get the Old Man patched up, drugged up, bucked up sufficiently to carry the battalion at least to the end of the retreat of the next few days. It was obvious that that must be done if there was no one else to take command— no one else that was pretty well certain to handle the men all right. But if there *was* anyone else to take over, didn't the C.O.'s condition make it too risky to let him remain in authority? Did it, or didn't it? Did it, or didn't it?

Looking at McKechnie coolly as if to see where next he should plant his fist, he had thus speculated. And he was aware that, at the most dreadful moment of his whole life, his besetting sin, as the saying is, was getting back on him. With the dreadful dread of the approaching strafe all over him, with a weight on his forehead, his eyebrows, his heavily labouring chest, he had to take . . . responsibility. And to realize that he was a fit person to take responsibility.

He said to McKechnie:

"The M.O. is the person who has to dispose of the colonel."

McKechnie exclaimed:

"By God, if that drunken little squit dares . . ."

Tietjens said:

"Derry will act along the lines of my suggestions. He doesn't have to take orders from me. But he has said that he will act along the lines of my suggestions. I shall accept the moral responsibility."

He felt the desire to pant: as if he had just drunk at a

draught a too great quantity of liquid. He did not pant. He looked at his wrist-watch. Of the time he had decided to give McKechnie, thirty seconds remained.

McKechnie made wonderful use of the time. The Germans sent over several shells. Not such very long-distance shells either. For ten seconds McKechnie went mad. He was always going mad. He was a bore. If that were only the German customary pooping off. . . . But it was heavier. Unusual obscenities dropped from the lips of McKechnie. There was no knowing where the German projectiles were going. Or aimed at. A steam laundry in Bailleul as like as not. He said:

"Yes! Yes! Aranjuez!"

The tiny subaltern had peeped again, with his comic hat, round the corner of the pinkish gravel buttress. . . . A good, nervous boy. Imagining that the fact that he had reported had not been noticed! The gravel certainly looked more pink now the sun was come up . . . It was rising on Bemerton! Or perhaps not so far to the west yet. The parsonage of George Herbert, author of "Sweet day so cool, so calm, so bright, the bridal of the earth and sky!"

It was odd where McKechnie, who was still shouting, got his words for unnatural vice. He had been Latin Prize man. But he was probably quite pure. The words very likely meant nothing to him. . . . As to the Tommies! . . . Then, why did they use them?

The German artillery thumped on! Heavier than the usual salvos with which methodically they saluted the dawn. But there were no shells falling in that neighbourhood. So it might not be the barrage opening the Great Strafe! Very likely they were being visited by some little German prince and wanted to show him what shooting was. Or by Field-Marshal Count von Brunkersdorf! Who had ordered them to shoot down the chimney of the Bailleul steam laundry. Or it might be sheer irresponsibility such as distinguished all gunners. Few Germans were imaginative enough to be irresponsible, but no doubt their gunners were more imaginative than other Germans.

He remembered being up in the artillery O.P.—what the devil was its name?—before Albert. On the Albert-Bécourt-Bécordel Road! What the *devil* was its name? A gunner had been looking through his glasses. He had said to Tietjens: "Look at that fat . . ." And through the glasses lent him, Tietjens had seen, on a hill-side in the direction of Martinpuich, a fat Hun, in shirt and trousers, carrying in his right hand a food tin from which he was feeding himself with his left. A fat, lousy object: suggesting an angler on a quiet day. The gunner had said to Tietjens:

"Keep your glass on him!"

And they had chased that miserable German about that naked hill-side, with shells, for ten minutes. Whichever way he bolted, they put a shell in front of him. Then they let him go. His action, when he had realized that they were really attending to him, had been exactly that of a rabbit dodging out of the wheat the reapers have just reached. At last he just lay down. He wasn't killed. They had seen him get up and walk off later. Still carrying his bait can!

His antics had afforded those gunners infinite amusement. It afforded them almost more when all the German artillery on that front, imagining that God knew what was the matter, had awakened and plastered heaven and earth and everything between for a quarter of an hour with every imaginable kind of missile. And had then, abruptly, shut up. . . . Yes. . . . Irresponsible people, gunners!

The incident had really occurred because Tietjens had happened to ask that gunner how much he imagined it had cost in shells to smash to pieces an indescribably smashed field of about twenty acres that lay between Bazentin-le-petit and Mametz Wood. The field was unimaginably smashed, pulverized, powdered. . . . The gunner had replied that with shells from all the forces employed it might have cost three million sterling. Tietjens asked how many men the gunner imagined might have been killed there. The gunner said he didn't begin to know. None at all, as like as not! No one was very likely to have been strolling about there for pleasure, and it hadn't contained any trenches. It was just a field. Nevertheless, when Tietjens had remarked that in that case two Italian labourers with a steam-plough could have pulverized that field about as completely for, say, thirty shillings, the gunner had taken it quite badly. He had made his men poop off after that inoffensive Hun with the bait can, just to show what artillery *can* do.

. . . At that point Tietjens had remarked to McKechnie:

"For my part, I shall advise the M.O. to recommend that the colonel should be sent back on sick leave for a couple of months. It is within his power to do that."

McKechnie had exhausted all his obscene expletives. He was thus sane. His jaw dropped.

"Send the C.O. back!" he exclaimed lamentably. "At the very moment when . . ."

Tietjens exclaimed:

"Don't be an ass. Or don't imagine that I'm an ass. No one is going to reap any glory. In this army. Here and now!"

McKechnie said:

"But what price the money? Command pay! Nearly four quid a day. You could do with two-fifty quid at the end of his two months!"

Not so very long ago it would have seemed impossible that any man *could* speak to him about either his private financial affairs or his intimate motives.

He said:

"I have obvious responsibilities . . ."

"Some say," McKechnie went on, "that you're a b——y millionaire. One of the richest men in England. Giving coalmines to duchesses. So they say. Some say you're such a pauper that you hire your wife out to generals. . . . Any generals. That's how you get your jobs."

To that Tietjens had had to listen before. . . .

Max Redoubt . . . It had come suddenly on to his tongue —just as, before, the name of Bemerton had come, belatedly. The name of the artillery observation-post between Albert and Bécourt-Bécordel had been Max Redoubt! During the intolerable waitings of that half-forgotten July and August the name had been as familiar on his lips as . . . say, as Bemerton itself. . . . When I forget thee, oh, my Bemerton . . . or, oh, my Max Redoubt . . . may my right hand forget its cunning! . . . The unforgettables! . . . Yet he had forgotten them! . . .

If only for a time he had forgotten them. Then, his right hand might forget its cunning. If only for a time. . . . But even that might be disastrous: might come at a disastrous moment. . . . The Germans had suppressed themselves. Perhaps they had knocked down the laundry chimney. Or hit some G.S. waggons loaded with coal. . . . At any rate, that was not the usual morning strafe. That was to come. "Sweet day so cool——" began again.

McKechnie hadn't suppressed himself. He was going to get suppressed. He had just been declaring that Tietjens had not displayed any chivalry in not reporting the C.O. if he, Tietjens, considered him to be drunk—or even chronically alcoholic. No chivalry . . .

This was like a nightmare! . . . No it wasn't. It was like fever when things appear stiffly unreal. . . . And exaggeratedly real! Stereoscopic, you might say!

McKechnie, with an accent of sardonic hate, begged to remind Tietjens that if he considered the C.O. to be a drunkard he ought to have him put under arrest. King's Regs. exacted that. But Tietjens was too cunning. He meant to have that two-fifty quid. He might be a poor man and need it. Or a millionaire and mean. They said that was how millionaires became millionaires: by snapping up trifles of money that, God knows, would be Godsends to people like himself, McKechnie.

It occurred to Tietjens that two hundred and fifty pounds after this was over might be a Godsend to himself, in a manner of speaking. And then he thought:

"Why the devil shouldn't I earn it?"

What was he going to do? After this was over.

And it was going over. Every minute the Germans were not advancing they were losing. Losing the power to advance. . . . Now, this minute! It was exciting.

"No!" McKechnie said. "You're too cunning. If you got poor Bill cashiered for drunkenness you'd have no chance of commanding. They'd put in another pukka colonel. As a stop-gap, whilst Bill's on sick leave, you're pretty certain to get it. That's why you're doing the damnable thing you're doing."

Tietjens had a desire to go and wash himself. He felt physically dirty.

Yet what McKechnie said was true enough! It was true! . . . The mechanical impulse to divest himself of money was so strong that he began to say:

"In that case . . ." He was going to finish: "I'll *get* the damned fellow cashiered." But he didn't.

He was in a beastly hole. But decency demanded that he shouldn't act in panic. He had a mechanical, normal panic that made him divest himself of money. Gentlemen don't earn money. Gentlemen, as a matter of fact, don't do anything. They exist. Perfuming the air like Madonna lilies. Money comes into them as air through petals and foliage. Thus the world is made better and brighter. And, of course, thus political life can be kept clean! . . . So you can't make money.

But look here: This unit was the critical spot of the whole affair. The weak spots of brigade, division, army, British Expeditionary Force, Allied forces. . . . If the Hun went through there. . . . *Fuit Ilium et magna gloria.* . . . Not much glory!

He was bound to do his best for that unit. That poor

b——y unit. And for the poor b——y knock-about come-
dians to whom he had lately promised tickets for Drury Lane
at Christmas. . . . The poor devils had said they preferred
the Shoreditch Empire or the old Balham. . . . That was
typical of England. The Lane was the *locus classicus* of the
race, but these rag-time . . . heroes—call them heroes!—
preferred Shoreditch and Balham!

An immense sense of those grimy, shuffling, grouching,
dirty-nosed pantomime-supers came over him and an intense desire to give them a bit of luck, and he said:

"Captain McKechnie, you can fall out. And you will return to duty. Your own duty. In proper head-dress."

McKechnie, who had been talking, stopped with his head
on one side like a listening magpie. He said:

"What's this? What's this?" stupidly. Then he remarked:

"Oh, well, I suppose if you're in command . . ."

Tietjens said:

"It's usual to say 'sir' when addressing a senior officer on
parade. Even if you don't belong to his unit."

McKechnie said:

"Don't belong! . . . *I* don't . . . To the poor b——y old
pals! . . ."

Tietjens said:

"You're attached to division headquarters, and you'll get
back to it. Now! At once! . . . And you won't came back
here. Not while I'm in command. . . . Fall out. . . ."

That was really a duty—a feudal duty!—performed for
the sake of the rag-time fellows. They wanted to be rid—
and at once!—of dipsomaniacs in command of that unit and
having the disposal of their lives. . . . Well, the moment
McKechnie had uttered the words: "To the poor b——y old
pals," an illuminating flash had presented Tietjens with the
conviction that, alone, the C.O. was too damn good an officer
to appear a dipsomaniac, even if he were observably drunk
quite often. But seen together with this fellow McKechnie,
the two of them must present a formidable appearance of
being alcoholic lunatics!

The rest of the poor b——y old pals didn't really any
more exist. They were a tradition—of ghosts! Four of them
were dead: four in hospital: two awaiting court martial for
giving stumer cheques. The last of them, practically, if you
excepted McKechnie, was the collection of putrescence and
rags at that moment hanging in the wire apron. . . . The
whole complexion of headquarters would change with the
going of McKechnie.

He considered with satisfaction that he would command a very decent lot. The adjutant was so inconspicuous you did not even notice him. Beady-eyed, like a bird! Always preoccupied. And little Aranjuez, the signalling officer! And a fat fellow called Dunne, who had represented intelligence since the night before last! A Company commander was fifty, thin as a pipe-stem and bald; B was a good, fair boy: of good family; C and D were subalterns, just out. But clean. . . . Satisfactory!

What a handful of frail grass with which to stop an aperture in the dam of—of the empire! Damn the empire! It was England! It was Bemerton Parsonage that mattered! What did we want with an empire! It was only a jerry-building Jew like Disraeli that could have provided us with that jerry-built name! The Tories said they had to have someone to do their dirty work. . . . Well, they'd had it!

He said to McKechnie:

"There's a fellow called Bemer—I mean Griffiths, O Nine Griffiths, I understand you're interested in for the Divisional Follies. I'll send him along to you as soon as he's had his breakfast. He's first-rate with the cornet."

McKechnie said:

"Yes, sir," saluted rather limply and took a step.

That was McKechnie all over. He never brought his mad fits to a crisis. That made him still more of a bore. His face would be distorted like that of a wild-cat in front of its kittens' hole in a stone wall. But he became the submissive subordinate. Suddenly! Without rhyme or reason!

Tiring people! Without manners! . . . They would presumably run the world now. It would be a tiresome world.

McKechnie, however, was saluting. He held a sealed envelope, rather small and crumpled, as if from long carrying. He was talking in a controlled voice after permission asked. He desired Tietjens to observe that the seal on the envelope was unbroken. The envelope contained "The Sonnet."

McKechnie must, then, have gone mad! His eyes, if his voice was quiet, though with an Oxford-Cockney accent—his prune-coloured eyes were certainly mad. . . . Hot prunes!

Men shuffled along the trenches, carrying by rope-handles very heavy, lead-coloured wooden cases: two men to each case. Tietjens said:

"You're D Company? . . . Get a move on! . . ."

McKechnie, however, wasn't mad. He was only pointing out that he could pit his intellect and his Latinity against those of Tietjens: that he could do it when the great day came!

The envelope, in fact, contained a sonnet. A sonnet Tietjens, for distraction, had written to rhymes dictated by Mc-Kechnie . . . for distraction in a moment of stress. . . .

Several moments of stress they had been in together. It ought to have formed a bond between them. It hadn't. . . . Imagine having a bond with a Highland-Oxford-Cockney!

Or perhaps it had! There was certainly the sonnet. Tietjens had written it in two and a half minutes, he remembered, to stave off the thought of his wife, who was then being a nuisance. . . . Two and a half minutes of forgetting Sylvia! A bit of luck! . . . But McKechnie had insisted on regarding it as a challenge. A challenge to his Latinity. He had then and there undertaken to turn that sonnet into Latin hexameters in two minutes. Or perhaps four. . . .

But things had got in the way. A fellow called 09 Morgan had got himself killed over their feet. In the hut. Then they had been busy: with the draft!

Apparently McKechnie had sealed up that sonnet in an envelope. In *that* envelope. Then and there. Apparently Mc-Kechnie had been inspired with a blind, Celtic, snorting rage to prove that he was better as a Latinist than Tietjens as a sonneteer. Apparently he was still so inspired. He was mad to engage in competition with Tietjens.

It was perhaps that that made him not quite mad. He kept sane in order to be fit for this competition. He was now repeating, holding out the envelope, seal upwards:

"I suppose you believe I have not read your sonnet, sir. I suppose you believe I have not read your sonnet, sir. . . . To prepare myself to translate it more quickly."

Tietjens said:

"Yes! No! . . . I don't care."

He couldn't tell the fellow that the idea of a competition was loathsome to him. Any sort of competition was loathsome to Tietjens. Even competitive games. He liked playing tennis. Real tennis. But he very rarely played, because he couldn't get fellows to play with that beating would not be disagreeable. . . . And it would be loathsome to be drawn into any sort of competition with this Prize man. . . . They were moving very slowly along the trench, McKechnie retreating sideways and holding out the seal.

"It's your seal, sir!" he was repeating. "Your own seal. You see, it isn't broken. . . . You don't perhaps imagine that I read the sonnet quickly and made a copy from memory?"

. . . The fellow wasn't even a decent Latinist. Or verse-maker, though he was always boasting about it to the impossible, adenoidy, Cockney subalterns who made up the battalion's mess. He would translate their chits into Latin verse. . . . But it was always into tags. Generally from the *Aeneid*. Like:

"Conticuere omnes or *Vino somnoque sepultum!"*

That was, presumably, what Oxford of just before the war was doing.

He said:

"I'm not a beastly detective. . . . Yes, of course, I quite believe it."

He thought of emerging into the society of little Aranjuez, who was some sort of gentle earnest Levantine, with pleasure. Think of thinking of a Levantine with pleasure! He said:

"Yes. It's all right, McKechnie."

He felt himself solid. He was really in a competition with this fellow. It was deterioration. He, Tietjens, was crumpling up morally. He had accepted responsibility: he had thought of two hundred and fifty pounds with pleasure: now he was competing with a Cockney-Celtic Prize man. He was reduced to that level. . . . Well, as like as not he would be dead before the afternoon. And no one would know.

Think of thinking about whether anyone would know or no! . . . But it was Valentine Wannop that wasn't to know. That he had deteriorated under the strain! . . . That enormously surprised him. He said to his subconscious self:

"What! Is *that* still there?"

That girl was at least an admirable Latinist. He remarked, with a sort of sardonic glee, that years before, in a dog-cart, emerging from mist, somewhere in Sussex—Udimore! —she had made him look silly. Over Catullus! Him, Tietjens! . . . Shortly afterwards old Campion had run into them with his motor that he couldn't drive but *would* drive.

McKechnie, apparently assuaged, said:

"I don't know if you know, sir, that General Campion is to take over this army the day after to-morrow. . . . But, of course, you would know."

Tietjens said:

"No. I didn't. . . . You fellows in touch with headquarters get to hear of things long before us." He added:

"It means that we shall be getting reinforcements. . . . It means the single command."

4 ~

IT MEANT that the end of the war was in sight.

In the next sector, in front of the headquarters' dug-out sacking, they found only Second-Lieutenant Aranjuez and Lance-Corporal Duckett of the orderly room. Both good boys, the lance-corporal with very long graceful legs. He picked up his feet well, but continually rubbed his ankles with his shoe when he talked earnestly. Somebody's bastard.

McKechnie plunged at once into the story of the sonnet. The lance-corporal had, of course, a large number of papers for Tietjens to sign. An untidy, buff-and-white sheaf, so Mc-Kechnie had time to talk. He wished to establish himself as on a level with the temporary C.O. At least intellectually.

He didn't. Aranjuez kept on exclaiming:

"The major wrote a sonnet in two and a half minutes! The major! Who would have thought it!" Ingenuous boy!

Tietjens looked at the papers with some attention. He had been so kept out of contact with the affairs of the battalion that he wanted to know. As he had suspected, the paper business of the unit was in a shocking state. Brigade, division, even army and, positively, Whitehall were strafing for information about everything imaginable, from jam, tooth-brushes and braces, to religions, vaccination and barrack damages. . . . This was interesting matter. A relief to contemplate. . . . You would almost think all-wise Authority snowed under and broke the backs of commanding officers with papers in order to relieve their minds of affording alternative interests . . . alternative to the exigencies of active hostilities! It was certainly a relief whilst waiting for a strafe to come to the right stage—to have to read a violent inquiry about P.R.I. funds, whilst the battalion had been resting near a place called Béhencourt. . . .

It appeared that Tietjens might well be thankful that he had not been allowed to handle the P.R.I. funds.

The second-in-command is the titular administrator of the Regimental Institute: he is the President, supposed to attend to the men's billiard-tables, almanacs, backgammon-boards, football boots. . . . But the C.O. had preferred to keep these books in his own hands. Tietjens regarded that as a slight. Perhaps it had not been!

It went quickly through his head that the C.O. perhaps had financial difficulties—though that was no real affair of

his. . . . The Horse Guards was pressingly interested in the
pre-enlistment affairs of a private called 64 Smith. They
asked violently and for the third time for particulars of his
religion, previous address and real name. . . . That was no
doubt the espionage branch at work. . . . But Whitehall was
also more violently interested in answers to queries about
the disposal of regimental funds of a training camp in Janu-
ary, 1915. . . . As long ago as that! The mills of God grind
slowly. . . . That query was covered by a private note from
the brigadier saying that he wished for goodness' sake the
C.O. would answer these queries or there would have to be
a Court of Inquiry.

These particular two papers ought not to have been
brought to Tietjens. He held them between the thumb and
forefinger of his left hand and the query upon 64 Smith S.—
which seemed rather urgent—between his first and second,
and so handed them to Lance-Corporal Duckett. That nice,
clean, fair boy was, at the moment, talking in intimate
undertones to Second-Lieutenant Aranjuez about the resem-
blances between the Petrarchan and the Shakespearean sonnet form. . . .

This was what His Majesty's Expeditionary Force had
come to. You had four of its warriors, four minutes before
the zero of a complete advance of the whole German line,
all interested in sonnets. . . . Drake and his game of bowls—
in fact repeated itself! . . . Differently, of course! But times
change.

He handed the two selected papers to Duckett.

"Give this one to the commanding officer," he said, "and
tell the sergeant-major to find what company Sixty-four Smith
is in and have him brought to me, wherever I am. . . . I'm going
right along the trenches now. Come after me when you've
been to the C.O. and the sergeant-major. Aranjuez will make
notes of what I want done about revetting; you can put
down anything about the personnel of the companies. . . .
Get a move on!"

He told McKechnie amiably to be out of those lines forth-
with. He didn't want him killed on his hands.

The sun was now shining into the trench.

He looked again through brigade's that-morning communication concerning dispositions the unit was to make in the
event of the expected German attack. . . . Due to begin—
the preparatory artillery at least—in three minutes' time.

Don't we say prayers before battle? . . . He could not
imagine himself doing it. . . . He just hoped that nothing

would happen that would make him lose control of his mind. . . . Otherwise he found that he was meditating on how to get the paper affairs of the unit into a better state. . . . "Who sweeps a room as for Thy cause . . ." It was the equivalent of prayer, probably. . . .

He noted that brigade's injunctions about the coming fight were not only endorsed with earnestness by division but also by very serious exhortations from army. The chit from brigade was in handwriting, that from division in fairly clear type-script, that from army in very pale typed characters. . . . It amounted to this: that they were that day to stick it till they burst. . . . That meant that there was nothing behind their backs—from there to the North Sea! . . . The French were hurrying along, probably. . . . He imagined a lot of little blue fellows in red breeches trotting along pink, sunlit plains.

(You cannot control your imagination's pictures. Of course the French no longer wore red trousers.) He saw the line breaking just where the blue section came to: the rest, swept back into the sea. He saw the whole of the terrain behind them. On the horizon was a glistening haze. That was where they were going to be swept to. Or of course they would not be swept. They would be lying on their faces, exposing the seats of their breeches. Too negligible for the large dust-pan and broom. . . . What was death like: the immediate process of dissolution? He stuffed the papers into his tunic pocket.

He remembered with grimmish amusement that one chit promised him reinforcements. Sixteen men! Sixteen! Worcesters! From a Worcester training-camp. . . . Why the deuce weren't they sent to the Worcester battalion just next door? Good fellows, no doubt. But they hadn't got the drill quiffs of our lot: they were not pals with our men: they did not know the officers by name. There would be no welcome to cheer them. . . . It was a queer idea, the deliberate destruction of regimental esprit de corps that the Home Authorities now insisted on. It was said to be imitated at the suggestion of a civilian of advanced social views from the French, who in turn had imitated it from the Germans. It is, of course, lawful to learn of the enemy: but is it sensible?

Perhaps it is. The Feudal Spirit was broken. Perhaps it would therefore be harmful to trench warfare. It used to be comfortable and cosy. You fought beside men from your own hamlet under the leadership of the parson's son. Perhaps that was not good for you?

At any rate, as at present arranged, dying was a lonely affair.

He, Tietjens, and little Aranjuez there, if something hit them, would die—a Yorkshire territorial magnate's son and the son of, positively, an Oporto Protestant minister, if you can imagine such a thing!—the dissimilar souls winging their way to heaven side by side. You'd think God would find it more appropriate if Yorkshiremen went with other North Country fellows, and dagoes with other papists. For Aranjuez, though the son of a Nonconformist of sorts, had reverted to the faith of his fathers.

He said:

"Come along, Aranjuez. . . . I want to see that wet bit of trench before the Hun shells hit it."

Well. . . . They were getting reinforcements. The Home Authorities had awakened to their prayers. They sent them sixteen Worcesters. They would be three hundred and forty-four—no, forty-three, because he had sent back O Nine Griffiths, the fellow with the cornet—three hundred and forty-three lonely souls against . . . say, two divisions! Against about eighteen thousand, very likely. And they were to stick it till they burst. Reinforced!

Reinforced. Good God! . . . Sixteen Worcesters!

What was at the bottom of it all?

Campion was going to command that army. That meant that real reinforcements had been promised from the millions of men that filled the base camps. And it meant the single command! Campion would not have consented to take the command of that army if he had not had those very definite promises.

But it would take time. Months! Anything like adequate reinforcements would take months.

And at that moment, in the most crucial point of the line of the Army, of the Expeditionary Force, the Allied Forces, the Empire, the Universe, the Solar-system, they had three hundred and sixty-six men commanded by the last surviving Tory. To face wave on wave of the Enemy.

In one minute the German barrage was due.

Aranjuez said to him:

"You can write a sonnet in two and a half minutes, sir. . . . And your siphon works like anything in that damp trench. . . . It took my mother's great-uncle, the canon of Oporto, fifteen weeks to finish his celebrated sonnet. I know because my mother told me. . . . But you oughtn't to be here, sir."

Aranjuez, then, was the nephew of the author of the *Son-*

net to Night. He could be. You had to have that sort of oddity to make up this world. So naturally he was interested in sonnets.

And having got hold of a battalion with a stretch of damp trench, Tietjens had had the opportunity of trying a thing he had often thought of—of drying out vertically cut, damp soil by means of a siphon of soil-pipes put in, not horizontally, but vertically. Fortunately Hackett, the commander of B Company, that had the wet trench, had been an engineer in civil life. Aranjuez had been along, out of sheer hero-worship, to B trenches to see how his hero's siphons had worked. He reported that they worked like a dream.

Little Aranjuez said:

"These trenches are like Pompeii, sir."

Tietjens had never seen Pompeii, but he understood that Aranjuez was referring to the empty square-cut excavations in the earth. Particularly to their emptiness. And to the deadly stillness in the sunlight. . . . Admirable trenches. Made to hold an establishment of several thousand men. To bustle with Cockney life. Now dead empty. They passed three sentries in the pinkish gravel passage and two men, one with a pick, the other with a shovel. They were exactly squaring the juncture of the wall and the path, as they might have done in Pompeii. Or in Hyde Park! A perfect devil for tidiness, A Company commander. But the men seemed to like it. They were sniggering, though they stopped that, of course, when Tietjens passed. . . .

A nice, dark, tiny boy, Aranjuez: his adoration was charming. From the very first—and naturally, frightened out of his little life—he had clung to Tietjens as a child clings to an omnipotent father. Tietjens, all-wise, could direct the awful courses of war and decree safety for the frightened! Tietjens needed that sort of worship. The boy said it would be awful to have anything happen to your eyes. Your girl naturally would not look at you. Not more than three miles away, Nancy Truefitt was now. Unless they had evacuated her. Nancy was his flame. In a tea-shop at Bailleul.

A man was sitting outside the mouth of A dug-out, just after they passed the mouth of the communication trench. . . . Comforting that channel in the soil looked, running uphill. You could saunter away up there, out of all this. . . . But you couldn't! There was no turning here either to the right or to the left!

The man writing in a copy-book had his tin hat right over his eyes. Engrossed, he sat on a gravel-step, his copy-book

on his knees. His name was Slocombe and he was a dramatist.
Like Shakespeare. He made fifty pounds a time writing music-
hall sketches: for the outer halls. The outer halls were the
cheap music-halls that go in a ring round the suburbs of
London. Slocombe never missed a second, writing in his
copy-books. If you fell the men out for a rest when march-
ing, Slocombe would sit by the roadside—and out would
come his copy-book and his pencil. His wife would type out
what he sent home. And write him grumbling letters if the
supply of copy failed. How was she to keep up the Sunday
best of George and Flossie if he did not keep on writing
one-act sketches? Tietjens had this information through cen-
soring one of the man's letters containing manuscript. . . .
Slocombe was slovenly as a soldier, but he kept the other
men in a good humour, his mind being a perfect repertoire
of Cockney jests at the expense of Big and Little Willy and
Brother Fritz. Slocombe wrote on, wetting his pencil with
his tongue.

The sergeant in the mouth of A Company headquarters'
dug-out started to turn out some sort of a guard, but Tietjens
stopped him. A Company ran itself on the lines of Regulars
in the depot. The O.C. had a conduct-sheet book as neat as
a ledger! The old, bald, grim fellow. Tietjens asked the sergeant questions. Had they their Mills bombs all right? They
weren't short of rifles—first-class order? . . . But how could
they be! Were there any sick? . . . Two! . . . Well, it was
a healthy life! . . . Keep the men under cover until the
Hun barrage began. It was due now.

It was due now. The second hand of Tietjens' watch,
like an animated pointer of hair, kicked a little on the stroke
of the minute. . . . "Crumb!" said the punctual, distant
sound.

Tietjens said to Aranjuez:

"It's presumably coming now!" Aranjuez pulled at the chin-
strap of his tin hat.

Tietjens' mouth filled itself with a dreadful salty flavour, the
back of his tongue being dry. His chest and heart laboured
heavily. Aranjuez said:

"If I stop one, sir, you'll tell Nancy Truefitt that . . ."

Tietjens said:

"Little nippers like you don't stop things. . . . Besides, feel
the wind!"

They were at the highest point of the trenches that ran
along a hill-side. So they were exposed. The wind had undoubtedly freshened, coming down the hill. In front and be-

hind, along the trench, they could see views. Land, some green, greyish trees.

Aranjuez said:

"You think the wind will stop them, sir," appealingly.

Tietjens exclaimed with gruffness:

"Of course it will stop them. They won't work without gas. Yet their men hate to have to face the gas-screens. It's our great advantage. It saps their *moral*. Nothing else would. They can't put up smoke-screens either."

Aranjuez said:

"I know you think their gas has ruined them, sir. . . . It was wicked of them to use it. You can't do a wicked thing without suffering for it, can you, sir?"

It remained indecently quiet. Like Sunday in a village with the people in church. But it was not pleasurable.

Tietjens wondered how long physical irregularities would inconvenience his mind. You cannot think well with a parched back to your tongue. This was practically his first day in the open during a strafe. His first whole day for quite a time. Since Noircourt! . . . How long ago? . . . Two years? . . . Maybe! . . . Then he had nothing to go on to tell him how long he would be inconvenienced!

It remained indecently quiet! Running footsteps, at first on duckboards, then on the dry path of trench! They made Tietjens start violently, inside himself. The house must be on fire!

He said to Aranjuez:

"Someone is in a hurry!"

The lad's teeth chattered. They must have made him feel bad too, the footsteps. . . . The knocking on the gate in *Macbeth*!

They began. It had come. Pam . . . Pamperi . . . Pam! Pam! . . . Pa . . . Pamperi . . . Pam! Pam! . . . Pampamperipampampam . . . Pam . . . They were the ones that sound like drums. They continued incessantly. Immensely big drums, the ones that go at it with real zest. . . . You know how it is, looking at an opera orchestra when the fellow with the big drumsticks really begins. Your own heart beats like hell. Tietjens' heart did. The drummer appears to go mad.

Tietjens was never much good at identifying artillery by the sound. He would have said that these were anti-aircraft-guns. And he remembered that, for some minutes, the drone of plane engines had pervaded the indecent silence. . . . But that drone was so normal it was part of the silence. Like your own thoughts. A filtered and engrossed sound, drifting down from overhead. More like fine dust than noise.

A familiar noise said: "We . . . e . . . e . . . ry!" Shells always appeared tired of life. As if after a long, long journey they said: "Weary!" Very much prolonging the *e* sound. Then "Whack!" when they burst.

This was the beginning of the strafe. . . . Though he had been convinced the strafe was coming, he had hoped for a prolongation of the . . . say, Bemerton! . . . conditions. The life Peaceful. And Contemplative. But here it was beginning. "Oh, well . . ."

This shell appeared heavier and to be more than usually tired. Desultory. It seemed to pass within six feet over the heads of Aranjuez and himself. Then, just twenty yards up the hill, it said, invisibly, "Dud!. . ." And it *was* a dud!

It had not, very likely, been aimed at their trench at all. It was probably just an aircraft shrapnel shell that had not exploded. The Germans were firing a great number of duds —these days.

So it might not be a sign of the beginning! It was tantalizing. But as long as it ended the right way one could bear it.

Lance-Corporal Duckett, the fair boy, ran to within two foot of Tietjens' feet and pulled up with a guardee's stamp and a terrific salute. There was life in the old dog yet. Meaning that a zest for spit and polish survived in places in these rag-time days.

The boy said, panting—it might have been agitation, or that he had run so fast. . . . But why had he run so fast if he were not agitated:

"If you please, sir" . . . pant. . . . "Will you come to the colonel?" . . . pant. "With as little delay as possible!" He remained panting.

It went through Tietjens' mind that he was going to spend the rest of that day in a comfortable, dark hole. Not in the blinding daylight. . . . Let us be thankful!

Leaving Lance-Corporal Duckett . . . it came suddenly into his head that he liked that boy because he suggested Valentine Wannop! . . . to converse in intimate tones with Aranjuez and so to distract him from the fear of imminent death or blindness that would mean the loss of his girl, Tietjens went smartly back along the trenches. He didn't hurry. He was determined that the men should not see him hurry. Even if the colonel should refuse to be relieved of the command, Tietjens was determined that the men should have the consolation of knowing that headquarters numbered one cool, sauntering soul amongst its members.

They had had, when they took over the Trasna Valley trenches before the Mametz Wood affair, a rather good major who wore an eye-glass and was of good family. He had something the matter with him, for he committed suicide later. . . . But as they went in, the Huns, say fifty yards away, began to shout various national battle-cries of the Allies or the melodies of regimental quick steps of British regiments. The idea was that if they heard, say: "Some talk of Alexander . . ." resounding from an opposite trench, H.M. Second Grenadier Guards would burst into cheers and Brother Hun would know what he had before him.

Well, this Major Grosvenor shut his men up, naturally, and stood listening with his eye-glass screwed into his face and the air of a connoisseur at a quartette party. At last he took his eye-glass out, threw it in the air and caught it again.

"Shout *Banzai!* men," he said.

That, on the off-chance, might give the enemy a scunner at the thought that we had Japanese troops in the line in front of them, or it would show them that we were making game of them, a form of offensive that sent these owlish fellows mad with rage. . . . So the Huns shut up!

That was the sort of humour in an officer that the men still liked. . . . The sort of humour Tietjens himself had not got: but he could appear unconcernedly reflective and all there—and he could tell them at trying moments that, say, their ideas about skylarks were all wrong. . . . That was tranquillizing.

Once he had heard a papist padre preaching in a barn, under shell-fire. At any rate shells were going overhead and pigs underfoot. The padre had preached about very difficult points in the doctrine of the Immaculate Conception, and the men had listened raptly. He said that was common sense. They didn't want lachrymose or mortuary orations. They wanted their minds taken off. . . . So did the padre!

Thus you talk to the men, just before the event, about skylarks or the hind legs of the elephant at the old Lane! And you don't hurry when the colonel sends for you.

He walked along, for a moment or two, thinking nothing. The pebbles in the gravel of the trench grew clear and individual. Someone had dropped a letter. Slocombe, the dramatist, was closing his copy-book. Sighing, apparently, he reached for his rifle. A Company sergeant-major was turn-

ing out some men of sorts. He said: "Get a move on!"
Tietjens said as he passed: "Keep them under cover as much
as you can, sergeant-major."

It occurred to him suddenly that he had committed a
military misdemeanour in leaving Lance-Corporal Duckett
with Aranjuez. An officer should not walk along a stretch of
lonely trench without escort. Some Hun offering might hit
him and there would be loss of property to His Majesty.
No one to fetch a doctor or stretcher-bearers while you
bled to death. That was the army. . . .

Well, he had left Duckett with Aranjuez to comfort him.
That minute subaltern was suffering. God knew what little
agonies ran about in his little mind, like mice! He was as
brave as a lion when strafes were on: when they weren't,
his little, blackamoor, nobbly face quivered as the thoughts
visited him. . . .

He had really left Valentine Wannop with Aranjuez! That,
he realized, was what he had done. The boy Duckett *was*
Valentine Wannop. Clean, blond, small: with the ordinary
face, the courageous eyes, the obstinately, slightly peaked
nose. . . . It was just as if, Valentine Wannop being in his
possession, they had been walking along a road and seen
someone in distress. And he, Tietjens, had said:

"I've got to get along. You stop and see what you can
do!"

And, amazingly, he was walking along a country road beside Valentine Wannop, silent, with the quiet intimacy that
comes with possession. She belonged to him. . . . Not a
mountain road: not Yorkshire. Not a valley road: not Bemerton. A country parsonage was not for him. So he wouldn't
take orders!

A down-land road, with some old thorn-trees. They only
grew really in Kent. And the sky coming down on all sides.
The flat top of a down!

Amazing! He had not thought of that girl for over a
fortnight now, except in moments of great strafes, when he
had hoped she would not be too worried if she knew where
he was. Because he had the sense that all the time she knew
where he was.

He had thought of her less and less. At longer intervals.
. . . As with his nightmare of the mining Germans who
desired that a candle should be brought to the captain. At
first, every night, three or four times every night, it had
visited him. . . . Now it came only once every night. . . .

The physical semblance of that boy had brought the girl

back to his mind. That was accidental, so it was not part of any psychological rhythm. It did not show him, that is to say, whether, in the natural course of events and without accidents, she was ceasing to obsess him.

She was certainly now obsessing him! Beyond bearing or belief. His whole being was overwhelmed by her . . . by her mentality, really. For of course the physical resemblance of the lance-corporal was mere subterfuge. Lance-corporals do not resemble young ladies. . . . And, as a matter of fact, he did not remember exactly what Valentine Wannop looked like. Not vividly. He had not that sort of mind. It was words that his mind found that let him know that she was fair, snub-nosed, rather broad-faced and square on her feet. As if he had made a note of it and referred to it when he wanted to think of her. His mind didn't make any mental picture: it brought up a sort of blur of sunlight.

It was the mentality that obsessed him: the exact mind, the impatience of solecisms and facile generalizations! . . . A queer catalogue of the charms of one's lady-love! . . . But he wanted to hear her say: "Oh, chuck it, Edith Ethel!" when Edith Ethel Duchemin, now of course Lady Macmaster, quoted some of the opinions expressed in Macmaster's critical monograph about the late Mr. Rossetti. . . . How *very* late now!

It would rest him to hear that. She was, in effect, the only person in the world that he wanted to hear speak. Certainly the only person in the world that he wanted to talk to. The only clear intelligence! . . . The repose that his mind needed from the crackling of thorns under all the pots of the world. . . . From the eternal, imbecile "Pampamperipam Pam Pamperi Pam Pam!" of the German guns that all the while continued. . . .

Why couldn't they chuck that? What good did it do them to keep that mad drummer incessantly thundering on his stupid instrument? . . . Possibly they might bring down some of our planes, but they generally didn't. You saw the black ball of their shells exploding and slowly expand like pocket-handkerchiefs about the unconcerned planes, like black peas aimed at dragon-flies against the blue: the illuminated, pinkish, pretty things! . . . But his dislike of those guns was just dislike—a Tory prejudice. They were probably worthwhile. Just. . . .

You naturally tried every argument in the unseen contest of wills that went on across the firmament.

"Ho!" says our staff, "they are going to attack in force

at such an hour ackemma," because naturally the staff
thought in terms of ackemma years after the twenty-four-
hour day had been established. "Well, we'll send out a million machine-gun planes to wipe out any men they've got
moving up into support!"

It was of course unusual to move bodies of men by daylight. But this game had only two resources: you used the
usual. Or the unusual. *Usually* you didn't begin your barrage
after dawn and launch your attack at ten-thirty or so. So
you might do it—the Huns might be trying it on—as a surprise measure.

On the other hand, our people might be sending over the
planes, whose immense droning was then making your very
bones vibrate, in order to tell the Huns that we were ready
to be surprised: that the time had now about come round
when we might be expecting the Hun brain to think out a
surprise. So we sent out those deathly, dreadful things to
run along just over the tops of the hedgerows, in spite of
all the guns! For there was nothing more terrifying in the
whole war than that span of lightness, swaying, approaching
a few feet above the heads of your column of men: instinct
with wrath: dispensing the dreadful rain! So we had sent
them. In a moment they would be tearing down. . . .

Of course if this were merely a demonstration: if, say,
there were no reinforcements moving, no troops detraining
at the distant rail-head, the correct Hun answer would be to
hammer some of our trenches to hell with all the heavy
stuff they could put on to them. That was like saying sar-
donically:

"God, if you interfere with our peace and quiet on a fine
day we'll interfere with yours!" And . . . Kerumph . . . the
waggons of coal would fly over until we recalled our planes
and all went to sleep again over the chess-board. . . . You
would probably be just as well off if you refrained from
either demonstration or counter-demonstration. But Great
General Staff liked to exchange these witticisms in iron. And
a little blood!

A sergeant of sorts approached him from Bn. H.Q. way,
shepherding a man with a head wound. His tin hat, that is
to say, was perched jauntily forward over a bandage. He
was Jewish-nosed, appeared not to have shaved, though he
had, and appeared as if he ought to have worn pince-nez to
complete his style of Oriental manhood. Private Smith. Tietjens said:

"Look here, what was your confounded occupation before the war?"

The man replied with an agreeable, cultured, throaty intonation:

"I was a journalist, sir. On a Socialist paper. Extreme Left!"

"And what," Tietjens asked, "was your agreeable name? . . . I'm obliged to ask you that question. I don't want to insult you."

In the old Regular army it was an insult to ask a private if he was not going under his real name. Most men enlisted under false names.

The man said:

"Eisenstein, sir!"

Tietjens asked if the man were a Derby recruit or compulsorily enlisted. He said he had enlisted voluntarily. Tietjens said: "Why?" If the fellow was a capable journalist and on the right side he would be more useful outside the army. The man said he had been foreign correspondent of a Left paper. Being correspondent of a Left paper with a name like Eisenstein deprived one of one's chance of usefulness. Besides, he wanted to have a whack at the Prussians. He was of Polish extraction. Tietjens asked the sergeant if the man had a good record. The sergeant said: "First-class man. First-class soldier." He had been recommended for the D.C.M. Tietjens said:

"I shall apply to have you transferred to the Jewish regiment. In the meantime you can go back to the First Line Transport. You shouldn't have been a Left journalist and have a name like Eisenstein. One or the other. Not both." The man said the name had been inflicted on his ancestry in the Middle Ages. He would prefer to be called Esau, as a son of that tribe. He pleaded not to be sent to the Jewish regiment, which was believed to be in Mesopotamia, just when the fighting there was at its most interesting.

"You're probably thinking of writing a book," Tietjens said. "Well, there are all Abanar and Pharpar to write about. I'm sorry. But you're intelligent enough to see that I can't take . . ." He stopped, fearing that if the sergeant heard any more the men might make it hot for the fellow as a suspect. He was annoyed at having asked his name before the sergeant. He appeared to be a good man. Jews could fight. . . . And hunt! . . . But he wasn't going to take any risks. The man, dark-eyed and erect, flinched a little, gazing into Tietjens' eyes.

"I suppose you can't, sir," he said. "It's a disappointment.
I'm not writing anything. I want to go on in the army. I
like the life."

Tietjens said:

"I'm sorry, Smith. I can't help it. Fall out!" He was sorry.
He believed the fellow. But responsibility hardens the heart.
It must. A very short time ago he would have taken trouble
over that fellow. A great deal of trouble, very likely. Now
he wasn't going to. . . .

A large capital A in whitewash decorated the piece of
corrugated iron that was derelictly propped against a channel
at right angles to the trench. To Tietjens' astonishment a
strong impulse like a wave of passion influenced his being
towards the left—up that channel. It wasn't funk: it wasn't
any sort of funk. He had been rather irritatedly wrapped
up in the case of Private Smith-Eisenstein. It had undeniably
irritated him to have to break the chances of a Jew and
Red Socialist. It was the sort of thing one did not do if one
were omnipotent—as he was. Then . . . this strong impulse?
. . . It was a passionate desire to go where you could find
exact intellect: rest.

He thought he suddenly understood. For the Lincolnshire
sergeant-major the word *peace* meant that a man could stand
up on a hill. For him it meant someone to talk to.

$\int \sim$

THE COLONEL SAID:

"Look here, Tietjens, lend me two hundred and fifty quid.
They say you're a damn beastly rich fellow. My accounts
are all out. I've got a loathsome complaint. My friends have
all gone back on me. I shall have to face a Court of Inquiry
if I go home. But my nerve's gone. I've got to go home."

He added:

"I dare say you knew all that."

From the sudden fierce hatred that he felt at the thought
of giving money to this man, Tietjens knew that his inner
mind based all its calculations on the idea of living with
Valentine Wannop . . . when men could stand up on hills.

He had found the colonel in his cellar—it really, actually
was a cellar, the remains of a farm—sitting on the edge
of his camp-bed, in his shorts, his khaki shirt very open at
the neck. His eyes were a little bloodshot, but his cropped
silver-grey hair was accurately waved, his grey moustache

beautifully pointed. His silver-backed hairbrushes and a small mirror were indeed on the table in front of him. By the rays of the lamp that, hung overhead, rendered that damp stone place faintly nauseating, he looked keen, clean and resolute. Tietjens wondered how he would look by daylight. He had remarkably seldom seen the fellow by daylight. Beside the mirror and the brushes lay, limply, an unfilled pipe, a red pencil and the white-buff papers from Whitehall that Tietjens had already read.

He had begun by looking at Tietjens with a keen, hard, bloodshot glance. He had said:

"You think you can command this battalion? Have you had any experience? It appears you suggest that I take two months' leave."

Tietjens had expected a violent outbreak. Threats even. None had come. The colonel had continued to regard him with intentness, nothing more. He sat motionless, his long arms, bare to the elbow, dependent over each of his knees, which were far apart. He said that if he decided to go he didn't want to leave his battalion to a man that would knock it about. He continued staring hard at Tietjens. The phrase was singular in that place and at that hour, but Tietjens understood it to mean that he did not want his battalion discipline to go to pieces.

Tietjens answered that he did not think he would let the discipline go to pieces. The colonel had said:

"How do you know? You're no soldier, are you?"

Tietjens said he had commanded in the line a company at full strength—nearly as large as the battalion—and, out of it, a unit of exactly eight times its present strength. He did not think any complaints had been made of him. The colonel said frostily:

"Well! I know nothing about you." He had added:

"You seem to have moved the battalion all right the night before last. I wasn't in a condition to do it myself. I'm not well. I'm obliged to you. The men appear to like you. They're tired of me."

Tietjens felt himself on tenter-hooks. He had, now, a passionate desire to command that battalion. It was the last thing he would have expected of himself. He said:

"If it becomes a question of a war of motion, sir, I don't know that I should have much experience."

The colonel answered:

"It won't become a war of motion before I come back. If I ever do come back."

Tietjens said:

"Isn't it rather like a war of motion now, sir?" It was perhaps the first time in his life he had ever asked for information from a superior in rank—with an implicit belief that he would get an exact answer. The colonel said:

"No. This is only falling back on prepared positions. There will be positions prepared for us right back to the sea. If the staff has done its work properly. If it hasn't, the war's over. We're done, finished, smashed, annihilated, non-existent."

Tietjens said:

"But if the great strafe that, according to division, is due now . . ."

The colonel said: "What?" Tietjens repeated his words and added:

"We might get pushed beyond the next prepared position."

The colonel appeared to withdraw his thoughts from a great distance.

"There isn't going to be any great strafe," he said. He was beginning to add: "Division has got . . ." A considerable thump shook the hill behind their backs. The colonel sat listening without much attention. His eyes gloomily rested on the papers before him. He said, without looking up:

"Yes: I don't want my battalion knocked about!" He went on reading again—the communication from Whitehall. He said: "You've read this?" and then:

"Falling back on prepared positions isn't the same as moving in the open. You don't have to do more than you do in a trench-to-trench attack. I suppose you can get your direction by compass all right. Or get someone to, for you."

Another considerable "Crump" of sound shook the earth, but from a little further away. The colonel turned the sheet of paper over. Pinned to the back of it was the private note of the brigadier. He perused this also with gloomy and unsurprised eyes.

"Pretty stiff, all this," he said; "you've read it? I shall have to go back and see about this."

He exclaimed:

"It's rough luck. I should have liked to leave my battalion to someone that knew it. I don't suppose you do. Perhaps you do, though."

An immense collection of fire-irons—all the fire-irons in the world—fell just above their heads. The sound seemed to prolong itself in echoes, though of course it could not have. It was repeated.

The colonel looked upwards negligently. Tietjens proposed to go to see. The colonel said:

"No, don't. Notting will tell us if anything's wanted. . . . Though nothing can be wanted!" Notting was the beady-eyed adjutant in the adjoining cellar. "How could they expect us to keep accounts straight in August, 1914? How can they expect me to remember what happened? At the depot. Then!" He appeared listless, but without resentment. "Rotten luck . . ." he said. "In the battalion and . . . with this!" He rapped the back of his hand on the papers. He looked up at Tietjens.

"I suppose I could get rid of you; with a bad report," he said. "Or perhaps I couldn't. . . . General Campion put you here. You're said to be his bastard."

"He's my godfather," Tietjens said. "If you put in a bad report of me I should not protest. That is, if it were on the grounds of lack of experience. I should go to the brigadier over anything else."

"It's the same thing," the colonel said. "I mean a godson. If I had thought you were General Campion's bastard, I should not have said it. . . . No; I don't want to put in a bad report of you. It's my own fault if you don't know the battalion. I've kept you out of it. I didn't want you to see what a rotten state the papers are in. They say you're the devil of a paper soldier. You used to be in a government office, didn't you?"

Heavy blows were being delivered to the earth with some regularity on each side of the cellar. It was as if a boxer of the size of a mountain were delivering rights and lefts in heavy alternation. And it made hearing rather difficult.

"Rotten luck," the colonel said. "And McKechnie's dotty. Clean dotty." Tietjens missed some words. He said that he would probably be able to get the paper-work of the battalion straight before the colonel came back.

The noise rolled downhill like a heavy cloud. The colonel continued talking and Tietjens, not being very accustomed to his voice, lost a good deal of what he said but, as if in a rift, he did hear:

"I'm not going to burn my fingers with a bad report on you that may bring a general on my back—to get back McKechnie, who's dotty. . . . Not fit to . . ."

The noise rolled in again. Once the colonel listened to it, turning his head on one side and looking upwards. But he appeared satisfied with what he heard and recommenced his perusal of the Horse Guards letter. He took the pencil, underlined words and then sat idly stabbing the paper with the point.

With every minute Tietjens' respect for him increased. This man at least knew his job—as an engine-dresser does, or the captain of a steam tramp. His nerves might have gone to pieces. They probably had; probably he could not go very far without stimulants: he was probably under bromides now.

And all things considered, his treatment of Tietjens had been admirable and Tietjens had to revise his view of it. He realized that it was McKechnie who had given him the idea that the colonel hated him: but he would not have said anything. He was too old a hand in the army to give Tietjens a handle by saying anything definite. . . . And he had always treated Tietjens with the sort of monumental deference that, in a mess, the colonel should bestow on his chief assistant. Going through a door at meal-times, for instance, if they happened to be side by side, he would motion with his hand for Tietjens to go first, naturally though, taking his proper precedence when Tietjens halted. And here he was, perfectly calm. And quite ready to be instructive.

Tietjens was not calm: he was too much bothered by Valentine Wannop and by the thought that if the strafe was on, he ought to be seeing about his battalion. And of course by the bombardment. But the colonel said, when Tietjens with the aid of signs again made proposals to take a look around:

"No. Stop where you are. This isn't the strafe. There is not going to be a strafe. This is only a little extra Morning Hate. You can tell by the noise. That's only four-point-twos. There's nothing really heavy. The really heavies don't come so fast. They'll be turning on to the Worcesters now and only giving us one every half-minute. . . . That's their game. If you don't know that, what are you doing here?" He added: "You hear?" pointing his forefinger to the roof. The noise shifted. It went away to the right as a slow coal-waggon might. He went on:

"This is your place. Not doing things up above. They'll come and tell you if they want things. And you've got a first-rate adjutant in Notting, and Dunne's a good man. . . . The men are all under cover: that's an advantage in having your strength down to three hundred. There's dug-outs for all and to spare. . . . All the same, this is no place for you. Nor for me. This is a young man's war. We're old uns.

Three and a half years of it have done for me. Three and a half months will do for you."

He looked gloomily at his reflection in the mirror that stood before him.

"You're a gone coon!" he said to it. Then he took it and, holding it for a moment poised at the end of a bare white arm, flung it violently at the rough stones of the wall behind Tietjens. The fragments tinkled to the ground.

"There's seven years' bad luck," he said. "God take 'em, if they can give me seven years worse than this last, I'd find it instructive!"

He looked at Tietjens with infuriated eyes.

"Look here, you!" he said. "You're an educated man. . . . What's the worst thing about this war? What's the *worst* thing? Tell me that!" His chest began to heave. "It's that they won't let us alone. Never! Not one of us! If they'd let us alone we could fight. But never. . . . No one! It's not only the beastly papers of the battalion, though I'm no good with papers. Never was and never shall be. . . . But it's the people at home. One's own people. God help us, you'd think that when a poor devil was in the trenches they'd let him alone. . . . Damn it: I've had solicitors' letters about family quarrels when I was in hospital. Imagine that! . . . Imagine it! I don't mean tradesmen's dunnings. But one's own people. I haven't even got a bad wife as McKechnie has and they say you have. My wife's a bit extravagant and the children are expensive. That's worry enough. . . . But my father died eighteen months ago. He was in partnership with my uncle. A builder. And they tried to do his estate out of his share of the business and leave my old mother with nothing. And my brother and sister threw the estate into Chancery in order to get back the little bit my father spent on my wife and children. My wife and children lived with my father whilst I was in India. . . . And out here. . . . My solicitor says they can get it out of my share: the cost of their keep. He calls it the doctrine of ademption. . . . Ademption . . . Doctrine of . . . I was better off as a sergeant," he added gloomily. "But sergeants don't get let alone. They've always got women after them. Or their wives take up with Belgians and they get written to about it. Sergeant Cutts of D Company gets an anonymous letter every week about his wife. How's he to do his duty! But he does. So have I till now. . . ." He added with renewed violence:

"Look here. You're an educated man, aren't you? The

sort of man that could write a book. You write a book about that. You write to the papers about it. You'd be more use to the army doing that than being here. I dare say you're a good enough officer. Old Campion is too keen a commander to stick a rotten officer into this job, godson or no godson. . . . Besides, I don't believe the whole story about you. If a general wanted to give a soft godson's job to a fellow, it would be a soft job and a fat one. He wouldn't send him here. So take the battalion with my blessing. You won't worry over it more than I have: the poor bloody Glamorgans."

So he had his battalion! He drew an immense breath. The bumps began to come back along the line. He figured those shells as being like sparrow-hawks beating along a hedge. They were probably pretty accurate. The Germans were pretty accurate. The trenches were probably being knocked about a good deal, the pretty, pinkish gravel falling about in heaps as it would lie in a park, ready to be spread on paths. He remembered how he had been up on the Montagne Noire, still, thank God, behind where they were now. Why did he thank God? Did he really care where the army was? Probably! But enough to say "Thank God" about? Probably too. . . . But as long as they kept on at the job, did anything matter? Anything else? It was keeping on that mattered. From the Montagne Noire he had seen our shells bursting on a thinnish line in the distance, in shining weather. Each shell existing in a white puff, beautifully. Forward and backward along the line. . . . Under Messines village. He had felt exhilaration to think that our gunners were making such good practice. Now some Hun on a hill was feeling exhilaration over puffs of smoke in our line! . . . But he, Tietjens, was . . . Damn it, he was going to make two hundred and fifty quid towards living with Valentine Wannop—when you really *could* stand up on a hill . . . anywhere!

The adjutant, Notting, looked in and said:

"Brigade wants to know if we're suffering any, sir?"

The colonel surveyed Tietjens with irony:

"Well, what are you going to report?" he asked. . . . "This officer is taking over from me," he said to Notting. Notting's beady eyes and red-varnished cheeks expressed no emotions.

"Oh, tell brigade," the colonel said, "that we're all as happy as sand-boys. We could stand this till kingdom come." He asked: "We *aren't* suffering any, are we?"

Notting said: "No, not in particular. C Company was

grumbling that all its beautiful revetments had been knocked to pieces. The sentry near their own dug-out complained that the pebbles in the gravel were nearly as bad as shrapnel."

"Well, tell brigade what I said. With Major Tietjens' compliments, not mine. He's in command."

". . . You may as well make a cheerful impression to begin with," he added to Tietjens.

It was then that, suddenly, he burst out with:

"Look here! Lend me two hundred and fifty quid!"

He remained staring fixedly at Tietjens with an odd air of a man who has just asked a teasing, jocular conundrum. . . .

Tietjens had recoiled—really half an inch. The man said he was suffering from a loathsome disease: it was being near something dirty. You don't contract loathsome diseases except from the cheapest kind of women or through being untidy-minded. . . . The man's pals had gone back on him. That sort of man's pals do go back on him! His accounts were all out. . . . He was in short the sort of swindling, unclean scoundrel to whom one lent money. . . . Irresistibly!

A crash of the sort that you couldn't ignore, as is the case with certain claps in thunder-storms, sent a good deal of gravel down their cellar steps. It crashed against their shaky door. They heard Notting come out of his cellar and tell someone to shovel the beastly stuff back again where it had come from.

The colonel looked up at the roof. He said that had knocked their parapet about a bit. Then he resumed his fixed gaze at Tietjens.

Tietjens said to himself:

"I'm losing my nerve. . . . It's the damned news that Campion is coming. . . . I'm becoming a wretched, irresolute Johnny."

The colonel said:

"I'm not a beastly sponger. I never borrowed before!" His chest heaved. . . . It really expanded and then got smaller again, the orifice in the khaki at his throat contracting. . . . Perhaps he never had borrowed before. . . .

After all, it didn't matter what kind of man this was, it was a question of what sort of a man Tietjens was becoming. He said:

"I can't lend you the money. I'll guarantee an overdraft to your agents. For two hundred and fifty."

Well, then, he remained the sort of man who automatically lent money. He was glad.

The colonel's face fell. His martially erect shoulders indeed collapsed. He exclaimed ruefully:

"Oh, I say, I thought you were the sort one could go to."

Tietjens said:

"It's the same thing. You can draw a cheque on your bank exactly as if I paid the money in."

The colonel said:

"I *can?* It's the same thing? You're *sure?*" His questions were like the pleas of a young woman asking you not to murder her.

. . . He obviously was not a sponger. He was a financial virgin. There could not be a subaltern of eighteen in the whole army who did not know what it meant to have an overdraft guaranteed after a fortnight's leave. . . . Tietjens only wished they didn't. He said:

"You've practically got the money in your hand as you sit there. I've only to write the letter. It's impossible your agents should refuse my guarantee. If they do, I'll raise the money and send it you."

He wondered why he didn't do that last in any case. A year or so ago he would have had no hesitation about overdrawing his account to any extent. Now he had an insupportable objection. Like a hatred!

He said:

"You'd better let me have your address." He added, for his mind was really wandering a little—there was too much talk!—"I suppose you'll go to Number Nine Red Cross at Rouen for a bit."

The colonel sprang to his feet:

"My God, what's that?" he cried out. "Me . . . to Number Nine."

Tietjens exclaimed:

"I don't know the procedure. You said you had . . ."

The other cried out:

"I've got cancer. A big swelling under the arm-pit." He passed his hand over his bare flesh through the opening of his shirt, the long arm disappearing to the elbow. "Good God . . . I suppose when I said my pals had gone back on me you thought I'd asked them for help and been refused. I haven't. . . . They're all killed. That's the worst way you can go back on a pal, isn't it? Don't you understand men's language?"

He sat heavily down on his bed again.

He said:

"By Jove: if you hadn't promised to let me have the

money there would have been nothing for me but to make a hole in the water."

Tietjens said:

"Well, don't contemplate it now. Get yourself well looked after. What does Derry say?"

The colonel again started violently:

"Derry! The M.O. . . . Do you think I'd tell him! Or little squits of subalterns? Or any man! You understand now why I wouldn't take Derry's beastly pill. How do I know what it mightn't do to . . ."

Again he passed his hand under his arm-pit, his eyes taking on a yearning and calculating expression. He added:

"I thought it a duty to tell you, as I was asking you for a loan. You might not get repaid. I suppose your offer still holds good?"

Drops of moisture had hitherto made beads on his forehead; it now shone, uniformly wet.

"If you haven't consulted anybody," Tietjens said, "you mayn't have got it. I should have yourself seen to right away. My offer still holds good!"

"Oh, I've got it, all right," the colonel answered with an air of infinite sapience. "My old man—my governor—had it. Just like that. And he never told a soul till three days before his death. Neither shall I."

"I should get it seen to," Tietjens maintained. "It's a duty to your children. And the King. You're too damn good a soldier for the army to lose."

"Nice of you to say so," the colonel said. "But I've stood too much. I couldn't face waiting for the verdict."

. . . It was no good saying he had faced worse things. He very likely hadn't, being the man he was.

The colonel said:

"Now if I could be any good!"

Tietjens said:

"I suppose I may go along the trenches now. There's a wet place . . ."

He was determined to go along the trenches. He had to . . . what was it . . . "find a place to be alone with Heaven." He maintained also his conviction that he must show the men his meal-sack of a body, mooning along; but attentive.

A problem worried him. He did not like putting it since it might seem to question the colonel's military efficiency. He wrapped it up: Had the colonel any special advice as to keeping in touch with units on the right and left? And as to passing messages.

. . . That was a mania with Tietjens. If he had had his
way he would keep the battalion day and night at communication drill. He had not been able to discover that any precautions of that sort were taken in that unit at all. Or in
the others alongside. . . .

He had hit on the colonel's heel of Achilles.

In the open it became evident: more and more and more
and always more evident! The news that General Campion
was taking over that command had changed Tietjens' whole
view of the world.

The trenches were much as he had expected. They con-
formed indeed exactly to the image he had had in the cellar.
They resembled heaps of reddish gravel laid out ready to
distribute over the roads of parks. Getting out of the dug-
out had been like climbing into a trolley that had just been
inverted for the purpose of discharging its load. It was a
nasty job for the men, cleaving a passage and keeping under
cover. Naturally the German sharpshooters were on the look-
out. Our problem was to get as much of the trench as you
could set up by daylight. The German problem was to get
as many of our men as possible. Tietjens would see that our
men stayed under cover until nightfall; the commander of
the unit opposite would attend to the sniping of as many
men as he could. Tietjens himself had three first-class snipers
left: they would attempt to get as many of the German
snipers as they could. That was self-defence.

In addition a great many enemy attentions would direct
themselves to Tietjens' stretch of the line. The artillery would
continue to plunk in a shell or so from time to time. They
would not do this very often because it would invite the
attention of our artillery, and that might prove too costly.
More or less heavy masses of high explosives would be
thrown on to the line: what the Germans called *Minenwerfer*
might project what our people called sausages. These being
visible coming through the air, you posted look-outs, who
gave you warning in time to get under cover. So the Germans had rather abandoned the use of these, probably as
being costly in explosives and not so very effective. They
made, that is to say, good holes but accounted for few
men.

Aeroplanes with their beastly bullet-distributing hoppers—
that is what they seemed like—would now and then duck
along the trench, but not very often. The proceeding was,
again, too costly: they would limit themselves as a rule to

circling leisurely overhead and dropping things whilst the shrapnel burst round them—and spattered bullets over the trench. Flying pigs, aerial torpedoes, and other floating missiles, pretty, shining, silvery things with fins, would come through the air and would explode on striking the ground or after burying themselves. There was practically no end to their devices and the Huns had a new one every other week or so. They perhaps wasted themselves on new devices. A good many of them turned out to be duds. And a good many of their usually successful missiles turned out to be duds. They were undoubtedly beginning to feel the strain —mental and in their materials. So that if you had to be in these beastly places it was probably better to be in our trenches than theirs. Our war material was pretty good!

This was the war of attrition. . . . A mug's game! A mug's game as far as killing men was concerned, but not an uninteresting occupation if you considered it as a struggle of various minds spread all over the broad landscape in the sunlight. They did not kill many men and they expended an infinite number of missiles and a vast amount of thought. If you took six million men armed with loaded canes and stockings containing bricks or knives and set them against another six million men similarly armed, at the end of three hours four million on the one side and the entire six million on the other would be dead. So, as far as killing went, it really was a mug's game. That was what happened if you let yourself get into the hands of the applied scientist. For all these things were the products not of the soldier but of hirsute, bespectacled creatures who peered through magnifying glasses. Or of course, on our side, they would be shaven-cheeked and less abstracted. They were efficient as slaughterers in that they enabled the millions of men to be moved. When you had only knives you could not move very fast. On the other hand, your knife killed at every stroke: you would set a million men firing at each other with rifles from eighteen hundred yards. But few rifles ever registered a hit. So the invention was relatively inefficient. And it dragged things out!

And suddenly it had become boring.

They were probably going to spend a whole day during which the Germans would strain themselves, their intelligences flickering across the world, to kill a couple of Tietjens' men, and Tietjens would exercise all his care in the effort not to have even one casualty. And at the end of the day they would all be very tired and the poor b——y men would have to set to work to repair the trenches in earnest. That was the ordinary day's work.

He was going about it. . . . He had got A Company commander to come up and talk to him about his fatigues. To the right of headquarters the trenches appeared to have suffered less than to the left, and it was possible to move quite a number of men without risk. A Company commander was an astonishingly thin, bald man of fifty. He was so bald that his tin hat slid about all over his skull. He had been a small ship-owner and must have married very late in life, for he spoke of having two children, one of five, one of seven. A pigeon pair. His business was now making fifty thousand a year for him. It pleased Tietjens to think that his children would be well provided for if he were killed. A nice, silent, capable man who usually looked into the distance rather abstractedly when he talked. He was killed two months later, cleanly, by a bullet.

He was impatient that things had not got a move on. What had become of the big Hun strafe?

Tietjens said:

"You remember the Hun company sergeant-major that surrendered to your crowd the night before last? The fellow who said he was going to open a little sweet-stuff shop in the Tottenham Court Road with the company money he had stolen? . . . Or perhaps you did not hear?"

The remembrance of that shifty-looking N.C.O. in blue-grey that was rather smart for a man coming in during a big fight stirred up intensely disagreeable feelings from the bottom of Tietjens' mind. It was detestable to him to be in control of the person of another human being—as detestable as it would have been to be himself a prisoner . . . that thing that he dreaded most in the world. It was indeed almost more detestable, since to be taken prisoner was at least a thing outside your own volition, whereas to control a prisoner, even under the compulsion of discipline on yourself, implies a certain free will of your own. And this had been an especially loathsome affair. Even normally, though it was irrational enough, prisoners affected him with the sense that they were unclean. As if they were maggots. It was not sensible, but he knew that if he had had to touch a prisoner he would have felt nausea. It was no doubt the product of his passionate Tory sense of freedom. What distinguished man from the brutes was his freedom. When, then, a man was deprived of freedom he became like a brute. To exist in his society was to live with brutes: like Gulliver amongst the Houyhnhnms!

And this unclean fellow had been a deserter in addition! He had been brought into the H.Q. dug-out at three in the morning after the strafe had completely died out. It appeared that he had come over, ostensibly, in the ordinary course of the attack. But he had lain all night in a shell-hole, creeping in to our lines only when things were quiet. Previously to starting, he had crammed his pockets with all the company money and even the papers that he could lay his hands on. He had been brought to H.Q. at that disagreeable hour because of the money and the papers, A Company judging that such things ought to be put in the hands at least of the adjutant as quickly as possible.

The C.O., McKechnie, the intelligence officer and the doctor had all, in addition to Tietjens himself, just settled in there, and the air of the smallish place was already fetid and reeking with service rum and whisky. The appearance of the German had caused Tietjens almost to vomit, and he was already in a state of enervation from having had to bring the battalion in. His temples were racked with a sort of neuralgia that he believed to be caused by eyestrain.

Normally the questioning of prisoners before they reached division was strongly discountenanced, but a deserter excites more interest than an ordinary prisoner, and the C.O., who was by then in a state of hilarious mutiny, absolutely ordered Tietjens to get all he could out of the prisoner. Tietjens knew a little German: the intelligence officer who knew that language well had been killed. Dunne, replacing him, had no German.

The shifty, upright, thin, dark fellow with even unusually uneasy eyes had answered questions readily enough: Yes, the Huns were fed up with the war; discipline had become so difficult to maintain that one of his reasons for deserting had been sheer weariness over the effort to keep the men under him in order. They had no food. It was impossible to get the men, in an advance, past any kind of food dumps. He was continually being unjustly reprimanded for his want of success, and standing there he cursed his late officers! Nevertheless, when the C.O. made Tietjens ask him some questions about an Austrian gun that the Germans had lately introduced to that front and that threw a self-burying shell containing an incredible quantity of H.E., the fellow had clicked his heels together and had answered:

"Nein, Herr Offizier, das wäre Landesverratung!" . . . to

answer that would be to betray one's country. His psychology had been difficult to grasp. He had explained as well as he could, using a few words of English, the papers that he had brought over. They were mostly exhortations to the German soldiers, circulars containing news of disasters to and the demoralization of the Allied troops; there were also a few returns of no great interest—mostly statistics of influenza cases. But when Tietjens had held before the fellow's eyes a typewritten page with a heading that he had now forgotten, the sergeant had exclaimed: *"Ach, nicht das!"* . . . and had made as if to snatch the paper from Tietjens' fingers. Then he had desisted, realizing that he was risking his life, no doubt. But he had become as pale as death and had refused to translate the phrases that Tietjens did not understand; and indeed Tietjens understood practically none of the words, which were all technical.

He knew the paper contained some sort of movement orders, but he was by that time heartily sick of the affair and he knew that that was just the sort of paper that the staff did not wish men in the line to meddle with. So he dropped the matter, and the colonel and the pals being by that time tired of listening and not grasping what was happening, Tietjens had sent the fellow at the double back to brigade under the charge of the intelligence officer and a heavier escort than was usual.

What remained to Tietjens of the affair was the expression that the fellow had used when asked what he was going to do with the company money he had stolen. He was going to open a little sweet shop in the Tottenham Court Road. He had, of course, been a waiter: in old Compton Street. Tietjens wondered vaguely what would become of him. What did they do with deserters? Perhaps they interned them: perhaps they made them N.C.O.s in prisoners' units. He could never go back to Germany. . . . That remained to him—and the horror and loathing he had felt at the episode: as if it had caused him personal deterioration. He had put the matter out of his mind.

It occurred to him now that very likely the urgent announcements from staff of all sorts had been inspired by that very paper! The paper that loathsome fellow had tried to grab at. He remembered that he had been feeling so sick that he hadn't bothered to have the man handcuffed. . . . It raised a number of questions: Does a man desert and at the same time refuse to betray his country? Well, he might. There was no end to the contradictions in men's characters.

Look at the C.O. An efficient officer and a muddled ass in one: even in soldiering matters!

On the other hand, the whole thing might be a plant of the Huns. The paper—the movement order—might have been meant to reach our army headquarters. On the face of it, important movement orders do not lie about in company offices. Not usually. The Huns might be trying to call our attention to this part of the line whilst their real attack might be coming somewhere else. That again was unlikely, because that particular part of the line was so weak owing to poor General Puffles' unpopularity with the great ones at home that the Huns would be mad if they attacked anywhere else. And the French were hurrying up straight to that spot in terrific force. He might then be a hero! . . . But he didn't look like a hero!

This sort of complication was wearisome now-a-days, though once it would have delighted him to dwell on it and work it out with nice figures and calculations of stresses. Now his only emotion about the matter was that, thank God, it was none of his job. The Huns didn't appear to be coming.

He found himself regretting that the strafe was not coming after all. That was incredible. How could he regret not being put into immediate danger of death?

Long, thin, scrawny and mournful, with his tin hat now tilted forwards over his nose, the O.C. A Company gazed into futurity and remarked:

"I'm sorry the Huns aren't coming!"

He was sorry the Huns were not coming. Because if they came they might as well come according to the information supplied by that prisoner. He had captured that fellow. He might as well therefore get the credit. It might get him remembered if he put in for leave. He wanted leave. He wanted to see his children. He had not seen them for two years now. Children of five and seven change a good deal in two years. He grumbled on. Without any shame at the revelation of his intimate motives. The quite ordinary man! But he was perfectly to be respected. He had a rather grating chest voice. It occurred to Tietjens that that man would never see his children.

He wished these intimations would not come to him. He found himself at times looking at the faces of several men and thinking that this or that man would shortly be killed. He wished he could get rid of the habit. It seemed indecent. As a rule he was right. But then, almost every man you looked at there was certain to get killed. . . . Himself excepted. He himself was going to be wounded in the soft place behind the right collar-bone.

He regretted that the strafe was not that morning coming! Because if they came they might as well come according to the information supplied by the prisoner he had examined in the stinking dug-out. His unit had captured the fellow. He would now be signing its H.Q. chits as acting O.C. Ninth Glamorganshires. So he, Tietjens, had captured that fellow. And his perspicacity in having him sent immediately back to brigade with his precious paper might get him, Tietjens, remembered favourably at brigade H.Q. Then they would leave him in temporary command of his battalion. And if they did that he might do well enough to get a battalion of his own!

He astounded himself. . . . His mentality was that of O.C. A Company!

He said:

"It was damn smart of you to see that fellow was of importance and have him sent at the double to me." O.C. A Coy. grew red over all his grim face. So, one day, he, Tietjens, might flush with pleasure at the words of some squit with a red band round his hat!

He said:

"Even if the Germans don't come it might have been helpful. It might have been even more helpful. It might have been the means of keeping them back." Because of course if the Germans knew that we had got hold of their movement order they might change their plans. That would inconvenience them. It was not likely. There was perhaps not time for the news that we knew to have got through to their Important Ones. But it was possible. Such things had happened.

Aranjuez and the lance-corporal stood still and so silent in the sunlight that they resembled fragments of the reddish trench. The red gravel of the trenches began here, however, to be smirched with more agricultural marl. Later the trenches became pure alluvial soil and then ran down more smartly into stuff so wet that it was like a quicksand. A bog. It was there he had tried revetting with a siphon-drain. The thought of that extreme of his line reminded him. He said:

"You know all about keeping in communication with immediately neighbouring units?"

The grim fellow said:

"Only what they taught in the training-camps at the beginning of the war, sir. When I joined up. It was fairly thorough but it's all forgotten now."

Tietjens said to Aranjuez:

"You're signalling officer. What do you know about keeping in communication with units on your right and left?"

Aranjuez, blushing and stammering, knew all about buzzers and signals. Tietjens said:

"That's only for trenches, all that. But, in motion. At your O.T.C. Didn't they practise you in keeping communication between troops in motion?"

They hadn't at the O.T.C. . . . At first it had been in the program. But it had always been crowded out by some stunt. Rifle-grenade drill. Bomb-throwing. Stokes-gun drill. Any sort of machine drill as long as it was not moving bodies of men over difficult country—sand-hills, say—and hammering into them that they must keep in touch unit with unit or drop connecting files if a unit itself divided up.

It was perhaps the dominant idea of Tietjens, perhaps the main idea that he got out of warfare—that at all costs you must keep in touch with your neighbouring troops. When, later, he had to command the escorts over immense bodies of German prisoners on the march, it several times occurred to him to drop so many connecting files for the benefit of the men or N.C.O.s—or even the officers—of his escort who had fallen out through sheer fatigue or disease, that he would arrive in a new camp at the day's end with hardly any escort left at all—say thirty for three thousand prisoners. The business of an escort being to prevent the escape of prisoners, it might have been thought better to retain the connecting files for that purpose. But, on the other hand, he never lost a prisoner except by German bombs, and he never lost any of his stragglers at all.

. . . He said to O.C. A Company:

"Please look after this matter in your company. I shall arrange as soon as I can to transfer you to the outside right of the unit. If the men are doing nothing, lecture them, please, yourself on this subject and talk very seriously to all lance-corporals, section leaders and oldest privates of platoons. And be good enough to get into communication at once with the company commander of the Wiltshires immediately on our right. In one of two ways the war is over. The war of trenches. Either the Germans will immediately drive us into the North Sea or we shall drive them back. They will then be in a state of demoralization and we shall need to move fast. Lieutenant Aranjuez, you will arrange to be present when Captain Gibbs talks to his company, and you will repeat what he says in the other companies."

He was talking quickly and distinctly, as he did when he was well, and he was talking stiltedly on purpose. He could not obviously call an officers' conference with a German attack possibly impending; but he was pretty certain that something of what he said would penetrate to nearly every ear of the battalion if he said it before a company commander, a signalling lieutenant and an orderly-room lance-corporal. It would go through that the Old Man was dotty on this joke, and sergeants would see that some attention was paid to the matter. So would the officers. It was all that could be done at the moment.

He walked behind Gibbs along the trench, which at this point was perfectly intact and satisfactory, the red gravel gradually giving place to marl. He remarked to the good fellow that in that way they would do something to checkmate the blasted civilians whose meddling with the processes of war had put them where they were. Gibbs agreed gloomily that civilian interference had lost the war. They so hated the Regular army that whenever a civilian saw a trace of Regular training remaining in this mud-fighting that they liked us to indulge in, he wrote a hundred letters under different names to the papers, and the War Secretary at once took steps to retain that hundred votes; Gibbs had been reading a home newspaper that morning.

Tietjens surprised himself by saying:

"Oh, we'll beat them yet!" It was an expression of impracticable optimism. He sought to justify his words by saying that their army commanders, having put up such a damn good fight in spite of the most criminal form of civilian interference, had begun to put a stopper on their games. Campion's coming was a proof that soldiers were going to be allowed to have some say in the conduct of the war. It meant the single command. . . . Gibbs expressed a muted satisfaction. If the French took over those lines, as they certainly would if they had the single command, he would no doubt be able to go home and see his children. All their divisions would have to be taken out of the lines to be reorganized and brought up to strength.

Tietjens said:

"As to what we were talking about. . . . Supposing you detailed outside section leaders and another file to keep in touch with the Wiltshires and they did the same. Supposing that for purposes of recognition they wore handkerchiefs round their right and left arms respectively. . . . It has been done. . . ."

"The Huns," Captain Gibbs said grimly, "would probably pick them off specially. They'd probably pick off specially anyone who had any sort of badge. So you would be worse off."

They were going at his request to look at a section of his trench. Orderly room had ordered him to make arrangements for machine-gun performances there. He couldn't. It didn't exist. Nothing existed. He supposed that to have been the new Austrian gun. New, probably, but why Austrian? The Austrians did not usually interest themselves much in high explosives. This one, whatever it was, threw something that buried itself and then blew up half the universe. With astonishingly little noise and commotion. Just lifted up. Like a hippopotamus. He, Gibbs, had hardly noticed anything, as you would have if it had been, say, a mine. When they came and told him that a mine had gone off there, he would not believe them. . . . But you could see for yourself that it looked exactly as if a mine had been chucking things about. A small mine. But still a mine. . . .

In the shelter of the broken end of the trench a fatigue of six men worked with pick and shovel, patiently, two at a time. They threw up mud and stones and patted them and, stepping down into the thus created vacancy, threw up more mud and stones. Water oozed about, uncertain where to go. There must be a spring there. That hill-side was honeycombed with springs. . . .

You would certainly have said there had been a mine there. If we had been advancing it would have been a small mine left by the Huns to cheer us up. But we had retreated onto ground we had always held. So it couldn't have been a mine.

Also it kicked the ground forward and backward and relatively little laterally, so that the deep hole it had created more resembled the entry into a rudimentary shaft than the usually circular shell-hole. A mound existed between Tietjens and B Company trench, considerably higher than you could see over. A vast mound, a miniature Primrose Hill. But much bigger than anything they had seen created by flying pigs or other aerial missiles as yet. Anyhow the mound was high enough to give Tietjens a chance to get round it in cover and shuffle down into B Company's line. He said to Gibbs:

"We shall have to see about that machine-gun place. Don't

come any further with me. Make those fellows keep their
heads down, and send them back if the Huns seem like sending over any more dirt."

6 ~

TIETJENS RECLINED on the reverse slope of the considerable
mound. In the sunlight. He had to be alone. To reflect on his
sentimental situation and his machine-guns. He had been
kept so out of the affairs of the unit that he had suddenly
remembered that he knew nothing whatever about his
machine-guns, or even about the fellow who had to look
after him. A new fellow called Cobbe, who looked rather
vacant, with an immense sunburnt nose and an open mouth.
Not, on the face of him, alert enough for his job. But you
never knew.

He was hungry. He had eaten practically nothing since
seven the night before, and had been on his feet the greater
part of the time.

He sent Lance-Corporal Duckett to A Company dug-out
to ask if they could favour him with a sandwich and some
coffee with rum in it: he sent Second-Lieutenant Aranjuez
to B Company to tell them that he was coming to take a
look round on their men and quarters. B Company commander for the moment was a very young boy, just out from
an O.T.C. It was annoying that he had an outside company.
But Constantine, the former commander, had been killed the
night before last. He was, in fact, said to be the gentleman
whose remains hung in the barbed wire, which was what
made Tietjens doubtful whether it could be he. He should not
have been so far to the left if he had been bringing his
company in. Anyhow, there had been no one to replace him
but this boy—Bennett. A good boy. So shy that he could
hardly give a word of command on parade, but yet with
all his wits about him. And blessed with an uncommonly
experienced company sergeant-major. One of the original
old Glamorganshires. Well, beggars could not be choosers!
The company had reported that morning five cases of the
influenza that was said to be ravaging the outside world. Here
then was another thing for which they had to thank the
outside world—this band of rag-time solitaries! They let the
outside world severely alone; they were, truly, hermits. Then
the outside world did this to them. Why not leave them
to their monastic engrossedness?

Even the rotten and detestable Huns had it! They were said by the divisional news-sheets to have it so badly that whole divisions were incapable of effective action. That might be a lie, invented for the purpose of heartening us; but it was probably true. The German men were apparently beastly underfed, and, at that, only on substitute foods of relatively small percentage of nutritive value. The papers brought over by that N.C.O. had certainly spoken urgently of the necessity of taking every precaution against the spread of this flail. Another circular violently and lachrymosely assured the troops that they were as well fed as the civilian populations and the Corps of Officers. Apparently there had been some sort of scandal. A circular of which he had not had time to read the whole ended up with an assertion something like: "Thus the honour of the Corps of Officers has been triumphantly vindicated."

It was a ghastly thought, that of that whole vast territory that confronted them, filled with millions of half-empty stomachs that bred disorders in the miserable brains. Those fellows must be the most miserable human beings that had ever existed. God knows, the life of our own Tommies must be hell. But those fellows . . . It would not bear thinking of.

And it was curious to consider how the hatred that one felt for the inhabitants of those regions seemed to skip in a wide trajectory over the embattled ground. It was the civilian populations and their rulers that one hated with real hatred. Now the swine were starving the poor devils in the trenches!

They were detestable. The German fighters and their intelligence and staffs were merely boring and grotesque. Unending nuisances. For he was confoundedly irritated to think of the mess they had made of his nice clean trenches. It was like when you go out for an hour and leave your dog in the drawing-room. You come back and find that it has torn to pieces all your sofa-cushions. You would like to knock its head off. . . . So you would like to knock the German soldiers' heads off. But you did not wish them much real harm. Nothing like having to live in that hell on perpetually half-empty, windy stomachs with the nightmares they set up! Naturally influenza was decimating them.

Anyhow, Germans were the sort of people that influenza *would* bowl over. They were bores because they came forever true to type. You read their confounded circulars and they made you grin whilst a little puking. They were like continual caricatures of themselves and they were continually hysterical. . . . Hypochondriacal. . . . Corps of Officers. . . .

Proud German Army. . . . His Glorious Majesty. . . . Mighty
Deeds. . . . Not much of the Rag-Time Army about that,
and that was welling out continuously all the time. . . .
Hypochondria!

A rag-time army was not likely to have influenza so badly.
It felt neither its moral nor its physical pulse. . . . Still,
here was influenza in B Company. They must have got it
from the Huns the night before last. B Company had had
them jump in on top of them; then and there had been hand-
to-hand fighting. It was a nuisance. B Company was a nuisance. It had naturally been stuck into the dampest and
lowest part of their line. Their company dug-out was reported
to be like a well with a dripping roof. It would take B
Company to be afflicted with such quarters. . . . It was difficult to see what to do—not to drain their quarters, but
to exorcise their ill luck. Still, it would have to be done. He
was going into their quarters to make a strafe, but he sent
Aranjuez to announce his coming so as to give the decent
young company commander a chance to redd up his
house. . . .

The beastly Huns! They stood between him and Valentine
Wannop. If they would go home he could be sitting talking
to her for whole afternoons. That was what a young woman
was for. You seduced a young woman in order to be able
to finish your talks with her. You could not do that without
living with her. You could not live with her without seducing her; but that was the by-product. The point is that you
can't otherwise talk. You can't finish talks at street-corners,
in museums, even in drawing-rooms. You mayn't be in the
mood when she is in the mood—for the intimate conversation that means the final communion of your souls. You
have to wait together—for a week, for a year, for a lifetime
—before the final intimate conversation may be attained . . .
and exhausted. So that . . .

That in effect was love. It struck him as astonishing. The
word was so little in his vocabulary. . . . Love, ambition,
the desire for wealth. They were things he had never known
of as existing—as capable of existing within him. He had
been the Younger Son, loafing, contemptuous, capable, idly
contemplating life, but ready to take up the position of the
Head of the Family if Death so arranged matters. He had
been a sort of eternal Second-in-Command.

Now: what the hell was he? A sort of Hamlet of the
Trenches? No, by God he was not. . . . He was perfectly
ready for action. Ready to command a battalion. He was

presumably a lover. They did things like commanding battalions. And worse!

He ought to write her a letter. What in the world would she think of this gentleman who had once made improper proposals to her, balked, said "So long!" or perhaps not even "So long!" and then walked off. With never a letter! Not even a picture postcard! For two years! A sort of a Hamlet all right! Or a swine!

Well, then, he ought to write her a letter. He ought to say: "This is to tell you that I propose to live with you as soon as this show is over. You will be prepared immediately on cessation of active hostilities to put yourself at my disposal; please. Signed, 'Xtopher Tietjens, Acting O.C. 9th Glams.'" A proper military communication. She would be pleased to see that he was commanding a battalion. Or perhaps she would not be pleased. She was a pro-German. She loved these tiresome fellows who tore his, Tietjens', sofa-cushions to pieces.

That was not fair. She was a pacifist. She thought these proceedings pestilential and purposeless. Well, there were times when they appeared purposeless enough. Look at what had happened to his neat gravel-walks. And to the marl too. Though that served the purpose of letting him sit sheltered. In the sunlight. With any number of larks. Someone once wrote:

A myriad larks in unison sang o'er her, soaring out of sight!

That was imbecile really. Larks cannot sing in unison. They make a heartless noise like that produced by the rubbing of two corks one on the other. . . . There came into his mind an image. Years ago: years and years ago: probably after having watched that gunner torment the fat Hun, because it had been below Max Redoubt . . . The sun was now for certain shining on Bemerton! Well, he could never be a country parson. He was going to live with Valentine Wannop! . . . he had been coming down the reverse side of the range, feeling good. Probably because he had got out of that O.P. which the German guns had been trying to find. He went down with long strides, the tops of thistles brushing his hips. Obviously the thistles contained things that attracted flies. They are apt to after a famous victory. So myriads of swallows pursued him, swirling round and round him, their wings touching; for a matter of twenty yards all round and their wings brushing him and the tops of the thistles. And

as the blue sky was reflected in the blue of their backs—
for their backs were below his eyes—he had felt like a Greek
god striding through the sea. . . .

The larks were less inspiring. Really, they were abusing
the German guns. Imbecilely and continuously, they were
screaming imprecations and threats. They had been relatively
sparse until just now. Now that the shells were coming back
from a mile or so off, the sky was thick with larks. A myriad
—two myriad—corks at once. Not in unison. Sang o'er him,
soaring out of sight! . . . You might almost say that it was a
sign that the Germans were going to shell you again. Wonderful "hinstinck" set by the Almighty in their little bosoms! It
was perhaps also accurate. No doubt the shells as they approached more and more shook the earth and disturbed the
little bosoms on their nests. So they got up and shouted;
perhaps warning each other; perhaps mere defiance of the
artillery.

He was going to write to Valentine Wannop. It was a
clumsy swine's trick not to have written to her before. He
had proposed to seduce her; hadn't done it and had gone off
without a word. . . . Considering himself rather a swell,
too!

He said:

"Did you get a bit to eat, corporal?"

The corporal balanced himself before Tietjens on the slope
of the mound. He blushed, rubbing his right sole on his
left instep, holding in his right hand a small tin-can and a
cup, in his left an immaculate towel containing a small cube.

Tietjens debated whether he should first drink of the coffee
and army rum to increase his zest for the sandwiches or
whether he should first eat the sandwiches and so acquire
more thirst for the coffee. . . . It would be reprehensible to
write to Valentine Wannop. The act of the cold-blooded
seducer. Reprehensible! . . . It depended on what was in
the sandwiches. It would be agreeable to fill the void below
and inwards from his breastbone. But whether do it first
with a solid or warm moisture?

The lance-corporal was deft. . . . He set the coffee-tin,
cup and towel on a flat stone that stuck out of that heap;
the towel, unfolded, served as a table-cloth; there appeared
three heaps of ethereal sandwiches. He said he had eaten half
a tin of warm mutton and haricot beans whilst he was cutting
the sandwiches. The meat in the sandwiches consisted of
foie gras, that pile: bully beef reduced to a paste with butter
that was margarine, anchovy paste out of a tin and minced

onion out of pickles; the third pile was bully beef *nature*, seasoned with Worcester sauce. . . . All the materials he had at disposal!

Tietjens smiled on the boy at his work. He said this must be a regular chef. The boy said:

"Not a chef yet, sir!" He had a camp-stool hung on his trenching-tool behind his hip. He had been chief assistant to one of the chief cooks in the Savoy. He had been going to go to Paris. "What you call a marmiton, sir!" he said. With his trenching-tool he was scooping out a level place in front of the flat rock. He set the camp-stool on the flattened platform.

Tietjens said:

"You used to wear a white cap and white overalls?"

He liked to think of the blond boy resembling Valentine Wannop dressed all in slim white. The lance-corporal said:

"It's different now, sir!" He stood at Tietjens' side, always caressing his instep. He regarded cooking as an Art. He would have preferred to be a painter, but Mother hadn't enough money. The source of supply dried up during the war. . . . If the C.O. would say a word for him after the war . . . He understood it was going to be difficult to get jobs after the war. All the blighters who had got out of serving, all the R.A.S.C., all the Lines-of-Communication men would get first chance. As the saying was, the further from the line the better the pay. And the chance, too!

Tietjens said:

"Certainly I shall recommend you. You'll get a job all right. I shall never forget your sandwiches." He would never forget the keen, clean flavour of the sandwiches or the warm generosity of the sweet, be-rummed coffee! In the blue air of that April hill-side. All the objects on that white towel were defined: with iridescent edges. The boy's face, too! Perhaps not physically iridescent. His breath, too, was very easy. Pure air! He was going to write to Valentine Wannop: "Hold yourself at my disposal. Please. Signed . . ." Reprehensible! Worse than reprehensible! You do not seduce the child of your father's oldest friend. He said:

"I shall find it difficult enough to get a job after the war!"

Not only to seduce the young woman, but to invite her to live a remarkably precarious life with him. It isn't done!

The lance-corporal said:

"Oh, sir; no, sir! . . . You're Mr. Tietjens, of Groby!"

He had often been to Groby of a Sunday afternoon. His

mother was a Middlesbrough woman. Southbank, rather. He had been to the grammar school and was going to Durham University when . . . supplies stopped. On the Eight Nine Fourteen. . . .

They oughtn't to put North Riding, Yorkshire, boys in Welsh-traditioned units. It was wrong. But for that he would not have run against this boy of disagreeable reminiscences.

"They say," the boy said, "that the well at Groby is three hundred and twenty feet deep, and the cedar at the corner of the house a hundred and sixty. The depth of the well twice the height of the tree!" He had often dropped stones down the well and listened: they made an astonishingly loud noise. Long: like echoes gone mad! His mother knew the cook at Groby. Mrs. Harmsworth. He had often seen . . . he rubbed his ankles more furiously, in a paroxysm . . . Mr. Tietjens, the father, and him, and Mr. Mark and Mr. John and Miss Eleanor. He once handed Miss Eleanor her riding-crop when she dropped it. . . .

Tietjens was never going to live at Groby. No more feudal atmosphere! He was going to live, he figured, in a four-room attic flat, on the top of one of the Inns of Court. With Valentine Wannop. *Because* of Valentine Wannop.

He said to the boy:

"Those German shells seem to be coming back. Go and request Captain Gibbs as soon as they get near to take his fatigues under cover until they have passed."

He wanted to be alone with Heaven. . . . He drank his last cup of warm, sweetened coffee, laced with rum. . . . He drew a deep breath. Fancy drawing a deep breath of satis-faction after a deep draught of warm coffee, sweetened with condensed milk and laced with rum! . . . Reprehensible! Gastronomically reprehensible! . . . What would they say at the club? . . . Well, he was never going to be at the club! The club-claret was to be regretted! Admirable claret. And the cold sideboard!

But, for the matter of that, fancy drawing deep breaths of satisfaction over the mere fact of lying—in command of a battalion!—on a slope, in the clear air, with twenty thou-sand—two myriad!—corks making noises overhead and the German guns directing their projectiles so that they were slowly approaching! Fancy!

They were, presumably, trying out their new Austrian gun. Methodically, with an infinite thoroughness. If, that is to say, there really was a new Austrian gun. Perhaps there wasn't. Division had been in a great state of excitement over such a weapon. It stood in orders that everyone was to try to obtain every kind of information about it, and it was said to throw a projectile of a remarkable, high-explosive efficiency. So Gibbs had jumped to the conclusion that the thing that had knocked to pieces his projected machine-gun emplacement had been the new gun. In that case they were trying it out very thoroughly.

The actual report of the gun or guns—they fired every three minutes, so that might mean that there was only one and that it took about three minutes to reload—was very loud and rather high in tone. He had not yet heard the actual noise made by the projectile, but the reports from a distance had been singularly dulled. When, presumably, the projectile had effected its landing, it bored extraordinarily into the ground and then exploded with a time-fuse. Very likely it would not be very dangerous to life, but if they had enough of the guns and the H.E. to plaster the things all along the line, and if the projectiles worked as efficiently as they had done on poor Gibbs' trench, there would be an end of trench warfare on the Allied side. But, of course, they probably had not either enough guns or enough high explosive and the thing would very likely act less efficiently in other sorts of soils. They were very likely trying that out. Or, if they were firing with only one gun they might be trying how many rounds could be fired before the gun became ineffective. Or they might be trying only the attrition game: smashing up the trenches, which was always useful, and then sniping the men who tried to repair them. You could bag a few men in that way, now and then. Or, naturally, with planes. . . . There was no end to these tiresome alternatives! Presumably, again, our planes might spot that gun or battery. Then it would stop!

Reprehensible! . . . He snorted! If you don't obey the rules of your club you get hoofed out, and that's that! If you retire from the post of second-in-command of Groby, you don't have to . . . oh, attend battalion parades! He had refused to take any money from Brother Mark on the ground of a fantastic quarrel. But he had not any quarrel with Brother Mark. The sardonic pair of them were just matching obstinacies. On the other hand, you had to set to the tenantry an example of chastity, sobriety, probity, or you could not take their beastly money. You provided them with the best Canadian seed-corn, with agricultural experiments suited to their soils; you sat on the head of your agent; you kept their buildings in repair; you apprenticed their sons;

you looked after their daughters when they got into trouble
and after their bastards, your own or another man's. But you
must reside on the estate. *You must reside on the estate.*
The money that comes out of those poor devils' pockets must
go back into the land so that the estate and all on it, down
to the licensed beggars, may grow richer and richer and
richer. So he had invented his fantastic quarrel with Brother
Mark: because he was going to take Valentine to live with
him. You could not have a Valentine Wannop having with
you in a Groby the infinite and necessary communings. You
could have a painted doxy from the servants' hall, quarrelling with the other maids, who would want her job, and
scandalizing the parsons for miles round. In their sardonic
way the tenants appreciated that: it was in the tradition and
all over the Riding they did it themselves. But not a lady:
the daughter of your father's best friend! They wanted Quality women to *be* Quality and they themselves would go to
ruin, spend their dung-and-seed money on whores and wreck
the fortunes of the estate sooner than that you should indulge
in infinite conversations. . . . So he hadn't taken a penny
of their money from his brother, and he wouldn't take a
penny when he in turn became Groby. Fortunately, there was
the heir. . . . Otherwise he could not have gone with that
girl!

Two pangs went through him. His son had never written
to him: the girl might have married a War Office clerk! On
the rebound! That was what it would be: a civilian War
Office clerk would be the most exact contrast to himself! . . .
But the son's letters would have been stopped by the mother.
That was what they did to people who were where *he* was.
As the C.O. had said! And Valentine Wannop, who had
listened to his conversation, would never want to mingle in-
timately in another's! Their communion was immutable and
not to be shaken!

So he was going to write to her: freckled, downright,
standing square on feet rather widely planted apart, just
ready to say: "Oh, *chuck* it, Edith Ethel! . . ." She made the
sunlight!

Or no: by heavens, he could not write to her! If he stopped
one or went dotty . . . Wouldn't it make it infinitely worse
for her to know that his love for her had been profound
and immutable? It would make it far worse, for by now
the edges of passion had probably worn less painful. Or there
was the chance of it! . . . But impenitently he would go on
willing her to submit to his will: through mounds thrown up

by Austrian projectiles and across the seas. They would do what they wanted and take what they got for it!

He reclined on his right shoulder, feeling like some immense and absurd statue: a collection of meal-sacks done in mud: with grotesque shorts revealing his muddy knees. . . . The figure on one of Michelangelo's Medici tombs. Or perhaps his *Adam* . . . He felt the earth move a little beneath him. The last projectile must have been pretty near. He would not have noticed the sound, it had become such a regular sequence. But he noticed the quiver in the earth. . . .

Reprehensible! he said. For God's sake *let* us be reprehensible! And have done with it! We aren't Hun strategists forever balancing pros and cons of militant morality!

He took, with his left hand, the cup from the rock. Little Aranjuez came round the mound. Tietjens threw the cup downhill at a large bit of rock. He said to Aranjuez's wistful, inquiring eyes:

"So that no toast more ignoble may ever be drunk out of it!"

The boy gasped and blushed:

"Then you've got someone that you love, sir!" he said in his tone of hero-worship. "Is she like Nancy, in Bailleul?"

Tietjens said:

"No, not like Nancy. . . . Or, perhaps, yes, a little like Nancy!" He did not want to hurt the boy's feelings by the suggestion that anyone unlike Nancy could be loved. He felt a premonition that that child was going to be hurt. Or, perhaps, it was only that he was already so suffering.

The boy said:

"Then you'll get her, sir. You'll certainly get her!"

"Yes, I shall probably get her!" Tietjens said.

The lance-corporal came, too, round the mound. He said that A Company were all under cover. They went all together round the heap in the direction of B Company's trench, down into which they slid. It descended sharply. It was certainly wet. It ended practically in a little swamp. The next battalion had even some yards of sand-bag parapet before entering the slope again with its trench. This was Flanders. Duck country. The bit of swamp would make personal keeping in communication difficult. Where Tietjens had put in his tile-siphons a great deal of water had exuded. The young O.C. Company said that they had had to bale the trench out until they had made a little drain down into the bog. They baled out with shovels. Two of the shovels still stood against the brushwood revetments of the parapet.

"Well, you should not leave your shovels about!" Tietjens shouted. He was feeling considerable satisfaction at the working of his siphon. In the meantime we had begun a considerable artillery demonstration. It became overwhelming. There was some sort of Bloody Mary somewhere a few yards off, or so it seemed. She pooped off. The planes had perhaps reported the position of the Austrian gun. Or we might be strafing their trenches to make them shut up that weapon. It was like being a dwarf at a conversation, a conflict—of mastodons. There was so much noise it seemed to grow dark. It was a mental darkness. You could not think. A Dark Age! The earth moved.

He was looking at Aranjuez from a considerable height. He was enjoying a considerable view. Aranjuez's face had a rapt expression—like that of a man composing poetry. Long dollops of liquid mud surrounded them in the air. Like black pancakes being tossed. He thought: "Thank God I did not write to her. We are being blown up!" The earth turned like a weary hippopotamus. It settled down slowly over the face of Lance-Corporal Duckett, who lay on his side, and went on in a slow wave.

It was slow, slow, slow . . . like a slowed-down movie. The earth manoeuvred for an infinite time. He remained suspended in space. As if he were suspended as he had wanted to be in front of that cockscomb in whitewash. Coincidence!

The earth sucked slowly and composedly at his feet.

It assimilated his calves, his thighs. It imprisoned him above the waist. His arms being free, he resembled a man in a life-buoy. The earth moved him slowly. It was solidish.

Below him, down a mound, the face of little Aranjuez, brown, with immense black eyes in bluish whites, looked at him. Out of viscous mud. A head on a charger! He could see the imploring lips form the words: "Save me, captain!" He said: "I've got to save myself first!" He could not hear his own words. The noise was incredible.

A man stood over him. He appeared immensely tall because Tietjens' face was on a level with his belt. But he was a small Cockney Tommy really. Name of Cockshott. He pulled at Tietjens' two arms. Tietjens tried to kick with his feet. Then he realized it was better not to kick with his feet. He was pulled out. Satisfactorily. There had been two men at it. A second, a corporal, had come. They were all three of them grinning. He slid down with the sliding earth towards Aranjuez. He smiled at the pallid face. He slipped a lot. He felt a frightful burning on his neck, below and behind the ear. His hand came down from feeling the place. The finger-tips had no end of mud and a little pinkishness on them. A pimple had perhaps burst. He had at least two men not killed. He signed agitatedly to the Tommies. He made gestures of digging. They were to get shovels.

He stood over Aranjuez, on the edge of liquid mud. Perhaps he would sink in. He did not sink in. Not above his boot-tops. He felt his feet to be enormous and sustaining. He knew what had happened. Aranjuez was sunk in the issuing hole of the spring that made that bog. It was like being on Exmoor. He bent down over an ineffable, small face. He bent down lower and his hands entered the slime. He had to get on his hands and knees.

Fury entered his mind. He had been sniped at. Before he had had that pain he had heard, he realized, an intimate drone under the hellish tumult. There was reason for furious haste. Or, no . . . They were low. In a wide hole. There was no reason for furious haste. Especially on your hands and knees.

His hands were under the slime, and his forearms. He battled his hands down greasy cloth; under greasy cloth. *Slimy*, not greasy! He pushed outwards. The boy's hands and arms appeared. It was going to be easier. His face was now quite close to the boy's, but it was impossible to hear what he said. Possibly he was unconscious. Tietjens said: "Thank God for my enormous physical strength!" It was the first time that he had ever had to be thankful for great physical strength. He lifted the boy's arms over his own shoulders so that his hands might clasp themselves behind his neck. They were slimy and disagreeable. He was short in the wind. He heaved back. The boy came up a little. He was certainly fainting. He gave no assistance. The slime was filthy. It was a condemnation of a civilization that he, Tietjens, possessed of enormous physical strength, should never have needed to use it before. He looked like a collection of meal-sacks; but, at least, he could tear a pack of cards in half. If only his lungs weren't . . .

Cockshott, the Tommy, and the corporal were beside him. Grinning. With the two shovels that ought not to have stood against the parapet of their trench. He was intensely irritated. He had tried to indicate with his signs that it was Lance-Corporal Duckett that they were to dig out. It was probably no longer Lance-Corporal Duckett. It was probably by now "it." The body! He had probably lost a man, after all!

Cockshott and the corporal pulled Aranjuez out of the

slime. He came out reluctantly, like a lug-worm out of sand. He could not stand. His legs gave way. He drooped like a flower done in slime. His lips moved, but you could not hear him. Tietjens took him from the two men, who supported him between the arms, and laid him a little way up the mound. He shouted in the ear of the corporal: "Duckett! Go and dig out Duckett! At the double!"

He knelt and felt along the boy's back. His spine might have been damaged. The boy did not wince. His spine might be damaged all the same. He could not be left there. Bearers could be sent with a stretcher if one was to be found. But they might be sniped coming. Probably, he, Tietjens, could carry that boy: if his lungs held out. If not, he could drag him. He felt tender, like a mother, and enormous. It might be better to leave the boy there. There was no knowing. He said: "Are you wounded?" The guns had mostly stopped. Tietjens could not see any blood flowing. The boy whispered: "No, sir!" He was, then, probably just faint. Shell-shock, very likely. There was no knowing what shell-shock was or what it did to you. Or the mere vapour of the projectile.

He could not stop there.

He took the boy under his arm as you might do a roll of blankets. If he took him on his shoulders he might get high enough to be sniped. He did not go very fast; his legs were so heavy. He bundled down several steps in the direction of the spring in which the boy had been. There was more water. The spring was filling up that hollow. He could not have left the boy there. You could only imagine that his body had corked up the spring-hole before. This had been like being at home, where they had springs like that. On the moors, digging out badgers. Digging earth drains, rather. Badgers have dry lairs. On the moors above Groby. April sunlight. Lots of sunlight and skylarks.

He was mounting the mound. For some feet there was no other way. They had been in the shaft made by that projectile. He inclined to the left. To the right would take them quicker to the trench, but he wanted to get the mound between them and the sniper. His breathing was tremendous. There was more light falling on them.

Exactly! . . . Snap! Snap! Snap! . . . Clear sounds from a quarter of a mile away. . . . Bullets whined. Overhead. Long sounds, going away. Not snipers. The men of a battalion. A chance! Snap! Snap! Snap! Bullets whined overhead. Men of a battalion get excited when shooting at anything running. They fire high. Trigger pressure. *He* was now a fat, running object. Did they fire with a sense of hatred or fun? Hatred, probably. Huns have not much sense of fun.

His breathing was unbearable. Both his legs were like painful bolsters. He would be on the relatively level in two steps if he made them. . . . Well, make them! . . . He was on the level. He had been climbing: up clods. He *had* to take an immense breath. The ground under his left foot gave way. He had been holding Aranjuez in front of his own body as much as he could, under his right arm. As his left foot sank in, the boy's body came right on top of him. Naturally this stiffish earth in huge clods had fissures in it. Apertures. It was not like regular digging.

The boy kicked, screamed, tore himself loose. . . . Well, if he wanted to go! The scream was like a horse's in a stable on fire. Bullets had gone overhead. The boy rushed off, his hands to his face. He disappeared round the mound. It was a conical mound. He, Tietjens, could now crawl on his belly. It was satisfactory.

He crawled. Shuffling himself along with his hips and elbows. There was probably a text-book way of crawling. He did not know it. The clods of earth appeared friendly. For bottom soil thrown to the top they did not feel or smell so very sour. Still, it would take a long time to get them into cultivation or under grass. Probably, agriculturally speaking that country would be in pretty poor condition for a long time. . . .

He felt pleased with his body. It had had no exercise to speak of for two months—as second-in-command. He could not have expected to be in even the condition he was in. But the mind had probably had a good deal to do with that! He had, no doubt, been in a devil of a funk. It was only reasonable. It was disagreeable to think of those Hun devils hunting down the unfortunate. A disagreeable business. Still, we did the same. . . . That boy must have been in a devil of a funk. Suddenly. He had held his hands in front of his face. Afraid to see. Well, you couldn't blame him. They ought not to send out schoolgirls. He was like a girl. Still, he ought to have stayed to see that he, Tietjens, was not pipped. He might have thought he was hit from the way his left leg had gone down. He would have to be strafed. Gently.

Cockshott and the corporal were on their hands and knees digging with the short-handled shovels that are known as trenching-tools. They were on the rear side of the mound.

"We've found 'im, sir," the corporal said. "Regular buried.

Just seed 'is foot. Dursen't use a shovel. Might cut 'im in 'arf!"

Tietjens said:

"You're probably right. Give me the shovel!"

Cockshott was a draper's assistant, the corporal a milk-man. Very likely they were not good with shovels.

He had had the advantage of a boyhood crowded with digging of all sorts. Duckett was buried horizontally, running into the side of the conical mound. His feet at least stuck out like that, but you could not tell how the body was disposed. It might turn to either side or upwards. He said:

"Go on with your tools above! But give me room."

The toes being to the sky, the trunk could hardly bend downwards. He stood below the feet and aimed terrific blows with the shovel eighteen inches below. He liked digging. This earth was luckily dryish. It ran down the hill conveniently. This man had been buried probably ten minutes. It seemed longer but it was probably less. He ought to have a chance. Probably earth was less suffocating than water. He said to the corporal:

"Do you know how to apply artificial respiration?"

"To the drowned?"

Cockshott said:

"I do, sir. I was swimming champion of Islington baths!" A rather remarkable man, Cockshott. His father had knocked up the arm of a man who tried to shoot Mr. Gladstone in 1866 or thereabouts.

A lot of earth falling away, obligingly, after one withdrawal of the shovel Lance-Corporal Duckett's thin legs appeared to the fork, the knees drooping.

Cockshott said:

" 'E ain't rubbin' 'is ankles this journey!"

The corporal said:

"Company cmander is killed, sir. Bullet clean through the 'ed!"

It annoyed Tietjens that here was another head wound. He could not apparently get away from them. It was silly to be annoyed, because in trenches a majority of wounds had to be head wounds. But Providence might just as well be a little more imaginative. To oblige one. It annoyed him, too, to think that he had strafed that boy just before he was killed. For leaving his shovels about. A strafe leaves a disagreeable impression on young boys for quite half an hour. It was probably the last incident in his life. So he died depressed. . . . Might God be making it up to him!

He said to the corporal:

"Let me come." Duckett's left hand and wrist had appeared, the hand drooping and improbably clean, level with the thigh. It gave the line of the body; you could clear away beside him.

" 'E wasn't on'y twenty-two," the corporal said.

Cockshott said: "Same age as me. Very particular 'e was about your rifle pull-throughs."

A minute later they pulled Duckett out, by the legs. A stone might have been resting on his face; in that case his face would have been damaged. It wasn't, though you had had to chance it. It was black but asleep. . . . As if Valentine Wannop had been reposing in an ash-bin. Tietjens left Cockshott applying artificial respiration very methodically and efficiently to the prostrate form.

It was to him a certain satisfaction that, at any rate, in that minute affair he hadn't lost one of the men but only an officer. As satisfaction it was not militarily correct, though as it harmed no one there was no harm in it. But for his men he always felt a certain greater responsibility; they seemed to him to be there infinitely less of their own volition. It was akin to the feeling that made him regard cruelty to an animal as a more loathsome crime than cruelty to a human being, other than a child. It was no doubt irrational.

Leaning, in the communication trench, against the corrugated iron that boasted a great whitewashed A, in a very clean thin Burberry boasting half a bushel of badges of rank —worsted crowns and things!—and in a small tin hat that looked elegant, was a slight figure. How the *devil* can you make a tin hat look elegant! It carried a hunting-switch and wore spurs. An inspecting general. The general said benevolently:

"Who are you?" and then with irritation: "Where the devil is the officer commanding this battalion? Why can't he be found?" He added: "You're disgustingly dirty. Like a blackamoor. I suppose you've an explanation."

Tietjens was being spoken to by General Campion. In a hell of a temper. He stood to attention like a scarecrow.

He said:

"I am in command of this battalion, sir. I am Tietjens, second-in-command. Now in command temporarily. I could not be found because I was buried. Temporarily."

The general said:

"You. . . Good God!" and fell back a step, his jaw dropping. He said: "I've just come from London!" And then: "By God, you don't stop in command of a battalion of mine a second after I take over!" He said: "They said this was the smartest battalion in my unit!" and snorted with passion. He added: "Neither my galloper nor Levin can find you or get you found. And there you come strolling along with your hands in your pockets!"

In the complete stillness, for, the guns having stopped, the skylarks, too, were taking a spell, Tietjens could hear his heart beat, little dry scraping sounds out of his lungs. The heavy beats were very accelerated. It gave an effect of terror. He said to himself:

"What the devil has his having been in London to do with it?" And then: "He wants to marry Sylvia! I'll bet he wants to marry Sylvia!" That was what his having been to London had to do with it. It was an obsession with him: the first thing he said when surprised and passionate.

They always arranged these periods of complete silence for the visits of inspecting generals. Perhaps the Great General Staffs of both sides arrange that for each other. More probably our guns had split themselves in the successful attempt to let the Huns know that we wanted them to shut up—that we were firing with what papists call a special intention. That would be as effective as a telephone message. The Huns would know there was something up. Never put the other side in a temper when you can help it.

He said:

"I've just had a scratch, sir. I was feeling in my pockets for my field-dressing."

The general said:

"A fellow like you has no right to be where he can be wounded. Your place is the lines of communication. I was mad when I sent you here. I shall send you back."

He added:

"You can fall out. I want neither your assistance nor your information. They said there was a damn smart officer in command here. I wanted to see him. . . . Of the name of . . . Of the name of . . . It does not matter. Fall out. . . ."

Tietjens went heavily along the trench. It came into his head to say to himself:

"It *is* a land of Hope and Glory!" Then he exclaimed: "By God! I'll take the thing before the commander-in-chief. I'll take the thing before the King in Council if necessary. By God I will!" The old fellow had no business to speak to him like that. It was importing personal enmity into service matters. He stood still, reflecting on the terms of his letter to brigade. The adjutant Notting came along the trench. He said:

"General Campion wants to see you, sir. He takes over this army on Monday." He added: "You've been in a nasty place, sir. Not hurt, I trust!" It was a most unusual piece of loquacity for Notting.

Tietjens said to himself:

"Then I've got five days in command of this unit. He can't kick me out before he's in command." The Huns would be through them before then. Five days' fighting! Thank God!

He said:

"Thanks. I've seen him. No, I'm all right. Beastly dirty!"

Notting's beady eyes had a tinge of agony in them. He said:

"When they said you had stopped one, sir, I thought I should go mad. We *can't* get through the work!"

Tietjens was wondering whether he should write his letter to brigade before or after the old fellow took over. Notting was saying:

"The doctor says Aranjuez will get through all right."

It would be better, if he were going to base his appeal on the grounds of personal prejudice. Notting was saying:

"Of course he will lose his eye. In fact it . . . it is not practically there. But he'll get through."

PART THREE

I

COMING INTO the square was like being suddenly dead, it was so silent and so still to one so lately jostled by the innumerable crowd and deafened by unceasing shouts. The shouting had continued for so long that it had assumed the appearance of being a solid and unvarying thing: like life. So the silence appeared like death; and now she had death in her heart. She was going to confront a madman in a stripped house. And the empty house stood in an empty square all of whose houses were so eighteenth century and silver-grey and rigid and serene that they ought all to be empty too and contain dead, mad men. And was this the errand? For to-day, when all the world was mad with joy? To become bear-ward to a man who had got rid of all his furniture and did not know the porter—mad without joy!

It turned out to be worse than she expected. She had expected to turn the handle of a door of a tall empty room; in a space made dim with shutters she would see him, looking suspiciously round over his shoulder, a grey badger or a bear taken at its dim occupations. And in uniform. But she was not given time even to be ready. In the last moment she was to steel herself incredibly. She was to become the cold nurse of a shell-shock case.

But there was not any last moment. He charged upon her. There in the open. More like a lion. He came, grey all over, his grey hair—or the grey patches of his hair—shining, charging down the steps, having slammed the hall-door. And lop-sided. He was carrying under his arm a diminutive piece of furniture. A cabinet.

It was so quick. It was like having a fit. The houses tottered.

He regarded her. He had presumably checked violently in his clumsy stride. She hadn't seen because of the tottering of the houses. His stone-blue eyes came fishily into place in his wooden countenance—pink and white. *Too* pink where it was pink and too white where it was white. Too much so for health. He was in grey homespuns. He should not wear homespuns or grey. It increased his bulk. He could be made to look . . . oh, a fine figure of a man, let us say!

What was he doing? Fumbling in the pocket of his clumsy trousers. He exclaimed—she shook at the sound of his slightly grating, slightly gasping voice:

"I'm going to sell this thing. . . . Stay here." He had produced a latch-key. He was panting fiercely beside her. Up the steps. He was beside her. Beside her. Beside her. It was infinitely sad to be beside this madman. It was infinitely glad. Because if he had been sane he would not have been beside him. She could be beside him for long spaces of time if he were mad. Perhaps he did not recognize her! She might be beside him for long spaces of time with him not recognizing her. Like tending your baby!

He was stabbing furiously at the latch-hole with his little key. He *would*: that was normal. He was a stab-the-keyhole sort of clumsy man. She would not want that altered. But she would see about his clothes. She said: "I am deliberately preparing to live with him for a long time!" Think of that! She said to him:

"Did you send for me?"

He had the door open: he said, panting—his *poor* lungs!:

"No." Then: "Go in!" and then: "I was just going. . . ."

She was in his house. Like a child. . . . He had not sent for her. . . . Like a child faltering on the sill of a vast black cave.

It *was* black. Stone flags. Pompeian-red walls scarred pale pink where fixed hall-furniture had been removed. Was it *here* she was going to live?

He said, panting, from behind her back:

"Wait here!" A little more light fell into the hall. That was because he was gone from the doorway.

He was charging down the steps. His boots were immense. He lolloped all over on one side because of the piece of furniture he had under his arm. He was grotesque, really. But joy radiated from his homespuns when you walked beside him. It welled out; it enveloped you. . . . Like the warmth from an electric heater, only that did not make you want to cry and say your prayers—the haughty oaf.

No, but he was not haughty. Gauche, then! No, but he was not gauche. . . . She could not run after him. He was a bright patch, with his pink ears and silver hair. Gallumphing along the rails in front of the eighteenth-century houses. *He* was eighteenth century all right. . . . But then the eighteenth century never went mad. The only century that never went mad. Until the French Revolution: and that was either not mad or not eighteenth century.

She stepped irresolutely into the shadows; she returned irresolutely to the light. . . . A long hollow sound existed: the sea saying: "Ow, Ow, Ow" along miles and miles. It was the armistice. It was Armistice Day. She had forgotten it. She was to be cloistered on Armistice Day! Ah, not cloistered! Not cloistered there. My beloved is mine and I am his! But she might as well close the door!

She closed the door as delicately as if she were kissing him on the lips. It was a symbol. It was Armistice Day. She ought to go away; instead she had shut the door on . . . Not on Armistice Day! What was it like to be . . . changed!

No! She ought not to go away! She ought not to go away! She ought *not*! He had told her to wait. She was not cloistered. This was the most exciting spot on the earth. It was not her fate to live nunlike. She was going to pass her day beside a madman; her night, too. . . . Armistice Night! That night would be remembered down unnumbered generations. Whilst one lived that had seen it the question would be asked: What did you do on Armistice Night? My beloved is mine and I am his!

The great stone stairs were carpetless: to mount them would be like taking part in a procession. The hall came in straight from the front door. You had to turn a corner to the right before you came to the entrance of a room. A queer arrangement. Perhaps the eighteenth century was afraid of draughts and did not like the dining-room door near the front entrance. . . . My beloved is . . . Why does one go on repeating that ridiculous thing? Besides, it's from the Song of Solomon, isn't it? The Canticle of Canticles! Then to quote it is blasphemy when one is . . . No, the essence of prayer is volition, so the essence of blasphemy is volition. She did not want to quote the thing. It was jumped out of her by sheer nerves. She was afraid. She was waiting for a madman in an empty house. Noises whispered up the empty stairway!

She was like Fatima. Pushing open the door of the empty room. He might come back to murder her. A madness caused by sex obsessions is not infrequently homicidal. . . . What did you do on Armistice Night? "I was murdered in an empty house!" For, no doubt he would let her live till midnight.

But perhaps he had not got sex obsessions. She had not the shadow of a proof that he had; rather that he hadn't! Certainly, rather that he hadn't. Always the gentleman.

They had left the telephone! The windows were duly shuttered, but in the dim light from between cracks the nickel gleamed on white marble. The mantelshelf. Pure Parian marble, the shelf supported by rams' heads. Singularly chaste. The ceilings and rectilinear mouldings in an intricate symmetry. Chaste, too. Eighteenth century. But the eighteenth century was not chaste. . . . *He* was eighteenth century.

She ought to telephone to her mother to inform that Eminence in untidy black with violet tabs here and there of the grave step that her daughter was . . .

What was her daughter going to do?

She ought to rush out of the empty house. She ought to be trembling with fear at the thought that he was coming home very likely to murder her. But she wasn't. What was she? Trembling with ecstasy? Probably. At the thought that he was coming. If he murdered her . . . Can't be helped! She was trembling with ecstasy all the same. She must telephone to her mother. Her mother might want to know where she was. But her mother never *did* want to know where she was. She had her head too screwed on to get into mischief! . . . Think of *that*!

Still, on such a day her mother might like to. They ought to exchange gladnesses that her brother was safe for good now. And others, too. Normally her mother was irritated when she rang up. She would be at her work. It was amazing to see her at work. Perhaps she never would again. Such untidiness of papers. In a little room. Quite a little room. She never would work in a big room because a big room tempted her to walk about and she could not afford the time to walk about.

She was writing at two books at once now. A novel . . . Valentine did not know what it was about. Her mother never let them know what her novels were about till they were finished. And a woman's history of the war. A history by a woman for women. And there she would be sitting at a large table that hardly left room for more than getting round it. Grey, large, generous-featured and tired, she would be poking over one set of papers on one side of the table or just getting up from over the novel, her loose pince-nez falling off; pushing round the table between its edge and the

wall to peer at the sheets of the woman's history that were
spread all over that region. She would work for ten minutes
or twenty-five or an hour at the one and then for an hour
and a half or half an hour or three-quarters at the other.
What a muddle her dear old head must be in!

With a little trepidation she took the telephone. It had got
to be done. She could not live with Christopher Tietjens without first telling her mother. Her mother ought to be given
the chance of dissuading. They say you ought to give a lover
a chance of a final scene before leaving him or her for good.
Still more your mother. That was jannock.

It broke the word of promise to the ear, the telephone! . . .
Was it blasphemy to quote Shakespeare when one was going
to . . . Perhaps bad taste. Shakespeare, however, was not
spotless. So they said. . . . Waiting! Waiting! How much of
one's life wasn't spent waiting, with one's weight boring one's
heels into the ground. . . . But *this* thing was dead. No roar
came from its mouth and when you jabbed the little gadget
at the side up and down no bell tinkled. . . . It had probably
been disconnected. They had perhaps cut him off for not
paying. Or he had cut it off so that she might not scream
for the police through it whilst he was strangling her. Anyhow they were cut off. They would be cut off from the world
on Armistice Night. . . . Well, they would probably be cut
off for good!

What nonsense. He had not known that she was coming.
He had not asked her to come.

So, slowly, slowly she went up the great stone staircase,
the noises all a-whispering up before her. . . . "So, slowly,
slowly she went up and slowly looked about her. Henceforth
take warning by the fall . . ." Well, she did not need to
take warning: she was not going to fall in the way Barbara
Allen did. Contrariwise!

He had not sent for her. He had not asked Edith Ethel
to ring her up. Then presumably she felt humiliated. But
she did not feel humiliated! It was, in effect, fairly natural.
He *was* quite noticeably mad, rushing out, lop-sided, with
bits of furniture under his arm and no hat on his noticeable
hair. Noticeable! That was what he was. He would never
pass in a crowd! . . . He *had* got rid of all his furniture as
Edith Ethel had alleged. Very likely he had not recognized
the porter, too. She, Valentine Wannop, had seen him going
to sell his furniture. Madly! Running to do it. You do not
run when you are selling furniture if you are sane. Perhaps Edith Ethel had seen him running along with a table

on his head. And she was by no means certain that he had recognized her, Valentine Wannop!

So Edith Ethel might have been almost justified in ringing her up. Normally it would have been an offence, considering the terms on which they had parted. Considering that Edith Ethel had accused her of having had a child by this very man! It was pretty strong, even if she had seen him running about the square with furniture, and even if there had been no one else who could help. . . . But she ought to have sent her miserable rat of a husband. There was no excuse!

Still, there had been nothing else for her, Valentine, to do. So there was no call for her to feel humiliated. Even if she had not felt for this man as she did she would have come, and, if he had been very bad, would have stayed.

He had not sent for her! This man who had once proposed love to her and then had gone away without a word and who had never so much as sent her a picture postcard! Gauche! Haughty! Was there any other word for him? There could not be. Then she ought to feel humiliated. But she did not.

She felt frightened, creeping up the great staircase and entering a great room. A very great room. All white, again with stains on the walls from which things had been removed. From over the way the houses confronted her, eighteenth-centuryishly. But with a touch of gaiety from their red chimney-pots. . . . And now she was spying: with her heart in her mouth. She was terribly frightened. This room was inhabited. As if set down in a field, the room being so large, there camped . . . A camp-bed for the use of officers, G.S. #1, as the saying is. And implements of green canvas, supported on crossed white-wood staves: a chair, a bucket with a rope-handle, a washing-basin, a table. The bed was covered over with a flea-bag of brown wool. She was terribly frightened. The further she penetrated the house the more she was at his mercy. She ought to have stayed downstairs. She was spying on him.

These things looked terribly sordid and forlorn. Why did he place them in the centre of the room? Why not against a wall? It is usual to stand the head of a bed against a wall when there is no support for the pillows. Then the pillows do not slip off. She would change. . . . No, she would not. He had put the bed in the centre of the room because he did not want it to touch walls that had been brushed by the dress of . . . You must not think bad things about that woman!

They did not look sordid and forlorn. They looked frugal. And glorious! She bent down, and drawing down the flea-bag at the top, kissed the pillows. She would get him linen pillows. You would be able to get linen now. The war was over. All along that immense line men could stand up!

At the head of the room was a dais. A box of square boarding, like the model throne artists have in studios. Surely she did not receive her guests on a dais: like royalty. She was capable . . . *You must not* . . . It was perhaps for a piano. Perhaps she gave concerts. It was used as a library now. A row of calf-bound books stood against the wall on the back edge of the platform. She approached them to see what books he had selected. They must be the books he had read in France. If she could know what books he had read in France she would know what some of his thoughts there had been. She knew he slept between very cheap cotton sheets.

Frugal and glorious. That was he! And he had designed this room to love her in. It was the room she would have asked. . . . The furnishing . . . Alcestis never had . . . For she, Valentine Wannop, was of frugal mind, too. And his worshipper. Having reflected glory . . . Damn it, she was getting soppy. But it was curious how their tastes marched together. He had been neither haughty nor gauche. He had paid her the real compliment. He had said: "Her mind so marches with mine that she will understand."

The books were indeed a job lot. Their tops ran along against the wall like an ill-arranged range of hills; one was a great folio in calf, the title indented deep and very dim. The others were French novels and little red military textbooks. She leaned over the dais to read the title of the tall book. She expected it to be Herbert's *Poems* or his *Country Parson*. . . . *He* ought to be a country parson. He never would be now. She was depriving the church of . . . Of a Higher Mathematician, really. The title of the book was *Vir. Obscur.*

Why did she take it that they were going to live together? She had no official knowledge that he wanted to. But *they* wanted to TALK. You can't talk unless you live together. Her eye, travelling downwards along the dais, caught words on paper. They threw themselves up at her from among a disorder of half a dozen typed pages; they were in big, firm,

pencilled letters. They stood out because they were pencilled;
they were:

"A man could stand up on a bleedin' 'ill!"

Her heart stopped. She must be out of condition. She
could not stand very well, but there was nothing to lean on to.
She had—she didn't know she had—read also the typed
words:

"Mrs. Tietjens is leaving the model cabinet by Barker of
Bath, which she believes you claim. . . ."

She looked desperately away from the letter. She did not
want to read the letter. She could not move away. She believed she was dying. Joy never kills. . . . But it . . . *"Fait
peur."* "Makes afraid." Afraid! Afraid! Afraid! There was
nothing now between them. It was as if they were already
in each other's arms. For surely the rest of the letter must
say that Mrs. Tietjens had removed the furniture. And his
comment—amazingly echoing the words she had just thought
—was that he could stand up. But it wasn't in the least
amazing. My beloved is mine. . . . Their thoughts marched
together; not in the least amazing. They could now stand on
a hill together. Or get into a little hole. For good. And talk.
Forever. She must not read the rest of the letter. She must
not be certain. If she were certain, she would have no hope
of preserving her . . . Of remaining. . . . Afraid and unable
to move. She would be forced to read the letter because
she was unable to move. Then she would be lost. She looked
beseechingly out of the window at the house-fronts over the
way. They were friendly. They would help her. Eighteenth
century. Cynical, but not malignant. She sprang right off her
feet. She could move, then. She hadn't had a fit.

Idiot. It was only the telephone. It went on and on. Drrinn;
drinnnn; d-r-R-I-n-n. It came from just under her feet. No,
from under the dais. The receiver was on the dais. She hadn't
consciously noticed it because she had believed the telephone
was dead. Who notices a dead telephone?

She said—it was as if she were talking into his ear, he so
pervaded her—she said:

"Who are you?"

One ought not to answer all telephone calls, but one does
so mechanically. She ought not to have answered this. She
was in a compromising position. Her voice might be recognized. Let it be recognized. She desired to be known to be
in a compromising position! What did you do on Armistice
Day!

A voice, heavy and old, said:

"You *are* there, Valentine. . . ."

She cried out:

"Oh, poor *mother*. . . . But he's not here." She added: "He's not been here with me. I'm still only waiting." She added again: "The house is empty!" She seemed to be stealthy, the house whispering round her. She seemed to be whispering to her mother to save her and not wanting the house to hear her. The house was eighteenth century. Cynical. But not malignant. It wanted her undoing but it knew that women liked being . . . ruined.

Her mother said, after a long time:

"Have you *got* to do this thing? . . . My little Valentine. . . . My little Valentine!" She wasn't sobbing.

Valentine said:

"Yes, I've got to do it!" She sobbed. Suddenly she stopped sobbing.

She said quickly:

"Listen, mother. I've had no conversation with him. I don't know even whether he's sane. He appears to be mad." She wanted to give her mother hope. Quickly. She had been speaking quickly to get hope to her mother as quickly as possible. But she added: "I believe that I shall die if I cannot live with him."

She said that slowly. She wanted to be like a little child trying to get truth home to its mother.

She said:

"I have waited too long. All these years." She did not know that she had such desolate tones in her voice. She could see her mother looking into the distance with every statement that came to her, thinking. Old and grey. And majestic and kind. . . . Her mother's voice came:

"I have sometimes suspected . . . My poor child . . . It has been for a long time?" They were both silent. Thinking. Her mother said:

"There isn't any practical way out?" She pondered for a long time. "I take it you have thought it all out. I know you have a good head and you are good." A rustling sound. "But I am not level with these times. I should be glad if there were a way out. I should be glad if you could wait for each other. Or perhaps find a legal . . ."

Valentine said:

"Oh, mother, don't cry! . . .Oh, mother, I can't. . . .Oh, I will come. . . . Mother, I will come back to you if you order it." With each phrase her body was thrown about as

if by a wave. She thought they only did that on the stage.
Her eyes said to her:

. . ."Dear Sir,

Our client, Mrs. Christopher Tietjens, of Groby-in-Cleveland . . ."

They said:

"After the occurrence at the base camp at . . ."

They said:

"Thinks it useless . . ."

She was agonized for her mother's voice. The telephone
hummed in E flat. It tried B. Then it went back to E flat.
Her eyes said:

"Proposes when occasion offers to remove to Groby . . ."
in fat, blue type-script. She cried agonizedly:

"Mother. Order me to come back or it will be too late . . ."

She had looked down, unthinkingly . . . as one does when
standing at the telephone. If she looked down again and read
to the end of the sentence that contained the words: "It is
useless," it would be too late! She would know that his wife
had given him up!

Her mother's voice came, turned by the means of its conveyance into the voice of a machine of Destiny.

"No, I can't. I am thinking."

Valentine placed her foot on the dais at which she stood.
When she looked down it covered the letter. She thanked
God. Her mother's voice said:

"I cannot order you to come back if it would kill you
not to be with him." Valentine could feel her late-Victorian
advanced mind desperately seeking for the right plea—for
any plea that would let her do without seeming to employ
maternal authority. She began to talk like a book: an august
Victorian book; Morley's *Life of Gladstone*. That was reasonable: she wrote books like that.

She said they were both good creatures of good stock. If
their consciences let them commit themselves to a certain
course of action they were probably in the right. But she
begged them, in God's name, to assure themselves that their
consciences *did* urge that course. She *had* to talk like a book!

Valentine said:

"It is nothing to do with conscience." That seemed harsh.
Her mind was troubled with a quotation. She could not find
it. Quotations ease strain; she said: "One is urged by blind
destiny!" A Greek quotation, then! "Like a victim upon an
altar. I am afraid; but I consent! . . ." Probably Euripides;
the *Alcestis* very likely! If it had been a Latin author the

phrases would have occurred to her in Latin. Being with her mother made her talk like a book. Her mother talked like a book: then *she* did. They *must;* if they did not they would scream. . . . But they were English ladies. Of scholarly habits of mind. It was horrible. Her mother said:

"That is probably the same as conscience—race conscience!" She could not urge on them the folly and disastrousness of the course they appeared to propose. She had, she said, known too many irregular unions that had been worthy of emulation and too many regular ones that were miserable and a cause of demoralization by their examples. . . . She was a gallant soul. She could not in conscience go back on the teachings of her whole life. She wanted to. Desperately! Valentine could feel the almost physical strainings of her poor, tired brain. But she could not recant. She was not Cranmer! She was not even Joan of Arc. So she went on repeating:

"I can only beg and pray you to assure yourself that not to live with that man will cause you to die or to be seriously mentally injured. If you think you can live without him or wait for him, if you think there is any hope of later union without serious mental injury, I beg and pray . . ."

She could not finish the sentence. . . . It was fine to behave with dignity at the crucial moment of your life! It was fitting: it was proper. It justified your former philosophic life. And it was cunning. Cunning!

For now she said:

"My child! My little child! You have sacrificed all your life to me and my teaching. How can I ask you now to deprive yourself of the benefit of them?"

She said:

"I *can't* persuade you to a course that might mean your eternal unhappiness! . . ." The *can't* was like a flame of agony!

Valentine shivered. That was cruel pressure. Her mother was no doubt doing her duty, but it was cruel pressure. It was very cold. November is a cold month. There were footsteps on the stairs. She shook.

"Oh, he is coming. He is coming!" she cried out. She wanted to say: "Save me!" She said: "Don't go away! Don't . . . Don't go away!" What do men do to you: men you love? Madmen. He was carrying a sack. The sack was the first she saw as he opened the door. Pushed it open; it was already half open. A sack was a dreadful thing for a madman to carry. In an empty house. He dumped the sack down on the hearthstone. He had coal-dust on his right fore-head. It was a heavy sack. Bluebeard would have had in it the corpse of his first wife. Borrow says that the gipsies say: "Never trust a young man with grey hair! . . ." He had only half-grey hair and he was only half young. He was panting. He must be stopped carrying heavy sacks. Panting like a fish. A great, motionless carp, hung in a tank.

He said:

"I suppose you would want to go out. If you don't we will have a fire. You can't stop here without a fire."

At the same moment her mother said:

"If that is Christopher I will speak to him."

She said away from the mouthpiece:

"Yes, let's go out. Oh, oh, oh. Let's go out. . . . Armistice . . . My mother wants to speak to you." She felt herself to be suddenly a little Cockney shop-girl. A midinette in an imitation Girl Guide's uniform. "Afride of the gentleman, my dear?" Surely one could protect oneself against a great carp! She could throw him over her shoulder. She had enough ju-jitsu for that. Of course a little person trained to ju-jitsu can't overcome an untrained giant if he expects it. But if he doesn't expect it she can.

His right hand closed over her left wrist. He had swum towards her and had taken the telephone in his left. One of the window-panes was so old it was bulging and purplish. There was another. There were several. But the first one was the purplishest. He said:

"Christopher Tietjens speaking!" He could not think of any-thing more recherché to say than that—the great inarticulate fellow! His hand was cool on her wrist. She was calm but streaming with bliss. There was no other word for it. As if you had come out of a bath of warm nectar and bliss streamed off you. His touch had calmed her and covered her with bliss.

He let her wrist go very slowly. To show that the grasp was meant for a caress! It was their first caress!

Before she had surrendered the telephone she had said to her mother:

"He doesn't know. . . . Oh, realize that he doesn't know!"

She went to the other end of the room and stood watching him.

He heard the telephone from its black depths say:

"How are you, my dear boy? My dear, dear boy; you're safe for good." It gave him a disagreeable feeling. This was the mother of the young girl he intended to seduce. He intended to. He said:

"I'm pretty well. Weakish. I've just come out of hospital. Four days ago." He was never going back to that bloody show. He had his application for demobilization in his pocket. The voice said:

"Valentine thinks you are very ill. Very ill, indeed. She came to you because she thinks that." She hadn't come, then, because . . . But, of course, she would not have. But she might have wanted them to spend Armistice Day together! She might have! A sense of disappointment went over him. Discouragement. He was very raw. That old devil, Campion! Still, one ought not to be as raw as that. He was saying, deferentially:

"Oh, it was mental rather than physical. Though I had pneumonia all right." He went on saying that General Campion had put him in command over the escorts of German prisoners all through the lines of several armies. That really nearly had driven him mad. He couldn't bear being a beastly jailer.

Still—still!—he saw those grey spectral shapes that had surrounded and interpenetrated all his later days. The image came over him with the mood of repulsion at odd moments —at the very oddest; without suggestion there floated before his eyes the image, the landscape, of greyish forms. In thousands, seated on upturned buckets, with tins of fat from which they ate at their sides on the ground, holding up newspapers that were not really newspapers; on grey days. They were all round him. And he was their jailer. He said: "A filthy job!"

Mrs. Wannop's voice said:

"Still, it's kept you alive for us!"

He said:

"I sometimes wish it hadn't!" He was astonished that he had said it; he was astonished at the bitterness of his voice. He added: "I don't mean that in cold blood of course," and he was again astonished at the deference in his voice. He was leaning down, positively, as if over a very distinguished, elderly, seated lady. He straightened himself. It struck him as distasteful hypocrisy to bow before an elderly lady when you entertained designs upon her daughter. Her voice said:

"My dear boy . . . my dear, almost son. . . ."

Panic overcame him. There was no mistaking those tones. He looked round at Valentine. She had her hands together as if she were wringing them. She said, exploring his face painfully with her eyes:

"Oh, be kind to her. Be kind to her. . . ."

Then there had been revelation of their . . . you couldn't call it intimacy!

He never liked her Girl Guide's uniform. He liked her best in a white sweater and a fawn-coloured short skirt. She had taken off her hat—her cowboyish hat. She had had her hair cut. Her fair hair.

Mrs. Wannop said:

"I've got to think that you have saved us. To-day I have to think that you have saved us. . . . And of all you have suffered." Her voice was melancholy, slow, and lofty.

Intense, hollow reverberations filled the house. He said:

"That's nothing. That's over. You don't have to think of it."

The reverberations apparently reached her ear. She said:

"I can't hear you. There seems to be thunder."

External silence came back. He said:

"I was telling you not to think of my sufferings."

She said:

"Can't you wait? You and she? Is there *no* . . ." The reverberations began again. When he could again hear she was saying:

"Has had to contemplate such contingencies arising for one's child. It is useless to contend with the tendency of one's age. But I had hoped . . ."

The knocker below gave three isolated raps, but the echoes prolonged them. He said to Valentine:

"That's the knocking of a drunken man. But then half the population might well be drunk. If they knock again, go down and send them away."

She said:

"I'll go in any case before they can knock again."

She heard him say as she left the room—she could not help waiting for the end of the sentence: she *must* gather all that she could as to that agonizing interview between her mother and her lover. Equally, she must go or she would go mad. It was no good saying that her head was screwed on straight. It wasn't. It was as if it contained two balls of string with two ends. On the one her mother pulled, on the other he. . . . She heard him say:

"I don't know. One has desperate need. Of talk. I have not really spoken to a soul for two years!" Oh, blessed, adorable man! She heard him going on, getting into a stride of talk:

"It's that that's desperate. I'll tell you. I'll give you an instance. I was carrying a boy. Under rifle-fire. His eye got knocked out. If I had left him where he was his eye would not have been knocked out. I thought at the time that he might have been drowned, but I ascertained afterwards that the water never rose high enough. So I am responsible for the loss of his eye. It's a sort of monomania. You see, I am talking of it now. It recurs. Continuously. And to have to bear it in complete solitude . . ."

She was not frightened going now down the great stairs. They whispered, but she was like a calm Fatima. *He* was Sister Anne, and a brother, too. The enemy was fear. She must not fear. He rescued her from fear. It is to a woman that you must come for refuge from regrets about a boy's eyes.

Her physical interior turned within her. He had been under fire! He might never have been there, a grey badger, a tender, tender grey badger leaning down and holding a telephone. Explaining things with tender care. It was lovely how he spoke to her mother; it was lovely that they were all three together. But her mother would keep them apart. She was taking the only way to keep them apart if she was talking to him as she had talked to her.

There was no knowing. She had heard him say:

He was pretty well. . . . "Thank God! . . ." Weakish. . . . "Ah, give *me* the chance to cherish him! . . ." He had just come out of hospital. Four days ago. He had had pneumonia all right, but it had been mental rather than physical. . . .

Ah, the dreadful thing about the whole war was that it had been—the suffering had been—mental rather than physical. And they had not thought of it. . . . He had been under fire. She had pictured him always as being in a base, thinking. If he had been killed it would not have been so dreadful for him. But now he had come back with his obsessions and mental troubles. . . . And he needed his woman. And her mother was forcing him to abstain from his woman! That was what was terrible. He had suffered mental torture and now his pity was being worked on to make him abstain from the woman that could atone.

Hitherto, she had thought of the war as physical suffering only: now she saw it only as mental torture. Immense miles and miles of anguish in darkened minds. That remained. Men might stand up on hills, but the mental torture could not be expelled.

She ran suddenly down the steps that remained to her and was fumbling at the bolts of the front door. She was not skilful at that: she was thinking about the conversation that dreadfully she felt to be continuing. She must stop the knocking. The knocker had stayed for just long enough for the abstention of an impatient man knocking on a great door. Her mother was too cunning for them. With the cunning that makes the mother wild duck tumble apparently broken-winged just under your feet to decoy you away from her little things. STORGE, Gilbert White calls it! For, of course, she could never have his lips upon hers when she thought of that crafty, beloved, grey Eminence sitting at home and shuddering. . . . But she *would!*

She found the gadget that opened the door—the third she had tried amongst incomprehensible, painted, century-old fixings. The door came open exactly upon a frustrated sound. A man was being propelled towards her by the knocker to which he held. . . . She had saved *his* thoughts. Without the interruption of the knocker he might be able to see that mother's device was just cunning. They were cunning, the great Victorians. . . . Oh, poor mother!

A horrible man in uniform looked at her hatefully, with piercing, hollow, black eyes in a fallen-away face. He said:

"I must see that fellow Tietjens; you're not Tietjens!" As if she were defrauding him. "It's urgent," he said. "About a sonnet. I was dismissed the army yesterday. *His* doing. And Campion's. His wife's lover!"

She said fiercely:

"He's engaged. You can't see him. If you want to see him you must wait!" She felt horror that Tietjens should ever have had to do with such a brute beast. He was unshaven; black. And filled with hatred. He raised his voice to say:

"I'm McKechnie. Captain McKechnie of the Ninth. Vice-Chancellor's Latin Prize man! One of the Old Pals!" He added: "Tietjens forced himself in on the Old Pals!"

She felt the contempt of the scholar's daughter for the Prize man; she felt that Apollo with Admetus was as nothing for sheer disgust compared with Tietjens buried in a band of such beings.

She said:

"It is not necessary to shout. You can come in and wait."

At all costs Tietjens must finish his conversation with her mother undisturbed. She led this fellow round the corner of the hall. A sort of wireless emanation seemed to connect her with the upper conversation. She was aware of it going on, through the wall above, diagonally; then through the ceiling in perpendicular waves. It seemed to work inside her head, her end of it, like waves, churning her mind.

She opened the shutters of the empty room round the corner, on the right. She did not wish to be alone in the dark with this hating man. She did not dare to go up and warn Tietjens. At all costs he must not be disturbed. It was not fair to call what her mother was doing cunning. It was instinct, set in her breast by the Almighty, as the saying is. . . . Still, it was early-Victorian instinct! Tremendously cunning in itself.

The hateful man was grumbling:

"He's been sold up, I see. That's what comes of selling your wife to generals. To get promotion. They're a cunning lot. But he overreached himself. Campion went back on him. But Campion, too, overreached *him*self. . . ."

She was looking out of the window, across the green square. Light was an agreeable thing. You could breathe more deeply when it was light. . . . Early-Victorian instinct! . . . The mid-Victorians had had to loosen the bonds. Her mother, to be in the van of mid-Victorian thought, had had to allow virtue to "irregular unions." As long as they were high-minded. But the high-minded do not consummate irregular unions. So all her books had showed you high-minded creatures contracting irregular unions of the mind or of sympathy, but never carrying them to the necessary conclusion. They would have been ethically at liberty to but they didn't. They ran with the ethical hare but hunted with the ecclesiastical hounds. . . . Still, of course, she could not go back on her premises just because it was her own daughter!

She said:

"I beg your pardon!" to that fellow. He had been saying:

"They're too damn cunning. They overreach themselves!" Her mind spun. She did not know what he had been talking about. Her mind retained his words, but she did not understand what they meant. She had been sunk in the contemplation of early-Victorian thought. She remembered the long—call it "liaison"—of Edith Ethel Duchemin and little Vincent Macmaster. Edith Ethel, swathed in opaque crape, creeping widow-like along the very palings she could see across the square, to her high-minded adulteries, amidst the whispered applause of mid-Victorian England. So circumspect and right! . . . She had her thoughts to keep, all right. Well under control! . . . Well, she had been patient.

The man said agonizedly:

"My filthy, bloody, swinish uncle, Vincent Macmaster. *Sir* Vincent Macmaster! And this fellow Tietjens. All in a league against me. . . . Campion too. . . . But he overreached himself. . . . A man got into Tietjens' wife's bedroom. At the base. And Campion sent him to the front. To get him killed. Her other lover, you see?"

She listened. She listened with all her attention straining. She wanted to be able to . . . She did not know what she wanted to be able to do! The man said:

"Major-General Lord Edward Campion, V.C., K.C.M.G., tantivy tum tum, et cetera. Too cunning. Too b——y cunning by half. Sent Tietjens to the front too to get him killed. Me too. We all three went up to division in a box-car—Tietjens, his wife's lover, and me. Tietjens confessed that bleedin' swab. Like a beastly monk. Told him that when you die—*in articulo mortis;* but you won't understand what that means!—your faculties are so numbed that you feel neither pain nor fear. He said death was no more than an anaesthetic. And that trembling, whining pup drank it in. . . . I can see them now. In a box-car. In a cutting."

She said:

"You've had shell-shock? You've got shell-shock now!"

He said, like a badger snapping:

"I haven't. I've got a bad wife. Like Tietjens. At least she isn't a bad wife. She's a woman with appetites. She satisfies her appetites. That's why they're hoofing me out of the army. But at least, I don't sell her to generals. To Major-General Lord Edward Campion, V.C., K.C.M.G., et cetera. I got divorce leave and didn't divorce her. Then I got second divorce leave. And didn't divorce her. It's against my principles. She lives with a British Museum palaeontologist and he'd lose his job. I owe that fellow Tietjens a hundred and seventy quid. Over my second divorce leave. I can't pay him. I didn't divorce, but I've spent the money. Going about with my wife and her friend. On principle!"

He spoke so inexhaustibly and fast, and his topics changed so quickly, that she could do no more than let the words go into her ears. She listened to the words and stored them up. One main line of topic held her; otherwise she could not think. She only let her eyes run over the friezes of the opposite houses. She gathered that Tietjens had been unjustly dismissed by Campion, whilst saving two lives under fire.

McKechnie grudgingly admitted heroism to Tietjens in order to blacken the general. The general wanted Sylvia Tietjens. So as to get her he had sent Tietjens into the hottest part of the line. But Tietjens had refused to get killed. He had a charmed life. That was Provvy spiting the general. All the same, Providence could not like Tietjens, a cully who comforted his wife's lover. A dirty thing to do. When Tietjens would not be killed the general came down into the line and strafed him to hell. Didn't she, Valentine, understand why? He wanted Tietjens cashiered so that he, Campion, might be less disgustingly disgraced for taking up with the wife. But he had overreached himself. You can't be cashiered for not being on the spot to lick a general's boots when you are saving life under rifle-fire. So the general had to withdraw his words and find Tietjens a dirty scavenger's job. Made a bleedin' jailer of him!

She was standing in the doorway so that this fellow should not run upstairs to where the conversation was going on. The windows consoled her. She only gathered that Tietjens had had great mental trouble. He must have. She knew nothing of either Sylvia Tietjens or the general except for their beautiful looks. But Tietjens must have had great mental trouble. Dreadful!

It was hateful. How could she stand it! But she must, to keep this fellow from Tietjens, who was talking to her mother.

And . . . if his wife was a bad wife, didn't it . . .

The windows were consoling. A little dark boy of an officer passed the railings of the house, looking up at the windows.

McKechnie had talked himself hoarse. He was coughing. He began to complain that his uncle, Sir Vincent Macmaster, had refused him an introduction to the Foreign Office. He had made a scene at the Macmasters' already that morning. Lady Macmaster—a haggard wanton, if there ever was one—had refused him access to his uncle, who was suffering from nervous collapse. He said suddenly:

"Now, about this sonnet: I'm at least going to show this fellow . . ." Two more officers, one short, the other tall, passed the window. They were laughing and calling out. ". . . that I'm a better Latinist than he. . . ."

She sprang into the hall. Thunder again had come from the door.

In the light outside, a little officer with his half-profile towards her seemed to be listening. Beside him was a thin lady, very tall. At the bottom of the steps were the two laughing officers. The boy, his eye turned towards her, with a shrinking timidity you would have said, exclaimed in a soft voice:

"We've come for Major Tietjens. . . . This is Nancy. Of Bailleul, you know!" He had turned his face still more towards the lady. She was unreasonably thin and tall, the face of her skin drawn. She was much the older. Much. And hostile. She must have put on a good deal of colour. Purplish. Dressed in black. She ducked a little.

Valentine said:

"I'm afraid . . . He's engaged. . . ."

The boy said:

"Oh, but he'll see us. This is Nancy, you know!"

One of the officers said:

"We said we'd look old Tietjens up. . . ." He had only one arm. She was losing her head. The boy had a blue band round his hat. She said:

"But he's dreadfully urgently engaged. . . ."

The boy turned his face full on her with a gesture of entreaty.

"Oh, but . . ." he said. She nearly fell, stepping back. His eye-socket contained nothing; a disorderly reddish scar. It made him appear to be peering blindly; the absence of the one eye blotted out the existence of the other. He said in Oriental pleading tones:

"The major saved my life; I must see him!" The sleeveless officer called out:

"We said we'd look old Tietjens up. . . . It's Armi . . . hick . . . At Rouen in the pub . . ." The boy continued:

"I'm Aranjuez, you know! Aranjuez. . . ." They had only been married last week. He was going to the Indian Army to-morrow. They *must* spend Armistice Day with the major. Nothing would be anything without the major. They had a table at the Holborn.

The third officer: he was a very dark, silky-voiced, young major, crept slowly up the steps, leaning on a stick, his dark eyes on her face.

"It *is* an engagement, you know!" he said. He had a voice like silk and bold eyes. "We really did make an engagement to come to Tietjens' house to-day . . . whenever it happened . . . a lot of us. In Rouen. Those who were in Number Two."

Aranjuez said:

"The C.O.'s to be there. He's dying, you know. And it would be nothing without the major. . . ."

She turned her back on him. She was crying because of the pleading tones of his voice and his small hands. Tietjens was coming down the stairs, mooning slowly.

2 ⁓

STANDING AT the telephone, Tietjens had recognized at once that this was a mother, pleading with infinite statesmanship for her daughter. There was no doubt about that. How could he continue to . . . to entertain designs on the daughter of this voice? . . . But he *did*. He couldn't. He did. He *couldn't*. He did. . . . You may expel nature by pleading . . . *tamen usque recur*. . . . She must recline in his arms before midnight. Having cut her hair had made her face look longer. Infinitely attracting. Less downright: with a refinement. Melancholy! Longing! One must comfort.

There was nothing to answer to the mother on sentimental lines. He wanted Valentine Wannop enough to take her away. That was the overwhelming answer to Mrs. Wannop's sophistications of the advanced writer of a past generation. It answered her then; still more it answered her now, to-day, when a man could stand up. Still, he could not overwhelm an elderly, distinguished and inaccurate lady! It is not done.

He took refuge in the recital of facts. Mrs. Wannop, weakening her ground, asked:

"*Isn't* there any legal way out? Miss Wanostrocht tells me your wife . . ."

Tietjens answered:

"I can't divorce my wife. She's the mother of my child. I can't live with her, but I can't divorce her."

Mrs. Wannop took it lying down again, resuming her proper line. She said that he knew the circumstances and that if his conscience . . . And so on and so on. She believed, however, in arranging things quietly if it could be done. He was looking down mechanically, listening. He read that "Our client, Mrs. Tietjens, of Groby-in-Cleveland, requests us to inform you that after the late occurrences at a base camp in France she thinks it useless that you and she should contemplate a common life for the future. . . ." He had contemplated that set of facts enough already. Campion during his leave had taken up his quarters at Groby. He did not suppose that Sylvia had become his mistress. It was improbable in the extreme. Unthinkable! He had gone to Groby with Tietjens' sanction in order to sound his prospects as candidate for the division. That is to say that, ten months ago, Tietjens had told the general that he might make Groby his headquarters as it had been for years. But, in that communication trench he had not told Tietjens that he had been at Groby. He had said "London." Specifically.

That *might* be an adulterer's guilty conscience but it was more likely that he did not want Tietjens to know that he had been under Sylvia's influence. He had gone for Tietjens bald-headed, beyond all reason for a commander-in-chief speaking to a battalion commander. Of course he might have the wind up at being in the trenches and being kept waiting so near the area of a real strafe as he might well have taken that artillery lark to be. He might have let fly just to relieve his nerves. But it was more likely that Sylvia had bewildered his old brains into thinking that he, Tietjens, was such a villain that he ought not to be allowed to defile the face of the earth. Still less a trench under General Campion's control.

Campion had afterwards taken back his words very handsomely—with a sort of distant and lofty deprecation. He had even said that Tietjens had deserved a decoration, but that there were only a certain number of decorations now to be given and that he imagined that Tietjens would prefer it to be given to a man to whom it would be of more advantage. And he did not like to recommend for decoration an officer so closely connected with himself. He said this before members of his staff . . . Levin and some others. And he went on, rather pompously, that he was going to employ Tietjens on a very responsible and delicate duty. He had been asked by H.M. government to put the charge over all enemy prisoners between army H.Q. and the sea in charge of an officer of an exceptionally trustworthy nature, of high social position and weight. In view of the enemy's complaints to The Hague of ill treatment of prisoners.

So Tietjens had lost all chance of distinction, command pay, cheerfulness, or even equanimity. And all tangible proof that he had saved life under fire—if the clumsy mud-bath of his incompetence could be called saving life under fire. He could go on being discredited by Sylvia till kingdom come, with nothing to show on the other side but the uncreditable fact that he had been a jailer. Clever old general! Admirable old godfather-in-law!

Tietjens astonished himself by saying to himself that if he had had any proof that Campion had committed adultery with Sylvia he would kill him! Call him out and kill him. . . .

That of course was absurd. You do not kill a general officer commanding-in-chief an army. And a good general too. His reorganization of that army had been everything that was ship-shape and soldierly; his handling it in the subsequent fighting had been impeccably admirable. It was in fact the apotheosis of the Regular soldier. That alone was a benefit to have conferred on the country. He had also contributed by his political action to forcing the single command on the government. When he had gone to Groby he had let it be quite widely known that he was prepared to fight that division of Cleveland on the political issue of single command or no single command—and to fight it in his absence in France. Sylvia no doubt would have run the campaign for him!

Well, that, and the arrival of the American troops in large quantities, had no doubt forced the hand of Downing Street. There could no longer have been any question of evacuating the Western Front. Those swine in their corridors were scotched. Campion was a good man. He was good—impeccable!—in his profession; he had deserved well of his country. Yet, if Tietjens had had proof that he had committed adultery with his, Tietjens', wife, he would call him out. Quite properly. In the eighteenth-century traditions for soldiers. The old fellow could not refuse. He was of eighteenth-century tradition too.

Mrs. Wannop was informing him that she had had the news of Valentine's having gone to him from a Miss Wanostrocht. She had, she said, at first agreed that it was proper that Valentine should look after him if he were mad and destitute. But this Miss Wanostrocht had gone on to say that she had heard from Lady Macmaster that Tietjens and her daughter had had a liaison lasting for years. And . . . Mrs. Wannop's voice hesitated . . . Valentine seemed to have announced to Miss Wanostrocht that she intended to live with Tietjens. "Maritally," Miss Wanostrocht had expressed it.

It was the last word alone of Mrs. Wannop's talk that came home to him. People would talk. About him. It was his fate. And hers. Their identities interested Mrs. Wannop, as novelist. Novelists live on gossip. But it was all one to him.

The word "Maritally!" burst out of the telephone like a blue light! That girl with the refined face, the hair cut longish, but revealing its thinner refinement. . . . That girl longed for him as he for her! The longing had refined her face. He must comfort . . .

He was aware that for a long time, from below his feet, a voice had been murmuring on and on. Always one voice. Who could Valentine find to talk to or to listen to for so long? Old Macmaster was almost the only name that came to his mind. Macmaster would not harm her. He felt her being united to his by a current. He had always felt that her being was united to his by a current. This, then, was the day!

The war had made a man of him! It had coarsened him and hardened him. There was no other way to look at it. It had made him reach a point at which he would no longer stand unbearable things. At any rate from his equals! He counted Campion as his equal; few other people, of course. And what he wanted he was prepared to take. . . . What he had been before, God alone knew. A Younger Son? A Perpetual Second-in-Command? Who knew. But to-day the world changed. Feudalism was finished; its last vestiges were gone. It held no place for him. He was going—he was damn well going!—to make a place in it for . . . A man could now stand up on a hill, so he and she could surely get into some hole together!

He said:

"Oh, I'm not destitute, but I was penniless this morning. So I ran out and sold a cabinet to Sir John Robertson. The old fellow had offered me a hundred and forty pounds for it before the war. He would only pay forty to-day—because of the immorality of my character." Sylvia had completely got hold of the old collector. He went on: "The armistice came too suddenly. I was determined to spend it with Valentine. I expected a cheque to-morrow. For some books I've sold. And Sir John was going down to the country. I had got into an old suit of mufti and I hadn't a civilian hat." Reverberations came from the front door. He said earnestly: "Mrs. Wannop. . . . If Valentine and I can, we will. . . . But to-day's to-day! . . . If we can't we can find a hole to get into. . . . I've heard of an antiquity-shop near Bath. No special regularity of life is demanded of old-furniture dealers. We should be quite happy! I have also been recommended to apply for a vice-consulate. In Toulon, I believe. I'm quite capable of taking a practical hold of life!"

The Department of Statistics would transfer him. All the government departments, staffed of course by non-combatants, were aching to transfer those who had served to any other old department.

A great many voices came from below-stairs. He could not leave Valentine to battle with a great number of voices. He said:

"I've got to go!" Mrs. Wannop's voice answered:

"Yes, do. I'm very tired."

He came mooning slowly down the stairs. He smiled. He exclaimed:

"Come up, you fellows. There's some hooch for you!" He had a royal aspect. An all-powerfulness. They pushed past her and then past him on the stairs. They all ran up the stairs, even the man with the stick. The armless man shook hands with his left hand as he ran. They exclaimed enthusiasms. . . . On all celebrations it is proper for His Majesty's officers to exclaim and to run upstairs when whisky is mentioned. How much the more so to-day!

They were alone now in the hall, he on a level with her. He looked into her eyes. He smiled. He had never smiled at her before. They had always been such serious people. He said:

"We shall have to celebrate! But I'm not mad. I'm not destitute!" He had run out to get money to celebrate with her. He had meant to go and fetch her. To celebrate that day together.

She wanted to say: "I am falling at your feet. My arms are embracing your knees!"

Actually she said:

"I suppose it is proper to celebrate together to-day!"

Her mother had made their union. For they looked at each other for a long time. What had happened to their eyes? It was as if they had been bathed in soothing fluid: they could look the one at the other. It was no longer the one looking and the other averting the eyes, in alternation. Her mother had spoken between them. They might never have spoken of themselves. In one heart-beat apiece whilst she had been speaking they had been made certain that their union had already lasted many years. . . . It was warm; their hearts beat quietly. They had already lived side by side for many years. They were quiet in a cavern. The Pompeian red bowed over them; the stairways whispered up and up. They would be alone together now. Forever!

She knew that he desired to say "I hold you in my arms.

My lips are on your forehead. Your breasts are being hurt by my chest!"

He said:

"Who have you got in the dining-room? It used to be the dining-room!"

Dreadful fear went through her. She said:

"A man called McKechnie. Don't go in!"

He went towards danger, mooning along. She would have caught at his sleeve, but Caesar's wife must be as brave as Caesar. Nevertheless she slipped in first. She had slipped past him before at a hanging-stile. A Kentish kissing-gate. She said:

"Captain Tietjens is here!" She did not know whether he was a captain or a major. Some called him one, some another.

McKechnie looked merely grumbling: not homicidal. He grumbled:

"Look here, my bloody swine of an uncle, your pal, has had me dismissed from the army!"

Tietjens said:

"Chuck it. You know you've been demobilized to go to Asia Minor for the government. Come and celebrate." McKechnie had a dirty envelope. Tietjens said: "Oh, yes. The sonnet. You can translate it under Valentine's inspection. She's the best Latinist in England!" He said: "Captain McKechnie: Miss Wannop!"

McKechnie took her hand:

"It isn't fair if you're such a damn good Latinist as that. . . ." he grumbled.

"You'll have to have a shave before you come out with us!" Tietjens said.

They three went up the stairs together, but they two were alone. They were going on their honeymoon journey. . . . The bride's going away! . . . She ought not to think such things. It was perhaps blasphemy. You go away in a neatly shining coupé with cockaded footmen!

He had rearranged the room. He had positively rearranged the room. He had removed the toilet-furnishings in green canvas: the camp-bed—three officers on it—was against the wall. That was his thoughtfulness. He did not want these people to have it suggested that she slept with him there. . . . Why not? Aranjuez and the hostile thin lady sat on green-canvas pillows on the dais. Bottles leaned against each other on the green-canvas table. They all held glasses.

There were in all five of H.M. officers. Where had they come from? There were also three mahogany chairs with green rep, sprung seats. Fat seats. Glasses were on the mantelshelf. The thin, hostile lady held a glass of dark red in an unaccustomed manner.

They all stood up and shouted:

"McKechnie!" "Good old McKechnie!" "Hurray McKechnie!" "McKechnie!" opening their mouths to the full extent and shouting with all their lungs. You could see that!

A swift pang of jealousy went through her.

McKechnie turned his face away. He said:

"The pals! The old pals!" He had tears in his eyes.

A shouting officer sprang from the camp-bed—her nuptial couch! Did she *like* to see three officers bouncing about on her nuptial couch? What an Alcestis! She sipped sweet port! It had been put into her hand by the soft, dark, armless major! The shouting officer slapped Tietjens violently on the back. The officer shouted:

"I've picked up a skirt. . . . A proper little bit of fluff, sir!"

Her jealousy was assuaged. Her lids felt cold. They had been wet for an instant or so: the moisture had cooled! It's salt of course! . . . She belonged to this unit! She was attached to him . . . for rations and discipline. So she was attached to it. Oh, happy day! Happy, happy day! . . . There was a song with words like that. She had never expected to see it. She had never expected . . .

Little Aranjuez came up to her. His eyes were soft, like a deer's, his voice and little hands caressing. . . . No, he had only one eye! Oh, dreadful! He said:

"You are the major's dear friend. . . . He made a sonnet in two and a half minutes!" He meant to say that Tietjens had saved his life.

She said:

"Isn't he wonderful!" Why?

He said:

"He can do anything! Anything! . . . He ought to have been . . ."

A gentlemanly officer with an eye-glass wandered in. . . . Of course they had left the front door open. He said with an exquisite voice:

"Hullo, major! Hullo, Monty! . . . Hullo, the pals!" and strolled to the mantelpiece to take a glass. They all yelled "Hullo, Duckfoot. . . . Hullo, Brassface!" He took his glass delicately and said: "Here's to hoping! . . . The mess!"

Aranjuez said:

"Our only V.C. . . ." Swift jealousy went through her.

Aranjuez said:

"*I say* . . . that *he* . . ." Good boy! Dear boy! Dear little brother! . . . Where was her own brother? Perhaps they were not going to be on terms any more! All around them the world was roaring. They were doing their best to make a little roaring unit there: the tide creeping into silent places!

The thin woman in black on the dais was looking at them. She drew her skirts together. Aranjuez had his little hands up as if he were going to lay them pleadingly on her breast. Why pleadingly? . . . Begging her to forget his hideous eye-socket. He said:

"Wasn't it splendid . . . wasn't it ripping of Nancy to marry me like this? . . . We shall all be such friends."

The thin woman caught her eye. She seemed more than ever to draw her skirts away, though she never moved. . . . That was because she, Valentine, was Tietjens' mistress. . . . There's a picture in the National Gallery called *Titian's Mistress.* . . . She passed, perhaps with them all, for having. . . The woman smiled at her: a painfully forced smile. For armistice. . . . She, Valentine, was outside the pale. Except for holidays and days of national rejoicing. . . .

She felt . . . nakedish, at her left side. Sure enough Tietjens was gone. He had taken McKechnie to shave. The man with the eye-glass looked critically round the shouting room. He fixed her and bore towards her. He stood over, his legs wide apart. He said:

"Hullo! Who'd have thought of seeing *you* here? Met you at the Prinseps'. Friend of friend Hun's, aren't you?"

He said:

"Hullo, Aranjuez! Better?"

It was like a whale speaking to a shrimp: but still more like an uncle speaking to a favourite nephew! Aranjuez blushed with sheer pleasure. He faded away as if in awe before tremendous eminences. For him she too was an eminence. His life-hero's . . . woman!

The V.C. was in the mood to argue about politics. He always was. She had met him twice during evenings at friends called Prinsep. She had not known him because of his eye-glasses: he must have put that up along with his ribbon. It took your breath away: like a drop of blood illuminated by a light that never was.

He said:

"They say you're receiving for Tietjens! Who'd have thought it? You a pro-German and he such a sound Tory. Squire of Groby and all, eh what?"

He said:

"Know Groby?" He squinted through his glasses round the room. "Looks like a mess this . . . Only needs the *Vie Parisienne* and the *Pink Un.* . . . Suppose he has moved his stuff to Groby. He'll be going to live at Groby now. The war's over!"

He said:

"But you and old Tory Tietjens in the same room . . . By Jove, the war's over. . . . The lion lying down with the lamb's nothing. . . ." He exclaimed: "Oh, damn! Oh, damn, damn, damn. . . . I say . . . I didn't mean it. . . . Don't cry. My dear little girl. My dear Miss Wannop. One of the best, I always thought you. You don't suppose . . ."

She said:

"I'm crying because of Groby . . . . It's a day to cry on anyhow. . . . You're quite a good sort, really!"

He said:

"Thank you! Thank you! Drink some more port! He's a good fat old beggar, old Tietjens. A good officer!" He added: "Drink a *lot* more port!"

He had been the most asinine, creaking, "what-about-your-king-and-country," shocked, outraged and speechless creature of all the many who for years had objected to her objecting to men being unable to stand up. . . . Now he was a rather kind brother!

They were all yelling.

"Good old Tietjens! Good old Fat Man! Pre-war hooch! He'd be the one to get it." No one like Fat Man Tietjens! He lounged at the door, easy, benevolent. In uniform now. That was better. An officer, yelling like an enraged Redskin, dealt him an immense blow behind the shoulder-blades. He staggered, smiling, into the centre of the room. An officer gently pushed her into the centre of the room. She was against him. Khaki encircled them. They began to yell and to prance, joining hands. Others waved the bottles and smashed underfoot the glasses. Gipsies break glasses at their weddings. The bed was against the wall. She did not like the bed to be against the wall. It had been brushed by . . .

They were going round them: yelling in unison:

"Over here! Pom Pom Over here! Pom Pom!
That's the word that's the word; Over here. . . ."

At least they weren't over there! They were prancing. The whole world round them was yelling and prancing round. They were the centre of unending roaring circles. The man with the eye-glass had stuck a half-crown in his other eye. He was well-meaning. A brother. She had a brother with the V.C. All in the family.

Tietjens was stretching out his two hands from the waist. It was incomprehensible. His right hand was behind her back, his left in her right hand. She was frightened. She was amazed. Did you ever! He was swaying slowly. The elephant! They were dancing! Aranjuez was hanging on to the tall woman like a kid on a telegraph-pole. The officer who had said he had picked up a little bit of fluff . . . well, he had! He had run out and fetched it. It wore white-cotton gloves and a flowered hat. It said: "Ow! Now! . . ." There was a fellow with a most beautiful voice. He led: better than a gramophone. Better . . .

Les petites marionettes, font! font! font. . . .

On an elephant. A dear, meal-sack elephant. She was setting out on . . .

Last Post

Oh, Rokehope is a pleasant place
If the fause thieves would let it be.

Border Ballad

PART ONE

I ⁓

HE LAY staring at the withy binders of his thatch; the grass
was infinitely green; his view embraced four counties; the
roof was supported by six small oak-sapling trunks, roughly
trimmed and brushed from above by apple-boughs. French
crab-apple! The hut had no sides.

The Italian proverb says: "He who allows the boughs of
trees to spread above his roof invites the doctor daily." Words
to that effect. He would have grinned, but that might have
been seen.

For a man who never moved, his face was singularly
walnut-coloured; his head, indenting the skim-milk white of
the pillows, should have been a gipsy's, the dark, silvered
hair cut extremely close, the whole face very carefully shaven
and completely immobile. The eyes moved, however, with
unusual vivacity, all the life of the man being concentrated
in them and their lids.

Down the path that had been cut in swaths from the
knee-high grass, and came from the stable to the hut, a heavy,
elderly peasant rolled in his gait. His overlong, hairy arms
swung as if he needed an axe or a log or a full sack to
make him a complete man. He was broad-beamed, in cord
breeches, very tight in the buttock; he wore black leggings,
an unbuttoned blue waistcoat, a striped flannel shirt, open
at the perspiring neck, and a square, high hat of black felt.

He said:

"Want to be shifted?"

The man in the bed closed his eyelids slowly.

" 'Ave a droper cider?"

The other again similarly closed his eyes. The standing man supported himself with an immense hand, gorilla-like, by one of the oaken posts.

"Best droper cider ever I tasted," he said. " 'Is lordship give me. 'Is lordship sester me: 'Gunning,' 'e ses, 'the day the vixen got into keeper's coop enclosure . . .' "

He began and slowly completed a very long story, going to prove that English noble landlords preferred foxes to pheasants. Or should! English landowners of the right sort. 'Is lordship would no more 'ave that vixen killed or so much as flurried, she no being gravid-like than. . . . Dreadful work a gravid vixen can do among 'en-coops with pheasant poults. . . . Have to eat fer six or seven, she have! All a-growing . . . So 'is lordship sester Gunning . . .

And then the description of the cider. . . . 'Ard! Thet cider was 'arder than a miser's 'art or 'n ole maid's tongue. Body it 'ad. Strength it 'ad. Stan's to reason. Ten-year cider. Not a drop was drunk in lordship's 'ouse under ten years in cask. Killed three sheep a week fer his indoor and outdoor servants. An' three hundred pigeons. The pigeon-cotes is a hundred feet high, an' the pigeons' nesteses in 'oles in the inside walls. Clap-nests a 'ole wall at a go an' takes the squabs. Times is not what they was, but 'is lordship keeps on. An' always will!

The man in the bed—Mark Tietjens—continued his own thought.

Old Gunning lumbered slowly up the path towards the stable, his hands swinging. The stable was a tile-heled, thatched affair, no real stable in the North Country sense— a place where the old mare sheltered among chickens and ducks. There was no tidiness amongst South Country folk. They hadn't it in them, though Gunning could bind a tidy thatch and trim a hedge properly. All-round man. Really an all-round man; he could do a great many things. He knew all about fox-hunting, pheasant-rearing, woodcraft, hedging, diking, pig-rearing, and the habits of King Edward when shooting. Smoking endless great cigars! One finished, light another, throw away the stub. . . .

Fox-hunting, the sport of kings with only twenty per cent of the danger of war! He, Mark Tietjens, had never cared for hunting; now he would never do any more; he had never cared for pheasant-shooting. He would never do any more. Not couldn't; wouldn't. "From henceforth . . ." It annoyed him that he had not taken the trouble to ascertain what it was Iago said, before he had taken Iago's resolution. . . . "From henceforth he never would speak word. . . ." Something to that effect: but you could not get that into a blank-verse line.

Perhaps Iago had not been speaking blank verse when he had taken his, Mark Tietjens', resolution. ". . . Took by the throat the circumciséd dog and smote him. . . ." Good man, Shakespeare! All-round man in a way, too. Probably very like Gunning. Knew Queen Elizabeth's habits when hunting; also very likely how to hedge, thatch, break up a deer or a hare or a hog, and how to serve a writ and write bad French. Lodged with a French family in Crutched Friars or the Minories. Somewhere.

The ducks were making a great noise on the pond up the hill. Old Gunning in the sunlight lumbered between the stable-wall and the raspberry canes, uphill. The garden was all uphill. He looked across the grass up at the hedge. When they turned him round he looked downhill at the house. Rough, grey stone!

Half round, he looked across the famous four counties; half round the other way on, he could see up the grass slope to the hedge on the roadside. Now he was looking uphill across the tops of the hay-grass, over the raspberry canes at the hedge that Gunning was going to trim. Full of consideration for him, they were, all the lot of them. Forever thinking of developing his possible interests. He didn't need it. He had interests enough.

Up the pathway that was above and beyond the hedge on a grass slope went the Elliott children, a lanky girl of ten, with very long, corn-coloured hair; a fat boy of five, unspeakably dirty. The girl too long and thin in the legs and ankles, her hair limp. War-starvation in early years. . . . Well, that was not his fault. He had given the nation the transport it needed; they should have found the stuff. They hadn't, so the children had long, thin legs and protruding wrists on pipe-stem arms. All that generation! . . . No fault of his. He had managed the nation's transport as it should be managed. His department had. His own department, made by himself from junior temporary clerk to senior permanent official, from the day of his entrance thirty-five years before to the day of his resolution never more to speak a word.

Nor yet stir a finger. He had to be in this world, in this nation. Let them care for him; he was done with them. . . . He knew the sire and dam of every horse from Eclipse to

Perlmutter. That was enough for him. They let him read all that could be read about racing. He had interests enough!

The ducks on the pond up the hill continued to make a great noise, churning boisterously the water with their wings and squawking. If they had been hens there would have been something the matter—a dog chasing them. Ducks did not signify; they went mad, contagiously. Like nations and all the cattle of a county.

Gunning, lumbering past the raspberry canes, took a bud or so and squeezed the pale things between finger and thumb, then examined his thumb. Looking for maggots, no doubt. Pale-green leaves the raspberry had; a fragile plant amongst the robuster rosaceae. That was not war-starvation but race. *Their* commissariat was efficient enough, but they were presumably not gross feeders. Gunning began to brush the hedge, sharp, brushing blows with his baggin hook. There was still far too much bramble amongst the quickset; in a week the hedge would be unsightly again.

That was part of their consideration again! They kept the hedge low so that he should be amused by passers-by on the path, though they would have preferred to let it grow high so that the passers-by should not see into the orchard. . . . Well, he had seen passers-by. More than they knew. . . . What the hell was Sylvia's game? And that old ass Edward Campion's? . . . Well, *he* was not going to interfere. There was, however, undoubtedly something up! . . . Marie Léonie—formerly Charlotte!—knew neither of them by sight, though she had undoubtedly seen them peering over the hedge!

They—it was more of their considerateness—had contrived a shelf on the left corner-post of his shelter. So that birds should amuse him! A hedge-sparrow, noiseless and quaker-grey, ghostlike, was on this shelf. A thin, undervitalized being that you never saw. It flitted, hiding itself deep in hedgerows. He had always thought of it as an American bird: a voiceless nightingale, thin, long, thin-billed, almost without markings as becomes a bird that seldom sees the sun but lives in the twilight of deep hedges. American because it ought to wear a scarlet letter. He only knew of Americans because of a book he had once read—a woman like a hedge-sparrow, creeping furtive in shadows and getting into trouble with a priest.

This desultory, slim bird, obviously Puritan, inserted its thin bill into the dripping that Gunning had put on the shelf for the tom-tits. The riotous tom-tit, the bottle-tit, the great-tit, all that family love dripping. The hedge-sparrow obviously did not; the dripping on that warmish June day had become oleaginous; the hedge-sparrow, its bill all greased, mumbled its upper and lower mandible but took no more dripping. It looked at Mark's eyes. Because these regarded it motionlessly, it uttered a long warning note and flitted, noiseless, into invisibility. All hedge things ignore you whilst you move on and do not regard them. The moment you stay still and fix your eyes on them they warn the rest of the hedge and flit off. This hedge-sparrow no doubt had its young within earshot. Or the warning might have been just co-operative.

Marie Léonie, *née* Riotor, was coming up the steps and then the path. He could hear her breathing. She stood beside him, shapeless in her long pinafore of figured cotton, and breathed heavily, holding a plate of soup and saying:

"*Mon pauvre homme! Mon pauvre homme! Ce qu'ils ont fait de toi!*"

She began a breathless discourse in French. She was of the large, blond, Norman type; in the middle forties, her extremely fair hair very voluminous and noticeable. She had lived with Mark Tietjens for twenty years now, but she had always refused to speak a word of English, having an invincible scorn for both language and people of her adopted country.

Her discourse poured on. She had set the little tray with the plate of reddish-yellowish soup on a flat shelf of wood that turned out on a screw from underneath the bed; in the soup was a shining clinical thermometer that she moved and regarded from time to time, beside the plate a glass syringe, graduated. She said that *ils—they—*had combined to render her soup of vegetables uneatable. They would not give her *navets de Paris* but round ones, like buttons; they contrived that the carrots should be *pourris* at their bottom ends; the leeks were of the consistency of wood. They were determined that he should not have vegetable soup because they wanted him to have meat juice. They were anthropophagi. Nothing but meat, meat, meat! That girl! . .

She had always in the Gray's Inn Road had Paris turnips from Jacopo's in Old Compton Street. There was no reason why you should not grow *navets de Paris* in this soil. The Paris turnip was barrel-shaped, round, round, round like an adorable little pig till it turned into its funny little tail. That was a turnip to amuse you; to change and employ your thoughts. *Ils*—he and she—were incapable of having their thoughts changed by a turnip.

Between sentences she ejaculated from time to time:

"My poor man! What they have made of you!"

Her volubility flowed over Mark like a rush of water over a grating, only a phrase or so now and then coming to his attention. It was not unpleasant; he liked his woman. She had a cat that she made abstain from meat on Friday. In the Gray's Inn Road that had been easier, in a large room decorated with innumerable miniatures and silhouettes representing members of the Riotor family and its branches. Mme. Riotor *mère* and Mme. Riotor *grand'mère* too had been miniature painters, and Marie Léonie possessed some astonishingly white statuary by the distinguished sculptor Monsieur Casimir-Bar, a lifelong friend of her family who had only never been decorated because of a conspiracy. So he had a great contempt for decorations and the decorated. Marie Léonie had been accustomed to repeat the voluminous opinions of Monsieur Casimir-Bar on the subject of decorations at great length on occasion. Since he, Mark, had been honoured by his sovereign she had less frequently recited them. She admitted that the democracy of to-day had not the sterling value that had distinguished democrats of the day of her parents, so it might be better to *caser* oneself —to find a niche amongst those whom the state distinguished.

The noise of her voice, which was deep-chested and not unpleasing, went on. Mark regarded her with the ironic indulgence that you accord to a child, but indeed, when he had been still in harness, it had rested him always to come home to her as he had done every Thursday and Monday, and not infrequently on a Wednesday when there had been no racing. It had rested him to come home from a world of incompetent imbeciles and to hear this brain comment on that world. She had views on virtue, pride, downfalls, human careers, the habits of cats, fish, the clergy, diplomats, soldiers, women of easy virtue, Saint Eustachius, President Grévy, the purveyors of comestibles, custom-house officers, pharmacists, Lyons silk-weavers, the keepers of boarding-houses, garrotters, chocolate-manufacturers, sculptors other than M. Casimir-Bar, the lovers of married women, house-maids . . . Her mind, in fact, was like a cupboard, stuffed, packed with the most incongruous materials, tools, vessels and debris. Once the door was opened you never knew what would tumble out or be followed by what. That was restful to Mark as foreign travel might have been—only he had never been abroad except when his father, before his accession to Groby, had lived in Dijon for his children's education. That was how he knew French.

Her conversation had another quality that continually amused him: she always ended it with the topic with which she had chosen to begin. Thus, to-day having chosen to begin with *navets de Paris,* with Paris turnips she would end, and it amused him to observe how on each occasion she would bring the topic back. She might be concluding a long comment on ironclads and have to get back suddenly to custards because the door-bell rang while her maid was out, but accomplish the transition she would before she answered the bell. Otherwise she was frugal, shrewd, astonishingly cleanly and healthy.

Whilst she was giving him his soup, inserting the glass syringe in his lips at half-minute intervals, which she timed by her wrist-watch, she was talking about furniture. . . . *Ils* would not let her apply to the species of rabbit-hutches in the salon a varnish that she imported from Paris; Monsieur her brother-in-law had really exhibited when she had actually varnished a truly discreditable chair—had exhibited a distraction that had really filled her with amusement. It was possible that the fashion of the day was for furniture of decrepitude, or gross forms. That *they* would not let her place in the salon the newly gilt arm-chair of her late mother or the sculptural group representing Niobe and some of her offspring by the late Monsieur Casimir-Bar, or the overmantel clock that was an exact reproduction in bronze of the Fountain of the Médicis in the gardens of the Luxembourg at Paris—that was a matter of taste. *Elle* might very well feel umbrage that she, Marie Léonie, should possess articles of such acknowledged prestige. For what could be more unapproachable than a Second Empire *fauteuil* newly gilt and maintained, she could assure the world, at such a pitch of glitter as dazzled the eyes? *Elle* might very well feel umbrage when you considered that the skirt that she wore when gardening was . . . Well, in short was what it was! Nevertheless, in that skirt she allowed herself to be seen by the clergyman. But why did *il,* who was admittedly a man of honour and sensibility and reputed to know all the things of this world and perhaps of the next—why did *he* join in the infinitely stupid conspiracy against the work of the great genius Casimir-Bar? She, Marie Léonie, could understand that he, in his difficult situation, would not wish to give permission to install in the salon works at which

elle took umbrage because her possessions did not include
objects of art which all the world acknowledged to be of
classic rank, not to mention the string of pearls which she,
Marie Léonie, Riotor by birth, owed to the generosity of
him, Mark, and her own economies. And other objects of
value and taste. That was reasonable. If your woman is
poorly *dot*-ed . . . Let us call it *dot*-ed . . . because certainly she, Marie Léonie, was not one to animadvert upon
those in situations of difficulty. . . . It would ill become
her so to do. Nevertheless, a great period of years of honesty, frugality, regularity of life and cleanliness . . . And
she asked Mark if he had ever seen in *her* parlour traces
of mud such as on wet days she had certainly observed in
the salon of a certain person. . . . And certain revelations
she could make as to the condition of a cupboard under
the stairs and the state to be observed behind certain presses
in the kitchen. But if you have not had experience in the
control of domestics, what would you? . . . Nevertheless,
a stretch of years passed in the state of housewifeliness
such as she had already adumbrated upon gave one the
right to comment—of course with delicacy—upon the *ménage* of a young person even though her delicate situation
might avert from her comment of an unchristian nature as
to certain other facts. It did, however, seem to her, Marie
Léonie, that to appear before a clergyman in a skirt decorated with no less than three visible *taches* of petrol, wearing
gloves encrusted with mud as you encrust a truffle with paste
before baking it under the cinders—and holding, of all implements, a common gardening-trowel . . . And to laugh
and joke with him! . . . Surely the situation called for a
certain—let them call it retirement of demeanour. She was
far from according to the priest as such the extravagant
privileges to which he laid claim. The late Monsieur Casimir-
Bar was accustomed to say that if we accorded to our *soi-
disant* spiritual advisers all that they would take, we should
lie upon a bed that had neither sheets, *eidredons,* pillows,
bolsters, nor settle. And she, Marie Léonie, was inclined to
agree with Monsieur Casimir-Bar, though, as one of the
heroes of the barricades in 1848, he was apt to be a little
extreme in his tenets. Still, a vicar is in England a functionary of the state and as such should be received with a
certain modesty and reserve. Yet she, Marie Léonie, formerly Riotor, her mother having been born Lavigne-Bourdreau
and having in consequence a suspicion of Huguenot blood,
so that she, Marie Léonie, might be expected to know how

the Protestant clergy should be received—she then, Marie
Léonie, from the little window on the side of the stairs,
had distinctly seen *elle* lay one hand on the shoulder of
that clergyman and point—point, mind you, with the *trowel*
—to the open front door and say—she had distinctly heard
the words: "Poor man, if you have hunger you will find
Mr. Tietjens in the dining-room. He is just eating a sandwich. It's hungry weather!" That was six months ago, but
Marie Léonie's ears still tingled at the words and the gesture.
A trowel! To point with a *trowel; pensez y!* If a trowel
why not a *main de fer,* a dust-pan? Or a vessel even more
homely! . . . And Marie Léonie chuckled.

Her grandmother Bourdreau remembered a crockery-
merchant of the ambulating sort who had once filled one
of those implements—a *vase de nuit,* but of course new—
with milk and had offered the whole gratuitously to any
passer-by who would drink the milk. A young woman called
Laborde accepted his challenge there in the market-place of
Noisy-Lebrun. She had lost her fiancé, who found the gesture exaggerated. But he was a farceur, that crockery-dealer!

She drew from the pocket of her pinafore several folded
pages of a newspaper and from under the bed a double
picture-frame—two frames hinged together so that they
would close. She inserted a sheet of the paper between the
two frames and then hung the whole on a piece of picture-
wire that depended from the roof-tree beneath the thatch.
Two braces of picture-wire, too, came from the supporting
posts, to right and left. They held the picture-frames motionless and a little inclined towards Mark's face. She was agreeable to look at, stretching up her arms. She lifted his torso
with great strength and infinite solicitude, propped it a little
with the pillows and looked to see that his eyes fell on the
printed sheet. She said:

"You can see well, like that?"

His eyes took in the fact that he was to read of the
Newbury Summer Meeting and the one at Newcastle. He
closed them twice to signify yes. The tears came into hers.
She murmured:

"*Mon pauvre homme! Mon pauvre homme!* What they
have done to you!" She drew from another pocket in her
pinafore a flask of eau-de-Cologne and a wad of cotton-
wool. With that, moistened, she wiped even more solicitously
his face and then his thin, mahogany hands, which she un-
covered. She had the air of women in France when they

change the white-satin clothes and wash the faces of favourite Virgins at the church-doors in August.

Then she stood back and apostrophized him. He took in that the King's filly had won the Berkshire Foal plate and the horse of a friend the Seaton Delaval Handicap, at Newcastle. Both might have been expected. He had meant to go to the Newcastle meeting this year and give Newbury a by. The last year he had gone racing he had done rather well at Newbury, so he had then thought he would try Newcastle for a change, and, whilst he was there, take a look at Groby and see what that bitch Sylvia was doing with Groby. Well, that was done with. They would presumably bury him at Groby.

She said in deep, rehearsed tones:

"My man!"—she might almost have well said: "My Deity!"—"What sort of life is this we lead here? Was there ever anything so singular and unreasonable? If we sit to drink a cup of tea, the cup may at any moment be snatched from our mouths; if we recline upon a divan—at any moment the divan may go. I do not comment on this that you lie by night as by day forever here in the open air, for I understand that it is by your desire and consent that you lie here and I will never exhibit aversion from that which you desire and that to which you consent. But cannot you bring it about that we should inhabit a house of some reason, one more suited to human beings of this age, and one that is less of a procession of goods and chattels? You can bring that about. You are all-powerful here. I do not know what are your resources. It was never your habit to tell me. You kept me in comfort. Never did I express a desire that you did not satisfy, though it is true that my desires were always reasonable. So I know nothing, though I read once in a paper that you were a man of extravagant riches, and that can hardly all have vanished, for there can have been fewer men of as great a frugality, and you were always fortunate and moderate in your wagers. So I know nothing and I would scorn to ask of these others, for that would imply doubt of your trust in me. I do not doubt that you have made arrangements for my future comfort, and I am in no uncertainty of the continuance of those arrangements. It is not material fears that I have. But all this appears to be a madness. Why are we here? What is the meaning of all this? Why do you inhabit this singular erection? It may be that the open air is of necessity for your malady. I do not believe that you lived in perpetual currents of air in your chambers, though I never saw them. But on the days you gave to me you had everything of the most comfortable and you seemed contented with my arrangements. And your brother and his woman appear so mad in all the other affairs of life that they may well be mad in this also. Why then will you not end it? You have the power. You are all-powerful here. Your brother will spring from one corner to the other of this lugubrious place in order to anticipate your slightest wish. *Elle*, too!"

Stretching out her hands, she had the air of a Greek woman who invoked a deity, she was so large and fair and her hair was so luxuriantly blond. And indeed, to her, in his mystery and silence he had the air of a deity who could discharge unthinkable darts and vouchsafe unimaginable favours. Though all their circumstances had changed, that had not changed, so that even his immobility enhanced his mystery. In all their life together, not merely here, he had been silent whilst she had talked. On the two regular days of the week on which he had been used to visit her, from the moment when she would open her door exactly at seven in the evening and see him in his bowler hat with his carefully rolled umbrella and with his racing-glasses slung diagonally across him, to the moment when, next morning at half-past ten, she would brush his bowler and hand him that and his umbrella, he would hardly speak a word—he would speak such few words as to give the idea of an absolute taciturnity, whilst she entertained him with an unceasing flow of talk and of comments on the news of the Quartier—of the French colonists of that part of London, or on the news in the French papers. He would remain seated on a hard chair, bending slightly forward, with, round the corners of his mouth, little creases that suggested an endless, indulgent smile. Occasionally he would suggest that she should put half a sovereign upon a horse; occasionally he would bring her an opulent present, heavy gold bangles floridly chased and set with large emeralds, sumptuous furs, expensive travelling trunks for when she had visited Paris or went to the sea-side in the autumn. That sort of thing. Once he had bought her a complete set of the works of Victor Hugo, bound in purple morocco, and all the works that had been illustrated by Gustave Doré, in green calf; once a hoof of a race-horse, trained in France, set in silver in the form of an inkstand. On her forty-first birthday—though she had no idea how he had ascertained that it was her forty-first birthday—he had given her a string of pearls and had taken

her to a hotel at Brighton kept by an ex-prize-fighter. He
had told her to wear the pearls at dinner, but to be careful
of them because they had cost five hundred pounds. He
asked her once about her investment of her savings, and
when she had told him that she was investing in French
rentes viagères he had told her that he could do better than
that for her, and afterwards from time to time he had told
her of odd but very profitable ways of investing small sums.

In this way, because his gifts filled her with rapture on
account of their opulence and weightiness, he had assumed
for her the aspect by degrees of a godhead who could bless
—and possibly blast—inscrutably. For many years after he
had first picked her up in the Edgware Road outside the
old Apollo, she had regarded him with suspicion, since he
was a man and it is the nature of men to treat women
with treachery, lust and meanness. Now she regarded herself as the companion of a godhead, secure and immune
from the evil workings of Fortune—as if she had been seated
on the shoulder of one of Jove's eagles, beside his throne.
The Immortals had been known to choose human compan-
ions: when they had so done, fortunate indeed had been the
lot of the chosen. Of them she felt herself to be one.

Even his seizure had not deprived her of her sense of
his wide-spreading and inscrutable powers, and she could not
rid herself of the conviction that if he would, he could talk,
walk and perform the feats of strength of a Hercules. It
was impossible not to think so; the strength of his glance
was undiminished, and it was the dark glance of a man,
proud, vigorous, alert and commanding. And the mysterious
nature and occurrence of the seizure itself only confirmed
her subconscious conviction. The fit had come so undramat-
ically that although the several pompous and, for her, nearly
imbecile, English physicians who had been called in to attend on him agreed that some sort of fit must have visited
him as he lay in his bed, that had done nothing to change
her mind. Indeed, even when her own doctor, Drouant-
Rouault, asserted with certitude and knowledge that this was a
case of fulminant hemiplegia of a characteristic sort, though
her reason accepted his conclusion, her subconscious intuition remained the same. Doctor Drouant-Rouault was
a sensible man; that he had proved by pointing out the
anatomical excellence of the works of sculpture by Monsieur Casimir-Bar and agreeing that only a conspiracy of
rivals could have prevented his arriving at the post of president of the École des Beaux Arts. He was, then, a man

of sense, and his reputation amongst the French tradesmen
of the Quarter stood very high: she had never herself needed
the attentions of a doctor. But if you needed a doctor, obviously you went to a Frenchman and acquiesced in what
he said.

But although she acquiesced in words to others, and indeed to herself, she could not convince herself in her *for
intérieur,* nor indeed had she arrived at that amount of
exterior conviction without some argument at least. She had
pointed out, not only to Doctor Drouant-Rouault, but she
had even conceived it to be her duty to point out to the
English practitioners to whom she would not otherwise have
spoken, that the man lying there in her bed was a North
Country man, from Yorkshire, where men were of an in-
conceivable obstinacy. She had asked them to consider that
it was not unusual for Yorkshire brothers and sisters or other
relatives to live for decades together in the same house and
never address a word to each other, and she had pointed
out that she knew Mark Tietjens to be of an unspeakable
determination. She knew it from their lifelong intimacy. She
had never, for instance, been able to make him change his
diet by an ounce in weight, or the shaking of a pepper-pot
as to flavour—not once in twenty years during which she
had cooked for him. She pleaded with these gentlemen to
consider as a possibility that the terms of the armistice were
of such a nature as to make a person of Mark's determination and idiosyncrasies resolve to withdraw himself forever
from all human contacts, and that if he did so determine,
nothing would cause him to change his determination. The
last word he had spoken had been whilst one of his col-
leagues at the ministry had been telephoning to tell her, for
Mark's information, what the terms of the armistice were.
At the news, which she had had to give him over her shoulder, he had made from the bed some remark. He had been
recovering from double pneumonia at the time. What the
remark had been she could not exactly repeat; she was almost certain that it had been to the effect—in English—
that he would never speak again. But she was aware that
her own predilection was sufficient to bias her hearing. She
had felt herself, at the news that the Allies did not intend
to pursue the Germans into their own country—she had felt
herself as if she could say to the High Permanent Official
at the other end of the telephone that she would never speak
word to him and his race again. It was the first thing that

had come into her mind, and no doubt it had been the first thing to come into Mark's.

So she had pleaded with the doctors. They had paid practically no attention to her, and she was aware that that was very likely due to her ambiguous position as the companion for long, without any legal security, of a man whom they considered as now in no position to continue his protection of her. That she in no way resented; it was in the nature of English male humanity. The Frenchman had naturally listened with deference, bowing even a little. But he had remarked with a sort of deaf obstinacy: Madame must consider that the occasion of the stroke only made more certain that it *was* a stroke. And that argument to her, as Frenchwoman, must seem almost incontrovertible. For the betrayal of France by her Allies at the supreme moment of triumph had been a crime, the news of which might well cause the end of the world to seem desirable.

2 ~

SHE CONTINUED to stand beside him and to apostrophize him until it should be time to turn round the framed newspaper so that he could read the other side of the sheet. What he read first contained the remarks of various writers on racing. That he took in rapidly, as if it were a mere *bonne bouche*. She knew that he regarded with contempt the opinions of all writers on racing, but the two who wrote in this particular sheet with less contempt than the others. But the serious reading began when she turned the page. Here were endless, serried columns of the names of race-horses, their jockeys and entrants at various race-meetings, their ages, ancestries, former achievements. That he would peruse with minute attention that would cost him just under an hour. She would have liked to stay with him whilst he read it, for the intensive study of matters connected with race-horses had always been their single topic of communion. She had spent almost sentimental hours leaning over the back of his arm-chair reading news of the turf simultaneously with himself, and the compliments he had been used to pay her over her predictions of form, if they were the only compliments he ever paid her, had filled her with the warm pleasure and confusion that she might have felt had he addressed the same compliments to her on the subject of her person. She did not indeed need compliments from him as to her person;

his complete contentment with her sufficed—but she had rejoiced in, and now missed, those long, quiet times of communing. She remarked to him indeed that Seattle had won her race as she had several days ago predicted because there had been no other competitors in any way of the same class as the filly, but there had been no answering, half-contemptuous grunt of acquiescence such as in the old days had been hers.

An aeroplane had droned overhead and she had stepped out to look up at the bright toy that, shone upon by the sun, progressed slowly across the pellucid sky. When she went in, in answer to the double closing of his lids that meant that he acquiesced in the turning of his news-sheet, she unhitched one brace from the oaken post to his right and, walking round his bed, attached the brace on the post to his left, doing the reverse with the brace that had gone to the left. In that way the picture-frames turned completely round and exhibited the other side of the newspaper-frame.

It was a contrivance that daily excited her annoyance and, as usual, she expressed herself. This was another instance of the madness of They—of her brother-in-law and his woman. Why had they not obtained one of those ingenious machines, like an arm of bright brass supporting a reading-shelf of agreeably varnished mahogany that you clamped to a bedstead and could adjust at any angle? Why indeed had they not procured one of those huts for the tuberculous that she had seen depicted in a catalogue? Such huts could be painted in agreeable stripes of green and vermilion, thus presenting a gay appearance, and they could be turned upon a pivot so as to meet the rays of the sun or avoid the currents of air caused by the wind. What could be the explanation of this mad and gross structure? A thatched roof supported on posts without walls? Did they desire him to be blown out of his bed by the draughts? Did they merely desire to enrage her? Or could it be that their resources were of such exiguity that they could not afford the conveniences of modern civilization?

She might well have thought that to be the case. But how could it, in face of the singular behaviour of Monsieur her *beau-frère* in the matter of the statuary of Casimir-Bar, the great sculptor? She had offered to contribute to the expenses of the establishment even at the cost of the sacrifice of what she held most dear, and how singular had been his behaviour. During their absence on the occasion of the great sale at

Wingham Priory she had ordered the amiable if gross Gunning and the semi-imbecile carpenter to descend from her room to the salon that admirable *Niobe* and the admittedly incomparable *Thetis Informing Neptune of the Death of a Son-in-law,* not to mention her newly regilt Second Empire *fauteuil.* And in that gloomy wilderness how had they not shone in their respective whiteness and auriference! The pose of the *Niobe* how passionate, the action of the *Thetis* how spirited and how at the same time pathetic! And she had seized the opportunity to varnish with a special preparation imported from the City of the Arts the only chair in the salon that was not too rough to be susceptible of varnish even though it came from Paris herself. A clumsy affair at that—of the epoch of Louis the Thirteenth of France, though heaven knew whose epoch that was here. Without doubt that of Cromwell the regicide!

And Monsieur must needs seize the moment of his entry on this thus enlivened scene to exhibit the only display of emotion that she had ever known him vouchsafe. For otherwise Monsieur had the pose of being at least as self-contained if not as absolutely taciturn as Mark himself. She asked Mark: Was that the moment for what was, after all, if you analysed it, a manifestation of attachment for his young woman? What else could it be? *Il*—Monsieur their relative —passed for a man of unbounded knowledge. He knew all knowledge. He could not but be aware of the supreme value of the work of Casimir-Bar, who, but for the machinations of his rival Monsieur Rodin and his *confrères,* must have attained to the highest honours in France. But not only had Monsieur with hisses and tut-tuts of anger ordered Gunning and the carpenter at once to remove the statuary and the *fauteuil* from the salon where she had exhibited them—with heaven knew how much reluctance—with a view to their attracting the attention of a chance customer—for chance customers did come in Their absence without rendezvous. . . . Not only that, but Monsieur, to gratify the perhaps not unnatural envy of *elle,* had cast meretricious doubts on the pecuniary value of the works of Casimir-Bar themselves. Everyone knew how the Americans to-day were stripping the unfortunate land of France of her choicest art treasures; the enormous prices they paid; the avidity they showed. Yet that man had tried to persuade her that her statues were worth no more than a few shillings apiece. It was incomprehensible. He was in want of money to the extent of turning their house into a mere depot for dilapidated ob-

jects in rough wood and battered brass. He had contrived
to obtain singular prices for these forlorn objects from insane Yankees who came great distances to purchase these
debris from him. Yet when he was offered pieces of the
utmost beauty in the most perfect condition he just simply
turned the objects down with scoffing.

For herself, she respected passion—though she could have
imagined an object of passion more calculated to excite that
feeling than *elle,* whom for convenience she would call her
belle-soeur. She at least was broad-minded, and moreover
she understood the workings of the human heart. It was
creditable for a man to ruin himself for the object of his
affections. But this at least she found exaggerated.

And what, then, was this determination to ignore the developments of modern genius? Why would they not purchase
for Mark a reading-desk with a brass arm that should indicate to the neighbours and dependents that at least he
was a person of condition? Why no revolving hut? There
were certain symptoms of that age that were disquieting.
She would be the first to acknowledge that. They had only
to read in the papers of the deeds of assassins, highway robbers, of the subversive and the ignorant who everywhere
seized the reins of power. But what was to be said against
such innocent things as the reading-desk, the revolving hut
and the aeroplane. Yes, the aeroplane!

Why did they ignore the aeroplane? They had told her
that the reason why they had been unable to provide her
with *navets de Paris* was that the season was becoming too
advanced for the sowing of the seeds of those admirable
and amusing vegetables which, seen advancing through the
pale electric lights of the early hours of the morning, piled
symmetrically as high as the first floors of the hotels, on
the market-carts, provided one of the gayest spectacles of
the night-life of La Ville Lumière. They had said that to
procure the seeds from Paris would demand at least a month.
But supposing they had sent a letter by aeroplane, request-
ing the dispatch of the seeds equally by aeroplane, to procure
them, as all the world knew, would be a matter merely of
a few hours. And, having thus brought the matter back to
turnips again, she concluded:

"Yes, *mon pauvre homme,* they have singular natures, our
relatives—for I will include the young woman in that cate-
gory. I, at least, am broad-minded enough for that. But they
have singular natures. It is a singular affair!"

She departed up the path towards the stable, speculating

on the nature of her man's relatives. They were the relatives of a godhead—but godheads had relatives of a singular nature. Let Mark figure as Jupiter; well, Jupiter had a son called Apollo who could not be regarded as exactly *fils de famille*. His adventures had been of the most irregular. Was it not known that he had spent a long space of time with the shepherds of King Admetus, singing and carousing? Well, Monsieur Tietjens might for convenience be regarded as a sort of Apollo, now amongst the shepherds of Admetus and complete with female companion. If he did not often sing, he also concealed the tendencies that had brought about his downfall. He was quiet enough about the house, extraordinary as the house might be. *Elle* also. If their relationship was irregular it presented no aspects of reprehensible festivity. It was a sufficiently serious *collage*. That at least ran in the family.

She came round the rough balks of the side of the stable upon Gunning, seated on the stone sill of the door, cutting with a broad-bladed clasp-knife considerable chunks out of a large meat pasty. She surveyed his extended leggings, his immense bemired boots and his unshaven countenance and remarked in French that the shepherds of Admetus were probably differently dressed. They certainly were in all the performances of the *Alceste* that she had seen. But perhaps he served his turn.

Gunning said that he supposed he had to go on duty again. She, he supposed, was going to bottle off the cider or she would not have had him bring down that 'ere cask. She was to be careful to tie the carks tight; it would get itself a 'ed proper.

She said that if she, a Norman of a hundred generations, did not know how to handle cider it would be a strange thing, and he said that it would be a pity if that cider went wrong after all the trouble they 'ad 'ad.

He brushed the crumbs of his demolished pie off the cords of his breeches, carefully picking up the larger fragments of crust and inserting them into his mouth between his broad red lips. He asked if 'er ladyship knew whether the cahptn wanted the mare that afternoon. If not 'e might 's well turn 'er on the Common. She said that she did not know; the captain had said nothing to her about it. He said he supposed 'e might 's well. Cramp said 'e would not have the settee ready to go to the station 'fore mornin'. If she would wait there he would go git some tepid water and they would moisten the eggs. She did not ask better.

He scrambled to his feet and lumbered down the stone path towards the house. She stood in the bright day regarding the long grass of the orchard, the gnarled, whitened trunks of the fruit-trees, the little lettuces like aligned rosettes in the beds, and the slope of the land towards the old stones of the house that the boughs of the apple-trees mostly hid. And she acknowledged that, in effect, she did not ask better. A Norman, if Mark had died in the ordinary course, she would no doubt have gone back to the neighbourhood either of Falaise or Bayeux, from which places came the families of her grandfather and grandmother respectively. She would probably have married a rich farmer or a rich grazier, and, by choice, she would have pursued a life of bottling off cider and moistening the eggs of sitting hens. She had had her training as a *coryphée* at the Paris opera, and no doubt if she had not made her visit to London with the Paris opera troupe and if Mark had not picked her up in the Edgware Road, where her lodgings had been, she would have lived similarly with some man in Clichy or Auteuil until with her economies she would have been able, equally, to retire to one or other of the *pays* of her families and marry a farmer, a butcher, or a grazier. She acknowledged, for the matter of that, that she would probably not have raised more succulent *poulets au grain* or more full-bodied cider than came from the nest-boxes and the presses here, and that she was leading no other life than that which she had always contemplated. Nor, indeed, would she have wanted any other henchman than Gunning, who, if you had given him a blue blouse with stitchery and a *casquette* with a black-leather peak, would have passed for any peasant in Caen market.

He swung up the path, carrying gingerly a large blue bowl, just as if his blouse bellied out round him; he had the same expression of the mouth; the same intonation. It was nothing that she obstinately spoke French to him. On his subjects he could tell by intuition what her answers to his questions were, and she understood him well enough.

He said that he had better take the 'ens off the nesteses fer fear they peck 'er 'ands, and giving her the bowl, brought out from the shadows a protesting, ruffled and crooning hen, before which he dropped a handful of bran-paste and a lettuce leaf. He came out with another and yet others. Then he said she could go in and sprinkle the eggs. He said that it always bothered him to turn the eggs; his clumsy ol' 'ands bruk 'em 's often as not. He said:

"Wait whilst I brings out ol' mare. Bit o' grass wunt do 'er much mischief."

The hens, swollen to an enormous size, paraded hostilely against one another about her feet; they clucked, crooned, pecked at lumps of paste, drank water eagerly from an iron dog-trough. With an exaggerated clatter of hoofs old mare emerged from the stable. She was aged nineteen, obstinate, bitter, very dark bay, extremely raw-boned. You might fill her with oats and mash five times a day but she would not put on flesh. She emerged into the light from the door with the trot of a prima-donna, for she knew she had once been a famous creature. The hens fled; she bit into the air, showing immense teeth. Gunning opened the orchard-gate, just at hand; she went out at a canter, checked, crumpled her knees together, fell on her side and rolled and rolled; her immense lean legs were incongruous, up in the air.

"Yes," Marie Léonie said, *"pour moi-même je ne demanderais pas mieux!"*

Gunning remarked:

"Don't show 'er age, do she? Gambolling like a five-day lamb!" His voice was full of pride, his grey face joyful. 'Is lordship once said that ol' mare had orter be put in the 'Orse Show up to Lunnon. Some years ago, that was!

She went into the dark, warm, odorous depths of the hen-house-stable shed, the horse-box being divided off from the hen half by wire netting, nest-boxes, blankets extended on use-poles. She had to bend down to get into the hen half. The cracks of light between the uprights of the walls blinked at her. She carried the bowl of tepid water gingerly and thrust her hand into the warm hay hollows. The eggs were fever-heat or thereabouts; she turned them and sprinkled in the tepid water; thirteen, fourteen, fourteen, eleven—that hen was a breaker!—and fifteen. She emptied out the tepid water and from other nests took out egg after egg. The acquisition gratified her.

In an upper box a hen brooded low. It crooned menacingly, then screamed with the voice of poultry disaster as her hand approached it. The sympathetic voices of other hens outside came to her, screaming with poultry disaster—and other hens on the Common. A rooster crowed.

She repeated to herself that she did not demand a better life than this. But was it not self-indulgence to be so contented? Ought she not to be, still, taking steps for her future —near Falaise or Bayeux? Did one not owe that to oneself? How long would this life last here? And, still more, when it broke up, *how* would it break up? What would *ils*—the strange people—do to her, her savings, her furs, trunks, pearls, turquoises, statuary, and newly gilt Second Empire chairs and clocks? When the sovereign died what did the heir, his concubines, courtiers and sycophants do to the Maintenon of the day? What precautions ought she not to be taking against that wrath to come? There must be French lawyers in London. . . .

Was it to be thought that *il*—Christopher Tietjens—clumsy, apparently slow-witted but actually gifted with the insight of the supernatural . . . Gunning would say: The captain, he never says anything, but who knows what he thinks? He perceives everything. . . . Was it to be thought, then, that once Mark was dead and he actual owner of the place called Groby and the vast stretch of coal-bearing land that the newspaper had spoken of, Christopher Tietjens would maintain his benevolent and frugal dispositions of to-day? It was truly thinkable. But, just as he appeared slow-witted and was actually gifted with the insight of the supernatural, so he might well now maintain this aspect of despising wealth and yet develop into a true Harpagon as soon as he held the reins of power. The rich are noted for hardness of heart, and brother will prey upon brother's widow sooner than on another.

So that, certainly, she ought to put herself under the protection of the authorities. But then, what authorities? The long arm of France would no doubt protect one of her nationals even in this remote and uncivilized land. But would it be possible to put that machinery in motion without the knowledge of Mark—and what dreadful steps might Mark not take in his wrath if he thought that she had set machinery in motion?

There appeared nothing for it but to wait, and that side of her nature being indolent, perhaps being alone indolent, she was aware that she was contented to wait. But was such a course right? Was it doing justice to herself or to France? For it is the duty of the French citizen, by industry, frugality and vigilance, to accumulate goods; and it was above all the duty of the French citizen to carry back accumulated hoards to that distressed country, stripped bare as she was by the perfidious Allies. She might herself rejoice in these circumstances, these grasses, orchards, poultry, cider-presses, vegetable-gardens—even if the turnips were not of the Paris *navet* variety! She might not ask for better. But there might be a little *pays*, near Falaise, or, in the alternative, near

Bayeux, a little spot that she might enrich with these spoils from the barbarians. If every inhabitant of a *pays* in France did the same, would not France again be prosperous, with all its *clochers* tolling out contentment across smiling acres? Well, then!

Standing gazing at the poultry, whilst Gunning with a hone smoothed out some notches from his baggin hook, previous to again going on duty, she began to reflect on the nature of Christopher Tietjens, for she desired to estimate what were her chances of retaining her furs, pearls and gilt articles of virtu. . . . By the orders of the doctor who attended daily on Mark—a dry, sandy, no doubt perfectly ignorant person—Mark was never to be left out of sight. He was of opinion, this doctor, that one day Mark might move—physically. And there might be great danger if ever he did move. The lesions, if lesions there were in his brain, might then be restarted with fatal effects—some such talk. So they must never let him out of their sight. For the night they had an alarm that was connected by a wire from his bed to hers. Hers was in a room that gave onto the orchard. If he so much as stirred in his bed the bell would ring in her ear. But indeed she rose every night, over and over again, to look from her window into his hut; a dim lantern illuminated his sheets. These arrangements appeared to her to be barbarous, but they met the views of Mark and she was thus in no position to question them. . . . So she had to wait whilst Gunning honed out his sickle-shaped, short-handled blade.

It had all then begun—all the calamities of the world had begun amidst the clamours and intoxications of that dreadful day. Of Christopher Tietjens till then she had known little or nothing. For the matter of that, of Mark himself she had known little or nothing until a very few years ago. She had known neither his name, nor how he occupied himself, nor yet where he lived. It had not been her business to inquire, so she had never made inquiries. Then one day—after thirteen years—he had awakened one morning with an attack of bronchitis after a very wet Newmarket Craven Meeting. He had told her to go to his office with a note addressed to his chief clerk, to ask for his letters and to tell them to send a messenger to his chambers to get some clothes and necessaries.

When she had told him that she did not know what his office was nor where were his chambers, nor even his surname, he had grunted. He had expressed neither surprise nor gratification, but she knew that he had been gratified—probably with himself for having chosen a woman companion who displayed no curiosity rather than with her for having displayed none. After that he had had a telephone installed in her rooms, and not infrequently he would stay later of a morning than had been his habit, letting a messenger from the office bring letters or fetch documents that he had signed. When his father had died he had put her into mourning.

By that date, gradually, she had learned that he was Mark Tietjens of Groby, an immense estate somewhere in the North. He employed himself at an office of the government's in Whitehall—apparently with questions of railways. She gathered, chiefly from ejaculations of the messenger, that he treated his ministry with contempt, but was regarded as so indispensable that he never lost his post. Occasionally the office would ring up and ask her if she knew where he was. She would gather from the papers afterwards that that was because there had been a great railway accident. On those occasions he would have been absent at a race-meeting. He gave the office, in fact, just as much of his time as he chose, no more and no less. She gathered that, with his overpowering wealth, it was of no account to him except as an occupation of leisure time between meetings, and she gathered that he was regarded as an occult power amongst the rulers of the nation. Once, during the war when he had hurt his hand, he dictated to her a note of a confidential nature to one of the Cabinet ministers. It had concerned itself with transport, and its tone had been that of singular, polite contempt.

For her he was in no way astonishing. He was the English Milor with *le spleen*. She had read of him in the novels of Alexander Dumas, Paul de Kock, Eugene Sue and Ponson du Terrail. He represented the England that the Continent applauded—the only England that the Continent applauded. Silent, obstinate, inscrutable, insolent but immensely wealthy and uncontrollably generous. For herself, *elle ne demandait pas mieux*. For there was about him nothing of the unexpected. He was as regular as the Westminster chimes; he never exacted the unexpected of her and he was all-powerful and never in the wrong. He was, in short, what her countrywomen called *sérieux*. No Frenchwoman asks better than that of lover or husband. It was the serious *collage par excellence:* they, as a *ménage*, were sober, honest, frugal, industrious, immensely wealthy, and seriously saving. For his dinner, twice a week, she cooked him herself two mutton-chops with all but an eighth of an inch of the fat pared off, two mealy potatoes, as light and as white as flour, an apple-pie with a very flaky crust which he ate with a wedge of Stilton and some pulled bread and butter. This dinner was never varied once in twenty years, except during the season of game, when on alternate weeks a pheasant, a brace of grouse or of partridges would come from Groby. Nor in the twenty years had they once been separated for a whole week, except that every late summer he spent a month at Harrogate. She always had his dress-shirts washed for him by her own laundress in the Quartier. He spent almost every week-end in one country-house or another, using at most two dress-shirts and that only if he stayed till Tuesday. English people of good class do not dress for dinner on Sundays. That is a politeness to God, because theoretically you attend evening service and you do not go to church in the country in evening dress. As a matter of fact you never go to evening service—but it is complimentary to suggest by your dress that you might be visited by the impulse. So, at least, Marie Léonie Tietjens understood the affair.

She was looking out on the Common that sloped up to beech-trees, at the poultry—bright chestnut birds, extremely busy on the intense green of the browsed grass. The great rooster reminded her of the late Monsieur Rodin, the sculptor who had conspired against Casimir-Bar. She had once seen him in his studio, conducting some American ladies round his work, and he had precisely resembled a rooster kicking its leg back and drooping its wings in the dust round a new hen. Only round a new one. Naturally! . . . This rooster was a tremendous Frenchman. *Un vrai de la vraie.* You could imagine nothing more unlike Christopher Tietjens! . . . The backward-raking legs on the dancing toes, the gait of a true master of deportment at an academy of young ladies! The vigilant clear eye cocking up every minute. . . . Hark! A swift shadow ran over the ground: the sparrow-hawk! The loud, piercing croon of that Father of his Country. How the hens all re-echoed it; how the chickens ran to their mothers and all together to the shadow of the hedge. Monsieur the hawk would have no chance amidst that outcry. The hawk flits silent and detests noise. It will bring the poultry-keeper with his gun! . . . All is discovered because of the vigilance of Milord Chantecler. . . . There are those who reprove him because his eyes are always on the sky, because he has a proud head. But that is his function—that and gallantry. Perceive him with a grain of corn, how

he flies upon it, how he invites with cries! His favourite—
the newest—hens run clucking joyously to him. How he bows,
droops and prances, holding the grain of corn in his powerful bill, depositing it, pecking to bruise it and then depositing
it before his sultana of the moment. Nor will he complain
if a little ball of fluff runs quickly and pecks the grain
from his bill before Madame Partlet can take it from him.
His gallantry has been wasted, but he is a good father!
. . . Perhaps there is not even a grain of corn when he
issues his invitations; perhaps he merely calls his favourites
to him that he may receive their praise or perform the act
of love. . . .

He is then the man that a woman desires to have vouch-
safed her. When he smites his wing-feathers behind his back
and utters his clarion cry of victory over the hawk that
now glides far away down the hill, his hens come out again
from the shadows, the chickens from beneath their mothers'
wings. He has given security to his country and in confidence
they can return to their avocations. Different, indeed, from
that Monsieur Christopher, who, even when he was still a
soldier, more than anything resembled a full, grey, coarse
meal-sack short in the wind and with rolling, hard-blue eyes.
Not hard eyes, but of a hard blue! And yet, curiously, he
too had some of the spirit of Chantecler beneath his rolling
shoulders of a farm-yard boar. Obviously you could not be
your brother's brother and not have some traces of the
Milor. . . . The spleen too. But no one could say that her
Mark was not a proper man, *chic* in an eccentric manner,
but, oh yes, *chic!* And that was his brother.

Naturally he might try to despoil her. That is what
brother does to brother's widow and children. . . . But, on
occasion, he treated her with a pompous courtesy—a parade.
On the first time he had seen her—not so long ago that;
only during that period of the war that had been without
measurable time—he had treated her to heavy but expressive
gestures of respect and words of courtesy in an old-fashioned
language that he must have learned at the Théâtre Français
while they still played *Ruy Blas*. French was a different thing
now, that she must acknowledge. When she went to Paris—
which she did every late summer whilst her man went to
Harrogate—the language her nephews spoke was a different
affair—without grace, courtesy, intelligibility. Certainly without respect! Oh, *là, là!* When they came to divide up her inheritance that would be a sharper kind of despoilment than
ever Christopher Tietjens'! Whilst she lay on her bed of

death those young fellows and their wives would be all
through her presses and armoires like a pack of wolves. . . .
La famille! Well, that was very proper. It showed the appropriate spirit of acquisition. What was a good mother for
if not to despoil her husband's relatives in the interests of
their joint children!

So Christopher had been as courteous as a well-trained
meal-sack of the *dix-huitième*. Eighteenth century. Older still,
période Molière! When he had come into her room that had
been dimly lit with a *veilleuse*—a night-light; they are so
much more economical than shaded electric lights!—he had
precisely suggested to her a lumbering character from Molière as presented at the Comédie Française; elaborate of
phrase and character but protuberant in odd places. She
might in that case have supposed that he entertained designs
on her person; but with his eyes sticking out in elaborate
considerateness, he had only come to break to her the news
that his brother was about to make an honest woman of
her. That had been Mark's phrase. It is of course only God
that can do that. . . . But the enterprise had had the full
concurrence of Monsieur the heir-apparent.

He had indeed been active whilst she had slumbered in a
hooded chair after four days and three nights on her feet.
She would have surrendered the body of Mark to no human
being but his brother. Now the brother had come to tell
her not to be alarmed—panting with nervousness and short-
ness of breath. . . . Bad lungs both the brothers had! Panting,
he had come to tell her not to be alarmed at finding in
her man's room a priest, a lawyer and a lawyer's clerk. . . .
These black-robed people attend on death, bringing will-forms
and the holy oils. The doctor and a man with oxygen
cylinders had been there when she had gone to repose herself. It was a pretty congregation of the vultures that attend
on us during life.

She had started at once to cry out. That undoubtedly was
what had made him nervous—the anticipation that she would
cry out sharply in the black, silent London that brooded between air raids. In that silence, before sleep had visited her
peignoir-enveloped and therefore clumsyish form, she had
been aware of Christopher's activities on the telephone in
the passage. It had struck her that he might have been
warning the Pompes Funèbres! . . . So she had begun to
scream: the sound that irresistibly you make when death is
about to descend. But he had agitated himself to soothe her
—for all the world like Monsieur Sylvain on the boards of

Molière's establishment! He spoke that sort of French, in a hoarse whisper, in the shadows of the night-light . . . assuring her that the priest was for marriage, with licence of the Archevêque de Cantorbéri such as in London you got in those days from Lambeth Palace for thirty pounds sterling. That enabled you to make any woman honest at any hour of the day or night. The lawyer was there to have a will re-signed. Marriage in this singular country invalidates any previous will. So Tietjens (Christophère) assured her.

But then, if there was that haste, there was danger of death. She had often speculated as to whether he would or would not marry her as an act of death-bed contrition. Rather contemptuously as great lords with *le spleen* make their peace with God. She screamed. In silent, black London. The night-light wavered in its saucer.

He crepitated out that his brother was doubling, in this new will, his posthumous provision for her with provision for the purchase of a house in France if she would not inhabit the dower-house at Groby. A Louis Treize dower-house. It was his idea of consolation. He affected to be business-like. . . . These English. But then, perhaps they do not go through your presses and wardrobes whilst your corpse is still warm!

She screamed out that they might take away their marriage papers and will-forms, but to give her her man again. If they had let her give him her tisanes instead of . . .

With her breast heaving, she had cried into that man's face:

"I swear that my first act when I am Madame Tietjens and have the legal power will be to turn out all these men and give him infusions of poppy-heads and lime-flowers." She expected to see him recoil, but he had said:

"In heaven's name do, my dear sister. It might save him and the nation."

It was silly of him to talk like that. These fellows had too much pride of family. Mark did no more than attend to transport. Well, perhaps transport in those days had its importance. Still, probably Tietjens, Christopher, overrated the indispensableness of Tietjens, Mark. . . . That would have been a month before the armistice. They were black days. . . . A good brother, though. . . .

In the other room, whilst papers were signing, after the *curé* in his *calotte* and all had done reading from his book, Mark had signed to her to bend her head down to him and had kissed her. He whispered:

"Thank God there is one woman-Tietjens who is not a whore and a bitch!" He winced a little; her tears had fallen on his face. For the first time she had said: *"Mon pauvre homme, ce qu'ils ont fait de toi!"* She had been hurrying from the room when Christopher had stopped her. Mark had said:

"I regret to put you to further inconvenience . . ." in French. He had never spoken to her in French before. Marriage makes a difference. They speak to you with ceremony out of respect for themselves and their station in life. You also are at liberty to address them as your *pauvre homme*.

There had to be another ceremony. A man looking like a newly dressed jail-bird stepped out with his book like an office register. With a blue-black jowl. He married them over again. A civil marriage this time.

It was then that, for the first time, she had become aware of the existence of another woman-Tietjens, Christopher's wife. . . . She had not known that Christopher had a wife. Why was not she there? But Mark with his labouring politeness and chest had told her that he exaggerated the formality of the marriage because if both he and Christopher died, she, Marie Léonie Tietjens, might have trouble with a certain Sylvia. The bitch! . . . Well, she, Marie Léonie, was prepared to face her sister-in-law.

3 ~

THE LITTLE maid, Beatrice, as well as Gunning, regarded Marie Léonie with paralysed but bewildered obedience. She was 'er ladyship, a good mark; a foreign Frenchy, bad; extraordinarily efficient about the house and garden and poultry-yard, a matter for mixed feelings. She was fair, not black-avised, a good mark; she was buxom, not skinny, like the real Quality. A bad mark because she was, then, not real Quality; but a qualifiedly good mark because, if you 'as to 'ave Quality all about you in the 'ouse, 'tis better not to 'ave real Quality. . . . But on the whole the general feeling was favourable, because like themselves she was floridly blond. It made 'er 'uman-like. Never you trust a dark woman, and if you marries a dark man 'e will treat you bad. In the English country-side it is like that.

Cabinet-maker Cramp, who was a remnant of the little dark persistent race that once had peopled Sussex, regarded Marie Léonie with distrust that mingled with admiration for the quality of the varnish that she imported from Paris. Proper French polish that were. He lived in the cottage just across the path, on the Common. 'E couldn' say as 'ow 'e liked the job the governors give 'im. He had to patch up and polish with beeswax—not varnish—rough stuff such 's 'is granf'er 'ad 'ad. An' 'ad got rid of. Rough ol' truck. More'n 'undred years old. 'N' more!

He had to take bits of old wood out of one sort of old truck and fit it into missing bits of other old truck. Bought old Moley's pig-pound boards that had been Little Kingsworth church-stalls. The cahptn 'ad 'ad 'im, Cramp, use 'em for all manner of patchin's-up. The captain had brought, too, ol' Miss Cooper's rabbit-'utch. Beautifully bevelled the panels was, too, when cleaned up 'n' beeswaxed. Cramp would acknowledge that. Made him match the bevelling in the timber from Kingsworth church-stalls for one of the missing doors, an' more of the timber for the patching. Proper job, he, Cramp, had made of it, too; he would say that. 'N' it looked proper when it was finished—a long, low press, with six bevelled doors; beautiful purfling on the edges. Like some of the stuff 'is lordship 'ad in the Tujer Room at Fittleworth House. More'n a 'undred years old. Three 'undred. Four. . . . There's no knowin'.

'N' no accountin' fer tastes, 'E would say 'e 'ad 'n eye —the cahptn 'ad. Look at a bit of ol' rough truck, the cahptn would, 'n' see it was older than the monument to Sir Richard Atchison on Tadworth 'Ill that was set up in the year 1842 to celebrate the glorious victory of Free Trade. So the monument said. Lug a bit of rough ol' truck out of the back of a cow-house where it had been throwed— the cahptn would. And his, Cramp's, heart would sink to see the ol' mare come back, some days, the cart full of 'en-coops, 'n' leaden pig-truffs, 'n' pewter plates that 'ad been used to stop up 'oles in cow-byres.

'N' off it would all go to Murrikay. Queer place Murrikay must be—full of the leavin's of ol' England. Pig-troughs, hen-coops, rabbit-hutches, wash-house coppers that no one now had any use for. He loaded 'em, when he'd scrubbed, and silver-sanded and beeswaxed-'n'-turpentined 'em, onto the ol' cart, 'n' put to ol' mare, 'n' down to station, 'n' on to Southampton 'n' off to New York. Must be a queer place, yon! Hadn't they no cabinet-makers or ol' rough truck of ther own?

Well, it took all sorts to make a world 'n' thank God fer that. He, Cramp, had a good job likely to last 'im 'is

lifetime because some folks wus queer in the 'ed. The ol'
lumber went out yon and his, Cramp's missus was gettin'
together a proper set of goods. A tidy treat their sittin'-
room looked, with aspidistras in mahogany tripods, 'n' a Wilton
carpet 'n' bamboo cheers 'n' mahogany whatnots. A proper woman Missus Cramp was, if sharp in the tongue.

Missus Cramp, she didn' give so much fer 'er ladyship.
She was agin' Foreigners. All German spies, they wus. Have
no truck with them, she wouldn't. Oo noo if they wus
's much 's married. Some says they wuz, some says they
wusn'. But you couldn' take in Missus Cramp. . . . 'N'
Quality! What was to show that they were real Quality?
Livin' how they did wasn' Quality manners. Quality wus stuck
up 'n' wore shiny clothes 'n' had motor cars 'n' statues 'n'
palms 'n' ball-rooms 'n' conservatories. 'N' didn' bottle off
the cider 'n' take the eggs 'n' speak queer lingo to the handy-
man. 'N' didn' sell the cheers they sat on. The four younger
children also didn't like 'er ladyship. Never called 'em pretty
dears, she didn't, nor give 'em sweeties nor rag-dolls nor
apples. Smacked 'em if she found 'em in the orchard. Never
so much 's give 'em red-flannel capes in the winter.

But Bill, the eldest, liked 'er ladyship. Called 'er a proper right un. Never stopped tarkin' of 'er. 'N' *she* 'ad statues
in 'er bedroom, 'n' fine gilt cheers, 'n' clocks, 'n' flowerin'
plants. Bill, 'e'd made fer 'er ladyship what she called 'n
eightyjare. In three stories, to stand in a corner 'n' hold
knick-knacks out of fretwork to a pettern she'd give 'im.
Varnished proper, too. A good piece of work if he shouldn't
say so. . . . But Missus Cramp, she'd never been allowed in
'er ladyship's bedroom. A proper place it was. Fit fer a countess! If Missus Cramp could be allowed to see it, she'd maybe
change her opinions. . . . But Missus Cramp, she said:
"Never you trust a fair woman," bein' dark.

The matter of the cider, however, did give him to think.
Proper cider it was, when they was given a bottle or two.
But it wasn't Sussex cider. A little like Devonshire cider,
more like Herefordshire. But not the same as any. More
head it had 'n' was sweeter, 'n' browner. 'N' not to be drunk
's freely! Fair scoured you, it did, if you drunk 's much 's
a quart!

The little settlement was advancing furtively to the hedge.
Cramp put his bald poll out of his work-shed and then crept
out. Mrs. Cramp, an untidy, dark, very thin woman,
emerged over her door-sill, wiping her hands on her apron.
The four Cramp children, at different stages of growth,

crept out of the empty pig-pound. Cramp was not going to buy his winter pigs till next fortnightly fair at Little Kingsnorth. The Elliott children, with the milk-can, came at a snail's pace down the green path from the farm; Mrs. Elliott, an enormous woman with untidy hair, peered over her own hedge, which formed a little enclosure on the Common; Young Hogben, the farmer's son, a man of forty, very thick-set, appeared on the path in the beech-wood, ostensibly driving a great black sow. Even Gunning left his brushing and lumbered to the edge of the stable. From there he could still see Mark in his bed, but also, looking downwards between the apple-trunks, he could see Marie Léonie bottle the cider, large, florid and intent, in the open dairying-shed, where water ran in a V-shaped wooden trough.

"Runnin' t' cider out of cask with a chube!" Mrs. Cramp screamed up the hill to Mrs. Elliott. "Ooever 'eared!" Mrs. Elliott rumbled huskily back at Mrs. Cramp. All these figures closed in furtively, the children peering through tiny interstices in the hedge and muttering one to the other: "Ooever 'eared. . . . Foreign ways, I call it. . . . A glass chube. . . . Ooever 'eared." Even Cramp, though, wiping his bald head with his carpenter's apron, he admonished Mrs. Cramp to remember that he had a good job—even Cramp descended from the path to the hedge-side and stood so close —peering over—that the thorns pricked his perspiring chest through his thin shirt. They said to the baker, who wearily followed his weary horse up the steep path, coming from the deep woods below: It had ought to be stopped. The police had ought to know. Bottling cider by means of a glass tube. And standing the cider in running water. Where was the excise? Rotting honest folks' guts! Poisoning them. No doubt the governor could tell them a tale if he could speak or move. The police had ought to know. . . . Showing off, with cider in running water—to cool it when first bottled! Ooever 'eared! Just because they 'ad a ladyship to their tail. 'N' more money than better folks. Not so much money either. Reckon they'd come to smash 'n' be sold up like 'Igginson at Fittleworth. Set 'isself up fer Quality, 'e did too! . . . 'N' not so much of a ladyship, neither. Not so much more of a ladyship as us if the truth was known. Not an earl or a lord, only a baronite-ess at that, supposin' we all 'ad our rights. . . . The police had ought to be brought into this affair!

A number of members of the Quality, on shining horses, their leathers creaking beautifully, rode at a walk up the path. They were the real Quality. A fine old gentleman, thin as a lath, clean face, hooky nose, white moustache, lovely cane, lovely leggings. On 'is lordship's favourite hack. A bay mare. A fine lady, slim as a boy, riding astride as they do to-day, though they did not use to. But times change. On the countess's own chestnut with white forehead. A bad-tempered horse. She must ride well, that lady. Another lady, grey-haired, but slim too, riding side-saddle in a funny sort of get-up. Long skirt with panniers and three-cornered hat like the ones you see in pictures of highwaymen in the new pub in Queen's Norton. Sort of old-fashioned, she looked. But no doubt it was the newest pattern. Things is so mixed up now-a-days. 'Is lordship's friends could afford to do as they pleased. A boy, eighteen maybe. Shiny leggings too: all their clothes is shiny. Rides well, too, the boy. Look how his legs nip into Orlando—the chief whip's horse. Out for an airing. 'Is lordship's groom of the stud only too glad if the horses can get exercise in hay-cutting time. The real Quality.

They reined in their horses and sat staring, a little further up the road, down into the orchard. They had ought to be told what was going on down there. Puts white powder into the cider along o' the sugar. The Quality ought to be told. . . . But you do not speak to the Quality. Better if they do not notice you. You never know. They sticks together. Might be friends of Tietjenses for all you know. You don't know Tietjenses ain't Quality. Better git a move on or something might 'appen to you. You hear!

The boy in the shiny leggings and clothes—bare-headed he was, with shiny fair hair and shiny cheeks—exclaimed in a high voice:

"I say, mother, I don't like this spying!" And the horses started and jostled.

You see. They don't like this spying. Get a move on. And all that peasantry got a move on whilst the horses went slowly uphill. Queer things the gentry can do to you still if they notice you. It is all very well to say this is a land fit for whatever the word is that stands for simple folk. They have the police and the keepers in their hands and your cottages and livings.

Gunning went out at the garden-gate beside the stable and shouted objurgations at Young Hogben.

"Hey, don't you drive that sow. She's as much right on Common as you."

The great sow was obstinately preceding the squat figure of Young Hogben, who hissed and squeaked behind her. She flapped her great ears and sniffed from side to side, a monument of black imperturbability.

"You keep your 'ogs out of our swedes!" Young Hogben shouted amidst objurgations. "In our forty-acre she is all day 'n' all night too!"

"You keep your swedes outen our 'ogs," Gunning shouted back, swinging his gorilla arms like a semaphore. He advanced onto the Common. Young Hogben descended the slope.

"You fence your 'ogs in same's other folks 'as to do," Young Hogben menaced.

"Folks as abuts on Commons 'as to fence out, not fence in," Gunning menaced. They stood foot to foot on the soft sward, menacing each other with their chins.

" 'Is lordship sold Tietjens' to the cahptn without Common rights," the farmer said. "Ask Mr. Fuller."

" 'Is lordship could no more sell Tietjens' 'thout Common rights 'n' you could milk without drinking rights. Ast Lawyer Sturgis!" Gunning maintained. Put arsenic in among 'is roots, Young Hogben maintained that he would. Spend seven years up to Lewes jail if 'e did, Gunning maintained. They continued for long the endless quarrel that obtains between tenant-farmer who is not Quality but used to brutalizing his hinds and gentlemen's henchman who is used to popularity amongst his class and the peasantry. The only thing upon which they agreed was that you wouldn't think there 'adn't been no war. The war ought to have given tenant-farmers the complete powers of local tyrants; it should have done the same for gentlemen's bailiffs. The sow grunted round Gunning's boots, looking up for grains of maize that Gunning usually dropped. In that way sows come to heel when you call them, however far away they may be on the Common.

From the hard road up the hill—Tietjens' went up the slope to the hedge there—descended the elderly lady who was singularly attired in the eyes of the country-people. She considered that she was descended, not by blood, but by moral affinity from Madame de Maintenon; therefore she wore a long grey riding-skirt with panniers, and a three-cornered, grey-felt hat, and carried a riding-switch of green shagreen. Her thin grey face was tired but authoritative; her hair, which she wore in a knot beneath her hat, was luminously grey; her pince-nez rimless.

Owing to the steepness of the bank on which the garden rose, the path of sea-pebbles zigzagged across most of its width, orange-coloured because it had been lately sanded. She went furtively between quince-trunks, much like the hedge-sparrow, flitting a stretch and then stopping for the boy with the shining leggings stolidly to overtake her.

She said that it was dreadful to think that the sins of one's youth could so find one out. It ought to make her young companion think. To come at the end of one's life to inhabiting so remote a spot. You could not get there with automobiles. Her own Delarue-Schneider had broken down on the hill-road in the attempt to get there yesterday.

The boy, slim in the body, but heavy in the bright red cheeks, with brown hair, truly shiny leggings and a tie of green, scarlet and white stripes, had a temporarily glum expression. He said, nevertheless, with grumbling determination, that he did not think this was playing the game. Moreover, hundreds of motors got up that hill; how else would people come to buy the old furniture? He had already told Mrs. de Bray Pape that the carburettors of Delarue-Schneiders were a wash-out.

It was just that, Mrs. Pape maintained, that was so dreadful a thought. She went swiftly down another zigzag of the path and then faltered.

It was that that was dreadful in these old countries, she said. Why could they never learn? Take example? Here were the descendants of a great family, the Tietjens of Groby, a haunt of ancient peace, the one reduced to a no doubt dreadful state by the sins of his youth, the other to making a living by selling old furniture.

The youth said she was mistaken. She must not believe all that his mother hinted to her. His mother was all right, but her hints went further than facts warranted. If he wanted to let Groby to Mrs. de Bray Pape, it was because he hated swank. His uncle also hated swank. . . . He mumbled a little and added: "And . . . my father!" Moreover, it was not playing the game. He had soft brown eyes that were now clouded and he was blushing.

He mumbled that mother was splendid, but he did not think she ought to have sent him there. Naturally she had her wrongs. For himself he was a Marxist communist. All Cambridge was. He therefore of course approved of his father's living with whom he wished. But there were ways of doing things. Because you were advanced you did not have to treat women with discourtesy. The reverse, rather. He was painfully agitated by the time he overtook the tired lady at the corner of the next zigzag.

She wanted him not to misunderstand her. No discredit attached in her eyes to the pursuit of selling old furniture. Far from it. Mr. Lemuel of Madison Avenue might be called a dealer in old furniture. It was, of course, Oriental, which made a difference. But Mr. Lemuel was a most cultivated man. His country-house at Croogers in the state of New York was kept up in a style that would have done credit to the *grands seigneurs* of pre-Revolutionary France. But from that to this . . . what a downfall!

The house—the cottage—was by now nearly below her feet, the roof extremely high, the windows sunk very deep in grey stone and very small. There was a paved semicircular court before the door, the space having been cut out of the orchard bank and walled with stones. It was extravagantly green, sunk in greenery, and the grass that came nearly to Mrs. Pape's middle was filled with hiding profusions of flowers turning to seed. The four counties swept away from under her, hedges like string going away, enclosing fields, to the hills on the very distant horizon. The country near at hand wooded. The boy beside her took a deep breath as he always did when he saw a great view. On the moors above Groby, for instance. Purple they were.

"It *isn't* fit for human habitation!" the lady exclaimed with the triumphant intonation of one who sees a great truth confirmed. "The homes of the poor in these old countries beggar even pity. Do you suppose they so much as have a bath?"

"I should think my father and uncle were personally *clean!*" the boy said. He mumbled that this was supposed to be rather a show-place. He could trust his father indeed to find rather a show-place to live in. Look at the rock-plants in the sunk garden! He exclaimed: "Look here! Let's go back!"

Mrs. Pape's perturbation gave way to obstinacy. She exclaimed:

"Never!" She had a mission from the poor boy's injured mother. She would never look Sylvia Tietjens in the face if she flinched. Sanitation went before anything. She hoped to leave the world a better place before she passed over. She had Authority conferred on her. Metempsychosistically. She believed that the soul of Madame de Maintenon, the companion of Louis the Fourteenth, had passed into her. How many convents had not the Maintenon set up and how rigidly had she not looked after the virtue and the sanitation of the inhabitants? That was what she, Mrs. Millicent de Bray Pape, looked to. She had in the south of France—the Riviera

—a palace, erected by Mr. Behrens, the celebrated archi-
tect—after the palace of the Maintenon at Sans Souci. But
sanitated! She asked the young man to believe her. The
boudoir appeared to be only a panelled boudoir, very large
because of the useless vanity of le Raw Solale. Madame de
Maintenon would have been content without such vanity. . . .
But only touch a spring in the panels and every sort of
bathing arrangement presented itself to you hidden in the
wall. Sunken baths; baths above ground; douches with sea-
water extra-iodized; lateral douches with and without bath-
salts dissolved in the water. That was what she called making
the world a little better. Impossible not to be healthy with
all that. . . .

The boy mumbled that he was not in principle against
the old tree's coming down. He was, indeed, in principle
against his uncle's and his father's adoption of the peasant
life. This was an industrial age. The peasant had always
spoilt every advance in the ideas of the world. All the men
at Cambridge were agreed as to that. He exclaimed:

"Hi! You can't do that. . . . Not go through standing hay!"

Every fibre of his country-boy landowner's soul was outraged as he saw the long trail of satiny grey that followed
Mrs. de Bray Pape's long skirts. How were his father's men
to cut hay that had been trampled like that? But, unable to
bear any longer the suspense of the spectacular advance
towards Mark Tietjens along those orange zigzags, Mrs. de
Bray Pape was running straight down the bank towards the
unwalled, thatched hut. She could see it through the tops
of the apple-tree.

The boy, desperately nervous, continued to descend the
zigzag paths that would take him into the very purlieus of
his father's house—onto the paved court where there were
rock-plants between the interstices. His mother *ought* not to
have forced him to accompany Mrs. de Bray Pape. His
mother was splendid. Divinely beautiful: athletic as Atalanta
or Betty Nuthall in spite of her sufferings. But she ought
not to have sent Mrs. de Bray Pape. It was *meant* as a sort
of revenge. General Campion had not approved. He could
see that, though he had said: "My boy, you ought always to
obey your dear mother! She has suffered so much. It is your
duty to make it up to her by fulfilling her slightest whim.
An Englishman always does his duty to his mother!"

Of course it was the presence of Mrs. de Bray Pape that
forced the general to say that. Patriotism. General Campion
was deadly afraid of mother. Who wasn't? But he would

hardly have enjoined upon a son to go and spy upon his
father and his father's . . . companion if he had not wanted
to show Mrs. de Bray Pape how superior English family ties
were to those of her country. They ragged each other about
that all day long.

And yet he did not know. The dominion of women over
those of the opposite sex was a terrible thing. He had seen
the old general whimper like a whipped dog and mumble
in his poor white moustache. . . . Mother was splendid. But
wasn't sex a terrible thing? . . . His breath came short.

He covered two foot of pebbles with the orange sand
rolled into them. A tidy job it must be, rolling on that
slope! Still, the actual gradient was not so steep on the
zigzags. One in sixteen perhaps. He covered another two
foot of pebbles with orange sand rolled in. How could he?
How could he cover another two? His heels were trembling!

Four counties ran out below his feet. To the horizon!
"He showed him the kingdoms of the earth." As great a view
as above Groby, but not purple and with no sea. Trust father
to settle where you could see a great view by going uphill.
Vox adhaesit. . . . "His feet were rooted to the earth. . . ."
No, *vox adhaesit faucibus* meant that his voice stuck to his
jaws. Palate rather. His palate was as dry as sawdust! How
could he do it! . . . A terrible thing! They called it Sex! . . .
His mother had coerced him into this dry palate and trembling heels by the force of her sex fever. Dreadful good-
nights they had had in her boudoir, she forcing and forcing
and forcing him with arguments to go. To come here. Beautiful mother! . . . Cruel! Cruel!

The boudoir all lit up. Warm! Scented! Mother's shoulders!
A portrait of Nell Gwynn by Sir Peter Lely. Mrs. de Bray
Pape wanted to buy it. Thought she could buy the earth,
but Lord Fittleworth only laughed. . . . How had they all
got forced down there? By mother. . . . To spy on father.
Mother had never set any store by Fittleworth—good fellow
Fittleworth, good landlord!—till last winter, when she had
got to know that father had bought this place, Then it was
Fittleworth, Fittleworth, Fittleworth! Lunches, dinner,
dances at the Ambassadors. Fittleworth wasn't saying no.
Who could say no to mother with her figure in the saddle
and her hair?

If he had known when they came down to Fittleworth's
last winter what he knew now! He knew now that his mother,
come down for the hunting, though she had never taken
much stock in hunting . . . Still, she could ride. Jove, she

could ride. He had gone queer all over again and again at
first in taking those leaps that she took laughing. Diana,
that's what she was. . . . Well, no, Diana was . . . His
mother, come down for the hunting, was there to torment
father and his . . . companion. She had told him. Laughing
in that way she had. . . . It must be sex cruelty! . . . Laughing like those Leonardi-do-da . . . Well, Vinci women. A
queer laugh, ending with a crooked smile . . . In correspondence with Father's servants . . . Dressing up as a housemaid and looking over the hedge.

How *could* she do it? *How?* How could she force him
to be here? What would Monty, the Prime Minister's son,
Dobles, Porter—fat ass because his father was too beastly
rich—what would his set think at Cambridge? They were all
Marxist communists to a man. But still . . .

What would Mrs. Lowther think if she *really* knew? . . .
If she could have been in the corridor one night when he
came out from his mother's boudoir! He would have had
the courage to ask her then. Her hair was like floss silk,
her lips like cut pomegranates. When she laughed she threw
up her head. . . . He was now warm all over, his eyes wet
and warm.

When he had asked if he ought to—if *she* wanted him to
—do whatever his mother wanted whether or no he approved. . . . If his mother asked him to do what he thought
was a mean action. . . . But that had been on the Peacock
Terrace with the famous Fittleworth Seven Sister Roses. . . .
How she went against the roses. . . . In a yellow . . . No,
moth-coloured . . . Not yellow, not yellow. Green's forsaken,
but yellow's forsworn. Great pity filled him at the thought
that Mrs. Lowther might be forsaken. But she must not be
forsworn . . . moth-coloured silk. Shimmering. Against pink
roses. Her fine, fine hair, a halo. She had looked up and
sideways. She had been going to laugh with her lips like
cut pomegranates. . . . She had told him that as a rule it
was a good thing to do what one's mother wanted when she
was like Mrs. Christopher Tietjens. Her soft voice . . .
Soft Southern voice . . . Oh, when she laughed at Mrs. de
Bray Pape. . . . How could she be a friend of Mrs. de Bray
Pape's? . . .

If it hadn't been sunlight . . . If he had come on Mrs.
Lowther as he came out of his mother's boudoir! He would
have had courage. At night. Late. He would have said: "If
you are really interested in my fate, tell me if I ought to
spy upon my father and his . . . companion!" She would not

have laughed, late at night. She would have given him her hand. The loveliest hands and the lightest feet. And her eyes would have dimmed. . . . Lovely, lovely pansies! Pansies are heartsease. . . .

Why did he have these thoughts: these wafts of intolerable . . . oh, desire. He was his mother's son. . . . His mother was . . . He would kill anyone who said it. . . .

Thank God! Oh, thank God! He was down on the crazy paving level with the house. *AND there was another path went up to Uncle Mark's shed.* The blessed Virgin—who was like Helen Lowther!—had watched over him. He had not to walk under those little deep, small-paned windows.

His father's . . . companion might have been looking out. He would have fainted. . . .

His father was a good sort of man. But he, too, must be . . . like mother. If what they said was true. Ruined by dissolute living. But a good, grey man. The sort of man to be tormented by mother. Great spatulate fingers. But no one had ever tied flies like father. Some he had tied years ago were the best he, Mark Tietjens junior of Groby, had yet. And father loved the wine-coloured moor. *How* could he stifle under these boughs! A house overhung by trees is unsanitary. Italians say that . . .

But what a lovely glimpse under the trees! Sweet-williams along the path. Light filtered by boughs. Shadow. Gleams in the little window-panes. Wall-stones all lichen. That's England. If he could spend a while here with father . . .

Father had been matchless with horses. Women, too. . . . What an inheritance was his, Mark Tietjens junior's! If he could spend a while here. . . . But his father slept with . . . If she came out of the door . . . She must be beautiful. . . . No, they said she was not a patch on mother. He had overheard that at Fittleworth's. Or Helen Lowther. . . . But his father had had his pick? . . . If he chose then to sleep with . . .

If she came out of the door he would faint. . . . Like the Venus of Botti . . . A crooked smile . . . No, Helen Lowther would protect . . . He might fall in love with his father's . . . What do you know of what will happen to you when you come in contact with the Bad Woman. . . . Of advanced views. . . . They said she was of Advanced Views. And a Latinist. . . . He was a Latinist. Loved it!

Or his father might with Hel . . . Hot jealousy filled him. His father was the sort of man . . . She might . . . Why did ever . . . people like mother and father beget children?

He kept his eyes fascinatedly fixed on the stone porch of the cottage whilst he stumbled up the great stone slabs to the path. The path led to Uncle Mark's wall-less thatched hut. . . . No form filled the porch. What was to become of him? He had great wealth; terrific temptation would be his. His mother was no guide. His father might have been better. . . . Well, there was Marxian communism. They all looked to that now, in his set at Cambridge. Monty, the Prime Minister's son, with black eyes; Dobles, Campion's nephew, lean as a rat; Porter, with a pig's snout, but witty as hell. Fat ass.

4 ~

MARK TIETJENS thought that a cow or a hog must have got into the orchard, there was such a rushing in the grass. He said to himself that that damn Gunning was always boasting about his prowess as a hedger; he might see that his confounded hedges kept out the beasts from the Common. An unusual voice—unusual in its intonation—remarked:

"Oh, Sir Mark Tietjens, this is dreadful!"

It appeared to be dreadful. A lady in a long skirt—an apparently elderly Di Vernon out of *Waverley*, which was one of the few novels Mark had ever read—was making dreadful havoc with the standing grass. The beautiful, proud heads swayed and went down as she rushed knee-deep amongst it; stopped, rushed again across his view and then stopped apparently to wring her hands and once more explain that it was dreadful. A tiny rabbit, scared out by her approach, scuttered out under his bed and presumably down into the vegetable-beds. Marie Léonie's Mistigris would probably get it and, since it was Friday, Marie Léonie would be perturbed.

The lady pushed through the remaining tall grass that stood between them and had the air of rising up at his bed-foot. She was rather a faint figure—like the hedge-sparrow. In grey, with a grey short coat and a waistcoat with small round buttons and a three-cornered hat. A tired, thin face. . . . Well, she must be tired, pushing through that long grass with a long skirt. She had a switch of green shagreen. The hen-tom-tit that lived in the old shoe they had tucked on purpose under his thatch uttered long warning cries. The hen-tom-tit did not like the aspect of this apparition.

She was devouring his face with her not disagreeable eyes and muttering:

"Dreadful! Dreadful!" An aeroplane was passing close overhead. She looked up and remarked almost tearfully:

"Hasn't it struck you that but for the sins of your youth you might be doing stunts round these good-looking hills? Now!"

Mark considered the matter, fixedly returning her glance. For an Englishman the phrase "the sins of your youth," as applied to a gentleman's physical immobility, implies only one thing. It never had occurred to him that that implication might be tacked on to him. But of course it might. It was an implication of a disagreeable, or at least a discrediting, kind, because in his class they had been accustomed to consider that the disability was incurred by consorting with public women of a cheap kind. He had never consorted with any woman in his life but Marie Léonie, who was health exaggerated. But if he had had to do with women he would have gone in for the most expensive sort. And taken precautions! A gentleman owes that to his fellows!

The lady was continuing:

"I may as well tell you at once that I am Mrs. Millicent de Bray Pape. And hasn't it struck you that but for *his* depravity—unbridled depravity—your brother might to-day be operating in Capel Court instead of peddling old furniture at the end of the world?"

She added disconcertingly:

"It's nervousness that makes me talk like this. I have always been shy in the presence of notorious libertines. That is my education."

Her name conveyed to him that this lady was going to occupy Groby. He saw no objection to it. She had, indeed, written to ask him if he saw any objection to it. It had been a queerly written letter, in hieroglyphs of a straggling and convoluted kind. . . . "I am the lady who is going to rent your mansion, Groby, from my friend Mrs. Sylvia."

It had struck him then—whilst Valentine had been holding the letter up for him to read. . . . Pretty piece, Valentine, now-a-days. The country air suited her—that this woman must be an intimate friend of his brother's wife, Sylvia. Otherwise she would have said "Mrs. Sylvia Tietjens," at least.

Now he was not so certain. This was not the sort of person to be an intimate friend of that bitch's. Then she was a cat's paw. Sylvia's intimates—amongst women—were all

Bibbies and Jimmies and Marjies. If she spoke to any other woman it was to make use of her—as a lady's maid or a tool.

The lady said:

"It must be agony to you to be reduced to letting your ancestral home. But that does not seem to be a reason for not speaking to me. I meant to ask the earl's housekeeper for some eggs for you, but I forgot. I am always forgetting. I am so active. Mr. de Bray Pape says I am the most active woman from here to Santa Fé."

Mark wondered: Why Santa Fé? That was probably because Mr. Pape had olive-tree plantations in that part of California. Valentine had told him over Mrs. Pape's letter that Mr. Pape was the largest olive-oil merchant in the world. He cornered all the olive-oil and all the straw-coloured flasks in Provence, Lombardy, California, and informed his country that you were not really refined if you used in your salads oil that did not come out of a Pape Quality flask. He showed ladies and gentlemen in evening dress starting back from expensively laid dinner-tables, holding their noses and exclaiming: "Have you no *Papes!*" Mark wondered where Christopher got his knowledges, for naturally Valentine had the information from him. Probably Christopher had looked at American papers. But why should one look at American papers? Mark himself never had. Wasn't there the *Field?* . . . He was a queer chap, Christopher.

The lady said:

"It *isn't* a reason for not speaking to me! It isn't!"

Her greyish face flushed slowly. Her eyes glittered behind her rimless pince-nez. She exclaimed:

"You are probably too haughtily aristocratic to speak to me, Sir Mark Tietjens. But I have in me the soul of the Maintenon; you are only the fleshly decendant of a line of chartered libertines. That is what Time and the New World have done to redress the balance of the Old. It is we who are keeping up the status of the *grands seigneurs* of old in your so-called ancestral homes."

He thought she was probably right. Not a bad sort of woman: she would naturally be irritated at his not answering her. It was proper enough.

He never remembered to have spoken to an American or to have thought about America. Except, of course, during the war. Then he had spoken to Americans in uniform about transport. He hadn't liked their collars, but they had known their jobs as far as their jobs went—which had been asking to be provided with a disproportionate amount of transport for too few troops. He had had to wring that transport out of the country.

If he had had his way he wouldn't have. But he hadn't had his way. Because the Governing Classes were no good. Transport is the soul of a war: the spirit of an army had used to be in its feet, Napoleon had said. Something like that. But those fellows had starved the army of transport; then flooded it with so much it couldn't move; then starved it again. Then they had insisted on his finding enormously too much transport for those fellows with queer collars who used it for disposing of typewriters and sewing-machines that came over on transports. . . . It had broken his back. That and solitude. There had not been a fellow he could talk to in the government towards the end. Not one who knew the difference between the ancestry of Persimmon and the stud form of Sceptre or Isinglass. Now they were paying for it.

The lady was saying to him that her spiritual affinity was probably a surprise to Sir Mark. There was none the less no mistake about it. In every one of the Maintenon's houses she felt instantly at home; the sight in any museum of any knick-knack or jewel that had belonged to the respectable companion of Louis Quatorze startled her as if with an electric shock. Mr. Quarternine, the celebrated upholder of the metempsychosistic school, had told her that those phenomena proved beyond doubt that the soul of the Maintenon had returned to earth in her body. What, as against that, were the mere fleshly claims of Old Family?

Mark considered that she was probably right. The old families of his country were a pretty inefficient lot that he was thankful to have done with. Racing was mostly carried on by English nobles from Frankfort-on-the-Main. If this lady could be regarded as speaking allegorically she was probably right. And she had had to get a soul from somewhere.

But she talked too much about it. People ought not to be so tremendously fluent. It was tiring; it failed to hold the attention. She was going on.

He lost himself in speculations as to her reason for being there, trampling on his brother's grass. It would give Gunning and the extra hands no end of an unnecessary job to cut. The lady was talking about Marie Antoinette. Marie Antoinette had gone sledging on salt in summer. Trampling down hay-grass was really worse. Or no better. If everyone in the country trampled on grass like that it would put up the price of fodder for transport animals to something prohibitive.

Why had she come there? She wanted to take Groby furnished. She might for him. He had never cared about Groby. His father had never had a stud worth talking about. A selling plater or two. He had never cared for hunting or shooting. He remembered standing on Groby lawn watching the shooting-parties take to the hills on the Twelfth and feeling rather a fool. Christopher of course loved Groby. He was younger and hadn't expected to own it.

A pretty muck Sylvia might have made of the place—if her mother had let her. Well, they would know pretty soon. Christopher would be back if the machine did not break his obstinate neck. . . . What, then, was this woman doing here? She probably represented a new turn of the screw that that unspeakable woman was administering to Christopher.

His sister-in-law, Sylvia, represented for him unceasing, unsleeping activities of a fantastic kind. She wanted, he presumed, his brother to go back and sleep with her. So much hatred could have no other motive. . . . There could be no other motive for sending this American lady here.

The American lady was telling him that she intended to keep up at Groby a semi-regal state—of course with due democratic modesty. Apparently she saw her way to squaring that circle! . . . Probably there are ways. There must be quite a lot of deucedly rich fellows in that country! How did they reconcile doing themselves well with democracy? Did their valets sit down to meals with them, for instance? That would be bad for discipline. But perhaps they did not care about discipline. There was no knowing.

Mrs. de Bray Pape apparently approved of having footmen in powder and the children of the tenants kneeling down when she drove out in his father's coach-and-six. Because she intended to use his father's coach-and-six when she drove over the moors to Redcar or Scarborough. That, Mrs. de Bray Pape had been told by Sylvia, was what his father had done. And it was true enough. That queer old josser his father had always had out that monstrosity when he went justicing or to the Assizes. That was to keep up his state. He didn't see why Mrs. de Bray Pape shouldn't keep up hers if she wanted to. But he did not see the tenants' children kneeling to the lady! Imagine old Scutt's children at it, or Long Tom o' th' Clough's! . . . Their grandchildren, of course. They had called his father "Tietjens"—some of them even "Auld Mark"!—to his face. He himself had always been "Young Mark" to them. Very likely he was still. These things do not change any more than the heather on the moors. He wondered what the tenants would call her. She would have a tough time of it. They weren't her tenants; they were his and they jolly well knew it. These fellows who took houses and castles furnished thought they jolly well hired the family. There had been before the war a fellow from Frankfort-on-the-Main took Lindisfarne or Holly Island or some such place and hired a bagpiper to play round the table while they ate. And closed his eyes whilst the fellow played reels. As if it had been a holy occasion. . . . Friend of Sylvia's friends in the government. To do her credit she would not stop with Jews. The only credit she had to her tail!

Mrs. de Bray Pape was telling him that it was not undemocratic to have your tenants' children kneel down when you passed.

A boy's voice said:

"Uncle Mark!" Who the devil could that be? Probably the son of one of the people he had week-ended with. Bowlby's maybe; or Teddy Hope's. He had always liked children and they liked him.

Mrs. de Bray Pape was saying that, yes, it was good for the tenants' children. The Rev. Dr. Slocombe, the distinguished educationalist, said that these touching old rites should be preserved in the interests of the young. He said that to see the Prince of Wales at the coronation kneeling before his father and swearing fealty had been most touching. And she had seen pictures of the Maintenon having it done when she walked out. *She* was now the Maintenon, therefore it must be right. But for Marie Antoinette . . .

The boy's voice said:

"I hope you will excuse . . . I *know* it isn't the thing . . ."

He couldn't see the boy without turning his head on the pillow, and he was not going to turn his head. He had a sense of someone a yard or so away at his off-shoulder. The boy at least had not come through the standing hay.

He did not imagine that the son of anyone he had ever week-ended with would ever walk through standing hay. The young generation were a pretty useless lot, but he could hardly believe they would have come to that yet. Their sons might. . . . He saw visions of tall dining-rooms lit up, with tall pictures, and dresses, and the sunset through high windows over tall grasses in the parks. He was done with that. If any tenants' children ever knelt to him it would be when he took his ride in his wooden coat to the little church over the moors. . . . Where his father had shot himself.

That had been a queer go. He remembered getting the news. He had been dining at Marie Léonie's. . . .

The boy's voice was, precisely, apologizing for the fact that that lady had walked through the grass. At the same time, Mrs. de Bray Pape was saying things to the discredit of Marie Antoinette, whom apparently she disliked. He could not imagine why anyone should dislike Marie Antoinette. Yet very likely she was dislikable. The French, who were sensible people, had cut her head off, so they presumably disliked her. . . .

He had been dining at Marie Léonie's, she standing, her hands folded before her, hanging down, watching him eat his mutton-chops and boiled potatoes, when the porter from his club had 'phoned through that there was a wire for him. Marie Léonie had answered the telephone. He had told her to tell the porter to open the telegram and read it to her. That was a not unusual proceeding. Telegrams that came to him at the club usually announced the results of races that he had not attended. He hated to get up from the dinner-table. She had come back slowly, and said still more slowly that she had bad news for him; there had been an accident; his father had been found shot dead.

He had sat still for quite a time; Marie Léonie also had said nothing. He remembered that he had finished his chops, but had not eaten his apple-pie. He had finished his claret.

By that time he had come to the conclusion that his father had probably committed suicide, and that he—he, Mark Tietjens—was probably responsible for his father's having done that. He had got up, then, told Marie Léonie to get herself some mourning, and had taken the night-train to Groby. There had been no doubt about it when he got there. His father had committed suicide. His father was not the man unadvisedly to crawl through a quicken-hedge, with his gun at full cock behind him, after rabbits. . . . It had been purposed.

There was, then, something soft about the Tietjens stock —for there had been no real and sufficient cause for the suicide. Obviously his father had had griefs. He had never got over the death of his second wife; that was soft for a Yorkshireman. He had lost two sons and an only daughter in the war; other men had done that and got over it. He had heard through him, Mark, that his youngest son—Christopher—was a bad hat. But plenty of men had sons who

were bad hats. . . . Something soft then about the stock!
Christopher certainly was soft. But that came from the
mother. Mark's stepmother had been from the south of
Yorkshire. Soft people down there! A soft woman. Christo-
pher had been her ewe-lamb and she had died of grief when
Sylvia had run away from him! . . .

The boy with a voice had got himself into view towards
the bottom of the bed, near Mrs. de Bray Pape . . . a
tallish slip of a boy, with slightly chawbacony cheeks, high-
coloured, lightish hair, brown eyes. Upstanding but softish.
Mark seemed to know him, but could not place him. The
boy asked to be forgiven for the intrusion, saying that he
knew it was not the thing.

Mrs. de Bray Pape was talking improbably about Marie
Antoinette, whom she very decidedly disliked. She said that
Marie Antoinette had behaved with great ingratitude to
Madame de Maintenon—which must have been difficult. Apparently, according to Mrs. de Bray Pape, when Marie Antoinette had been a neglected little girl about the Court of
France, Madame de Maintenon had befriended her, lending
her frocks, jewels and perfumes. Later Marie Antoinette
had persecuted her benefactor. From that had arisen all the
woes of France and the Old World in general.

That appeared to Mark to be to mix history, but he was
not very certain. Mrs. de Bray Pape said, however, that
she had those little-known facts from Mr. Reginald Weiler,
the celebrated professor of social economy at one of the
western universities.

Mark returned to the consideration of the softness of the
Tietjens stock, whilst the boy gazed at him with eyes that
might have been imploring or that might have been merely
moon-struck. Mark could not see what the boy could have
to be imploring about, so it was probably just stupidity. His
breeches, however, were very nicely cut. Very nicely, indeed;
Mark recognized, indeed, the tailor—a man in Conduit
Street. If that fellow had the sense to get his riding-breeches
from that man, he could not be quite an ass. . . .

That Christopher was soft because his mother did not
come from the north of Yorkshire or Durham might be
true enough—but that was not enough to account for the
race dying out. His, Mark's, father had no descendants by
his sons. The two brothers who had been killed had been
childless. He himself had none. Christopher . . . Well, that
was debatable!

That he, Mark, had practically killed his own father he was

ready to acknowledge. One made mistakes; that was one. If
one made mistakes, one should try to repair them; otherwise,
one must, as it were, cut one's losses. He could not bring
his father back to life; he hadn't, equally, been able to do
anything for Christopher. . . . Not much, certainly. The fellow had refused his brass. . . . He couldn't really blame him.

The boy was asking him if he would not speak to them.
He said he was Mark's nephew, Mark Tietjens junior.

Mark took credit to himself because he did not stir a hair.
He had so made up his mind, he found, that Christopher's
son was not his son that he had almost forgotten the cub's
existence. But he ought not to have made up his mind so
quickly: he was astonished to find from the automatic working of his mind that he so had. There were too many factors
to be considered that he had never bothered really to consider. Christopher had determined that this boy should have
Groby: that had been enough for him, Mark. He did not
care who had Groby.

But the actual sight of this lad whom he had never seen
before presented the problem to him as something that needed
solution. It came as a challenge. When he came to think of
it, it was a challenge to him to make up his mind finally
as to the nature of Woman. He imagined that he had never
bothered his head about that branch of the animal kingdom.
But he found that, lying there, he must have spent quite a
disproportionate amount of his time in thinking about the
motives of Sylvia.

He had never spoken much with any but men—and then
mostly with men of his own class and type. Naturally you
addressed a few polite words to your week-end hostess. If
you found yourself in the rose-garden of a Sunday before
church with a young or old woman who knew anything
about horses, you talked about horses, or Goodwood, or
Ascot to her for long enough to show politeness to your
hostess' guests. If she knew nothing about horses you talked
about the roses or the irises, or the weather last week. But
that pretty well exhausted it.

Nevertheless, he knew all about women. Of that he was
confident. That is to say, that when in the course of conversation or gossip he had heard the actions of women nar-
rated or commented on, he had always been able to supply
a motive for those actions sufficient to account for them
to his satisfaction, or to let him predict with accuracy what
course the future would take. No doubt, twenty years of

listening to the almost ceaseless but never disagreeable conversation of Marie Léonie had been a liberal education.

He regarded his association with her with complete satisfaction—as the only subject for complete satisfaction to be
found in the contemplation of the Tietjens family. Christopher's Valentine was a pretty piece enough and had her head
screwed confoundedly well on. But Christopher's association
with her had brought such a peck of troubles down on his
head that, except for the girl as an individual, it was a
pretty poor choice. It was a man's job to pick a woman
who would neither worry him nor be the cause of worries.
Well, Christopher had picked two—and look at the results!

He himself had been completely unmistaken—from the
first minute. He had first seen Marie Léonie on the stage at
Covent Garden. He had gone to Covent Garden in attend-
ance on his stepmother, his father's second wife—the soft
woman. A florid, gentle, really saintly person. She had passed
around Groby for a saint. An Anglican saint, of course.
That was what was the matter with Christopher. It was
the soft streak. A Tietjens had no business with saintliness
in his composition! It was bound to get him looked on as
a blackguard!

But he had attended Covent Garden as a politeness to
his stepmother, who very seldom found herself in town.
And there, in the second row of the ballet, he had seen
Marie Léonie—slimmer, of course, in those days. He had at
once made up his mind to take up with her, and, an obliging
commissionaire having obtained her address for him from
the stage-door, he had, towards twelve-thirty next day,
walked along the Edgware Road towards her lodgings. He
had intended to call on her; he met her, however, in the
street. Seeing her there, he had liked her walk, her figure,
her neat dress.

He had planted himself, his umbrella, his billycock hat
and all, squarely in front of her—she had neither flinched nor
attempted to bolt round him—and had said that, if at the
end of her engagement in London, she cared to be placed
"dans ses draps," with two hundred and fifty pounds a
year and pin-money to be deliberated on, she might hang up
her cream-jug at an apartment that he would take for her
in St. John's Wood Park, which was the place in which, in
those days, most of his friends had establishments. She had
preferred the neighbourhood of the Gray's Inn Road, as reminding her more of France.

But Sylvia was quite another pair of shoes. . . .

That young man was flushing all over his face. The young of the tom-tit in the old shoe were getting impatient; they were chirruping in spite of the alarm-cries of the mother on the boughs above the thatch. It was certainly insanitary to have boughs above your thatch, but what did it matter in days so degenerate that even the young of tom-tits could not restrain their chirpings in face of their appetites.

That young man—Sylvia's by-blow—was addressing embarrassed remarks to Mrs. de Bray Pape. He suggested that perhaps his uncle resented the lady's lectures on history and sociology. He said he had come to talk about the tree. Perhaps that was why his uncle would not speak to them.

The lady said that it was precisely giving lessons in history to the dissolute aristocracy of the Old World that was her mission in life. It was for their good, resent it how they might. As for talking about the tree, the young man had better do it for himself. She now intended to walk around the garden to see how the poor lived.

The boy said that in that case he did not see why Mrs. de Bray Pape had come at all. The lady answered that she had come at the sacred behest of his injured mother. That ought to be answer enough for him. She flitted, disturbedly, from Mark's view.

The boy, swallowing visibly in his throat, fixed his slightly protruding eyes on his uncle's face. He was about to speak, but he remained for a long time silent and goggling. That was a Christopher Tietjens trick—not a Tietjens family trick. To gaze at you a long time before speaking. Christopher had it, no doubt, from his mother—exaggeratedly. She would gaze at you for a long time. Not unpleasantly, of course. But Christopher had always irritated him, even as a small boy. . . . It is possible that he himself might not be as he was if he hadn't gazed at him for a long time, like a stuck pig. On the morning of that beastly day. Armistice Day. . . . Beastly.

Cramp's eldest son, a bugler in the second Hampshires, went down the path, his bugle shining behind his khaki figure. Now they would make a beastly row with that instrument. On Armistice Day they had played the last post on the steps of the church under Marie Léonie's windows. . . . The Last Post! . . . The Last of England! He remembered thinking that. He had not by then had the full terms of that surrender, but he had had a dose enough of Christopher's stuck-piggedness! . . . A full dose! He didn't say he didn't deserve it. If you make mistakes you must take what you get for it. You shouldn't make mistakes.

The boy at the foot of the bed was making agonized motions with his throat: swallowing his Adam's apple. He said:

"I can understand, uncle, that you hate to see us. All the same, it seems a little severe to refuse to speak to us!"

Mark wondered a little at the breakdown in communications that there must have been. Sylvia had been spying round that property, and round and round and round again. She had had renewed interviews with Mrs. Cramp. It had struck him as curious taste to like to reveal to dependents—to reveal and to dwell upon the fact that you were distasteful to your husband. If his woman had left him he would have preferred to hold his tongue about it. He certainly would not have gone caterwauling about it to the carpenter of the man she had taken up with. Still, there was no accounting for tastes. Sylvia had, no doubt, been so full of her own griefs that very likely she had not listened to what Mrs. Cramp had said about his, Mark's, condition. On the one or two interviews he had had with that bitch she had been like that. She had sailed in with her grievances against Christopher with such vigour that she had gone away with no ideas at all as to the conditions on which she was to be allowed to inhabit Groby. Obviously it taxed her mind to invent what she invented. You could not invent that sort of sex-cruelty stuff without having your mind a little affected. She could not, for instance, have invented the tale that he, Mark, was suffering for the sins of his youth without its taking it out of her. That is the ultimate retribution of Providence on those who invent gossip frequently. They go a little dotty. . . . The fellow—he could not call his name to mind, half Scotch, half Jew—who had told him the worst tales against Christopher had gone a little dotty. He had grown a beard and wore a top-hat at inappropriate functions. Well, in effect, Christopher was a saint, and Provvy invents retributions of an ingenious kind against those who libel saints.

At any rate, that bitch must have become so engrossed in her tale that it had not come through to her that he, Mark, could not speak. Of course, the results of venereal disease are not pleasant to contemplate, and, no doubt, Sylvia, having invented the disease for him, had not liked to contemplate the resultant symptoms. At any rate, that boy did not know—and neither did Mrs. de Bray Pape—that he

did not speak. Not to them, not to anybody. He was finished
with the world. He perceived the trend of its actions, listened
to its aspirations, and even to its prayers, but he would
never again stir lip or finger. It was like being dead—or
being God.

This boy was apparently asking for absolution. He was of
opinion that it was not a very sporting thing of himself and
Mrs. Bray to come there. . . .

It was, however, sporting enough. He could see that they
were both as afraid of him, Mark, as of the very devil. Its
taste might, however, be questioned. Still, the situation was
unusual—as all situations are. Obviously it was not in good
taste for a boy to come to the house in which his father
lived with a mistress, nor for the wife's intimate friend either.
Still, they apparently wanted, the one to let, the other to
take, Groby. They could not do either if he, Mark, did not
give permission, or, at any rate, if he opposed them. It
was business, and business may be presumed to cover quite
a lot of bad taste.

And, in effect, the boy was saying that his mother was,
of course, a splendid person, but that he, Mark junior, found
her proceedings in many respects questionable. One could
not, however, expect a woman—and an injured woman . . .
The boy, with his shining eyes and bright cheeks, seemed to
beg Mark to concede that his mother was at least an injured
woman. . . . One could not expect, then, a wronged woman
to see things eye to eye with . . . with young Cambridge!
For, he hastened to assure Mark, his set—the son of the
Prime Minister, young Doble, and Porter—as well as himself, were unanimously of opinion that a man ought to be
allowed to live with whom he liked. He was not, therefore,
questioning his father's actions, and, for himself, if the occasion arose, he would be very glad to shake his father's . . .
companion . . . by the hand.

His bright eyes became a little humid. He said that he was
not in effect questioning anything, but he thought that he
himself would have been the better for a little more of
his father's influence. He considered that he had been too
much under his mother's influence. They noticed it, even
at Cambridge! That, in effect, was the real snag when it
came to be a question of dissolving unions once contracted.
Scientifically considered. Questions of . . . of sex attraction,
in spite of all the efforts of scientists, remained fairly mysterious. The best way to look at it . . . the safest way, was
that sex attraction occurred, as a rule, between tempera-

mental and physical opposites, because nature desired to correct extremes. No one, in fact, could be more different than his father and mother—the one so graceful, athletic and . . . oh, charming. And the other so . . . oh, let us say perfectly honourable, but . . . oh, lawless. Because, of course, you can break certain laws and remain the soul of honour.

Mark wondered if this boy was aware that his mother habitually informed everyone whom she met that his father lived on women. On the immoral earnings of women, she would infer when she thought it safe. . . .

The soul of honour, then, and masculinely clumsy and damn fine in his way. . . . Well, he, Mark Tietjens junior, was not there to judge his father. His uncle Mark could see that he regarded his father with affection and admiration. But if nature—he must be pardoned for using anthropomorphic expressions since they were the shortest way—if nature, then, meant unions of opposite characters to redress extremes in the children, the process did not complete itself with . . . in short, with the act of physical union. For just as there were obviously inherited physical characteristics, and, no doubt, inherited memory, there yet remained the question of the influence of temperament by means of personal association. So that for one opposite to leave the fruits of a union exclusively under the personal influence of the other opposite was very possibly to defeat the purposes of nature. . . .

That boy, Mark thought, was a very curious problem. He seemed to be a good, straight boy. A little loquacious; still, that was to be excused since he had to do all the talking himself. From time to time he had paused in his speech, as if, deferentially, he wished to have Mark's opinion. That was proper. He, Mark, could not stand hobbledehoys—particularly the hobbledehoys of that age, who appeared to be opinionative and emotional beyond the normal in hobbledehoys. Anyhow, he could not stand the young once they were beyond the age of childhood. But he was aware that if you want to conduct a scientific investigation, if you want to arrive, for yourself, at the truth of an individual's parentage—you must set aside your likes and dislikes.

Heaven knew, he had found Christopher, when he had been only one of the younger ones in his father's—he had found him irritating enough . . . a rather moony, fair brat, interested mostly in mathematics, with a trick of standing with those goggle eyes gazing bluely at you—years ago, in and around, at first the nursery, then the stables at Groby.

Then, if this lad irritated him, it was rather an argument in favour of his being Christopher's son than Sylvia's by-blow by another man. . . . What was the fellow's name? A rank bad hat, anyhow.

The probability was that he *was* the other fellow's son. That woman would not have trepanned Christopher into the marriage if she hadn't at least thought that she was with child. There was nothing to be said against any wench's tricking any man into marrying her if she were in that condition. But once having got a man to give a name to your bastard you ought to treat him with some loyalty; it is a biggish service he has done you. That Sylvia had never done. . . . They had got this young fellow into their—the Tietjenses'—family. There he was, with his fingers on Groby already. . . . That was all right. As great families as Tietjens had had that happen to them.

But what made Sylvia pestilential was that she should afterwards have developed this sex-madness for his unfortunate brother.

There was no other way to look at it. She had undoubtedly lured Christopher on to marry her because she thought, rightly or wrongly, that she was with child by another man. They would never know—she herself probably did not know!—whether this boy was Christopher's son or the other's. English women are so untidy—shamefaced—about these things. That was excusable. But every other action of hers from that date had been inexcusable—except regarded as actions perpetrated under the impulsion of sex viciousness.

It is perfectly proper—it is a mother's duty—to give an unborn child a name and a father. But afterwards to blast the name of that father is more discreditable than to leave the child nameless. This boy was now Tietjens of Groby—but he was also the boy who was the son of a father who had behaved unspeakably according to the mother. . . . And the son of a mother who had been unable to attract her man! . . . Who advertised the fact to the estate carpenter! If we say that the good of the breed is the supreme law, what sort of virtue was this?

It was all very well to say that every one of Sylvia's eccentricities had in view the sole aim of getting her boy's father to return to her. No doubt they might. He, Mark, was perfectly ready to concede that even her infidelities, notorious as they had been, might have been merely ways of calling his unfortunate brother's attention back to her—of keeping herself in his mind. After the marriage Christopher, finding

out that he had been a mere cat's paw, probably treated
her pretty coldly or ignored her—maritally. . . . And he was
a pretty attractive fellow, Christopher. He, Mark, was bound
now-a-days to acknowledge that. A regular saint and Christian martyr and all that. . . . Enough to drive a woman wild
if she had to live beside him and be ignored.

It is obvious that women must be allowed what means
they can make use of to maintain—to arouse—their sex
attraction for their men. That is what the bitches are for in
the scale of things. They have to perpetuate the breed. To
do that they have to call attention to themselves and to use
what devices they see fit to use, each one according to her
own temperament. That cruelty was an excitant, he was
quite ready, too, to concede. He was ready to concede
anything to the woman. To be cruel is to draw attention to
yourself; you cannot expect to be courted by a man whom
you allow to forget you. But there probably ought to be a
limit to things. You probably ought in this, as in all other
things, to know what you can do and what you can't—and
the proof of this particular pudding, as of all others, was
in the eating. Sylvia had left no stone unturned in the determination to keep herself in her man's mind, and she had
certainly irretrievably lost her man: to another girl. Then
she was just a nuisance.

A woman intent on getting a man back ought to have
some system, some sort of scheme at the very least. But
Sylvia—he knew it from the interminable talk that he had had
with Christopher on Armistice Night—Sylvia delighted most
in doing what she called pulling the strings of shower-baths.
She did extravagant things, mostly of a cruel kind, for the
fun of seeing what would happen. Well, you cannot allow
yourself fun when you are on a campaign. Not as to the
subject matter of the campaign itself! If then you do what
you want rather than what is expedient, you damn well have
to take what you get for it. *Damn* well!

What would have justified Sylvia, no matter what she did,
would have been if she had succeeded in having another child
by his brother. She hadn't. The breed of Tietjens was not
enriched. Then she was just a nuisance. . . .

An infernal nuisance. . . . For what was she up to now?
It was perfectly obvious that both Mrs. de Bray Pape and
this boy were here because she had had another outbreak
of . . . practically sadism. They were here so that Christopher might be hurt some more and she not forgotten. What,
then, was it? What the deuce was it?

The boy had been silent for some time. He was gazing at Mark with the goggle-eyed gasping that had been so irritating in his father—particularly on Armistice Day. . . . Well, he, Mark, was apparently now conceding that this boy was probably his brother's son. A real Tietjens after all was to reign over the enormously long grey house behind the fantastic cedar. The tallest cedar in Yorkshire. In England. In the empire. . . . He didn't care. "He who lets a tree overhang his roof calls the doctor in daily. . . ." The boy's lips began to move. No sound came out. He was presumably in a great state!

He was undoubtedly like his father. Darker . . . Brown hair, brown eyes, high-coloured cheeks all flushed now. Straight nose, marked brown eyebrows. A sort of . . . scared, puzzled . . . what was it? . . . expression. Well, Sylvia was fair; Christopher was dark-haired with silver streaks, but fair-complexioned. . . . Damn it: this boy was more attractive than Christopher had been at his age and earlier. . . . Christopher hanging round the schoolroom door in Groby, puzzled over the mathematical theory of waves. He, Mark, hadn't been able to stand him or, indeed, any of the other children. There was sister Effie—*born* to be a curate's wife. . . . Puzzled! That was it! . . . That bothering woman, his father's second wife—the Saint!—had introduced the puzzlement strain into the Tietjenses. . . . This was Christopher's boy, saintly strain and all. Christopher was probably born to be a rural dean in a fat living writing treatises on the integral calculus all the time except on Saturday afternoons. With a great reputation for saintliness. Well, he wasn't the one and hadn't the other. He was an old-furniture dealer who made a stink in virtuous nostrils. . . . Provvy works in a mysterious way. The boy was saying now:

"The tree . . . the great tree . . . It darkens the windows. . . ."

Mark said: "Oha!" to himself. Groby Great Tree was the symbol of Tietjens. For thirty miles round Groby they made their marriage vows by Groby Great Tree. In the other ridings they said that Groby Tree and Groby Well were equal in height and depth one to the other. When they were really imaginatively drunk, Cleveland villagers would declare—would knock you down if you denied—that Groby Great Tree was 365 foot high and Groby Well 365 feet deep. A foot for every day of the year. . . . On special occasions —he could not himself be bothered to remember what—they would ask permission to hang rags and things from the boughs. Christopher said that one of the chief indictments against Joan of Arc had been that she and the other village girls of Domrémy had hung rags and trinkets from the boughs of a cedar. Offerings to fairies. . . . Christopher set great store by the tree. He was a romantic ass. Probably he set more store by the tree than by anything else at Groby. He would pull the house down if he thought it incommoded the tree.

Young Mark was bleating, positively bleating:

"The Italians have a proverb. . . . 'He who lets a tree overhang his house invites a daily call from the doctor. . . .' I agree myself. . . . In principle, of course. . . ."

Well, that was that! Sylvia, then, was proposing to threaten to ask to have Groby Great Tree cut down. Only to threaten to ask. But that would be enough to agonize the miserable Christopher. You couldn't cut down Groby Great Tree. But the thought that the tree was under the guardianship of unsympathetic people would be enough to drive Christopher almost dotty—for years and years.

"Mrs. de Bray Pape," the boy was stammering, "is extremely keen on the tree's being . . . I agree in principle. . . . My mother wished you to see that—oh, in modern days —a house is practically unlettable if . . . So she got Mrs. de Bray Pape . . . She hasn't had the courage though she swore she had. . . ."

He continued to stammer. Then he started and stopped, crimson. A woman's voice had called:

"Mr. Tietjens. . . . Mr. Mark. . . . Hi . . . hup!"

A small woman, all in white, white breeches, white coat, white wideawake, was slipping down from a tall bay with a white star on the forehead—a bay with large nostrils and an intelligent head. She waved her hand obviously at the boy and then caressed the horse's nostrils. Obviously at the boy . . . for it was obviously unlikely that Mark senior would know a woman who could make a sound like "Hi, hup!" to attract his attention.

Lord Fittleworth, in a square, hard hat, sat on an immense, coffin-headed dapple-grey. He had bristling, close-cropped moustaches and sat like a limpet. He waved his crop in the direction of Mark and went on talking to Gunning, who was at his stirrup. The coffin-headed beast started forward and reared a foot or so; a wild, brazen, yelping sound had disturbed it. The boy was more and more scarlet and as emotion grew on him, more and more like Christopher on that beastly day. . . . Christopher with a piece of furniture

under his arm, in Marie Léonie's room, his eyes goggling
out at the foot of the bed.

Mark swore painfully to himself. He hated to be reminded
of that day. Now this lad and that infernal bugle that the
younger children of Cramp had got hold of from their
bugler-brother had put it back damnably in his mind. It
went on. At intervals. One child had a try, then another.
Obviously then Cramp the eldest took it. It blared out. . . .
Ta . . . Ta . . . Ta . . . Ta . . . ti . . . ta-ta-ti . . . Ta . . .
The last post. The b——y infernal last post. . . . Well,
Christopher, as that day Mark had predicted, had got
himself, with his raw sensibilities, into a pretty b——y
infernal mess while some drunken ass had played the last
post under the window. . . . Mark meant that whilst that
farewell was being played he had had that foresight. And
he hated the bugle for reminding him of it. He hated it
more than he had imagined. He could not have imagined
himself using profanity even to himself. He must have been
profoundly moved. Deucedly and profoundly moved at that
beastly noise. It had come over the day like a disaster. He
saw every detail of Marie Léonie's room as it had been
on that day. There was, on the marble mantelshelf, under
an immense engraving of the Sistine Madonna, a feeding-
cup over a night-light in which Marie Léonie had been
keeping some sort of pap warm for him. . . . Probably the
last food to which he had ever helped himself. . . .

BUT NO . . . that must have been about twelve, or earlier
or later, on that infernal day. In any case he could not
remember any subsequent meal he had had then; but he
remembered an almost infinitely long period of intense vex-
ation. Of mortification in so far as he could accuse himself
of ever having felt mortified. He could still remember the
fierce intaking of his breath through his nostrils that had
come when Christopher had announced what had seemed to
him then his ruinous intentions. . . . It had not been till
probably four in the morning that Lord Wolstonmark had
rung him, Mark, up to ask him to countermand the transport that was to have gone out from Harwich. . . . At four
in the morning, the idiotic brutes. His substitute had disappeared in the rejoicings, and Lord Wolstonmark had wanted
to know what code they used for Harwich, because the

transport must at all costs be stopped. There was going to
be no advance into Germany. . . . He had never spoken
after that!

His brother was done for; the country finished; he was
as good as down and out, as the phrase was, himself. In
his deep mortification—yes, mortification!—he had said to
Christopher that morning—the 11th November, 1918—that
he would never speak to him again. He hadn't at that moment meant to say that he would never speak to Christopher
at all again—merely that he was never going to speak to
him about affairs—the affairs of Groby! Christopher might
take that immense, far-spreading, grey bothersome house
and the tree and the well and the moors and all the John
Peel outfit. Or he might leave them. He, Mark, was never
going to speak about the matter any more.

He remembered thinking that Christopher might have
taken him to mean that he intended to withdraw, for what
it was worth, the light of his countenance from the Christopher Tietjens ménage. Nothing had been further from his
thoughts. He had a soft corner in his heart for Valentine
Wannop. He had had it ever since sitting, feeling like a fool,
in the anteroom of the War Office, beside her—gnawing at
the handle of his umbrella. But, then, he had recommended
her to become Christopher's mistress: he had, at any rate,
begged her to look after his mutton-chops and his buttons.
So that it wasn't likely that when, a year or so later, Christopher announced that he really was at last going to take
up with the young woman and to chance what came of it—
it wasn't likely that he intended to dissociate himself from
the two of them.

The idea had worried him so much that he had written
a rough note—the last time that his hand had ever held a
pen—to Christopher. He had said that a brother's backing
was not of great use to a woman, but in the special circumstances of the case, he being Tietjens of Groby, for
what it was worth, and Lady Tietjens—Marie Léonie—
being perfectly willing to be seen on all occasions with Valentine and her man, it might be worth something, at any
rate with tenantry and such like.

Well, he hadn't gone back on that!

But once the idea of retiring, not only from the office but
the whole world, had come into his head it had grown
and grown, on top of his mortification and his weariness.
Because he could not conceal from himself that he was
weary to death—of the office, of the nation, of the world

and people. . . . People . . . he was tired of them, and of the streets, and the grass, and the sky and the moors. He had done his job. That was before Wolstonmark had telephoned, and he still thought that he had done his job of getting things here and there about the world to some purpose.

A man is in the world to do his duty by his nation and his family. . . . By his own people first. Well, he had to acknowledge that he had let his own people down pretty badly—beginning with Christopher. Chiefly Christopher. But that reacted on the tenantry.

He had always been tired of the tenantry and Groby. He had been born tired of them. That happens. It happens particularly in old and prominent families. It was odd that Groby and the whole Groby business should so bore him; he supposed he had been born with some kink. All the Tietjenses were born with some sort of kink. It came from the solitude maybe, on the moors, the hard climate, the rough neighbours—possibly even from the fact that Groby Great Tree overshadowed the house. You could not look out of the schoolroom windows at all for its great, ragged trunk, and all the children's wing was darkened by its branches. Black! . . . Funeral plumes! The Hapsburgs were said to hate their palaces—that was no doubt why so many of them, beginning with Juan Ort, had come muckers. At any rate, they had chucked the royalty business.

And at a very early age he had decided that he would chuck the country-gentleman business. He didn't see that he was the one to bother with those confounded, hard-headed beggars or with those confounded wind-swept moors and wet valley bottoms. One owed the blighters a duty, but one did not have to live among them or see that they aired their bedrooms. It had been mostly swank that, always; since the Corn Laws, it had been almost entirely swank. Still, it is obvious that a landlord owes something to the estate from which he and his fathers have drawn their incomes for generations and generations.

Well, he had never intended to do it, because he had been born tired of it. He liked racing and talking about racing to fellows who liked racing. He had intended to do that to the end.

He hadn't been able to.

He had intended to go on living between the office, his chambers, Marie Léonie's and week-ends with race-horse owners of good family until his eyes closed. . . . Of course

God disposes in the end, even of the Tietjenses of Groby!
He had intended to give over Groby, on the death of his
father, to whichever of his brothers had heirs and seemed
likely to run the estate well. That would have been quite
satisfactory. Ted, his next brother, had had his head screwed
on all right. If he had had children he would have filled
the bill. So would the next brother. . . . But neither of them
had had children and both had managed to get killed in
Gallipoli. Even sister Mary, who was actually next to him
and a *maîtresse femme* if ever there was one, had managed
to get killed as a Red Cross matron. *She* would have run
Groby well enough—the great, blowsy, grey woman with a
bit of a moustache.

Thus God had let him down with a bump on Christopher.
. . . Well, Christopher would have run Groby well enough.
But he wouldn't. Wouldn't own a yard of Groby land;
wouldn't touch a penny of Groby money. He was suffering
for it now.

They were both, in effect, suffering, for Mark could not
see what was to become of either Christopher or the estate.

Until his father's death Mark had bothered precious little
about the fellow. He was by fourteen years the younger:
there had been ten children altogether, three of his own
mother's children having died young and one having been
soft. So Christopher had been still a baby when Mark had
left Groby for good—for good except for visits, when he
had brought his umbrella and seen Christopher mooning at
the schoolroom door or in his own mother's sitting-room.
So he had hardly seen the boy.

And at Christopher's wedding he had definitely decided
that he would not see him again—a mug who had got trepanned into marrying a whore. He wished his brother no
ill, but the thought of him made Mark sickish. And then,
for years, he had heard the worst possible rumours about
Christopher. In a way they had rather consoled Mark. God
knows, he cared little enough about the Tietjens family—
particularly for the children by that soft saint. But he would
rather have any brother of his be a wrong un than a mug.

Then gradually, from the gossip that went abroad, he had
come to think that Christopher was a very bad wrong un
indeed. He could account for it easily enough. Christopher
had a soft streak, and what a woman can do to deteriorate
a fellow with a soft streak is beyond belief. And the woman
Christopher had got hold of—who had got hold of him—
passed belief too. Mark did not hold any great opinion of

women at all; if they were a little plump, healthy, a little loyal and not noticeable in their dress, that was enough for him. . . . But Sylvia was as thin as an eel, as full of vice as a mare that's a wrong un, completely disloyal and dressed like any Paris cocotte. Christopher, as he saw it, had had to keep that harlot to the tune of six or seven thousand a year, in a society of all wrong uns too—and on an income of at most two. . . . Plenty for a younger son. But naturally he had had to go wrong to get the money.

So it had seemed to him . . . and it had seemed to matter precious little. He gave a thought to his brother perhaps twice a year. But then one day—just after the two brothers had been killed—their father had come up from Groby to say to Mark at the club:

"Has it occurred to you that since those two boys are killed, that fellow Christopher is practically heir to Groby? You have no legitimate children, have you?" Mark replied that he hadn't any bastards either and that he was certainly not going to marry.

At that date it had seemed to him certain that he was not going to marry papist Marie Léonie Riotor, and certainly he was not going to marry anyone else. So Christopher —or at any rate Christopher's heir—must surely come in to Groby. It had not really, hitherto, occurred to him. But when it was thus put forcibly into his mind he saw instantly that it upset the whole scheme of his life. As he saw Christopher then, the fellow was the last person in the world to have the charge of Groby—for you had to regard that as to some extent a cure of souls. And he himself would not be much better. He was hopelessly out of touch with the estate, and, even though his father's land-steward was a quite efficient fellow, he himself at that date was so hopelessly immersed in the affairs of the then war that he would hardly have a moment of time to learn anything about the property.

There was, therefore, a breakdown in his scheme of life. That was already a pretty shaking sort of affair. Mark was accustomed to regard himself as master of his fate—as being so limited in his ambitions and so entrenched behind his habits and his wealth that if circumstances need not of necessity bend to his will, fate could hardly touch him.

And it was one thing for a Tietjens younger son to be a bold sort of law-breaker—or at any rate that he should be contemptuous of restraint. It was quite another that the heir to Groby should be a soft sort of bad hat whose distasteful bunglings led his reputation to stink in the nostrils of all his

own class, if a younger son can be said to have a class. . . .
At any rate in the class to which his father and eldest brother
belonged. Tietjens was said to have sold his wife to her
cousin the duke at so contemptible a price that he was obviously penniless even after that transaction. He had sold
her to other rich men—to bank-managers, for instance. Yet
even after that he was reduced to giving stumer cheques.
If a man sold his soul to the devil he should at least insist
on a good price. Similar transactions were said to distinguish
the social set in which that bitch moved—but most of the
men who, according to Ruggles, sold their wives to members
of the government obtained millions by governmental financial tips—or peerages. Not infrequently they obtained both
peerages and millions. But Christopher was such a confounded ass that he had got neither the one nor the other.
His cheques were turned down for twopences. And he was
such a bungler that he must needs get with child the daughter
of their father's oldest friend, and let the fact be known to
the whole world. . . .

This information he had from Ruggles—and it killed their
father. Well, he, Mark, was absolutely to blame: that was
that. But—infinitely worse—it had made Christopher absolutely determined not to accept a single penny of the money
that had become Mark's and that had been his father's. And
Christopher was as obstinate as a hog. For that Mark did
not blame him. It was a Tietjens job to be as obstinate as
a hog.

He couldn't, however, disabuse his mind of the idea that
Christopher's refusal of Groby and all that came from Groby
was as much a manifestation of the confounded saintliness
that he got from his soft mother as of a spirit of resentment.
Christopher *wanted* to rid himself of his great possessions.
The fact that his father and brother had believed him to
be what Marie Léonie would have called *maquereau* and had
thus insulted him he had merely grasped at with eagerness
as an excuse. He wanted to be out of the world. That was
it. He wanted to be out of a disgustingly inefficient and
venial world, just as he, Mark, also wanted to be out of a
world that he found almost more fusionless and dishonest
than Christopher found it.

At any rate, at the first word that they had had about
the heirship to Groby after their father's death, Christopher
had declared that he, Mark, might take his money to the
devil and the ownership of Groby with it. He proposed never
to forgive either his father or Mark. He had only consented

to take Mark by the hand at the urgent solicitation of Valentine Wannop. . . .

That had been the most dreadful moment of Mark's life. The country was, even then, going to the devil; his brother proposed to starve himself; Groby, by his brother's wish, was to fall into the hands of that bitch. . . . And the country went further and further towards the devil, and his brother starved worse and worse . . . and as for Groby . . .

The boy who practically owned Groby had, at the first sound of the voice of the woman who wore white riding-kit and called "Hi, hup!"—at the very first sound of her voice the boy had scampered off through the raspberry canes and was now against the hedge, whilst she leaned down over him, laughing, and her horse leaned over behind her. Fittleworth was smiling at them benevolently and at the same time continuing his conversation with Gunning. . . .

The woman was too old for the boy, who had gone scarlet at the sound of her voice. Sylvia had been too old for Christopher: she had got him on the hop when he had been only a kid. . . . The world went on.

He was nevertheless thankful for the respite. He had to acknowledge to himself that he was not as young as he had been. He had a great deal to think of if he was to get the hang of—he was certainly not going to interfere with—the world, and having to listen to conversations that were mostly moral apophthegms had tired him. He had got too many at too-short intervals. If he had spoken he would not have, but, because he did not speak, both the lady who was descended from the Maintenon and that boy had peppered him with moral points of view that all required to be considered, without leaving him enough time to get his breath mentally.

The lady had called them a corrupt and effete aristocracy. They were probably not corrupt, but certainly, regarded as landowners, they were effete—both he and Christopher. They were simply bored at the contemplation of that terrific nuisance—and refusing to perform the duties of their post, they refused the emoluments too. He could not remember that, after childhood, he had ever had a penny out of Groby. They would not accept that post; they had taken others. . . . Well, this was his, Mark's, last post. . . . He could have smiled at his grim joke.

Of Christopher he was not so sure. That ass was a terrific sentimentalist. Probably he would have liked to be a great landowner, keeping up the gates on the estate—like Fittleworth, who was a perfect lunatic about gates. He was probably even now jaw-jawing Gunning about them, smacking his boot-top with his crop-handle. Yes—keeping up the gates and seeing that the tenants' land gave so many bushels of wheat to the acre or supported so many sheep the year round. . . . How many sheep would an acre keep all the year round, and how many bushels of wheat, under proper farming, should it give? He, Mark, had not the least idea. Christopher would know—with the difference to be expected of every acre of all the thousand acres of Groby. . . . Yes, Christopher had pored over Groby with the intentness of a mother looking at her baby's face!

So that his refusal to take on that stewardship might very well arise from a sort of craving for mortification of the spirit. Old Campion had once said that he believed—he positively believed with shudders—that Christopher desired to live in the spirit of Christ. That had seemed horrible to the general, but Mark did not see that it was horrible, per se. . . . He doubted, however, whether Christ would have refused to manage Groby had it been his job. Christ was a sort of an Englishman, and Englishmen did not, as a rule, refuse to do their jobs. . . . They had not used to. Now, no doubt, they did. It was a Russian sort of trick. He had heard that even before the revolution great Russian nobles would disperse their estates, give their serfs their liberty, put on a hair-shirt and sit by the roadside begging. . . . Something like that. Perhaps Christopher was a symptom that the English were changing. He himself was not. He was just lazy and determined—and done with it!

He had not at first been able to believe that Christopher was resolved—with a Yorkshire resolution—to have nothing to do with Groby or his, Mark's, money. He had, nevertheless, felt a warm admiration for his brother the moment the words had been said. Christopher would take none of his father's money; he would never forgive either his father or his brother. A proper Yorkshire sentiment, uttered coldly and, as it were, good-humouredly. His eyes, naturally, had goggled, but he had displayed no other emotion.

Nevertheless, Mark had imagined that he might be up to some game. He might be merely meaning to bring Mark to his knees. . . . But how could Mark be more brought to his knees than by offering to give over Groby to his brother? It is true he had kept that up his sleeve whilst his brother had been out in France. After all, there was no sense in offering a fellow who might be going to become food for powder the management of great possessions. He had felt a certain satisfaction in the fact that Christopher *was* going out, though he was confoundedly sorry too. He really admired Christopher for doing it—and he imagined that it might clear some of the smirchiness that must attach to Christopher's reputation, in spite of what he now knew to be his brother's complete guiltlessness of the crimes that had been attributed to him. He had, of course, been wrong —he had reckoned without the determined discredit that, after the war was over, the civilian population would contrive to attach to every man who had been to the front as a fighting soldier. After all, that was natural enough. The majority of the male population was civilian, and, once the war was over and there was no more risk, they would bitterly regret that they had not gone. They would take it out of the ex-soldiers, all right!

So that Christopher had rather been additionally discredited than much helped by his services to the country. Sylvia had been able to put it, very reasonably, that Christopher was by nature that idle and dissolute thing, a soldier. That, in times of peace, had helped her a great deal.

Still, Mark had been pleased with his brother, and once Christopher had been invalided back, and had returned to his old-tin saving depot near Ealing, Mark had at once set wheels in motion to get his brother demobilized so that he might look after Groby. By that time Groby was inhabited by Sylvia, the boy, and Sylvia's mother. The estate just had to be managed by the land-steward who had served his father, neither Sylvia nor her family having any finger in that; though her mother was able to assure him, Mark, that the estate was doing as well as the Agricultural Committees of grocers and stock-jobbers would let it. They insisted on wheat being sown on exposed moors where nothing but heather had a chance, and active moorland sheep being fattened in water-bottoms full of liver fluke. But the land-steward fought them as well as one man could be expected to fight the chosen of a nation of small shopkeepers. . . .

And at that date—the date of Christopher's return to Ealing—Mark had still imagined that Christopher had really only been holding out for the possession of Groby. He was, therefore, disillusioned rather nastily. He had managed to get Christopher demobilized—without telling him anything about it—by just about the time when the armistice came along. . . . And then he found that he really had put the fat in the fire!

He had practically beggared the wretched fellow, who,

counting on living on his pay for at least a year longer, had mortgaged his blood-money in order to go into a sort of partnership in an old-furniture business with a confounded American. And, of course, the blood-money was considerably diminished, being an allowance made to demobilized officers computed on the number of their days of service. So he had docked Christopher of two or three hundred pounds. That was the sort of mucky situation into which Christopher might be expected to be got by his well-wishers. . . . There he had been, just before Armistice Day, upon the point of demobilization and without an available penny! It appeared that he had to sell even the few books that Sylvia had left him when she had stripped his house.

That agreeable truth had forced itself on Mark at just the moment when he had been so rotten bad with pneumonia that he might be expected to cash in at any moment. Marie Léonie had indeed, of her own initiative, telephoned to Christopher that he had better come to see his brother if he wanted to meet him on this side of the grave.

They had at once started arguing—or, rather, each had started exposing his views. Christopher stated what he was going to do, and Mark his horror at what Christopher proposed. Mark's horror came from the fact that Christopher proposed to eschew comfort. An Englishman's duty is to secure for himself forever reasonable clothing, a clean shirt a day, a couple of mutton-chops grilled without condiments, two floury potatoes, an apple-pie with a piece of Stilton and pulled bread, a pint of Club Médoc, a clean room, in the winter a good fire in the grate, a comfortable arm-chair, a comfortable woman to see that all these were prepared for you, to keep you warm in bed and to brush your bowler and fold your umbrella in the morning. When you had that secure for life, you could do what you liked provided that what you did never endangered that security. What was to be said against that?

Christopher had nothing to advance except that he was not going to live in that way. He was not going to live in that way unless he could secure that, or something like it, by his own talents. His only available and at the same time marketable talent was his gift for knowing genuine old furniture. So he was going to make a living out of old furniture. He had had his scheme perfectly matured; he had even secured an American partner, a fellow who had as great a gift for the cajolement of American purchasers of old stuff as he, Christopher, had for its discovery. It was still the war then, but Christopher and his partner, between them, had predicted the American mopping up of the world's gold supply and the consequent stripping of European houses of old stuff. . . . At that you could make a living.

Other careers, he said, were barred to him. The Department of Statistics, in which he had formerly had a post, had absolutely cold-shouldered him. They were not only adamant, they were also vindictive against civil servants who had become serving soldiers. They took the view that those members of their staffs who had preferred serving were idle and dissolute fellows who had merely taken up arms in order to satisfy their lusts for women. Women had naturally preferred soldiers to civilians; the civilians were now getting back on them. That was natural.

Mark agreed that it was natural. Before he had been interested in his brother as a serving soldier, he had been inclined to consider most soldiers as incompetent over transport and, in general, nuisances. He agreed, too, that Christopher could not go back to the department. There he was certainly a marked man. He could possibly have insisted on his rights to be taken back even though his lungs, being by now pretty damaged by exposure, might afford them a pretext for legally refusing him. H.M. Civil Service and departments have the right to refuse employment to persons likely to become unfit for good. A man who has lost an eye may be refused by any department because he may lose the other and so become liable for a pension. But, even if Christopher forced himself on the department, they would have their bad mark against him. He had been too rude to them during the war when they had tried to force him to employ himself in the faking of statistics that the ministry had coerced the department into supplying in order to dish the French, who demanded more troops.

With that point of view, Mark found himself entirely in sympathy. His long association with Marie Léonie, his respect for the way in which she had her head screwed on, the constant intimacy with the life and point of view of French individuals of the *petite bourgeoisie* which her gossip had given him—all these things, together with his despair for the future of his own country, had given him a very considerable belief in the destinies and, indeed, in the virtues of the country across the channel. It would, therefore, have been very distasteful to him that his brother should take pay from an organization that had been employed to deal treacherously with our allies. It had, indeed, become extremely distasteful to him to take pay himself from a government that had forced such a course upon the nation, and he would thankfully have resigned from his office if he had not considered that his services were indispensable to the successful prosecution of the war which was then still proceeding. He wanted to be done with it, but, at the moment, he saw no chance. The war was by then obviously proceeding towards a successful issue. Owing to the military genius of the French, who, by then, had the supreme command, the enemy nations were daily being forced to abandon great stretches of territory. But that only made the calls on transport the greater, whilst, if we were successfully and unwastefully to occupy the enemy capital, as at that date he imagined that we obviously must, the demand for the provision of transport must become almost unmeasurable.

Still, that was no argument for the re-entry of his brother into the service of the country. As he saw things, public life had become—and must remain for a long period—so demoralized by the members of the then government, with their devious foreign policies and their intimacies with a class of shady financiers such as had never hitherto had any finger in the English political pie—public life had become so discreditable an affair that the only remedy was for the real governing classes to retire altogether from public pursuits. Things, in short, must become worse before they could grow better. With the dreadful condition of ruin at home and foreign discredit to which the country must almost immediately emerge under the conduct of the Scotch grocers, Frankfort financiers, Welsh pettifoggers, Midland armament-manufacturers and South Country incompetents who during the later years of the war had intrigued themselves into office—with that dreadful condition staring it in the face, the country must return to something like its old standards of North Country common sense and English probity. The old governing class to which he and his belonged might never return to power, but, whatever revolutions took place—and he did not care!—the country must reawaken to the necessity for exacting of whoever might be its governing class some semblance of personal probity and public honouring of pledges. He obviously was out of it, or he would be out of it with the end of the war, for even from his bed he had taken no small part in the directing of affairs at his office. . . . A state of war obviously favoured the coming to the top of all kinds of devious stormy petrels; that was inevitable and could not be helped. But in normal times a country—every country—was true to itself.

Nevertheless, he was very content that his brother should, in the interim, have no share in affairs. Let him secure his mutton-chop, his pint of claret, his woman and his umbrella, and it mattered not into what obscurity he retired. But how was that to be secured? There had seemed to be several ways.

He was aware, for instance, that Christopher was both a mathematician of no mean order and a Churchman. He might perfectly well take orders, assume the charge of one of the three family livings that Mark had in his gift, and, whilst competently discharging the duties of his cure, pursue whatever are the occupations of a well-cared-for mathematician.

Christopher, however, whilst avowing his predilection for such a life—which, as Mark saw it, was exactly fitted to his asceticism, his softness in general and his private tastes —Christopher admitted that there was an obstacle to his assuming such a cure of souls—an obstacle of an insuperable nature. Mark at once asked him if he were, in fact, living with Miss Wannop. But Christopher answered that he had not seen Miss Wannop since the day of his second proceeding to the front. They had then agreed that they were not the sort of persons to begin a hidden intrigue, and the affair had proceeded no further.

Mark was, however, aware that a person of Christopher's way of thinking might well feel inhibited from taking on a cure of souls if, in spite of the fact that he had abstained from seducing a young woman, he nevertheless privately desired to enter into illicit relations with her, and that that was sufficient to justify him in saying that an insuperable obstacle existed. He did not know that he himself agreed, but it was not his business to interfere between any man and his conscience in a matter of the Church. He was himself no very good Christian, at any rate as regards the relationships of men and women. Nevertheless, the Church of England was the Church of England. No doubt, had Christopher been a papist he could have had the young woman for his housekeeper and no one would have bothered.

But what the devil, then, was his brother to do? He had been offered, as a sop in the pan, and to keep him quiet, no doubt, over the affair of the Department of Statistics, a vice-consulate in some Mediterranean port—Toulon or Leghorn, or something of the sort. That might have done

well enough. It was absurd to think of a Tietjens, heir to
Groby, being under the necessity of making a living. It was
fantastic, but if Christopher was in a fantastic mood there
was nothing to be done about it. A vice-consulate is a potty
sort of job. You attend to ships' manifests, get members of
crews out of jail, give old lady tourists the addresses of
boarding-houses kept by English or half-castes, or provide
the vice-admirals of visiting British squadrons with the names
of local residents who should be invited to entertainments
given on the flagship. It was a potty job; innocuous too,
if it could be regarded as a sort of marking time. . . . And
at that moment Mark thought that Christopher was still holding out for some sort of concession on Mark's part before definitely assuming the charge of Groby, its tenants
and its mineral rights. . . . But there were insuperable ob-
jections to even the vice-consulate. In the first place, the
job would have been in the public service, a fact to which,
as has been said, Mark strongly objected. Then, the job was
offered as a sort of a bribe. And, in addition, the consular
service exacts from everyone who occupies a consular or
vice-consular post the deposit of a sum of four hundred
pounds sterling, and Christopher did not possess even so much
as four hundred shillings. . . . And, in addition, as Mark
was well aware, Miss Wannop might again afford an obstacle. A British vice-consul might possibly keep a Maltese
or Levantine in a back street and no harm done, but he
probably could not live with an English young woman of
family and position without causing so much scandal as to
make him lose his job. . . .

It was at this point that Mark again, but for the last
time, asked his brother why he did not divorce Sylvia.

By that time Marie Léonie had retired to get some rest.
She was pretty worn out. Mark's illness had been long and
serious; she had nursed him with such care that during the
whole time she had not been out into the streets except
once or twice to go across the road to the Catholic church,
where she would offer a candle or so for his recovery, and
once or twice to remonstrate with the butcher as to the
quality of the meat he supplied for Mark's broths. In addition, on many days, she had worked late, under Mark's directions, on papers that the office had sent him. She either
could not or would not put her man into the charge of any
kind of night-nurse. She alleged that the war had mopped
up every kind of available attendant on the sick, but Mark
shrewdly suspected that she had made no kind of effort to

secure an assistant. There was her national dread of draughts to account for that. She accepted with discipline, if with despair, the English doctor's dictum that fresh air must be admitted to the sick-room, but she sat up night after night in a hooded chair, watching for any change in the wind and moving in accordance a complicated arrangement of screens that she maintained between her patient and the open window. She had, however, surrendered Mark to his brother without a murmur, and had quietly gone to her own room to sleep, and Mark, though he carried on almost every kind of conversation with his brother, and though he would not have asked her to leave them in order that he might engage on topics that his brother might like to regard as private—Mark seized the opportunity to lay before Christopher what he thought of Sylvia and the relationships of that singular couple.

It amounted, in the end, to the fact that Mark wanted Christopher to divorce his wife, and to the fact that Christopher had not altered in his views that a man cannot divorce a woman. Mark put it that if Christopher intended to take up with Valentine, it mattered practically very little whether after an attempt at a divorce he married her or not. What a man has to do if he means to take up with a woman, and as far as possible to honour her, is to make some sort of fight of it—as a symbol. Marriage, if you do not regard it as a sacrament—as, no doubt, it ought to be regarded—was nothing more than a token that a couple intended to stick to each other. Now-a-days people—the right people—bothered precious little about anything but that. A constant change of partners was a social nuisance; you could not tell whether you could or couldn't invite a couple together to a tea-fight. And society existed for social functions. That was why promiscuity was no good. For social functions you had to have an equal number of men and women, or someone got left out of conversations, and so you had to know who, officially in the social sense, went with whom. Everyone knew that all the children of Lupus at the War Office were really the children of the Prime Minister, so that presumably the countess and the Prime Minister slept together most of the time, but that did not mean that you invited the Prime Minister and the woman to social-official functions, because they hadn't any ostensible token of union. On the contrary, you invited Lord and Lady Lupus together to all functions that would get into the papers, but you took care to have

the lady at any private, week-endish parties or intimate din-
ners to which the Chief was coming.

And Christopher had to consider that if it came to marriage ninety per cent of the inhabitants of the world regarded the marriages of almost everybody else as invalid.
A papist obviously could not regard a marriage before an
English registrar or a French *maire* as having any moral
validity. At best it was no more than a demonstration of
aspirations after constancy. You went before a functionary
publicly to assert that man and woman intended to stick
to each other. Equally for extreme Protestants a marriage
by a papist priest, or a minister of any other sect, or a
Buddhist lama, had not the blessing of their own brand of
Deity. So that really, to all practical intents, it was sufficient
if a couple really assured their friends that they intended
to stick together, if possible, forever; if not, at least for
years enough to show that they had made a good shot at it.
Mark invited Christopher to consult whom he liked in his,
Mark's, particular set and he would find that they agreed
with his views.

So he was anxious that if Christopher intended to take
up with the Wannop young woman he should take at least
a shot at a divorce. He might not succeed in getting one.
He obviously had grounds enough, but Sylvia might make
counter-allegations, he, Mark, couldn't say with what chance
of success. He was prepared himself to accept his brother's
assertions of complete innocence, but Sylvia was a clever
devil and there was no knowing what view a judge might
take. Where there had been such a hell of a lot of smoke
he might consider that there must be enough flame to justify
refusing a divorce. There would no doubt be, thus—a beastly
stink. But a beastly stink would be better than the sort of
veiled ill fame that Sylvia had contrived to get attached to
Christopher. And the fact that Christopher had faced the
stink and made the attempt would be at least that amount
of tribute to Miss Wannop. Society was good-natured and
was inclined to take the view that if a fellow had faced
his punishment and taken it he was pretty well absolved.
There might be people who would hold out against them,
but Mark supposed that what Christopher wanted for himself and his girl was reasonable material comfort with a
society of sufficient people of the right sort to give them a
dinner or so a week and a week-end or so a month in the
week-ending season.

Christopher had acquiesced in the justness of his views

with so much amiability that Mark began to hope that he would get his way in the larger matter of Groby. He was prepared to go further and to stake as much as his assurance that if Christopher would settle down at Groby, accept a decent income and look after the estate, he, Mark, would assure his brother and Valentine of bearable social circumstances.

Christopher, however, had made no answer at all beyond saying that if he tried to divorce Sylvia it would apparently ruin his old-furniture business. For his American partner assured him that in the United States if a man divorced his wife instead of letting her divorce him no one would do any business with him. He had mentioned the case of a man called Blum, a pretty warm stock-exchange man, who insisted on divorcing his wife against the advice of his friends; he found when he returned to the stock-market that all his clients cold-shouldered him, so that he was ruined. And as these fellows were shortly going to mop up everything in the world, including the old-furniture trade, Christopher supposed that he would have to study their prejudices.

He had come across his partner rather curiously. The fellow, whose father had been a German Jew but a naturalized American citizen, had been in Berlin mopping up German old furniture for sale in the American interior, where he had a flourishing business. So, when America had come in on the side that was not German, the Germans had just simply dropped on Mr. Schatzweiler in their pleasant way, incorporated him in their forces and had sent him to the front as a miserable little Tommy before the Americans had been a month in the show. And there, amongst the prisoners he had had to look after, Christopher had found the little, large-eyed sensitive creature, unable to speak a word of German but just crazy about the furniture and tapestries in the French châteaux that the prisoners passed on their marches. Christopher had befriended him; kept him as far as possible separated from the other prisoners, who naturally did not like him; and had a good many conversations with him.

It had appeared that Mr. Schatzweiler had had a good deal to do in the way of buying with Sir John Robertson, the old old-furniture millionaire, who was a close friend of Sylvia's and had been so considerable an admirer of Christopher's furniture-buying gifts that he had, years ago, proposed to take Christopher into partnership with himself. At that time Christopher had regarded Sir John's proposals as outside the range of his future; he had then been employed in the Department of Statistics. But the proposal had always amused and rather impressed him. If, that is to say, that hard-headed old Scotsman who had made a vast fortune at his trade made to Christopher a quite serious business proposition on the strength of Christopher's *flair* in the matter of old woods and curves, Christopher himself might take his own gifts with a certain seriousness.

And by the time he came to be in command of the escort over those miserable creatures, he had pretty well realized that after the necessity for escorts was over he would jolly well have to consider how he was going to make a living for himself. That was certain. He was not going to reinsert himself amongst the miserable collection of squits who occupied themselves in his old department; he was too old to continue in the army; he was certainly not going to accept a penny from Groby sources. He did not care what became of him—but his not caring did not take any tragico-romantic form. He would be quite prepared to live in a hut on a hill-side and cook his meals over three bricks outside the door—but that was not a method of life that was very practicable and even that needed money. Everyone who served in the army at the front knew how little it took to keep life going—and satisfactory. But he did not see the world, when it settled down again, turning itself into a place fit for old soldiers who had learned to appreciate frugality. On the contrary, the old soldiers would be chivvied to hell by a civilian population who abhorred them. So that merely to keep clean and out of debt was going to be a tough job.

So, in his long vigils in tents, beneath the moon, with the sentries walking, challenging from time to time, round the barbed-wire stockades, the idea of Sir John's proposition had occurred to him with some force. It had gathered strength from his meeting with Mr. Schatzweiler. The little fellow was a shivering artist, and Christopher had enough of superstition in him to be impressed by the coincidence of their having come together in such unlikely circumstances. After all, Providence must let up on him after a time, so why should not this unfortunate and impressively Oriental member of the Chosen People be a sign of a covenant? In a way he reminded Christopher of his former protégé Macmaster—he had the same dark eyes, the same shape, the same shivering eagerness.

That he was a Jew and an American did not worry Christopher; he had not objected to the fact that Macmaster had been the son of a Scotch grocer. If he had to go into partnership and be thrown into close contact with anyone at all, he did not care much who it was as long as it was not either a bounder or a man of his own class and race. To be in close mental communion with either an English bounder or an Englishman of good family would, he was aware, be intolerable to him. But for a little shivering, artistic Jew, as of old for Macmaster, he was quite capable of feeling a real fondness—as you might for an animal. Their manners were not your manners and could not be expected to be, and whatever their intelligences, they would have a certain little alertness, a certain exactness of thought. . . . Besides, if they did you in, as every business partner or protégé must be expected to do, you did not feel the same humiliation as you did if you were swindled by a man of your own race and station. In the one case it was only what was to be expected, in the other you were faced with the fact that your own tradition had broken down. And under the long strain of the war he had outgrown alike the mentality and the traditions of his own family and his own race. The one and the other were not fitted to endure long strains.

So he welcomed the imploring glances and the eventual Oriental gratitude of that little man in his unhappy tent. For, naturally, by communicating in his weighty manner with the United States headquarters when he happened to find himself in its vicinity, he secured the release of the little fellow, who was by now safely back somewhere in the interior of the North American continent.

But before that happened he had exchanged a certain amount of correspondence with Sir John, and had discovered from him and from one or two chance members of the American Expeditionary Force that the little man was quite a good old-furniture dealer. Sir John had by that time gone out of business and his letters were not particularly cordial to Tietjens—which was only what was to be expected if Sylvia had been shedding her charms over him. But it had appeared that Mr. Schatzweiler had had a great deal of business with Sir John, who had indeed supplied him with a great part of his material, and so, if Sir John had gone out of business, Mr. Schatzweiler would need to find in England someone to take Sir John's place. And that was not going to be extraordinarily easy, for what with the amount of his money that the Germans had mopped up— they had sold him immense quantities of old furniture and got paid for it, and had then enlisted him in the ranks of

their Brandenburgers, where naturally he could do nothing
with carved-oak chests that had elaborate steel hinges and
locks. . . . What then with that, and his prolonged absence
from the neighbourhood of Detroit, where he had mostly
found his buyers, Mr. Schatzweiler found himself extremely
hampered in his activities. It therefore fell to Christopher,
if he was to go into partnership with the now sanguine and
charming Oriental, to supply an immediate sum of money.
That had not been easy, but by means of mortgaging his
pay and his blood-money, and selling the books that Sylvia
had left him, he had been able to provide Mr. Schatzweiler
with enough to make at least a start somewhere across the
water. . . . And Mr. Schatzweiler and Christopher had between them evolved an ingenious scheme along lines that
the American had long contemplated, taking into account
the tastes of his countrymen and the nature of the times.

Mark had listened to his brother during all this with indulgence and even with pleasure. If a Tietjens contemplated
going into trade, he might at least contemplate an amusing
trade carried on in a spirited manner. And what Christopher
humorously projected was at least more dignified than stock-
broking or bill-discounting. Moreover, he was pretty well
convinced by this time that his brother was completely reconciled to him and to Groby.

It was about then and when he had again begun to introduce the topic of Groby that Christopher got up from
the chair at the bedside that he had been occupying and,
having taken his brother's wrist in his cool fingers, remarked:

"Your temperature's pretty well down. Don't you think
it is about time that you set about marrying Charlotte? I
suppose you mean to marry her before this bout is finished;
you might have a relapse."

Mark remembered that speech perfectly well, with the
addition that if he, Christopher, hurried about it they might
get the job done that night. It must therefore then have
been about one o'clock of an afternoon about three weeks
before the 11th November, 1918.

Mark had replied that he would be much obliged to Christopher, and Christopher, having roused Marie Léonie and
told her that he would be back in time to let her have a
good night's rest, disappeared, saying that he was going
straight to Lambeth. In those days, supposing you could command thirty pounds or so, there was no difficulty in getting
married at the shortest possible notice, and Christopher had

promoted too many last-minute marriages amongst his men not to know the ropes.

Mark viewed the transaction with a good deal of satisfaction. It had needed no arguing; if the proceeding had the approval of the heir-presumptive to Groby, there was nothing more to be said against it. And Mark took the view that if he agreed to a proceeding that Christopher could only have counselled as heir-presumptive, that was an additional reason for Mark's expecting that Christopher would eventually consent to administer Groby himself.

6 ～

THAT WOULD have been three weeks before the eleventh of November. His mind boggled a little at computing what the actual date in October must have been. With his then pneumonia his mind had not much registered the dates of that period; days had gone by in fever and boredom. Still, a man ought to remember the date of his wedding. Say it had been the twentieth of October, 1918. The twentieth of October had been his father's birthday. When he came to think of it he could remember remembering hazily that it was queer that he should be going out of life on the date his father had entered it. It made a sort of full stop. And it made a full stop that, practically on that day, papists entered into their own in Groby. He had, that is to say, made up his mind to the fact that Christopher's son would have Groby as a home even if Christopher didn't. And the boy was by now a full-fledged papist, pickled and oiled and wafered and all. Sylvia had rubbed the fact in about a week ago by sending him a card for his nephew's provisional baptism and first communion about a week before. It had astonished him that he had not felt more bitter.

He had not any doubt that the fact had reconciled him to his marriage with Marie Léonie. He had told his brother a year or so before that he would never marry her because she was a papist, but he was aware that then he was only chipping at Spelden, the fellow that wrote Spelden on Sacrilege, a book that predicted all sorts of disaster for fellows who owned former papist Church lands or who had displaced papists. When he had told Christopher that he would never marry Charlotte—he had called her Charlotte for reasons of camouflage before the marriage—he had been quite aware that he was chipping at Spelden's ghost—for Spelden must have been dead a hundred years or so. As it were, he had been saying grimly if pleasantly to that bogy:

"Eh, old un. You see. You may prophesy disaster to Groby because a Tietjens was given it over the head of one of your fellows in Dutch William's time. But you can't frighten me into making an honest woman—let alone a lady of Groby—out of a papist."

And he hadn't. He would swear that no idea of disaster to Groby had entered his head at the date of the marriage. Now, he would not say; but of what he felt then he was certain. He remembered thinking whilst the ceremony was going on of the words of Fraser of Lovat before they executed him in the Forty-Five. They had told him on the scaffold that if he would make some sort of submission to George II they would spare his body from being exhibited in quarters on the spikes of the buildings in Edinburgh. And Fraser had answered: "An' the King will have my heid, I care not what he may do with my ——," naming a part of a gentleman that is not now mentioned in drawing-rooms. So, if a papist was to inhabit Groby House, it mattered precious little if the first Lady Tietjens of Groby were papist or heathen.

A man as a rule does not marry his mistress whilst he has any kick in him. If he still aims at a career, it might hinder him if she were known to have been his mistress, or, of course, a fellow who wants to make a career might want to help himself on by making a good marriage. Even if a man does not want to make a career he may think that a woman who has been his mistress as like as not may cuckold him after marriage, for, if she has gone wrong with him, she would be more apt to go wrong elsewhere as well. But if a fellow is practically finished, those considerations disappear, and he remembers that you go to hell if you seduce virgins. It is as well at one time or another to make your peace with your Creator. "Forever" is a long word and God is said to disapprove of unconsecrated unions.

Besides, it would very likely please Marie Léonie, though she had never said a word about it, and it would certainly dish Sylvia, who was no doubt counting on being the first Lady Tietjens of Groby. And then, too, it would undoubtedly make Marie Léonie safer. In one way and another he had given his mistress quite a number of things that might well be desirable to that bitch, and neither his nor Christopher's lives were worth much, whilst Chancery can be a very expensive affair if you get into it.

And he was aware that he had always had a soft spot in his heart for Marie Léonie, otherwise he would not have provided her with the name of Charlotte for public consumption. A man gives his mistress another name if there is any chance of his marrying her, so that it may look as if he were marrying someone else when he does it. "Marie Léonie Riotor" looks different from a casual "Charlotte." It gives her a better chance in the world outside.

So it had been well enough. The world was changing and there was no particular reason why he should not change with it. . . . And he had not been able to conceal from himself that he was getting on the way. Time lengthened out. When he had come in drenched from one of the potty local meetings that they had had to fall back on during the war, he had known that something was coming to him, because after Marie Léonie had tucked him up in bed he could not remember the strain of the winner of some handicap of no importance. Marie Léonie had given him a goodish tot of rum with butter in it and that might have made him hazy—but, all the same, that had never happened to him in his life before, rum or no rum. And by now he had forgotten even the name of the winner and the meeting. . . .

He could not conceal from himself that his memory was failing, though otherwise he considered himself to be as sound a man as he had ever been. But when it came to memory, ever since that day, his brain had checked at times as a tired horse will at a fence. . . . A tired horse!

He could not bring himself to the computation of what three weeks back from the eleventh of November came to; his brain would not go at it. For the matter of that, he could remember precious little of the events of that three weeks in their due order. Christopher had certainly been about, relieving Marie Léonie at night and attending to him with a soft, goggle-eyed attentiveness that only a man with a saint for a mother could have put up. For hours and hours he would read aloud in Boswell's *Life of Johnson,* for which Mark had had a fancy.

And Mark could remember drowsing off with satisfaction to the sound of the voice and drowsing with satisfaction awake again, still to the sound of the voice. For Christopher had the idea that if his voice went droning on it would make Mark's slumbers more satisfactory.

Satisfaction. . . . Perhaps the last satisfaction that Mark was ever to know. For at that time—during those three weeks—he had not been able to believe that Christopher really meant to stick out about the matter of Groby. How could you believe that a fellow who waited on you with the softness of a girl built of meal-sacks was determined to . . . call it, break your heart. That was what it came to. . . . A fellow, too, who agreed in the most astounding manner with your views of things in general. A fellow, for the matter of that, who knew ten times as much as you did. A damn learned fellow. . . .

Mark had no contempt for learning—particularly for younger sons. The country was going to the dogs because of the want of education of the younger sons, whose business it was to do the work of the nation. It was a very old North Country rhyme that, that when land is gone and money spent, then learning is most excellent. No, he had no contempt for learning. He had never acquired any because he was too lazy: a little Sallust, a little Cornelius Nepos, a touch of Horace, enough French to read a novel and follow what Marie Léonie said. . . . Even to himself he called her Marie Léonie once he was married to her. It had made her jump at first!

But Christopher was a damn learned fellow. Their father, a younger son at the beginning, had been damn learned too. They said that even at his death he had been one of the best Latinists in England—the intimate friend of that fellow Wannop, the professor. . . . A great age at which to die by his own hand, his father's! Why, if that marriage had been on the 20th October, 1918, his father, then dead, must have been born on the 20th October, what? . . . 1834. . . . No, that was not possible. . . . No: '44. *His* father, Mark knew, had been born in 1812—before Waterloo!

Great stretches of time. Great changes! Yet father had not been an incult sort of a man. On the contrary, if he was burly and determined, he was quiet. And sensitive. He had certainly loved Christopher very dearly—and Christopher's mother.

Father was very tall, stooping like a toppling poplar towards the end. His head seemed very distant, as if he hardly heard you. Iron-grey; short-whiskered! Absent-minded towards the end. Forgetting where he had put his handkerchief and where his spectacles were when he had pushed them up on to his forehead. . . . He had been a younger son who had never spoken to his father for forty years. Father's father had never forgiven him for marrying Miss Selby of Biggen . . . not because it was marrying below him, but because his father had wanted their mother for his eldest son. . . . And they had been poor in their early childhood, wandering over the Continent, to settle at last in Dijon, where they had kept some sort of state . . . a large house in the middle of the town with several servants. He never could imagine how their mother had done it on four hundred a year. But she had. A hard woman. But father had kept in with French people and corresponded with Professor Wannop and Learned Societies. He had always regarded him, Mark, as rather a dunce. . . . Father would sit reading in elegantly bound books, by the hour. His study had been one of the showrooms of the house in Dijon.

Did he commit suicide? If so, then Valentine Wannop was his daughter. There could not be much getting away from that, not that it mattered much. In that case Christopher would be living with his half-sister. . . . Not that it mattered much. It did not matter much to him, Mark . . . but his father was the sort of man that it might drive to suicide.

A luckless sort of beggar, Christopher! . . . If you took the whole conglobulation at its worst—the father suiciding, the son living with his sister in open sin, the son's son not his son, and Groby going over to papist hands . . . That was the sort of thing that would happen to a Tietjens of the Christopher variety: to any Tietjens who would not get out or get under as he, Mark, had done. Tietjenses took what they damn well got for doing what they damn well wanted to. Well, it landed them in that sort of post. . . . A last post, for, if that boy was not Christopher's, Groby went out of Tietjens hands. There would be no more Tietjenses. Spelden might well be justified.

The grandfather of father scalped by Indians in Canada in the war of 1812; the father dying in a place where he should not have been—taking what he got for it and causing quite a scandal for the Court of Victoria; the elder brother of father killed drunk whilst fox-hunting; father suicided; Christopher a pauper by his own act with a by-blow in his shoes. If, then, there were to be any more Tietjenses by blood . . . Poor little devils! They would be their own cousins. Something like that. . . .

And possibly none the worse off for that. . . . Either Spelden or Groby Great Tree had perhaps done for the others. Groby Great Tree had been planted to commemorate the birth of great-grandfather, who had died in a whore-shop—and it had always been whispered in Groby, amongst the children and servants, that Groby Great Tree did not like the house. Its roots tore chunks out of the foundations, and two or three times the trunk had had to be bricked into the front wall. It had been brought as a sapling from Sardinia at a time when gentlemen still thought about landscape-gardening. A gentleman in those days consulted his heirs about tree-planting. Should you plant a group of copper beeches against a group of white maples over against the ha-ha a quarter of a mile from the house so that the contrast seen from the ball-room windows should be agreeable—in thirty years' time? In those days thought, in families, went in periods of thirty years, owner gravely consulting heir, who should see that development of light and shade that the owner never would.

Now-a-days the heir apparently consulted the owner as to whether the tenant who was taking the ancestral home furnished might not cut down trees in order to suit the sanitary ideas of the day. . . . An American day! Well, why not? Those people could not be expected to know how picturesque a contrast the tree would make against the roofs of Groby Great House when seen from Peel's Moorside. They would never hear of Peel's Moorside, or John Peel, or the coat so grey. . . .

Apparently that was the meaning of the visit of that young' colt and Mrs. de Bray Pape. They had come to ask his, Mark's, sanction as owner to cut down Groby Great Tree. And then they had funked it and bolted. At any rate the boy was still talking earnestly to the woman in white over the hedge. As to where Mrs. de Bray Pape was, he had no means of knowing; she might be among the potato rows studying the potatoes of the poor for all he knew. He hoped she would not come upon Marie Léonie, because Marie Léonie would make short work of Mrs. de Bray Pape and be annoyed on top of it.

But they were wrong to funk talking to *him* about cutting down Groby Great Tree. He cared nothing about it. Mrs. de Bray Pape might just as well have come and said cheerfully: "Hullo, old cock, we're going to cut down your bally old tree and let some light into the house. . . ." if that was the way Americans talked when they were cheerful; he had no means of knowing. He never remembered to have talked to an American. . . . Oh, yes, to Cammy Fittleworth! She had certainly been a dreadfully slangy young woman before her husband came into the title. But then Fittleworth was confoundedly slangy too. They said he had to give up in the middle of a speech he tried to make in the House of Lords because he could not do without the word "toppin'," which upset the Lord Chancellor. . . . So there was no knowing what Mrs. de Bray Pape might not have said if she had not thought she was addressing a syphilitic member of an effete aristocracy mad about an old cedar-tree. But she might just as well have cheerfully announced it. He did not care. Groby Great Tree had never seemed to like him. It never seemed to like anybody. They say it never forgave the Tietjenses for transplanting it from nice warm Sardinia to that lugubrious climate. . . . That was what the servants said to the children and the children whispered to each other in the dark corridors.

But poor old Christopher! He was going to go mad if the suggestion were made to him. The barest hint! Poor old Christopher, who was now probably at that very minute in one of those beastly machines overhead, coming back from Groby. . . . If Christopher *had* to buy a beastly South Country show-cottage, Mark wished he would not have bought it so near a confounded air-station. However, he expected, probably, that beastly Americans would come flying in the beastly machines to buy the beastly old junk. They did indeed do so—sent by Mr. Schatzweiler, who was certainly efficient except in the sending of cheques.

Christopher had nearly jumped out of his skin—that is to say, he had sat as still as a lump of white marble—when he gathered that Sylvia and, still more his own heir, wanted to let Groby furnished. He had said to Mark, over Sylvia's first letter: "You won't let 'em?" and Mark knew the agony that was behind his tallowy mask and goggle eyes. . . . Perfectly white around the nostrils he went—that was the sign!

And it had been as near to an appeal as he had ever come—unless the request for a loan on Armistice Day could be regarded as an appeal. But Mark did not think that that could be regarded as a score. In their game neither of them had yet made a real score. Probably neither of them ever would; they were a stout pair of North Country men whatever else could be said against them.

No: it hadn't been a score when Christopher had said: "You won't let 'em let Groby?" the day before yesterday: Christopher had been in an agony, but he was not *asking* Mark not to let Groby be let; he was only seeking information as to how far Mark would let the degradation of the old place go. Mark had let him pretty well know that Groby might be pulled down and replaced by a terra-cotta hotel before he would stir a finger. On the other hand, Christopher had only to stir a finger and not a blade of grass between the cobbles in the Stillroom Yard could be grubbed up. . . . But by the rules of the game neither of them could give an order. Neither. Mark said to Christopher: "Groby's yours!" Christopher said to Mark: "Groby's yours!" With perfect good humour and coldness. So probably the old place would fall to pieces or Sylvia would turn it into a bawdy-house. . . . It was a good joke! A good, grim Yorkshire joke!

It was impossible to know which of them suffered more. Christopher, it is true, was having his heart broken because the house suffered—but, damn it, wasn't Mark himself pretty well heart-broken because Christopher refused to accept the house from him? . . . It was impossible to know which!

Yes, his confounded heart had been broken on Armistice Day in the morning—between the morning and the morning after. . . . Yes: after Christopher had been reading Boswell aloud, night after night for three weeks. . . . Was that playing the game? Was it playing the game to get no sleep if you had not forgiven your brother. . . . Oh, no doubt it was playing the game. You don't forgive your brother if he lets you down in a damn beastly way. . . . And of course it *is* letting a fellow down in a beastly—a beastly!—way to let him know that you believe he lives on the immoral earnings of his wife. . . . Mark had done that to Christopher. It was unforgivable all right. And equally of course you do not hurt your brother except on the lines circumscribed by the nature of the offence: you are the best friend he has—except on the lines circumscribed by the offence; and he will nurse you like a blasted soft woman—except in so far as the lines circumscribed by the offence do not preclude your ministrations.

For, obviously, the best thing Christopher could have done for his brother's health would have been to have accepted the stewardship of Groby—but his brother could die and he himself could die before he would do that. It was neverthe-less a pretty cruel affair. . . . Over Boswell the two brothers had got as thick as thieves with an astonishing intimacy—and with an astonishing similarity. If one of them made a comment on Bennett Langton it would be precisely the com-ment that the other had on his lips. It was what asses call telepathy now-a-days . . . a warm, comfortable feeling, late at night with the light shaded from your eyes, the voice going on through the deep silence of London that awaited the crashes of falling bombs. . . . Well, Mark accepted Chris-

topher's dictum that he himself was an eighteenth-century
bloke and was only forestalled when he had wanted to tell
Christopher that he was more old-fashioned still—a sort of
seventeenth-century Anglican who ought to be strolling in a
grove with the Greek Testament beneath the arm and all.
. . . And, hang it all, there was room for him! The land
had not changed. . . . There were still the deep beech-woods
making groves beside the plough-lands and the rooks rising
lazily as the plough came towards them. The land had not
changed. . . . Well, the breed had not changed. . . . There
was Christopher. . . . Only, the times . . . they had changed.
. . . The rooks and the plough-lands and the beeches and
Christopher were there still. . . . But not the frame of mind
in the day. . . . The sun might rise and go above the plough
till it set behind the hedge, and the ploughman went off to
the inn settle; and the moon could do the same. But they
would—neither sun nor moon—look on the spit of Christopher in all their journeys. Never. They might as well expect
to see a mastodon. . . . And he, Mark, himself was an
old-fashioned buffer. That was all right. Judas Iscariot himself was an old-fashioned ass, once upon a time!

But it was almost on the edge of not playing the game
for Christopher to let that intimacy establish itself and all
the time to cherish that unforgivingness. . . . Not quite not
playing the game: but almost. For hadn't Mark held out
feelers? Hadn't he made concessions? Hadn't his very marrying of Marie Léonie been by way of a concession to Christopher? Didn't Christopher, if the truth was to be known,
want Mark to marry Marie Léonie because he, Christopher,
wanted to marry Valentine Wannop and hadn't a hope? If
the truth were known . . . Well, he had made that concession
to Christopher, who was a sort of a parson anyhow. But
ought Christopher to have exacted—to have telepathically
willed—that concession if he wasn't himself going to concede
something? Ought he to have forced him, Mark, to accept
his mooning womanly services when the poor devil was already worn out with his military duties of seeing old tins
cleaned out day after day, if he meant to become a beastly
old-furniture dealer and refuse Groby? For, upon his soul,
till the morning of Armistice Day, Mark had accepted Christopher's story of Mr. Schatzweiler as merely a good-
humoured, grim threat. . . . A sort of a feint at a threat. . . .

Well, probably it was playing the game all right: if Christopher thought it was jannock, jannock it was!

But . . . a damn beastly shock. . . . Why, he had been

practically convalescent, he had been out of bed in a dressing-gown and had told Lord Wolstonmark that he could pile in as many papers as he liked from the office. . . . And then Christopher, without a hat and in a beastly civilian suit of light mulberry-coloured Harris tweed, had burst into the room with a beastly piece of old furniture under his arm. . . . A sort of inlaid toy writing-desk. A model. For cabinet-makers! A fine thing to bring into a convalescent bedroom, to a man quietly reading Form T.O. LOUWR, 1962, E 17 of the 10/11/18, in front of a clean fire. . . . And chalk white about the gills the fellow was—with an awful lot of silver in his hair. . . . What age was he? Forty? Forty-three? God knew!

Forty. . . . He wanted to borrow forty quid on that beastly piece of furniture. To have an Armistice Day Bean-feast and set up house with his gal! Forty quid! My God! Mark felt his bowels turning over within him with disgust. . . . The gal—that fellow's half-sister as like as not—was waiting in an empty house for him to go and seduce her. In order to celebrate the salvation of the world by seven million deaths!

If you seduce a girl you don't do it on forty pounds: you accept Groby and three, seven, ten thousand a year. So he had told Christopher.

And then he had got it. Full in the face. Christopher was not going to accept a penny from him. Never. Not ever! . . . No doubt about that, either. That fact had gone into Mark as a knife goes into the stag's throat. It had hurt as much, but it hadn't killed! Damn it, it might as well have! It might as well have. . . . Does a fellow do that to his own brother just because his own brother has called him . . . what is the word? *Maquereau!* . . . Probably a *maquereau* is worse than a pimp. . . . The difference between a flea and a louse, as Dr. Johnson said.

Eh, but Christopher was bitter! . . . Apparently he had gone round first to Sir John Robertson's with the jigamaree. Years before, Sir John had promised to buy it for a hundred pounds. It was a special sort of model signed by some duke of a Bath cabinet-maker in 1762. . . . Wasn't that the year of the American Rebellion? Well, Christopher had bought it in a junk-shop of sorts for a fiver and Sir John had promised him a hundred quid. He collected cabinet-makers' models: extraordinarily valuable they were. Christopher had spat out that this was worth a thousand dollars. . . . Thinking of his old-furniture customers!

When Christopher had used that word—with the blue pebbles sticking out of his white-lard head—Mark had felt the sweat break out all over him. He had known it was all up. . . . Christopher had gone on: you expected him to spit electric sparks, but his voice was wooden. Sir John had said to him:

"Eh, no, mon. You're a fine soldier now, raping half the girls in Flanders and Ealing and asking us to regard you as heroes. Fine heroes. And now you're safe. . . . A hundred pounds is a price to a Christian that is faithful to his lovely wife. Five pounds is as much as I'll give you for the model, and be thankful it is five, not one, for old sake's sake!"

That was what Sir John Robertson had said to Christopher: that was what the world was like to serving soldiers in that day. You don't have to wonder that Christopher was bitter—even to his own brother with the sweat making his underlinen icy. Mark had said:

"My good chap. I won't lend you a penny on that idiotic jigamaree. But I'll write you a cheque for a thousand pounds this minute. Give me my cheque-book from the table. . . ."

Marie Léonie had come into the room on hearing Christopher's voice. She liked to hear the news from Christopher. And she liked Christopher and Mark to have heated discussions. She had observed that they did Mark good: on the day when Christopher had first come here, three weeks before, when they certainly had heatedly discussed, she had observed that Mark's temperature had fallen from ninety-nine point six to ninety-eight point two. In two hours. . . . After all, if a Yorkshire man can quarrel he can live. They were like that, those others, she said.

Christopher had turned on her and said:

"*Ma belle amie m'attend à ma maison; nous voulons célébrer avec mes camarades de régiment. Je n'ai pas le sou. Prêtez-moi quarante livres, je vous en prie, madame!*"

He had added that he would leave his cabinet as a pledge. He was as stiff as a sentry outside Buckingham Palace. She had looked at Mark with some astonishment. After all, she might well be astonished. He himself had made no sign and suddenly Christopher had exclaimed:

"*Prêtez les moi, prêtez les moi, pour l'amour de Dieu!*"

Marie Léonie had gone a little white, but she had turned up her skirt and turned down her stocking and took out the notes.

"*Pour le dieu d'Amour, monsieur, je veux bien,*" she had

said. . . . You never knew what a Frenchwoman would not
say. That was out of an old song.

But the sweat burst out all over his face at the recollection: great drops of sweat.

7 ~

MARIE LÉONIE, a strong taste of apples in her mouth, strong
savours of apples on the air, wasps around her and as if a
snow-drift of down descending about her feet, was frowning
seriously over Burgundy bottles into which ran cider from
a glass tube that she held to their necks. She frowned because the task was serious and engrossing, because the wasps
annoyed her and because she was resisting an impulse inside herself. It told her that something ailed Mark and urged
her to go and look at him.

It annoyed her because, as a rule—a rule so strong that
it had assumed the aspect of a regulation—she felt presages
of something ailing Mark only at night. Only at night. During the day usually she felt in her *for intérieur* that Mark
was like what he was only because he wanted so to be.
His glance was too virile and dominant to let you think
otherwise—the dark, liquid, direct glance! But at nightfall
—or at any rate shortly after supper, when she had retired
to her room—terrible premonitions of disaster to Mark
visited her. He was dying where he lay; he was beset by the
spectral beings of the country-side; robbers, even, had crept
upon him, though that was unreasonable. For all the country-
side knew that Mark was paralysed and unable to store
wealth in his mattress. . . . Still, nefarious strangers might
see him and imagine that he kept his gold repeater-watch
beneath his pillow. . . . So she would rise a hundred times
in a night and, going to the low, diamond-casement window,
would lean out and listen. But there would be no sound:
the wind in the leaves; the cry of water-birds overhead. The
dim light would be in the hut, seen unmoving through the
apple-boughs.

Now, however, in broad daylight, towards the hour of
tea, with the little maid on a stool beside her plucking the
boiling-hens that were to go to market next day, with the
boxes of eggs on their shelves, each egg wired to the bottom
of its box, waiting till she had time to date-stamp it—in the
open potting-shed in the quiet, broad light of a summer day

she was visited by a presage of something ailing Mark. She resented it, but she was not the woman to resist it.

There was, however, nothing to warrant it. From the corner of the house to which she proceeded she could see quite well the greater part of Mark's solitary figure. Gunning, being talked to by the English lord, held a spare horse by the bridle and was looking at Mark over the hedge. He exhibited no emotions. A young man was walking along the inside of the hedge between it and the raspberries. That was no affair of hers: Gunning was not protesting. The head and shoulders of a young woman—or it might be another young man—were proceeding along the outside of the hedge nearly level with the first one. That was equally no affair of hers. Probably they were looking at the bird's-nest. There was some sort of bird's-nest, she had heard, in that thick hedge. There was no end to the folly of the English in the country as in the town: they would waste time over everything. This bird was a bottle . . . bottle-something, and Christopher and Valentine and the parson and the doctor and the artist who lived down the hill were crazy about it. They walked on tiptoe when they were within twenty yards. Gunning was allowed to trim the hedge, but apparently the birds knew Gunning. . . . For Marie Léonie, all birds were "moineaux"; as who should say "sparrers"; in London they called them that—just as all flowers were "giroflées"—as you might say wallflowers. . . . No wonder this nation was going to rack and ruin when it wasted its time over preserving the nests of sparrers and naming innumerable wallflowers! The country was well enough—a sort of suburb of Caen: but the people! . . . no wonder William, of Falaise, in Normandy subjugated them with such ease.

Now she had wasted five minutes, for the glass tubes, hinged on rubber, that formed her siphon from barrel to bottle had had perforce to be taken out of the spile-hole; the air had entered into it, and she would have to put it back and suck once more at the tube until the first trickle of cider entered her mouth. She disliked having to do that; it wasted the cider and she disliked the flavour in the afternoon when one had lunched. The little maid also would say: "A-oh, meladyship, Ah *du* call thet queer!" . . . Nothing would cure that child of saying that though she was otherwise *sage et docile*. Even Gunning scratched his head at the sight of those tubes.

Could these savages never understand that if you want to have *cidre mousseux*—foaming—you must have as little sediment as possible? And that in the bottom of casks, even if they had not been moved for a long time, there will always be sediment—particularly if you set up a flow in the liquid by running it from a tap near the bottom. So you siphon off the top of the great casks for bottling *mousseux,* and drink the rest from the cask, and run the thickest into little thin-wood casks with many hoops for freezing in the winter. . . . To make *calvados,* where you cannot have alembics because of the excise. . . . In this unhappy country you may not have alembics for the distilling of apple-jack, plum-brandy or other *fines*—because of the excise! *Quel pays! Quels gens!*

They lacked industry, frugality—and, above all, spirit! Look at that poor Valentine, hiding in her room upstairs because there were people about whom she suspected of being people from the English lord's house. . . . By rights that poor Valentine should be helping her with the bottling and ready to sell that lugubrious old furniture to visitors whilst her lord was away buying more old rubbish. . . . And she was distracted because she could not find some prints. They represented—Marie Léonie was well aware because she had heard the facts several times—street-criers of ambulant wares in London years ago. There were only eight of these to be found. Where were the other four? The customer, an English lady of title, was anxious for them. As presents for an immediate wedding! Monsieur my brother-in-law had come upon the four that were to make up the set at a sale two days before. He had recounted with satisfaction how he had found them on the grass. . . . It was supposed that he had brought them home; but they were not in the warehouse at Cramp the carpenter's, they were not to be found left in the cart. They were in no drawer or press. . . . What was to prove that *mon beau frère* had brought them home from the sale? He was not there: he was gone for a day and a half. Naturally he would be gone for a day and a half when he was most needed. . . . And where was he gone, leaving his young wife in that nervous condition. For a day and a half! He had never before been gone for a day and a half. . . . There was then something brewing; it was in the air; it was in her bones. . . . It was like that dreadful day of the armistice, when this miserable land betrayed the beautiful *pays de France!* . . . When Monsieur had borrowed forty pounds of her. . . . In the name of heaven, why did not he borrow another forty—or eighty—or a hundred, rather than be distracted and distract Mark and his unhappy girl? . . .

She was not unsympathetic, that girl. She had civilization. She could talk of Philémon and Baucis. She had made her *bachot*, she was what you would call *fille de famille*. . . . But without *chic*. . . . Without . . . Without . . . Well, she neither displayed enough erudition to be a *bas bleu*—though she had enough erudition!—nor enough *chic* to be a *femme légère*—a *poule* who would *faire la noce* with her gallant. Monsieur the brother-in-law was no gay spark. But you never know with a man. . . . The cut of a skirt; a twist of the hair . . . Though to-day there was no hair to twist: but there is the equivalent.

And it was a fact that you never knew a man. Look at the case of Eleanor Dupont, who lived for ten years with Duchamp of the Sorbonne. . . . Eleanor would never attend scrupulously to her attire because her man wore blue spectacles and was a *savant*. . . . But what happened? There came along a little piece with a hat as large as cartwheel covered with green stuff and sleeves up above her ears—as the mode was then. . . .

That had been a lesson to her, Marie Léonie, who had been a girl at the time. She had determined that if she achieved a *collage sérieux* with a monsieur of eighty and as blind as a bat she would study the modes of the day right down to the latest perfume. These messieurs did not know it, but they moved among *femmes du monde* and the fashionable cocottes, and however much she at home might be the little brown bird of the domestic hearth, the lines of her dresses, her hair, her personal odour, must conform. Mark did not imagine; she did not suppose he had ever seen a fashionable journal in her apartments that were open to him, or had ever suspected that she walked in the Row on a Sunday when he was away. . . . But she had studied these things like another. And more. For it is difficult to keep with the fashion and at the same time appear as if you were a serious *petite bourgeoise*. But she had done it; and observe the results. . . .

But that poor Valentine. . . . Her man was attached enough: and well he ought to be, considering the affair in which he had landed her. But always there comes the *pic des tempêtes*, the Cap Horn, round which you must go. It is the day when your man looks at you and says: "H'm, h'm," and considers if the candle is not more valuable than the game! Ah, then. . . . There are wise folk who put that

at the seventh year, other wise ones at the second, others
again at the eleventh. . . . But in fact you may put it at
any day on any year—to the hundredth. . . . And that poor
Valentine with four spots of oil on her only skirt but two.
And that so badly hung, though the stuff no doubt was once
good. One must concede that! They make admirable tweeds
in this country: better certainly than in Roubaix. But is that
enough to save a country—or a woman dependent on a man
who has introduced her into a bad affair?

A voice behind her said:

"I see you have plenty of eggs!"—an unusual voice of a
sort of breathless nervousness. Marie Léonie continued to
hold the mouth of her tube into the neck of a burgundy
bottle; into this she had already introduced a small screw
of sifted sugar and an extremely minute portion of a powder
that she got from a pharmacist of Rouen. This, she understood, made the cider of a rich brownness. She did not see
why cider should be brown, but it was considered to be less
fortifying if it were light golden. She continued also to think
about Valentine, who would be twittering with nerves at the
window whose iron-leaded casement was open above their
heads. She would have put down her Latin book and have
crept to the window to listen.

The little girl beside Marie Léonie had risen from the
three-legged stool and held a dead, white fowl with a nearly
naked breast by its neck. She said hoarsely:

"These 'ere be 'er ladyship's settin's of prize Reds." She
was blond, red-faced and wore on her dull fair hair a rather
large cap, on her thin body a check-blue cotton gown. " 'Arf
a crownd apiece the heggs be, or twenty-four shillings a
dozen if you takes a gross."

Marie Léonie heard the hoarse voice with some satisfaction. This girl whom they had only had for a fortnight
seemed to be satisfactory mentally; it was not her business
to sell the eggs, but Gunning's; nevertheless she knew the
details. She did not turn round: it was not *her* business to
talk to anyone who wanted to buy eggs, and she had no
curiosity as to customers. She had too much else to think
about. The voice said:

"Half a crown seems a great deal for an egg. What is
that in dollars? This must be that tyranny over edibles by
the producer of which one has heard so much."

"Tidd'n nothin' in dollars," the girl said. " 'Arf a dollar
is two bob. 'Arf a crownd is two-'n'-six."

The conversation continued, but it grew dim in Marie

Léonie's thoughts. The child and the voice disputed as to what a dollar was—or so it appeared, for Marie Léonie was not familiar with either of the accents of the disputants. The child was a combative child. She drove both Gunning and the cabinet-maker Cramp with an organ of brass. Of tin perhaps, like a penny whistle. When she was not grubbily working she read books with avidity—books about blood if she could get them. She had an exaggerated respect for the Family, but none for any other soul in the world. . . .

Marie Léonie considered that, by now, she might have got down to the depth of the cask where you find sediment. She ran some cider into a clear glass, stopping the tube with her thumb. The cider was clear enough to let her bottle another dozen, she judged; then she would send for Gunning to take the spile-bung out of the next cask. Four sixty-gallon casks she had to attend to; two of them were done. She began to tire: she was not unfatiguable if she was indefatigable. She began, at any rate, to feel drowsy. She wished Valentine could have helped her. But that girl had not much backbone, and she, Marie Léonie, acknowledged that for the sake of the future it was good that she should rest and read books in Latin or Greek. And avoid nervous encounters.

She had tucked her up under an eiderdown on their four-post bed because They would have all the windows open and currents of air must, above all, be avoided by women. . . . *Elle* had smiled and said that it had once been her dream to read the works of Aeschyle beside the blue Mediterranean. They had kissed each other. . . .

The maid beside her was saying that orf'n 'n' orf'n she'd 'eared 'er farver, oo was a dealer, wen a lot of ol' 'ens, say, 'ad gone to three-an'-nine, say "Make it two 'arf-dollars!" They didn' 'ave dollars in thet country, but they did 'ave 'arf-dollars. 'N' Capt'n Kidd the pirate, 'e 'ad dollars, 'n' pieces of eight 'n' moi-dors too!

A wasp annoyed Marie Léonie; it buzzed almost on her nose, retired, returned, made a wide circuit. There were already several wasps struggling in the glass of cider she had just drawn; there were others in circles round spots of cider on the slats of wood on which the barrels were arranged. They drew in their tails and then expanded, ecstatically. Yet only two nights before she and Valentine had gone with Gunning all over the orchard with a lantern, a trowel and a bottle of prussic acid, stopping up holes along the paths and in banks. She had liked the experience, the darkness, the ring of light from the lantern on the rough grass, the feeling that she was out, near Mark, and that yet Gunning and his lantern kept spiritual visitors away. . . . What she suffered between the desire to visit her man in the deep nights and the possibility of coming up against *revenants*. . . . Was it reasonable? . . . What women had to suffer for their men! Even if they were faithful. . . .

What the unfortunate *elle* had not suffered. . . .

Even on what you might call her *nuit de noces*. . . . At the time it had seemed incomprehensible. Marie Léonie had had no details. It had merely seemed fantastic: possibly even tragic because Mark had taken it so hardly. Truly she believed he had become insane. At two in the morning, beside Mark's bed. They had—the two brothers—exchanged words of considerable violence whilst the girl shivered. And was determined. That girl had been determined. She would not go back to her mother. At two in the morning. . . . Well, if you refuse to go back to your mother at two in the morning you kick indeed your slipper over the mill!

The details of that night came back to her, amongst wasps and beneath the conversation of the unseen woman in the shed where the water ran in the trough. She had set the bottles in the trough because it is a good thing to cool cider before the process of fermentation in the bottles begins. The bottles with their shining necks of green glass were an agreeable spectacle. The lady behind her back was talking of Oklahoma. . . . The cowboy with the large nose that she had seen on the film at the Piccadilly Cinema had come from Oklahoma. It was, no doubt, somewhere in America. She had been used to go to the Piccadilly Cinema on a Friday. You do not go to the theatre on a Friday if you are *bien pensant,* but you may regard the cinema as being to the theatre what a *repas maigre* is as against a meal with meat. . . . The lady speaking behind her came apparently from Oklahoma: she had eaten prairie-chickens in her time. On a farm. Now, however, she was very rich. Or so she told the little maid. Her husband could buy half Lord Fittleworth's estate and not miss the money. She said that if only people here would take example . . .

On Armistice Evening they had come thumping on her door. The bell had failed to wake her after all the noise in the street of that day. . . . She had sprung into the middle of the floor and flown to save Mark . . . from an air raid. She had forgotten that it was the armistice. . . . But the knocking had gone on on the door.

Before it had stood Monsieur the brother-in-law and that
girl in a dark-blue Girl Guide's sort of uniform. Both
chalk white and weary to death. As if they leaned against
one another . . . She had been for bidding them go away, but
Mark had come out of the bedroom. In his night-shirt with
his legs bare. And hairy! He had bidden them come in,
roughly, and had got back into bed. . . . That had been the
last time he had been on his legs! Now, he having been in
bed so long, his legs were no longer hairy, but polished.
Like thin glazed bones!

She had recalled his last gesture. He had positively used
a gesture, like a man raving. . . . And, indeed, he was raving.
At Christopher. And dripping with sweat. Twice she had
wiped his face whilst they shouted at each other.

It had been difficult to understand what they said because
they had spoken a sort of *patois*. Naturally they returned to
the language they had spoken in their childhoods—when they
were excited, these unexcitable people! It resembled the *patois*
of the Bretons. Harsh. . . .

And, for herself, she had been all concerned for the girl.
Naturally she had been concerned for the girl. One is a woman. . . . At first she had taken her for a little piece from
the streets. . . . But even for a little piece from the streets . . .
Then she had noticed there had been no rouge; no imitation-
pearl necklace. . . .

Of course when she had gathered that Mark was pressing
money on them she had felt different. Different in two ways.
It could not be a little piece. And then her heart had contracted at the idea of money being given away. They might
be ruined. It might be these people instead of her Paris
nephews who would pillage her corpse. But the brother-in-
law pushed the thought of money away from him with both
hands. If she—*elle*—wanted to go with him she must share
his fortunes. . . . What a country! What people!

There had seemed to be no understanding them then. . . .
It had appeared that Mark insisted that the girl should stop
there with her lover: the lover, on the contrary, insisted that
she should go home to her mother. The girl kept saying that
on no account would she leave Christopher. He could not
be left. He would die if he was left. . . . And, indeed, that
brother-in-law had seemed sick enough. He panted worse
than Mark.

She had eventually taken the girl to her own room. A little,
agonized, fair creature. She had felt inclined to enfold her
in her arms but she had not done so. Because of the money.

. . . She might as well have. It was impossible to get these people to touch money. She would now give no little to lend that girl twenty pounds for a frock and some undergarments.

The girl had sat there without speaking. It had seemed for hours. Then some drunken man on the church-steps opposite had begun to play the bugle. Long calls. . . . Tee . . . Teee . . . Teeee . . . Ta-heee . . . To-hee . . . Continuing forever. . . .

Valentine had begun to cry. She had said that it was dreadful. But you could not object. It was the last post they were playing. For the dead. You could not object to their playing the last post for the dead that night. Even if it was a drunken man who played and even if it drove you mad. The dead ought to have all they could get.

If she had not made the necessary allowances, that would have seemed to Marie Léonie an exaggerated sentiment. The English bugle-notes could do no good to the French dead, and the English losses were so negligible in quantity that it hardly seemed worth while to become *émotionnée* when their funeral call was played by a drunken man. The French papers estimated the English losses at a few hundreds: what was that as against the millions of her own people? . . . But she gathered that this girl had gone through something terrible that night with the wife, and being too proud to show emotion over her personal vicissitudes, she pretended to find an outlet because of the sounds of that bugle. . . . Well, it was mournful enough. She had understood it when Christopher, putting his face in at the crack of the door, had whispered to her that he was going to stop the bugle because its sound was intolerable to Mark.

The girl apparently had been in a reverie, for she had not heard him. She, Marie Léonie, had gone to look at Mark, and the girl sat there, on the bed. Mark was by then quite quiescent. The bugle had stopped. To cheer him she had made a few remarks about the inappropriateness of playing, for a negligible number of dead, a funeral call at three in the morning. If it had been for the French dead—or if her country had not been betrayed! It was betraying her country to have given those monsters an armistice when they were far from their borders. Merely that was treachery on the part of these sham allies. They should have gone right through those monsters, slaying them by the million, defenceless, and then they should have laid waste their country with fire and sword. Let them, too, know what it was to suffer as France had suffered. It was treachery enough not to have done that, and the child unborn would suffer for it.

But there they waited, then, even after that treachery had been done, to know what were the terms of even that treachery. They might even now not intend to be going to Berlin. . . . What, then, was life for?

Mark had groaned. In effect he was a good Frenchman. She had seen to that. The girl had come into the room. She could not bear to be alone. . . . What a night of movement and cross-movement. She had begun to argue with Mark. Hadn't there, she had asked, been enough of suffering? He agreed that there had been enough of suffering. But there must be more. . . . Even out of justice to the poor bloody Germans. . . . He had called them the poor bloody Germans. He had said that it was the worst disservice you could do your foes not to let them know that remorseless consequences follow determined actions. To interfere in order to show fellows that if they did what they wanted they need not of necessity take what they got for it was in effect to commit a sin against God. If the Germans did not experience that in the sight of the world, there was an end of Europe and the world. What was to hinder endless recurrences of what had happened near a place called Gemmenich on the 4th of August, 1914, at six o'clock in the morning? There was nothing to hinder it. Any other state from the smallest to the largest might . . .

The girl had interrupted to say that the world had changed, and Mark, lying back exhausted on his pillows, had said with a sort of grim sharpness:

"It is you who say it. . . . Then you may run the world. . . . I know nothing about it. . . ." He appeared exhausted.

It was singular the way those two discussed—discussed "the situation" at three-thirty in the morning. Well, nobody wanted to be asleep that night, it seemed. Even in that obscure street mobs went by, shouting and playing concertinas. She had never heard Mark discuss before—and she was never to hear him discuss again. He appeared to regard that girl with a sort of aloof indulgence, as if he were fond of her but regarded her as overlearned, too young, devoid of all experience. And Marie Léonie had watched them and listened with intentness. In twenty years these three weeks had for the first time showed her her man in contact with his people. The contemplation had engrossed her.

She could, nevertheless, see that her man was exhausted in his inner being, and obviously that girl was tried beyond endurance. Whilst she talked she appeared to listen for distant sounds. . . . She kept on recurring to the idea that punishment was abhorrent to the modern mind. Mark stuck to his point that to occupy Berlin was not punishment, but that not to occupy Berlin was to commit an intellectual sin. The consequence of invasion is counter-invasion and symbolical occupation, as the consequence of overpride is humiliation. For the rest of the world, he knew nothing of it; for his own country, that was logic—the logic by which she had lived. To abandon that logic was to abandon clearness of mind: it was mental cowardice. To show the world Berlin occupied, with stands of arms and colours on her public places, was to show that England respected logic. Not to show the world that was to show that England was mentally cowardly. We dared not put the enemy nations to pain because we shrank from the contemplation.

Valentine had said: "There has been too much suffering!"

He had said:

"Yes, you are afraid of suffering. . . . But England is necessary to the world. . . . To my world. . . . Well, make it your world and it may go to rack and ruin how it will. I am done with it. But then . . . you must accept the responsibility. A world with England presenting the spectacle of moral cowardice would be a world on a lower plane. . . . If you lower the record for the mile, you lower the standard of blood-stock. Try to think of that. If Persimmon had not achieved what it did, the French Grand Prix would be less of an event and the trainers at Maisons Laffitte would be less efficient. And the jockeys. And the stable-lads. And the sporting-writers. . . . A world profits by the example of a steadfast nation. . . ."

Suddenly Valentine said:

"Where is Christopher?" with such intenseness that it was like a blow.

Christopher had gone out. She exclaimed:

"But you must not let him go out. . . . He is not fit to go out alone. . . . He has gone out to go back. . . ."

Mark said:

"Don't go. . . ." For she had got to the door. "He went out to stop the last post. But you may play the last post for me. Perhaps he has gone back to the square. He had presumably better see what has happened to his wife. I should not myself."

Valentine had said with extraordinary bitterness:

"He shall not. He shall not." She had gone.

It had come through to Marie Léonie partly then and partly subsequently that Christopher's wife had turned up at Christopher's empty house, that was in the square a few yards away only. They had gone back late at night probably for purposes of love and had found her there. She had come for the purpose of telling them that she was going to be operated on for cancer, so that with their sensitive natures they could hardly contemplate going to bed together at that moment.

It had been a good lie. That Mrs. Tietjens was a *maîtresse femme*. There was no denying that. She herself was engaged for those others both by her own inclinations and the strong injunctions of her husband, but Mme. Tietjens was certainly ingenious. She had managed to incommode and discredit that pair almost as much as any pair could be incommoded and discredited, although they were the most harmless couple in the world.

They had certainly not had an agreeable festival on that Armistice Day. Apparently one of the officers present at their dinner of celebration had gone raving mad; the wife of another of Christopher's comrades of the regiment had been rude to Valentine; the colonel of the regiment had taken the opportunity to die with every circumstance of melodrama. Naturally all the other officers had run away and had left Christopher and Valentine with the madman and the dying colonel on their hands.

An agreeable *voyage de noces*. . . . It appeared that they had secured a four-wheel cab in which, with the madman and the other, they had driven to Balham—an obscure suburb, with sixteen celebrants hanging all over the outside of the cab and two on the horse's back—at any rate for a couple of miles from Trafalgar Square. They were not, of course, interested in the interior of the cab; they were merely gay because there was to be no more suffering. No doubt Valentine and Christopher had got rid of the madman somewhere in Chelsea at an asylum for shell-shock cases; but the authorities would not take the colonel, so they had driven on to Balham, the colonel making dying speeches about the late war, his achievements, the money he owed Christopher. . . . Valentine had appeared to find that extremely trying. The man died in the cab.

They had had to walk back into town because the driver of the four-wheeler was so upset by the death in his cab that he could not drive. Moreover, the horse was foundered. It had been twelve midnight before they reached Trafalgar

Square. They had had to struggle through packed crowds nearly all the way. Apparently they were happy at the accomplishment of their duty—or their benevolence. They stood on the top step of St. Martin's Church, dominating the square, that was all illuminated and packed and roaring, with bonfires made of the paving-wood and omnibuses, and the Nelson Column going up and the fountain-basins full of drunkards, and orators and bands. . . . They stood on the top step, drew deep breaths and fell into each other's arms. . . . For the first time—though apparently they had loved each other for a lustre or more. . . . What people!

Then, at the top of the stairs in the house in the Inn, they had perceived Sylvia, all in white! . . .

Apparently she had been informed that Christopher and that girl were in communication—by a lady who did not like Christopher because she owed him money. A Lady Macmaster. Apparently there was no one in the world who did not dislike Christopher because they owed him money. The colonel and the lunatic and the husband of the lady who had been rude to Valentine . . . all! All! Right down to Mr. Schatzweiler, who had only paid Christopher one cheque for a few dollars out of a great sum and had then contracted a nervous break-down on account of the sufferings he had gone through as a prisoner of war. . . .

But what sort of a man was that Christopher to have in his hands the fortunes of a woman? . . . Any woman!

Those were practically the last words her Mark had ever spoken to her, Marie Léonie. She had been supporting him whilst he drank a tisane she had made in order that he might sleep, and he had said gravely:

"It is not necessary that I should ask you to be kind to Mademoiselle Wannop. Christopher is incapable of looking after her. . . ." His last words, for immediately afterwards the telephone bell had rung. He had just before seemed to have a good deal of temperature, and it had been whilst his eyes were goggling at her, the thermometer that she had stuck in his mouth gleaming on his dark lips, and while she was regretting letting him be tormented by his family, that the sharp drilling of the telephone had sounded from the hall. Immediately the strong German accent of Lord Wolstonmark had, with its accustomed disagreeableness, burred in her ear. He had said that the Cabinet was still sitting and they desired to know at once the code that Mark used in his communications with various ports. His second-in-command appeared to be lost amongst the celebrations of that night.

Mark had said with a sort of grim irony from the bedroom that if they wanted to stop his transport going out they might just as well not use cipher. If they wanted to use a twopenny-halfpenny economy as window-dressing for the elections they'd have to have, they might as well give it as much publicity as they could. Besides, he did not believe they would get into Germany with the transport they had. A good deal had been smashed lately.

The minister had said with a sort of heavy joy that they were not going into Germany: and that had been the most dreadful moment of Marie Léonie's life; but with her discipline she had just simply repeated the words to Mark. He had then said something she did not quite catch: and he would not repeat what he had said. She said as much to Lord Wolstonmark, and the chuckling accent said that he supposed that that was the sort of news that would rattle the old boy. But one must adapt oneself to one's day; the times were changed.

She had gone from the instrument to look at Mark. She spoke to him; she spoke to him again. And again—rapid words of panic. His face was dark purple and congested; he gazed straight before him. She raised him; he sank back inertly.

She remembered going to the telephone and speaking in French to the man at the other end. She had said that the man at the other end was a German and a traitor; her husband should never speak to him or his fellows again. The man had said: "Eh, what's that? Eh . . . Who are you?"

With appalling shadows chasing up and down in her mind, she had said:

"I am Lady Mark Tietjens. You have murdered my husband. Clear yourself from off my line, murderer!"

It had been the first time she had ever given herself that name; it was indeed the first time she had ever spoken in French to that ministry. But Mark had finished with the ministry, with the government, with the nation. . . . With the world.

As soon as she could get that man off the wire she had rung up Christopher. He had come round with Valentine in tow. It had certainly not been much of a *nuit de noces* for that young couple.

PART TWO

I ~

SYLVIA TIETJENS, using the persuasion of her left knee, edged her chestnut nearer to the bay mare of the shining general. She said:

"If I divorce Christopher, will you marry me?"

He exclaimed with the vehemence of a shocked hen:

"Good God, no!"

He shone everywhere except in such parts of his grey-tweed suit as would have shown by shining that they had been put on more than once. But his little white moustache, his cheeks, the bridge but not the tip of his nose, his reins, his Guards' tie, his boots, martingale, snaffle, curb, fingers, finger-nails—all these gave evidence of interminable rubbings. . . . By himself, by his man, by Lord Fittleworth's stable-hands, grooms. . . . Interminable rubbings and supervisions at the end of extended arms. Merely to look at him you knew that he was something like Lord Edward Campion, lieutenant-general retired, M.P., K.C.M.G. (MILITARY), V.C., M.C., D.S.O. . . .

So he exclaimed:

"Good God, no!" and using a little-finger touch on his snaffle-rein, made his mare recoil from Sylvia Tietjens' chestnut.

Annoyed at its mate's motion, the bad-tempered chestnut with the white forehead showed its teeth at the mare, danced a little and threw out some flakes of foam. Sylvia swayed backwards and forwards in her saddle and smiled down into her husband's garden.

"You can't, you know," she said, "expect to put an idea out of my head just by flurrying the horses. . . ."

"A man," the general said between "Come ups" to his mare, "does not marry his . . ."

His mare went backwards a pace or two into the bank and then a pace forwards.

"His what?" Sylvia asked with amiability. "You can't be going to call me your cast mistress. No doubt most men would have a shot at it. But I never have been even your mistress. . . . I have to think of Michael!"

"I wish," the general said vindictively, "that you would settle what that boy is to be called. . . . Michael or Mark!" He added: "I was going to say: 'His godson's wife,' . . . A man may not marry his godson's wife."

Sylvia leant over to stroke the neck of the chestnut.

"A man," she said, "cannot marry any other man's wife. . . . But if you think that I am going to be the second Lady Tietjens after that . . . French prostitute . . ."

"You would prefer," the general said, "to be India. . . ."

Visions of India went through their hostile minds. They looked down from their horses over Tietjens' in West Sussex, over a house with a high-pitched, tiled roof with deep windows of the grey local stone. He nevertheless saw names like Akhbar Khan, Alexander of Macedon, the son of Philip, Delhi, the Massacre at Cawnpore. . . . His mind, given over from boyhood to the contemplation of the largest jewel in the British crown, spewed up those romances. He was member for the West Cleveland Division and a thorn in the side of the government. They *must* give him India. They knew that if they did not he could publish revelations as to the closing days of the late war. . . . He would naturally never do that. One does not blackmail even a government.

Still, to all intents, he *was* India.

Sylvia also was aware that he was to all intents and purposes India. She saw receptions in government houses, in which, habited with a tiara, she too would be INDIA. . . . As someone said in Shakespeare:

> "I am dying, Egypt, dying! Only
> I will importune Death awhile until
> Of many thousand kisses this poor last
> Is laid upon thy lips. . . ."

She imagined it would be agreeable, supposing her to betray his old Pantaloon India, to have a lover, gasping at her feet, exclaiming: "I am dying, India, dying. . . ." And she with her tiara, very tall. In white, probably. Probably satin!

The general said:

"You know you cannot possibly divorce my godson. You are a Roman Catholic."

She said, always with her smile:

"Oh, *can't* I? . . . Besides, it would be of the greatest advantage to Michael to have for a stepfather the field-marshal commanding. . . ."

He said with impotent irritation:

"I wish you would settle whether that boy's name is Michael or Mark!"

She said:

"He calls himself Mark. . . . I call him Michael because I hate the name of Mark. . . ."

She regarded Campion with real hatred. She said to herself that upon occasion she would be exemplarily revenged upon him. "Michael" was a Satterthwaite name—her father's; "Mark," the name for a Tietjens eldest son. The boy had originally been baptized and registered as Michael Tietjens. At his reception into the Roman Church he had been baptized "Michael Mark." Then had followed the only real deep humiliation of her life. After his papist baptism the boy had asked to be called Mark. She had asked him if he really meant that. After a long pause—the dreadful long pauses of children before they render a verdict!—he had said that he intended to call himself Mark from then on. . . . By the name of his father's brother, of his father's father, grandfather, great-grandfather. . . . By the name of the irascible apostle of the lion and the sword. . . . The Satterthwaites, his mother's family, might go by the board.

For herself, she hated the name of Mark. If there was one man in the world whom she hated because he was insensible of her attraction it was Mark Tietjens, who lay beneath the thatched roof beneath her eyes. . . . Her boy, however, intended, with a child's cruelty, to call himself Mark Tietjens. . . .

The general grumbled:

"There is no keeping track with you. . . . You say now you would be humiliated to be Lady Tietjens after that Frenchwoman. . . . But you have always said that that Frenchwoman is only the concubine of Sir Mark. I heard you tell your maid so only yesterday. . . . You say one thing, then you say another. . . . What is one to believe?"

She regarded him with sunny condescension. He grumbled on:

"One thing, then another. . . . You say you cannot divorce my godson because you are a Roman Catholic. Nevertheless, you begin divorce proceedings and throw all the mud you can over the miserable fellow. Then you remember your creed and don't go on. . . . What sort of game is this?" She regarded him still ironically but with good humour across the neck of her horse.

He said:

"There's *really* no fathoming you. . . . A little time ago —for months on end, you were dying of . . . of internal cancer, in short . . ."

She commented with the utmost good temper:

"I didn't want that girl to be Christopher's mistress. . . . You would think that no man with any imagination at all *could* . . . I mean with his wife in that condition. . . . But, of course, when she insisted . . . Well, I wasn't going to stop in bed, in retreat, all my life. . . ."

She laughed good-humouredly at her companion.

"I don't believe you know anything about women," she said. "Why should you? Naturally Mark Tietjens married his concubine. Men always do as a sort of death-bed offering. You will eventually marry Mrs. Partridge if I do not choose to go to India. You think you would not, but you would. . . . As for me, I think it would be better for Michael if his mother were Lady Edward Campion—of India—than if she were merely Lady Tietjens the second of Groby, with a dowager who was once a cross-Channel fly-by-night. . . ." She laughed and added: "Anyhow, the sisters at the Blessed Child said that they never saw so many lilies—symbols of purity—as there were at my tea-parties when I was dying. . . . You'll admit yourself you never saw anything so ravishing as me amongst the lilies and the tea-cups with the great crucifix above my head. . . . You were singularly moved! You swore you would cut Christopher's throat yourself on the day the detective told us that he was really living here with that girl. . . ."

The general exclaimed:

"About the dower-house at Groby. . . . It's really damned awkward. . . . You swore to me that when you let Groby to that American madwoman I could have the dower-house and keep my horses in Groby stables. But now it appears I can't. . . . It appears . . ."

"It appears," Sylvia said, "that Mark Tietjens means to

leave the dower-house at the disposal of his French concubine. . . . Anyhow, you can afford a house of your own.
You're rich enough!"

The general groaned:

"Rich enough! My God!"

She said:

"You have still—trust *you!*—your younger son's settlement. You have still your general's pay. You have the interest
on the grant the nation made you at the end of the war.
You have four hundred a year as a member of Parliament.
You have cadged on me for your keep and your man's keep
and your horses' and grooms' at Groby for years and years.
. . ."

Immense dejection covered the face of her companion. He
said:

"Sylvia. . . . Consider the expenses of my constituency. . . .
One would almost say you hated me!"

Her eyes continued to devour the orchard and garden that
were spread out below her. A furrow of raw, newly turned
earth ran from almost beneath their horses' hoofs nearly
vertically to the house below. She said:

"I suppose that is where they get their water supply. From
the spring above here. Cramp the carpenter says they are always having trouble with the pipes!"

The general exclaimed:

"Oh, Sylvia. And you told Mrs. de Bray Pape that they
had no water supply so they could not take a bath!"

Sylvia said:

"If I hadn't she would never have thought of cutting down
Groby Great Tree. . . . Don't you see that for Mrs. de Bray
Pape people who do not take baths are outside the law?
So, though she's not really courageous, she will risk cutting
down their old trees. . . ." She added: "Yes, I almost believe I do hate misers, and you are more next door to a
miser than anyone else I ever honoured with my acquaintance. . . ." She added further: "But I should advise you to
calm yourself. If I let you marry me you will have my
Satterthwaite pickings. Not to mention the Groby pickings
till Michael comes of age, and the—what is it?—ten thousand a year you will get from India. If out of all that you
cannot skimp enough to make up for house-room at my
expense at Groby, you are not half the miser I took you
for!"

A number of horses, with Lord Fittleworth and Gunning,
came up from the soft track outside the side of the garden

and onto the hard road that bordered the garden's top. Gunning sat one horse without his feet in the stirrups and had the bridles of two others over his elbows. They were the horses of Mrs. de Bray Pape, Mrs. Lowther and Mark Tietjens. The garden with its quince-trees, the old house with its immensely high-pitched roof such as is seen in countries where wood was once plentiful, the thatch of Mark Tietjens' shelter and the famous four counties, ran from the other side of the hedge out to infinity. An aeroplane droned down towards them, many miles away. Up from the road ran a slope covered with bracken, to many great beech-trees, along a wire hedge. That was the summit of Cooper's Common. In the stillness the hoofs of all those horses made a noise like that of desultorily approaching cavalry. Gunning halted his horses at a little distance; the beast Sylvia rode was too ill-tempered to be approached.

Lord Fittleworth rode up to the general and said:

"God damn it, Campion, ought Helen Lowther to be down there? Her ladyship will give me no rest for a fortnight!" He shouted at Gunning: "Here you, blast you, you old scoundrel, where's the gate Speeding complains you have been interfering with?" He added to the general: "This old villain was in my service for thirty years, yet he's always counter-swinging the gates in your godson's beastly fields. Of course a man has to look after his master's interests, but we shall have to come to some arrangement. We can't go on like this." He added to Sylvia:

"It isn't the sort of place Helen ought to go to, is it? All sorts of people living with all sorts . . . If what you say is true!"

The Earl of Fittleworth gave in all places the impression that he wore a scarlet tail-coat, a white stock with a fox-hunting pin, white buckskin breeches, a rather painful eye-glass and a silk top-hat attached to his person by a silken cord. Actually he was wearing a square, high, black, felt hat, pepper-and-salt tweeds and no eye-glass. Still, he screwed up one eye to look at you, and his lucid dark pupils, his contracted swarthy face with its little bristling black-grey moustache, gave him, perched on his immense horse, the air of a querulous but very masterful monkey.

He considered that he was out of earshot of Gunning and so continued to the other two: "Oughtn't to give away masters before their servants. . . . But it *isn't* any place for the niece of the President of a Show that Cammie has most of her money in. Anyhow, she will comb my whiskers!" Before

marrying the earl, Lady Fittleworth had been Miss Camden
Grimm. "Regular Aga . . . Agapemone, so you say. A queer
go for old Mark at his age."

The general said to Fittleworth:

"Here, I say, she says I am a regular miser. . . . You
don't have any complaints, say, from your keepers that I
don't tip enough? Tell her, will you? That's the real sign of
a miser!"

Fittleworth said to Sylvia:

"You don't mind my talking like that of your husband's
establishment, do you?" He added that in the old days they
would not have talked like that before a lady about her
husband. Or perhaps, by Jove, they would have! His grandfather had had a . . .

Sylvia was of opinion that Helen Lowther could look
after herself. Her husband was said not to pay her the attentions that a lady had a right to expect of a husband. So
if Christopher . . .

She took an appraising sideways glance at Fittleworth. That
peer was going slightly purple under his brown skin. He
gazed out over the landscape and swallowed in his throat.
She felt that her time for making a decision had come.
Times changed, the world changed; she felt heavier in the
mornings than she had ever used to. She had had a long,
ingenious talk with Fittleworth the night before, on a long
terrace. She had been ingenious even for her, but she was
aware that afterwards Fittleworth had had a long bedroom
talk with his Cammie. Over even the greatest houses a certain sense of suspense broods when the master is talking to
the mistress. The master and the mistress—upon a word,
usually from the master—take themselves off, and the house-
guests, at any rate in a small party, straggle, are uncertain
as to who gives the signal to retire, suppress yawns even.
Finally the butler approaches the most intimate guests and
says that the countess will not be coming down again.

That night Sylvia had shot her bolt. On the terrace she
had drawn for the earl a picture of the ménage upon whose
roof she now looked down. It stretched out below her, that
little domain, as if she were a goddess dominating its destinies.
But she was not so certain of that. The dusky purple under
Fittleworth's skin showed no diminution. He continued to
gaze away over his territory, reading it as if it were in a
book—a clump of trees gone here, the red roof of a new
villa grown up there in among the trees, a hop-oast with its
characteristic cowl gone from a knoll. He was getting ready

to say something. She had asked him the night before to root that family out of that slope.

Naturally not in so many words. But she had drawn such a picture of Christopher and Mark as made it, if the peer believed her, almost a necessity for a conscientious nobleman to do the best to rid his country-side of a plague-spot. . . . The point was whether Fittleworth would choose to believe her because she was a beautiful woman with a thrilling voice. He was terribly domestic and attached to his transatlantic female, as only very wicked dark men late in life can contrive to be, when they come of very wicked, haughty and influential houses. They have, as it were, attended on the caprices of so many opera singers and famous professionals that when, later in life, they take capricious or influential wives, they get the knack of very stiffly but minutely showing every sort of elaborate deference to their life-partners. That is born with them.

So that the fate of that garden and that high-pitched roof was, in fact, in the hands of Cammie Fittleworth—in so far as great peers to-day have influence over the fates of their neighbours. And it is to be presumed that they have some.

But all men are curious creatures. Fittleworth stiffened at queer places. He had done so last night. He had stood a good deal. It had to be remembered that Mark Tietjens was an old acquaintance of his—not as intimate as he would have been if the earl had had children, for Mark preferred houses of married people who had children. But the earl knew Mark very well. . . . Now, a man listening to gossip about another man whom he knows very well will go pretty far towards believing what a beautiful woman will tell him. Beauty and truth have a way of appearing to be akin, and it is true that no man knows what another man is doing when he is out of sight.

So that in inventing or hinting at a ruinous, concealed harem, with consequent disease to account for Mark's physical condition and apparent ruin, she thought she was not going altogether too far. She had, at any rate, been ready to chance it. It is the sort of thing a man will believe . . . about his best friend even. He will say: "Only think. . . . All the while old X . . . was appearing such a quiet codger he was really . . . " And the words rivet conviction.

So that appeared to get through.

Her revelations as to Christopher's financial habits had not appeared to do so well. The earl had listened with his head

on one side, whilst she had let him gather that Christopher
lived on women—on the former Mrs. Duchemin, now Lady
Macmaster, for instance. Yes, to that the earl had listened
with deference, and it had seemed a fairly safe allegation to
make. Old Duchemin was known to have left a pot of money
to his widow. She had a very nice little place not six or
seven miles away from where they stood.

And it had seemed natural to bring in Edith Ethel, for,
not so long ago, Lady Macmaster had paid Sylvia a visit. It
was about the late Macmaster's debt to Christopher. That
was a point about which Lady Macmaster was and always
had seemed to be a little cracky. She had actually visited
Sylvia in order to see if Sylvia would not use her influence
with Christopher. To get him to remit the debt. Even in the
old days Lady Macmaster had been used to worry Sylvia
about that.

Apparently Christopher had not carried his idiocy as far
as might be expected. He had dragged that wretched girl
down into those penurious surroundings, but he was not going to let her and the child she appeared to be going to
have suffer actual starvation, or even too great worry. And
apparently, to satisfy a rather uneasy vanity, years before
Macmaster had given Christopher a charge on his life-insurance. Macmaster, as she well knew, had sponged unmerci-
fully on her husband, and Christopher had certainly regarded
the money he had advanced as a gift. She herself had many
times upbraided him about it; it had appeared to her one
of Christopher's worst unbearablenesses.

But apparently the charge on the life-insurance still existed
and was now a charge on that miserable fellow's rather ex-
tensive estate. At any rate, the insurance company refused
to pay over any money to the widow until the charge was
satisfied. . . . And the thought that Christopher was doing
for that girl what, she was convinced, he never would have
done for herself had added a new impulse to Sylvia's bitterness. Indeed, her bitterness had by now given way almost
entirely to a mere spirit of tormentingness—she wanted to
torture that girl out of her mind. That was why she was
there now. She imagined Valentine under the high roof suffering tortures because she, Sylvia, was looking down over
the hedge.

But the visit of Lady Macmaster had certainly revived
her bitterness, as it had suggested to her new schemes of
making herself a nuisance to the household below her. Lady
Macmaster, in widow's weeds of the most portentous crape

that gave to her at once the elegance and the direness of a funeral horse, had really seemed more than a little out of her mind. She had asked Sylvia's opinion of all sorts of expedients for making Christopher loosen his grip, and she had continued her supplications even in correspondence. At last she had hit on a singular expedient. . . . Some years before, apparently, Edith Ethel had had an affair of the heart with a distinguished Scottish littérateur, now deceased. Edith Ethel, as was well known, had acted the Egeria to quite a number of Scottish men of letters. That was natural; the Macmasters' establishment was Scottish, Macmaster had been a critic and had had government funds for the relief of indigent men of letters, and Edith Ethel was passionately cultured. You could see that even in the forms her crape took and in how she arranged it around her when she sat or agitatedly rose to wring her hands.

But the letters of this particular Scot had outpassed the language of ordinary Egerianishness. They spoke of Lady Macmaster's eyes, arms, shoulders, feminine aura. . . . These letters Lady Macmaster proposed to entrust to Christopher for sale to transatlantic collectors. She said they ought to fetch thirty thousand pounds at least, and with the ten-per-cent commission that Christopher might take, he might consider himself as amply repaid for the four-thousand-odd that Macmaster's estate owed him.

And this had appeared to Sylvia to be so eccentric an expedient that she had felt the utmost pleasure in suggesting that Edith Ethel should drive up to Tietjens' with her letters and have an interview—if possible with Valentine Wannop in the absence of Tietjens. This, she calculated, would worry her rival quite a little—and even if it did not do that, she, Sylvia, would trust herself to obtain subsequently from Edith Ethel a great many grotesque details as to the Wannop's exhausted appearance, shabby clothing, worn hands.

For it is to be remembered that one of the chief torments of the woman who has been abandoned by a man is the sheer thirst of curiosity for material details as to how that man subsequently lives. Sylvia Tietjens for a great number of years had tormented her husband. She would have said herself that she had been a thorn in his flesh. That was largely because he had seemed to her never to be inclined to take his own part. If you live with a person who suffers from being put upon a good deal, and if that person will not assert his own rights, you are apt to believe that your standards as gentleman and Christian are below his, and the experience is lastingly disagreeable. But, in any case, Sylvia Tietjens had had reason to believe that for many years, for better or for worse—and mostly for worse—she had been the dominating influence over Christopher Tietjens. Now, except for extraneous annoyances, she was aware that she could no longer influence him either for evil or for good. He was a solid, four-square lump of meal-sacks too heavy for her hauling about.

So that the only real pleasure that she had was when, at night, in a circle of cosy friends, she could assert that she was not even yet out of his confidence. Normally she would not—the members of her circle would not—have made confidantes of her ex-husband's domestics. But she had had to chance whether the details of Christopher's ménage as revealed by the wife of his carpenter would prove to her friends sufficiently amusing to make her friends forget the social trespass she committed in consorting with her husband's dependents, and she had to chance whether the carpenter's wife would not see that by proclaiming her wrongs over the fact that her husband had left her, she was proclaiming her own unattractiveness.

She had hitherto chanced both, but the time, she was aware, was at hand when she would have to ask herself whether she would not be better off if she were what the French call *rangée* as the wife of the commander-in-chief in India than as a free-lance woman owing her popularity entirely to her own exertions. It would be slightly ignominious to owe part of her prestige to a pantaloon like General Lord Edward Campion, K.C.B., but how restful might it not be! To keep your place in a society of Marjies and Beatties—and even of Cammies, like the Countess of Fittleworth—meant constant exertion and watchfulness, even if you were comfortably wealthy and well-born—and it meant still more exertion when your staple capital for entertainment was the domestic misfortunes of a husband that did not like you.

She might well point out to Marjie, Lady Stern, that her husband's clothes lacked buttons and the wife of his companion all imaginable *chic;* she might well point out to Beattie, Lady Elsbacher, that according to her husband's carpenter's wife, the interior of her husband's home resembled a cave encumbered with packing cases in dark-coloured wood, whereas in her day . . . Or she might even point out to Cammie, Lady Fittleworth, to Mrs. de Bray Pape and Mrs. Lowther that, having a defective water supply, her husband's woman probably provided him only with difficulty with baths.

. . . But every now and then someone—as had been the
case once or twice with the three American ladies—would
point out, a little tentatively, that her husband was by now
Tietjens of Groby to all intents and purposes. And people—
and in particular American ladies—would attach particular
importance before her to English country gentlemen who
had turned down titles and the like. Her husband had not
turned down a title; he had not been able to, for much as
Mark had desired to refuse a baronetcy, at the last moment
he had been given to understand that he couldn't. But her
husband had practically turned down a whole great estate,
and the romantic aspect of that feat was beginning to filter
through to her friends. For all her assertions that his seeming poverty was due to dissolute living and consequent bank-
ruptcy, her friends would occasionally ask her whether in fact
his poverty was not simply a voluntary affair, the result
either of a wager or a strain of mysticism. They would point
out that the fact that she and her son at least had all the
symptoms of considerable wealth looked like a sign rather
that Christopher did not desire wealth, or was generous, than
that he had no longer money to throw away. . . .

There were symptoms of that sort of questioning of the
mind rising up in the American ladies whom Cammie Fittleworth liked to have staying with her. Hitherto Sylvia had
managed to squash them. After all, the Tietjens household
below her feet was a singular affair for those who had not
the clue to its mystery. She had the clue herself; she knew
both about the silent feud between the two brothers and
about their attitude to life. And if it enraged her that Christopher should despise the things that money could buy and
that she so valued, it none the less gratified her to know
that, in the end, she was to be regarded as responsible for that
silent feud and the renunciation that it had caused. It
was her tongue that had set going the discreditable stories
that Mark had once believed against his brother.

But if she was to retain her power to blast that household with her tongue, she felt she ought to have details.
She must have corroborative details. Otherwise she could not
so very convincingly put over her picture of abandoned cor-
ruption. You might have thought that in her coercing Mrs.
de Bray Pape and her son into making that rather outrageous visit, and in awakening Mrs. Lowther's innocent curiosity as to the contents of the cottage, she had been inspired
solely by the desire to torment Valentine Wannop. But she
was aware that there was more than that to it. She might

get details of all sorts of queernesses that, triumphantly, to
other groups of listeners she could retail as proof of her
intimacy with that household.

If her listeners showed any signs of saying that it was
queer that a man like Christopher, who appeared like a
kindly group of sacks, should actually be a triply crossed
being, compounded by a Lovelace, Pandarus and a Satyr, she
could always answer: "Ah, but what can you expect of people
who have hams drying in their drawing-room!" Or if others
alleged that it was queer, if Valentine Wannop had Christopher as much under her thumb as she was said to have,
even by Sylvia, that she should still allow Christopher to run
an agapemone in what was, after all, her own house, Sylvia
would have liked to be able to reply: "Ah, but what can
you expect of a woman upon whose stairs you will find, side
by side, a hairbrush, a frying-pan and a copy of Sappho!"

That was the sort of detail that Sylvia needed. The one
item she had: The Tietjens, she knew from Mrs. Carpenter
Cramp, had an immense fire-place in their living-room and,
after the time-honoured custom, they smoked their hams in
that chimney. But to people who did not know that smoking hams in great chimneys was a time-honoured custom,
the assertion that Christopher was the sort of person who
dried hams in his drawing-room would bring up images of
your finding yourself in a sort of place where hams reclined
on the sofa-cushions. Even that was not a proof to the reflective that the perpetrator was a Sadic lunatic—but few
people are reflective and at any rate it was queer, and one
queerness might be taken as implying another.

But as to Valentine she could not get details enough. You
had to prove that she was a bad housekeeper and a blue-
stocking in order that it should be apparent that Christopher
was miserable—and you had to prove that Christopher was
miserable in order to make it apparent that the hold that
Valentine Wannop certainly had over him was something un-
holy. For that it was necessary to have details of misplaced
hairbrushes, frying-pans and copies of Sappho.

It had, however, been difficult to get those details. Mrs.
Cramp, when appealed to, had made it rather plain that,
far from being a bad housekeeper, Valentine Wannop did
no housekeeping at all, whereas Marie Léonie—lady Mark—
was a perfect devil of a *ménagère*. Apparently Mrs. Cramp
was allowed no further into the dwelling than the wash-house
—because of half-pounds of sugar and dusters that Mrs.

Cramp, in the character of charwoman, had believed to be her perquisites. Marie Léonie hadn't.

The local doctor and the parson, both of whom visited the house, had contributed only palely coloured portraits of the young woman. Sylvia had gone to call on them, and making use of the Fittleworth aegis—hinting that Lady Cammie wanted details of her humbler neighbours for her own instruction—Sylvia had tried to get behind the professional secrecy that distinguished parsons and doctors. But she had not got much behind. The parson gave her the idea that he thought Valentine rather a jolly girl, very hospitable and with a fine tap of cider at disposal and fond of reading under trees—the classics mostly. Very much interested also in rock-plants, as you could see by the bank under Tietjens' windows. . . . Their house was always called Tietjens'. Sylvia had never been under those windows, and that enraged her.

From the doctor Sylvia, for a faint flash, gained the impression that Valentine enjoyed rather poor health. But it had been only an impression arising from the fact that the doctor saw her every day—and it was rather discounted by the other fact that the doctor said that his daily visits were for Mark, who might be expected to pop off at any moment. So he needed careful watching. A little excitement and he was done for. . . . Otherwise Valentine seemed to have a sharp eye for old furniture, as the doctor knew to his cost, for in a small way, he collected himself. And he said that at small cottage sales and for small objects Valentine could drive a bargain that Tietjens himself never achieved.

Otherwise, from both the doctor and the parson, she had an impression of Tietjens' as a queer household—queer because it was so humdrum and united. She really herself had expected something more exciting! Really. It did not seem possible that Christopher should settle down into tranquil devotion to brother and mistress after the years of emotion she had given him. It was as if a man should have jumped out of a frying-pan into—a duck-pond.

So, as she looked at the red flush on Fittleworth's face, an almost mad moment of impatience had overcome her. This fellow was about the only man who had ever had the guts to stand up to her. . . . A fox-hunting squire: an extinct animal!

The trouble was, you could not tell quite how extinct he was. He might be able to bite as hard as a fox. Otherwise she would be running down, right now, running down that zigzag orange path to that forbidden land.

That she had hitherto never dared. From a social point
of view it would have been outrageous, but she was prepared to chance that. She was sure enough of her place in
Society, and if people will excuse a man's leaving his wife,
they will excuse the wife's making at least one or two dem-
onstrations that are a bit thick. But she had simply not dared
to meet Christopher: he might cut her.

Perhaps he would not. He was a gentleman and gentlemen do not actually cut women with whom they have slept.
. . . But he might. . . . She might go down there, and in a
dim, low room be making some sort of stipulation—God
knew what, the first that came into her head—to Valentine.
You can always make up some sort of reason for approaching the woman who has supplanted you. But he might come
in, mooning in, and suddenly stiffen into a great, clumsy—
oh, adorable—face of stone.

That was what you would not dare to face. That would
be death. She could imagine him going out of the room,
rolling his shoulders. Leaving the whole establishment indif-
ferently to her, closing only himself in invisible bonds—denied
to her by the angel with the flaming sword! . . . That was
what he would do. And that before the other woman. He
had come once very near it, and she had hardly recovered
from it. That pretended illness had not been so much pretended as all that! She had smiled angelically, under the great
crucifix, in the convent that had been her nursing home—
angelically, amongst lilies, upon the general, the sisters, the
many callers that gradually came to her teas. But she had
had to think that Christopher was probably in the arms of
his girl and he had let her go when she had, certainly
physically, needed his help.

But that had not been a calm occasion, in that dark,
empty house. . . . And he had not, at that date, enjoyed
the favours, the domesticity, of that young woman. He hadn't
had a chance of comparison, so the turning down had not
counted. He had treated her barbarously—as social counters
go it had been helpful to her—but only at the strong urge of
a young woman driven to fury: that could be palliated. It
hardly indeed affected her now as a reverse. Looked at reasonably: if a man comes home intending to go to bed with a
young woman who has bewitched him for a number of years
and finds another woman who tells him that she has cancer,
and then does a very creditable faint from the top of the
stairs and thus—in spite of practice and of being as hard
as nails—puts her ankle out of joint, he has got to choose

between the one and the other. And the other in this case had been vigorous, determined on her man, even vituperative. Obviously Christopher was not the sort of man who would *like* seducing a young woman whilst his wife was dying of internal cancer, let alone a sprained ankle. But the young woman had arrived at a stage when she did not care for any delicacies or their dictates.

No. That she had been able to live down. But if now the same thing happened, in dim, quiet daylight, in a tranquil old room . . . that she would not be able to face. It is one thing to acknowledge that your man has gone—there is no irrevocability about going. He may come back when the other woman is insignificant, a blue-stocking, entirely un-*chic*. . . . But if he took the step—the responsibility—of cutting you, that would be to put between you a barrier that no amount of weariness with your rival could overstep.

Impatience grew upon her. The fellow was away in an aeroplane. Gone North. It was the only time she had ever *known* of him as having gone away. It was her only chance of running down those orange zigzags. And now—it was all Lombard Street to a china apple that Fittleworth intended to disapprove of her running down. And you could not ignore Fittleworth.

2 ~

No, YOU could not ignore Fittleworth. As a fox-hunting squire he might be an extinct monster—though, then again, he might not: there was no knowing. But as a wicked, dark adept with bad women, and one come of a race that had been adepts with women good and bad for generations, he was about as dangerous a person as you could find. That gross, slow, earthy, obstinate fellow Gunning could stand grouchily up to Fittleworth, answer him back and chance what Fittleworth could do to him. So could any cottager. But, then, they were his people. She wasn't . . . she, Sylvia Tietjens, and she did not believe she could afford to outface him. Nor could half England.

Old Campion wanted India—probably she herself wanted Campion to have India. Groby Great Tree was cut down, and if you have not the distinction, if you rid yourself of the distinction, of Groby Great Tree just to wound a man to the heart—you may as well take India. Times were changing, but there was no knowing how the circumstances of a man like Fittleworth changed. He sat his horse like a monkey and gazed out over his land as his people had done for generations, bastard or legitimate. And it was all very well to regard him as merely a country squire married to a transatlantic nobody and so out of it. He hopped up to London —he and his Cammie too—and he passed unnoticeably about the best places and could drop a word or so here and there; and for all the countess' foreign and unknown origin, she had access to ears to which it was dangerous to have access —dangerous for aspirants to India. Campion might have his war services and his constituency. But Cammie Fittleworth was popular in the right places, and Fittleworth had his hounds and, when it came even to constituencies, the tradesmen of a couple of counties. And was wicked.

It had been obvious to her for a long time that God would one day step in and intervene for the protection of Christopher. After all, Christopher was a good man—a rather sickeningly good man. It is, in the end, she reluctantly admitted, the function of God and the invisible Powers to see that a good man shall eventually be permitted to settle down to a stuffy domestic life . . . even to chaffering over old furniture. It was a comic affair—but it was the sort of affair that you had to admit. God is probably—and very rightly —on the side of the stuffy domesticities. Otherwise the world could not continue—the children would not be healthy. And certainly God desired the production of large crops of healthy children. Mind doctors of to-day said that all cases of nervous break-down occurred in persons whose parents had not led harmonious lives.

So Fittleworth might well have been selected as the lightning conductor over the house of Tietjens. And the selection was quite a good one on the part of the Unseen Powers. And no doubt predestined. There was no accident about Mark's being under the aegis—if that was what you called it—of the earl. Mark had for long been one of the powers of the land; so had Fittleworth. They had moved in the same spheres—the rather mysterious spheres of Good People—who ruled the destinies of the nation in so far as the more decorative and more splendid jobs were concerned. They must have met about, here and there, constantly for years. And no doubt Mark had indicated that it was in that neighbourhood that he wanted to end his days simply because he wanted to be near the Fittleworths, who could be relied on to look after his Marie Léonie and the rest of them.

For the matter of that, Fittleworth himself, like God, was

on the side of the stuffy domesticities and on the side of
women who were in the act of producing healthy children.
Early in life he had had a woman to whom he was said
to have been hopelessly attached and whom he had acquired
in romantic circumstances—a famous dancer whom he had
snapped up under the nose of a very Great Person indeed.
And the woman had died in child-birth—or had given birth
to an infant child and gone mad and committed suicide after
that achievement. At any rate, for months and months, Fittleworth's friends had had to sit up night after night with him
so that he might not kill himself.

Later—after he had married Cammie in the search for a
domesticity that, except for his hounds, he too had made
really almost stuffy—he had interested himself—and of course
his countess—in the cause of providing tranquil conditions
for women before child-birth. They had put up a perfectly
lovely lying-in alms-house right under their own windows,
down there.

So there it was—and, as she took her sideways glance at
Fittleworth, high up there in the air beside her, she was perfectly aware that she might be in for such a duel with
him as had seldom yet fallen to her lot.

He had begun by saying: "God damn it, Campion, ought
Helen Lowther to be down there?" Then he had put it, as
upon her, Sylvia's information, that the cottage was in effect
a disorderly house. But he had added: "If what you say is
true."

That of course was distinctly dangerous, for Fittleworth
probably knew quite well that it had been at her, Sylvia's,
instigation that Helen Lowther *was* down there. And he was
letting her know that if it *was* at her instigation and if the
house was really in her belief a brothel, his countess would
be frightfully displeased. Frightfully.

Helen Lowther was of no particular importance, except to
the countess—and of course to Michael. She was one of
those not unattractive Americans that drift over here and enjoy themselves with frightfully simple things. She liked visiting
ruins and chattering about nothing in particular, and gal-
loping on the downs and talking to old servants, and she
liked the adoration of Michael. Probably she would have
turned down the adoration of anyone older.

And the countess probably liked to protect her innocence.
The countess was fiftyish now, and of a generation that preserved a certain stiffness along with a certain old-fashioned
broadness of mind and outspokenness. She was of a class of

American that had once seemed outrageously wealthy and
who, if in the present stage of things they did not seem
overwhelming, yet retained an aspect of impressive comfort
and social authority, and she moved in a set most of whose
individuals, American, English, or even French, were of much
the same class as herself. She tolerated—she even liked—
Sylvia, but she might well be mad if from under her roof
Helen Lowther, who was in her charge, should come into
social contact with an irregular couple. You never knew when
that point of view might not crop up in women of that date
and class.

Sylvia, however, had chanced it. She had to—and in the
end it was only pulling the string of one more shower-bath.
It was a shower-bath formidably charged—but in the end
that was her vocation in life, and, if Campion had to lose
India, she could always pursue her vocation in other country-
sides. She was tired, but not as tired as all that!

So Sylvia had chanced saying that she supposed Helen
Lowther could look after herself, and had added a salacious
quip to keep the speech in character. She knew nothing
really of Helen Lowther's husband, who was probably a lean
man with some dim avocation, but he could not be very
impressionné, or he would not let his attractive young wife
roam forever over Europe.

His lordship gave no further sign beyond repeating that if
that fellow was the sort of fellow Mrs. Tietjens said he was,
her ladyship would properly curl his whiskers. And, in face
of that, Sylvia simply had to make a concession to the extent of saying that she did not see why Helen Lowther could
not visit a show-cottage that was known, apparently over
half America. And perhaps buy some old sticks.

His lordship removed his gaze from the distant hills and
turned a cool, rather impertinent glance on her. He said:

"Ah, if it's only that . . ." and nothing more. And she
chanced it again:

"If," she said slowly too, "you think Helen Lowther is in
need of protection I don't mind if I go down and look after
her myself!"

The general, who had tried several interjections, now exclaimed:

"Surely you wouldn't meet that fellow! . . ." And that
rather spoilt it.

For Fittleworth could take the opportunity to leave her
to what he was at liberty to regard as the directions of her
natural protector. Otherwise he must have said something to

give away his attitude. So she had to give away more of her own with the words:

"Christopher is not down there. He has taken an aeroplane to York—to save Groby Great Tree. Your man Speeding saw him when he went to get your saddle. Getting into a plane." She added: "But he's too late. Mrs. de Bray Pape had a letter the day before yesterday to say the tree had been cut down. At her orders!"

Fittleworth said: "Good God!" Nothing more. The general regarded him as one fearing to be struck by lightning. Campion had already told her over and over again that Fittleworth would rage like a town bull at the bare idea that the tenant of a furnished house should interfere with its owner's timber. . . . But he merely continued to look away, communing with the handle of his crop. That called, Sylvia knew, for another concession, and she said:

"Now Mrs. de Bray Pape has got cold feet. Horribly cold feet. That's why she's down there. She's got the idea that Mark may have her put in prison!" She added further:

"She wanted to take my boy, Michael, with her to intercede. As the heir, he has some right to a view!"

And from those speeches of hers Sylvia had the measure of her dread of that silent man. Perhaps she was more tired than she thought, and the idea of India more attractive.

At that point Fittleworth exclaimed:

"Damn it all, I've got to settle the hash of that fellow Gunning!"

He turned his horse's head along the road and beckoned the general towards him with his crop-handle. The general gazed back at her appealingly, but Sylvia knew that she had to stop there and await Fittleworth's verdict from the general's lips. She wasn't even to have any duel of *sous-entendus* with Fittleworth.

She clenched her fingers on her crop and looked towards Gunning. . . . If she was going to be asked by the countess through old Campion to pack up, bag and baggage, and leave the house, she would at least get what she could out of that fellow whom she had never yet managed to approach.

The horses of the general and Fittleworth, relieved to be out of the neighbourhood of Sylvia's chestnut, minced companionably along the road, the mare liking her companion.

"This fellow Gunning," his lordship began. . . . He continued with great animation: "About these gates . . . You are aware that my estate carpenter repairs . . ."

Those were the last words she heard, and she imagined Fittleworth continuing for a long time about his bothering gates in order to put Campion quite off his guard—and no doubt for the sake of manners. Then he would drop in some shot that would be terrible to the old general. He might even cross-question him as to facts, with sly side-questions, looking away over the country.

For that she cared very little. She did not pretend to be a historian: she entertained rather than instructed. And she had conceded enough to Fittleworth. Or perhaps it was to Cammie. Cammie was a great, fat, good-natured dark thing with pockets under her liquid eyes. But she had a will. And by telling Fittleworth that she had not incited Helen Lowther and the two others to make an incursion into the Tietjens' household, Sylvia was aware that she had weakened.

She hadn't intended to weaken. It had happened. She had intended to chance conveying the idea that she intended to worry Christopher and his companion into leaving that country.

The heavy man with the three horses approached slowly, with the air of a small army in the narrow road. He was grubby and unbuttoned, but he regarded her intently with eyes a little bloodshot. He said from a distance something that she did not altogether understand. It was about her chestnut. He was asking her to back that 'ere chestnut's tail into the hedge. She was not used to being spoken to by the lower classes. She kept her horse along the road. In that way the fellow could not pass. She knew what was the matter. Her chestnut would lash out at Gunning's charges if they got near her stern. In the hunting season it wore a large K on its tail.

Nevertheless the fellow must be a good man with horses: otherwise he would not be perched on one with the stirrups crossed over the saddle in front of him and lead two others. She did not know that she would care to do that herself now-a-days; there had been a time when she would have. She had intended to slip down from the chestnut and hand it, too, over to Gunning. Once she was down on the road he could not very well refuse. But she felt disinclined—to cock her leg over the saddle. He looked like a fellow who could refuse.

He refused. She had asked him to hold her horse whilst she went down and spoke to his master. He had made no motion towards her; he had continued to stare fixedly at her. She had said:

"You're Captain Tietjens' servant, aren't you? I'm his wife. Staying with Lord Fittleworth!"

He had made no answer and no movement except to draw the back of his right hand across his left nostril—for lack of a handkerchief. He said something incomprehensible— but not conciliatory. Then he began a longer speech. That she understood. It was to the effect that he had been thirty years, boy and man, with his lordship and the rest of his time with the cahptn. He also pointed out that there was a hitching-post and chain by the gate there. But he did not advise her to hitch to it. The chestnut would kick to flinders any cart that came along the road. And the mere idea of the chestnut lashing out and injuring itself caused her to shudder; she was a good horsewoman.

The conversation went with long pauses. She was in no hurry; she would have to wait till Campion or Fittleworth came back—with the verdict probably. The fellow when he used short sentences was incomprehensible because of his dialect. When he spoke longer she got a word or two out of it.

It troubled her a little, now, that Edith Ethel might be coming along the road. Practically she had promised to meet her at that spot and at about that moment, Edith Ethel proposing to sell her love-letters to Christopher—or through him. . . . The night before, she had told Fittleworth that Christopher had bought the place below her with money he had from Lady Macmaster because Lady Macmaster had been his mistress. Fittleworth had boggled at that . . . it had been at that moment that he had gone rather stiff to her.

As a matter of fact, Christopher had bought that place out of a windfall. Years before—before even she had married him—he had had a legacy from an aunt, and in his visionary way had invested it in some colonial—very likely Canadian—property or invention or tramway concession, because he considered that some remote place, owing to its geographical position on some road—was going to grow. Apparently during the war it had grown, and the completely forgotten investment had paid nine-and-sixpence in the pound. Out of the blue. It could not be helped. With a monetary record of visionariness and generosity such as Christopher had behind him, some chickens must now and then come home—some visionary investment turn out sound, some debtor turn honest. She understood even that some colonel who had died on Armistice Night and to whom Christopher had lent a good sum in hundreds had turned honest.

At any rate his executors had written to ask her for Christopher's address with a view to making payments. She hadn't at the time known Christopher's address, but no doubt they had got it from the War Office or somewhere.

With windfalls like those he had kept afloat, for she did not believe the old-furniture business as much as paid its way. She had heard through Mrs. Cramp that the American partner had embezzled most of the money that should have gone to Christopher. You should not do business with Americans. Christopher, it is true, had years ago—during the war —predicted an American invasion—as he always predicted everything. He had, indeed, said that if you wanted to have money you must get it from where money was going to, so that if you wanted to sell you must prepare to sell what they wanted. And they wanted old furniture more than anything else. That was why there were so many of them here. She didn't mind. She was already beginning a little campaign with Mrs. de Bray Pape to make her refurnish Groby—to make her export all the clumsy eighteen-forty mahogany that the great house contained to Santa Fé, or wherever it was that Mr. Pape lived alone; and to refurnish with Louis Quatorze as befitted the spiritual descendant of the Maintenon. The worst of it was that Mr. Pape was stingy.

She was, indeed, in a fine taking that morning—Mrs. de Bray Pape. In hauling out the stump of Groby Great Tree the wood-cutters had apparently brought down two-thirds of the ball-room exterior wall, and that vast, gloomy room, with its immense lustres, was wrecked, along with the old school-rooms above it. As far as she could make out from the steward's letter, Christopher's boyhood bedroom had practically disappeared. . . . Well, if Groby Great Tree did not like Groby House it had finely taken its dying revenge. . . . A nice shock Christopher would get! Anyhow, Mrs. de Bray Pape had already pretty well mangled the great dovecote in erecting in it a new power station.

But apparently it was going to mangle the De Bray Papes to the tune of a pretty penny, and apparently Mr. Pape might be expected to give his wife no end of a time. . . . Well, you can't expect to be God's vicegerent of England without barking your shins on old, hard things.

No doubt Mark knew all about it by now. Perhaps it had killed him. She hoped it hadn't, because she still hoped to play him some tidy little tricks before she had done with him. . . . If he were dead or dying beneath that parallelogram of thatch down among the apple-boughs, all sorts of things might be going to happen. Quite inconvenient things.

There would be the title. She quite definitely did not want the title, and it would become more difficult to injure Christopher. People with titles and great possessions are vastly more difficult to discredit than impoverished commoners, because the scale of morality changes. Titles and great possessions expose you to great temptations: it is scandalous, on the other hand, that the indigent should have any fun!

So that, sitting rather restfully in the sunlight on her horse, Sylvia felt like a general who is losing the fruits of victory. She did not much care. She had got down Groby Great Tree: that was as nasty a blow as the Tietjenses had had in ten generations.

But then a queer, disagreeable thought went through her mind, just as Gunning at last made again a semi-comprehensible remark. Perhaps in letting Groby Great Tree be cut down God was lifting the ban off the Tietjenses. He might well. Gunning, however, had said something like:

"Shedd'n gaw dahn theer. Ride Boldero up to farm 'n' put he in loose-box." She gathered that if she would ride her horse to some farm he could be put in a loose-box and she could rest in the farmer's parlour. Gunning was looking at her with a queer intent look. She could not just think what it meant.

Suddenly it reminded her of her childhood. Her father had had a head gardener just as gnarled and just as apparently autocratic. That was it. She had not been much in the country for thirty years. Apparently country-people had not changed much. Times change; people not so much.

For it came back to her with sudden extraordinary clearness. The side of a greenhouse, down there in the west where she had been "Miss Sylvia, oh, Miss *Sylvia!*" for a whole army of protesting retainers, and that old, brown, gnarled fellow who was equally Mr. Carter for them all except her father. Mr. Carter had been potting geranium-shoots and she had been a little teasing a white kitten. She was thirteen, with immense plaits of blond hair. The kitten had escaped from her and was rubbing itself, its back arched, against the leggings of Mr. Carter, who had a special affection for it. She had proposed—merely to torment Mr. Carter—to do something to the kitten, to force its paws into walnut-shells perhaps. She had so little meant to hurt the kitten that she had forgotten what it was she had proposed to do. And suddenly the heavy man, his bloodshot eyes fairly blazing, had threatened if she so much as blew on that kitten's fur to

thrash her on a part of her anatomy on which public school-
boys rather than young ladies are usually chastised . . . so
that she would not be able to sit down for a week, he had
said.

Oddly enough, it had given her a queer pleasure, that returned always with the recollection. She had never otherwise
in her life been threatened with physical violence, and she
knew that within herself the emotion had often and often
existed: If only Christopher would thrash her within an inch
of her life . . . Or yes—there had been Drake . . . He had
half killed her: on the night before her wedding to Christopher. She had feared for the child within her! That emotion
had been unbearable!

She said to Gunning—and she felt for all the world as if
she were trying a torment on Mr. Carter of years ago:

"I don't see why I need go to the farm. I can perfectly
well ride Boldero down this path. I must certainly speak to
your master."

She had really no immediate notion of doing anything of
the sort, but she turned her horse towards the wicket-gate
that was a little beyond Gunning.

He scrambled off his horse with singular velocity and under
the necks of those he led. It was like the running of an
elephant, and, with all the reins bunched before him, he almost
fell with his back on the little wicket towards whose latch
she had been extending the handle of her crop. . . . She
had not meant to raise it. She swore she had not meant to
raise it. The veins stood out in his hairy open neck and
shoulders. He said: No, she didn'!

Her chestnut was reaching its teeth out towards the led
horses. She was not certain that he heard her when she
asked if he did not know that she was the wife of the
captain, his master, and guest of Lord Fittleworth, his ex-
master. Mr. Carter certainly had not heard her years ago
when she had reminded him that she was his master's daughter. He had gone on fulminating. Gunning was doing that
too—but more slowly and heavily. He said first that the
cahptn would tan her hide if she so much as disturbed his
brother by a look; he would hide her within an inch of her
life. As he had done already.

Sylvia said that by God he never had; if he said he had
he lied. Her immediate reaction was to resent the implication that she was not as good a man as Christopher. He
seemed to have been boasting that he had physically corrected her.

Gunning continued dryly:

"You put it in the papers yourself. My ol' missus read it me. Powerful set on Sir Mark's comfort, the cahptn is. Threw you downstairs, the cahptn did, 'n' give you cancer. It doesn't show!"

That was the worst of attracting chivalrous attentions from professional people. She had begun divorce proceedings against Christopher, in the way of a petition for restitution of conjugal rights, compounding with the shade of Father Consett and her conscience as a Roman Catholic by arguing that a petition for the restoration of your husband from a Strange Woman is not the same as divorce proceedings. In England at that date it was a preliminary and caused as much publicity as the real thing, to which she had no intention of proceeding. It caused quite a terrific lot of publicity, because her counsel in his enthusiasm for the beauty and wit of his client—in his chambers the dark, Gaelic, youthful K.C. had been impressively sentimental in his enthusiasm—learned counsel had overstepped the rather sober bounds of the preliminary aspects of these cases. He knew that Sylvia's aim was not divorce but the casting of all possible obloquy on Christopher, and in his fervid Erse oratory he had cast as much mud as an enthusiastic terrier with its hind legs out of a fox's hole. It had embarrassed Sylvia herself, sitting brilliantly in court. And it had roused the judge, who knew something of the case, having, like half London of his class, taken tea with the dying Sylvia beneath the crucifix and amongst the lilies of the nursing home that was also a convent. The judge had protested against the oratory of Mr. Sylvian Hatt, but Mr. Hatt had got in already a lurid picture of Christopher and Valentine in a dark, empty house on Armistice Night throwing Sylvia downstairs and so occasioning in her a fell disease from which, under the court's eyes, she was fading. This had distressed Sylvia herself, for, rather with the idea of showing the court and the world in general what a fool Christopher was to have left her for a little brown sparrow, she had chosen to appear all radiance and health. She had hoped for the appearance of Valentine in court. It had not occurred.

The judge had asked Mr. Hatt if he really proposed to bring in evidence that Captain Tietjens and Miss Wannop had enticed Mrs. Tietjens into a dark house—and on a shake of the head that Sylvia had not been able to refrain from giving Mr. Hatt, the judge had made some extremely rude remarks to her counsel. Mr. Hatt was at that time standing as parliamentary candidate for a Midland borough and was anxious to attract as much publicity as that or any other case would give him. He had therefore gone bald-headed for the judge, even accusing him of being indifferent to the sufferings he was causing to Mr. Hatt's fainting client. Rightly handled, impertinence to a judge will gain quite a number of votes on the radical side of Midland constituencies, judges being supposed to be all Tories.

Anyhow, the case had been a fiasco from Sylvia's point of view, and for the first time in her life she had felt mortification; in addition she had felt a great deal of religious trepidation. It had come into her mind in court—and it came with additional vividness there above that house, that, years ago in her mother's sitting-room in a place called Lobscheid, Father Consett had predicted that if Christopher fell in love with another woman, she, Sylvia, would perpetrate acts of vulgarity. And there she had been, not only toying with the temporal courts in a matter of marriage, which is a sacrament, but led undoubtedly into a position that she had to acknowledge was vulgar. She had precipitately left the court when Mr. Hatt had for the second time appealed for pity for her—but she had not been able to stop it. . . . Pity! She appeal for pity! She had regarded herself—she had certainly desired to be regarded—as the sword of the Lord smiting the craven and the traitor—to Beauty! And was it to be supported that she was to be regarded as such a fool as to be decoyed into an empty house! Or as to let herself be thrown downstairs! . . . But *qui facit per alium* is herself responsible, and there she had been in a position as mortifying as would have been that of any city clerk's wife. The florid periods of Mr. Hatt had made her shiver all over, and she had never spoken to him again.

And her position had been broadcasted all over England— and now, here in the mouth of this gross henchman, it had recurred. At the most inconvenient moment. For the thought suddenly recurred, sweeping over with immense force: God had changed sides at the cutting down of Groby Great Tree.

The first intimation she had had that God might change sides had occurred in that hateful court, and had, as it were, been prophesied by Father Consett. That dark saint and martyr was in Heaven, having died for the Faith, and undoubtedly he had the ear of God. He had prophesied that she would toy with the temporal courts; immediately she had felt herself degraded, as if strength had gone out from her.

Strength had undoubtedly gone out from her. Never before

in her life had her mind not sprung to an emergency. It was all very well to say that she could not move physically either backwards or forwards for fear of causing a stampede amongst all those horses and that therefore her mental uncertainty might be excused. But it was the finger of God— or of Father Consett who, as saint and martyr, was the agent of God. . . . Or perhaps God himself was here really taking a hand for the protection of his Christopher, who was undoubtedly an Anglican saint. . . . The Almighty might well be dissatisfied with the other relatively amiable saint's conduct of the case, for surely Father Consett might be expected to have a soft spot for her, whereas you could not expect the Almighty to be unfair even to Anglicans. . . . At any rate, up over the landscape, the hills, the sky, she felt the shadow of Father Consett, the arms extended as if on a gigantic cruciform—and then, above and behind that, an . . . an August Will!

Gunning, his bloodshot eyes fixed on her, moved his lips vindictively. She had, in face of those ghostly manifestations across hills and sky, a moment of real panic. Such as she had felt when they had been shelling near the hotel in France, when she had sat amidst palms with Christopher under a glass roof. . . . A mad desire to run—or as if your soul ran about inside you like a parcel of rats in a pit awaiting an unseen terrier.

What was she to do? What the devil was she to do? . . . She felt an itch. . . . She felt the very devil of a desire to confront at least Mark Tietjens . . . even if it should kill the fellow. Surely God could not be unfair! What was she given beauty for—the dangerous remains of beauty!—if not to impress it on the unimpressible! She ought to be given the chance at least once more to try her irresistible ram against that immovable post before . . . She was aware . . .

Gunning was saying something to the effect that if she caused Mrs. Valentine to have a miscarriage or an idiot child, 'is lordship would flay all the flesh off 'er bones with 'is own ridin'-crop. 'Is lordship 'ad fair done it to 'im, Gunning 'isself, when 'e lef' 's missus then eight and a 'arf munce gone, to live with old Mother Cressy! The child was bore dead.

The words conveyed little to her. . . . She was aware . . . She was aware . . . What was she aware of . . . She was aware that God—or perhaps it was Father Consett that so arranged it, more diplomatically, the dear!—desired that she should apply to Rome for the dissolution of her marriage with Christopher and that she should then apply to the civil courts. She thought that probably God desired that Christopher should be freed as early as possible, Father Consett suggesting to him the less stringent course.

A fantastic object was descending at a fly-crawl the hill-road that went almost vertically up to the farm amongst the beeches. She did not care!

Gunning was saying that that were why 'is lordship give 'im the sack. Took away the cottage an' ten bob a week that 'is lordship allowed to all as had been in his service thritty year.

She said: "What! What's that? . . ." Then it came back to her that Gunning had suggested that she might give Valentine a miscarriage. . . . Her breath made a little clittering sound, like the trituration of barley ears, in her throat; her gloved hands, reins and all, were over her eyes, smelling of morocco leather; she felt as if within her a shelf dropped away—as the platform drops away from beneath the feet of a convict they are hanging. She said: "Could . . ." Then her mind stopped, the clittering sound in her throat continuing. Louder. Louder.

Descending the hill at the fly's pace was the impossible. A black basket-work pony-phaeton: the pony—you always look at the horse first—four hands too big; as round as a barrel, as shining as a mahogany dining-table, pacing for all the world like a *haute école* circus steed, and in a panic bumping its behind into that black vehicle. It eased her to see . . . But . . . fantastically horrible, behind that grotesque coward of a horse, holding the reins, was a black thing, like a funeral charger; beside it a top-hat, a white face, a buff waistcoat, black coat, a thin, Jewish beard. In front of that a bare, blond head, the hair rather long—on the front seat, back to the view. Trust Edith Ethel to be accompanied by a boy-poet *cicisbeo*! Training Mr. Ruggles for his future condition as consort!

She exclaimed to Gunning:

"By God, if you do not let me pass, I will cut your face in half. . . ."

It was justified! This in effect was too much—on the part of Gunning and God and Father Consett. All of a heap they had given her perplexity, immobility and a dreadful thought that was gripping her vitals. . . . Dreadful! Dreadful!

She must get down to the cottage. She must get down to the cottage.

She said to Gunning:

"You damn fool. . . . You *damn* fool. . . . I want to save . . ."

He moved up—interminably—sweating and hairy, from the gate on which he had been leaning, so that he no longer barred her way. She trotted smartly past him and cantered beautifully down the slope. It came to her from the bloodshot glance that his eyes gave her that he would like to outrage her with ferocity. She felt pleasure.

She came off her horse like a circus performer to the sound of "Mrs. Tietjens! Mrs. Tietjens," in several voices from above. She let the chestnut go to hell.

It seemed queer that it did not seem queer. A shed of logparings set upright, the gate banging behind her. Applebranches spreading down; grass up to the middle of her grey breeches. It was Tom Tiddler's Ground; it was near a place called Gemmenich on the fourth of August, 1914! . . . But just quietude: quietude.

Mark regarded her boy's outline with beady, inquisitive eyes. She bent her switch into a half-hoop before her. She heard herself say:

"Where are all these fools? I want to get them out of here!"

He continued to regard her: beadily: his head like mahogany against the pillows. An apple-bough caught in her hair.

She said:

"Damn it all, I had Groby Great Tree cut down: not that tin Maintenon. But, as God is my saviour, I would not tear another woman's child in the womb!"

He said:

"You poor bitch! You poor bitch! The riding has done it!"

She swore to herself afterwards that she had heard him say that, for at the time she had had too many emotions to regard his speaking as unusual. She took, indeed, a prolonged turn in the woods before she felt equal to facing the others. Tietjens' had its woods onto which the garden gave directly.

Her main bitterness was that they had this peace. She was cutting the painter, but they were going on in this peace; her world was waning. It was the fact that her friend Bobbie's husband, Sir Gabriel Blantyre—formerly Bosenheim—was cutting down expenses like a lunatic. In her world there was the writing on the wall. Here they could afford to call her a poor bitch—and be in the right of it, as like as not!

3 ~

VALENTINE WAS awakened by the shrill overtones of the voice of the little maid coming through the open window. She had fallen asleep over the words: *"Saepe te in somnis vidi!"* to a vision of white limbs in the purple Adriatic. Eventually the child's voice said:

"We only sez 'mem' to friends of the family!" shrilly and self-assertively.

She was at the casement, dizzy and sickish with the change of position and the haste—and violently impatient of her condition. Of humanity she perceived only the top of a three-cornered grey hat and a grey panniered skirt in downward perspective. The sloping tiles of the potting-shed hid the little maid; aligned small lettuce plants, like rosettes on the dark earth, ran from under the window, closed by a wall of sticked peas, behind them the woods, slender grey ash-trunks going to a great height. They were needed for shelter. They would have to change their bedroom: they could not have a night nursery that faced the north. The spring onions needed pricking out: she had meant to put the garden pellitory into the rocks in the half-circle; but the operation had daunted her. Pushing the little roots into crevices with her fingers, removing stones, trowelling in artificial manure, stooping, dirtying her fingers would make her retch. . . .

She was suddenly intensely distressed at the thought of the lost coloured prints. She had searched the whole house—all imaginable drawers, cupboards, presses. It was like their fate that, when they had at last got a good—an English—client, their first commission from her should go wrong. She thought again of every imaginable, unsearched parallelogram in the house, standing erect, her head up, neglecting to look down on the intruder.

She considered all their customers to be intruders. It was true that Christopher's gifts lay in the way of old-furniture dealing—and farming. But farming was ruinous. Obviously if you sold old furniture straight out of use in your own house, it fetched better prices than from a shop. She did not deny Christopher's ingenuity—or that he was right to rely on her hardihood. He had at least the right so to rely. Nor did she mean to let him down. Only . . .

She passionately desired little Chrissie to be born in that
bed with the thin fine posts, his blond head with the thin
fine hair on those pillows. She passionately desired that he
should lie with blue eyes gazing at those curtains on the
low windows. . . . *Those!* With those peacocks and globes.
Surely a child should lie gazing at what his mother had seen
whilst she was awaiting him!

And, where were those prints? . . . Four parallelograms
of faint, silly colour. Promised for tomorrow morning. The
margins needed bread-crumbing. . . . She imagined her
chin brushing gently, gently back and forward on the floss
of his head; she imagined holding him in the air as, in that
bed, she lay, her arms extended upwards, her hair spread
on those pillows! Flowers perhaps spread on that quilt. Laven-
der!

But if Christopher reported that one of those dreadful
people with querulous voices wanted a bedroom complete? . . .
If she begged him to retain it for her. Well, he would.
He prized her above money. She thought—ah, she knew—
that he prized the child within her above the world.

Nevertheless, she imagined that she would go all on to
the end with her longings unvoiced. . . . Because there was
the game. . . . His game . . . oh, hang it, *their* game! And
you have to think whether it is worse for the unborn child
to have a mother with unsatisfied longings, or a father beaten
at his . . . No, you must not call it a game. . . . Still,
roosters beaten by other roosters lose their masculinity. . . .
Like roosters, men. . . . Then, for a child to have a father
lacking masculinity . . . for the sake of some peacock and
globe curtains, spindly bed-posts, old, old glass tumblers with
thumb-mark indentations. . . .

On the other hand, for the mother the soft feeling that
those things give! . . . The room had a barrel-shaped ceiling,
following the lines of the roof almost up to the roof-tree;
dark oak beams, beeswaxed—ah, that beeswaxing! Tiny, low
windows almost down to the oaken floor. . . . You would
say, too much of the show-place: but you lived into it. You
lived yourself into it in spite of the Americans who took,
sometimes embarrassed, peeps from the doorway.

Would they have to peek into the nursery? Oh, God, who
knew? What would he decree? It was an extraordinary thing
to live with Americans all over you, dropping down in aeroplanes, seeming to come up out of the earth. . . . There, all
of a sudden, you didn't know how. . . .

That woman below the window was one, now. How in the

world had she got below that window? . . . But there were
so many entrances—from the spinney, from the Common,
through the fourteen-acre, down from the road. . . . You
never knew who was coming. It was eerie; at times she shivered over it. You seemed to be beset—with stealthy people,
creeping up all the paths. . . .

Apparently the little tweeny was disputing the right of that
American woman to call herself a friend of the family and
thus to be addressed as "Mem"! The American was asserting
her descent from Madame de Maintenon. . . . It was astonishing the descents they all had! She herself was descended
from the surgeon-butler to Henry VII—Henry the Some-
thingth. And, of course, from the great Professor Wannop,
beloved of lady educators and by ladies whom he had educated. . . . And Christopher was eleventh Tietjens of Groby
—with an eventual burgomaster of Scheveningen or somewhere in some century or other: time of Alva. Number one
came over with Dutch William, the Protestant Hero! . . . If
he had not come, and if Professor Wannop had not educated
her, Valentine Wannop—or educated her differently—she
would not have . . . Ah, but she would have! If there had
not been any HE, looking like a great Dutch *treckschluyt*
or whatever you call it—she would have had to invent one to
live with in open sin. . . . But her father might have educated her so as to have—at least presentable underclothes. . . .

He could have educated her so as to be able to say—oh,
but tactfully:

"Look here, you. . . . Examine my . . . my *cache-corsets*.
. . . Wouldn't some new ones be better than a new pedigree
sow?" The fellow never had looked at her . . . *cache-corsets*.
Marie Léonie had!

Marie Léonie was of opinion that she would lose Christopher
if she did not deluge herself with a perfume called Houbigant
and wear pink silk next the skin. *Elle ne demandait pas
mieux*—but she could not borrow twenty pounds from Marie
Léonie. Nor yet forty. . . . Because, although Christopher
might never notice the condition of her all-wools, he jolly
well would be struck by the ocean of Houbigant and the
surf of pink. . . . She would give the world for them. . . .
But he would notice—and then she might lose his love. Because she had borrowed the forty pounds. On the other hand,
she might lose it because of the all-wools. And heaven knew
in what condition the other pair would be when they came
back from Mrs. Cramp's newest laundry attentions. . . . You

could never teach Mrs. Cramp that wool must not be put into boiling water!

Oh God, she ought to lie between lavendered linen sheets with little Chrissie on soft, pink silk, air-cushionish bosoms! . . . Little Chrissie, descended from surgeon-butler—surgeon-barber, to be correct!—and burgomaster. Not to mention the world-famous Professor Wannop. . . . Who was to become . . . who was to become, if it was as she wished it . . . But she did not know what she wished, because she did not know what was to become of England or the world. . . . But if he became what Christopher wished he would be a contemplative parson farming his own tithe-fields and with a Greek Testament in folio under his arm. . . . A sort of White of Selborne. . . . Selborne was only thirty miles away, but they had had never the time to go there. . . . As who should say: *Je n'ai jamais vu Carcassonne.* . . . For, if they had never found time, because of pigs, hens, pea-sticking, sales, selling, mending all-wool undergarments, sitting with dear Mark—before little Chrissie came with the floss silk on his palpitating soft poll and his spinning pebble-blue eyes: if they had never found time now, before, how in the world would there be time with, added on to all the other, the bottles, and the bandagings and the bathing before the fire with the warm, warm water, and feeling and the slubbing of the soap-saturated flannel on the adorable, adorable limbs? And Christopher looking on. . . . He would never find time to go to Selborne, nor Arundel, nor Carcassonne, nor after the Strange Woman. . . . Never. Never!

He had been away now for a day and a half. But it was known between them—without speaking!—that he would never be away for a day and a half again. Now, before her pains began he could . . . seize the opportunity! Well, he had seized it with a vengeance. . . . A day and a half! To go to Wilbraham sale! With nothing much that they wanted. . . . She believed . . . she believed that he had gone to Groby in an aeroplane. . . . He had once mentioned that. Or she knew that he had thought of it. Because the day before yesterday when he had been almost out of his mind about the letting of Groby, he had suddenly looked up at an aeroplane and had remained looking at it for long, silent . . . Another woman it could not be. . . .

He had forgotten about those prints. That was dreadful. She knew that he had forgotten about them. How could he, when they wanted to get a good, English client, for the sake of little Chrissie? How could he? How could he? It is true that he was almost out of his mind about Groby and Groby Great Tree. He had begun to talk about that in his sleep, as for years, at times, he had talked, dreadfully, about the war.

"Bringt dem Hauptmann eine Kerze. . . . Bring the major a candle," he would shout dreadfully beside her in the blackness. And she would know that he was remembering the sound of picks in the earth beneath the trenches. And he would groan and sweat dreadfully, and she would not dare to wake him. . . . And there had been the matter of the boy, Aranjuez's, eye. It appeared that he had run away over a shifting landscape, screaming and holding his hand to his eye. After Christopher had carried him out of a hole. . . . Mrs. Aranjuez had been rude to her at the Armistice Night dinner. . . . The first time in her life that anyone—except of course Edith Ethel—had been ever rude to her. Of course you did not count Edith Ethel Duchemin, Lady Macmaster! . . . But it's queer: your man saves the life of a boy at the desperate risk of his own. Without that there would not have been any Mrs. Aranjuez: then Mrs. Aranjuez is the first person that ever in your life is rude to you. Leaving permanent traces that made you shudder in the night? Hideous eyes!

Yet, but for a miracle there might have been no Christopher. Little Aranjuez—it had been because he had talked to her for so long, praising Christopher, that Mrs. Aranjuez had been rude to her!—little Aranjuez had said that the German bullets had gone over them as thick as the swarm of bees that came out when Gunning cut the leg off the skep with his scythe! . . . Well, there might have been no Christopher. Then there would have been no Valentine Wannop! She could not have lived. . . . But Mrs. Aranjuez should not have been rude to her. The woman must have seen with half an eye that Valentine Wannop could not live without Christopher. . . . Then, why should she fear for her little, imploring, eyeless creature!

It was queer. You would almost say that there was a Provvy who delighted to torment you with: "If it hadn't been that . . ." Christopher probably believed that there was a Provvy or he would not dream for his little Chrissie a country parsonage. . . . He proposed, if they ever made any money, to buy a living for him—if possible near Salisbury. . . . What was the name of the place? . . . a pretty name. . . . Buy a living where George Herbert had been parson. . . .

She must, by the bye, remember to tell Marie Léonie that

it was the Black Orpington labelled 42 not the Red 16 that
she had put the setting of Indian runners under. She had
found that Red 16 was not really broody, though she had come
on afterwards. It was queer that Marie Léonie had not
the courage to put eggs under broody hens because they
pecked her, whereas she, Valentine, had no courage to take
the chickens when the settings hatched, because of the shells
and gumminesses that might be in the nests. . . . Yet neither
of them wanted courage. . . . Hang it all, neither of them
wanted courage, or they would not be living with Tietjenses.
It was like being tied to buffaloes!

And yet . . . How you wanted them to charge!

Bremersyde. . . . No, that was the home of the Haigs.
. . . Tide what will and tide what tide, there shall be Haigs
at Bremersyde. . . . Perhaps it was Bemersyde! . . . Bemerton, then. George Herbert, rector of Bemerton, near Wilton,
Salisbury. . . . That was what Chrissie was to be like. . . .
She was to imagine herself sitting with her cheek on Chrissie's
floss-silk head, looking into the fire and seeing in the coals
Chrissie walking under elms beside plough-lands. *Elle ne demandait,* really, *pas mieux!*

If the country would stand it! . . .

Christopher presumably believed in England as he believed
in Provvy—because the land was pleasant and green and
comely. It would breed true. In spite of showers of Americans descended from Tiglath Pileser and Queen Elizabeth,
and the end of the industrial system and the statistics of the
shipping trade, England with its pleasant, green comeliness
would go on breeding George Herberts with Gunnings to
look after them. . . . Of course with Gunnings!

The Gunnings of the land were the rocks on which the
lighthouse was built—as Christopher saw it. And Christopher
was always right. Sometimes a little previous. But always
right. Always right. The rocks had been there a million years
before the lighthouse was built: the lighthouse made a deuce
of a movable flashing—but it was a mere butterfly. The rocks
would be there a million years after the light went for the
last time out.

A Gunning would be, in the course of years, painted
blue, a Druid-worshipper, a Duke Robert of Normandy, il-
literately burning towns and begetting bastards—and eventually—actually at the moment—a man of all works, half full
of fidelity, half blatant, hairy. A retainer you would retain
as long as you were prosperous and dispensed hard cider

and overlooked his peccadilloes with women. He would go on. . . .

The point was whether the time had come for another Herbert of Bemerton. Christopher thought it had: he was always right; always right. But previous. He had predicted the swarms of Americans buying up old things. Offering fabulous prices. He was right. The trouble was they did not pay when they offered the fabulous prices: when they did pay they were as mean as . . . she was going to say Job. But she did not know that Job was particularly mean. That lady down below the window would probably want to buy the signed cabinet of Barker of 1762 for half the price of one bought in a New York department store and manufactured yesterday. . . . And she would tell Valentine she was a blood-sucker, even if—to suppose the ridiculous!—Valentine let her have it at her own price. On the other hand, Mr. Schatzweiler talked of fantastic prices. . . .

Oh, Mr. Schatzweiler, Mr. Schatzweiler, if you would only pay us ten per cent of what you owe us I could have all the pink fluffies, and three new gowns, and keep the little old lace for Chrissie—and have a proper dairy and not milk-goats. And cut the losses over the confounded pigs, and put up a range of glass in the sunk garden where it would not be an eyesore. . . . As it was . . .

The age of fairy-tales was not, of course, past. They had had windfalls: lovely windfalls when infinite ease had seemed to stretch out before them. . . . A great windfall when they had bought this place; little ones for the pigs and old mare. . . . Christopher was the sort of fellow; he had sowed so many golden grains that he could not be always reaping whirlwinds. There must be some halcyon days. . . .

Only it was deucedly awkward now—with Chrissie coming and Marie Léonie hinting all day that, as she was losing her figure, if she could not get the grease stains out of her skirt she would lose the affections of Christopher. And they had not got a stiver. . . . Christopher had cabled Schatzweiler. . . . But what was the use of that? . . . Schatzweiler would be finely dished if she lost the affections of Christopher —because poor old Chris could not run any old junk-shop without her. . . . She imagined cabling Schatzweiler—about the four stains on the skirt and the necessity for elegant lying-in gowns. Or else he would lose Christopher's assistance. . . .

The conversation down below raised its tones. She heard the tweeny maid ask why if the American lady was a friend of the family she did not know 'er ladyship theere? . . .

Of course it was easy to understand: these people came, all of them, with letters of introduction from Schatzweiler. Then they insisted that they were friends of the family. It was perhaps nice of them—because most English people would not want to know old-furniture dealers.

The lady below exclaimed in a high voice:

"That Lady Mark Tietjens! That! Mercy me, I thought it was the cook!"

She, Valentine, ought to go down and help Marie Léonie. But she was not going to. She had the sense that hostile presences were creeping up the path and Marie Léonie had given her the afternoon off. . . . For the sake of the future, Marie Léonie had said. And *she* had said that she had once expected her own future to offer the reading of Aeschylus beside the Aegean Sea. Then Marie Léonie had kissed her and said she knew that Valentine would never rob her of her belongings after Mark died!

An unsolicited testimonial, that. But of course Marie Léonie would desire her not to lose the affections of Christopher. Marie Léonie would say to herself that in that case Christopher might take up with a woman who *would* want to rob Marie Léonie of her possessions after Mark died. . . .

The woman down below announced herself as Mrs. de Bray Pape, descendant of the Maintenon, and wanted to know if Marie Léonie did not think it reasonable to cut down a tree that overhung your house. Valentine desired to spring to the window: she sprang to the old panelled door and furiously turned the key in the lock. She ought not to have turned the key so carelessly: it had a knack of needing five or ten minutes manipulation before you could unlock the door again. . . . But she ought to have sprung to the window and cried out to Mrs. de Bray Pape: "If you so much as touch a leaf of Groby Great Tree we will serve you with injunctions that it will take half your life and money to deal with!"

She ought to have done that to save Christopher's reason. But she could not: she could not! It was one thing living with all the tranquillity of conscience in the world in open sin. It was another, confronting elderly Americans who knew the fact. She was determined to remain shut in there. An Englishman's house may no longer be his castle—but an Englishwoman's castle is certainly her own bedroom. When once, four months or so ago, the existence of little Chrissie being manifest, she had expressed to Christopher the idea that they ought no longer to go stodging along in penury, the case being so grave: they ought to take some of the Groby money—for the sake of future generations . . .

Well, she had been run down. . . . At that stage of parturition, call it, a woman is run down and hysterical. . . . It had seemed to her overwhelmingly the fact that a breeding woman ought to have pink fluffy things next her quivering skin and sprayings of, say, Houbigant, all over her shoulders and hair. For the sake of the child's health.

So she had let out violently at poor wretched old Chris, faced with the necessity for denying his gods, and had slammed to and furiously locked that door. Her castle had been her bedroom with a vengeance then—for Christopher had been unable to get in or she to get out. He had had to whisper through the keyhole that he gave in: he was dreadfully concerned for her. He had said that he hoped she would try to stick it a little longer, but, if she would not, he would take Mark's money.

Naturally she had not let him—but she *had* arranged with Marie Léonie for Mark to pay a couple of pounds more a week for their board and lodging, and as Marie Léonie had perforce taken over the housekeeping, they had found things easing off a little. Marie Léonie had run the house for thirty shillings a week less than she, Valentine, had ever been able to do—and run it streets better. Streets and streets! So they had had money at least nearly to complete their equipments of table-linen and the layette. . . . The long and complicated annals!

It was queer that her heart was nearly as much in Christopher's game as was his own. As house-mother, she ought to have grabbed after the last penny—and goodness knew the life was strain enough. Why do women back their men in unreasonable romanticisms? You might say that it was because, if their men had their masculinities abated—like defeated roosters!—the women would suffer in intimacies. . . . Ah, but it wasn't that! Nor was it merely that they wanted the buffaloes to which they were attached to charge.

It was really that she had followed the convolutions of her man's mind. And ardently approved. She disapproved with him of riches, of the rich, of the frame of mind that riches confer. If the war had done nothing else for them— for those two of them—it had induced them, at least, to install Frugality as a deity. They desired to live hard, even if it deprived them of the leisure in which to think high! She agreed with him that if a ruling class loses the capacity

to rule—or the desire!—it should abdicate from its privileges and get underground.

And having accepted that as a principle, she could follow
the rest of his cloudy obsessions and obstinacies.

Perhaps she would not have backed him up in his long
struggle with dear Mark if she had not considered that their
main necessity was to live high. . . . And she was aware
that why, really, she had sprung to the door rather than to
the window had been that she had not desired to make an
unfair move in that long chess-game. On behalf of Christopher. If she had had to see Mrs. de Bray Pape or to speak
to her it would have been disagreeable to have that descendant of a king's companion look at her with the accusing eyes
of one who thinks: "You live with a man without being
married to him!" Mrs. de Bray Pape's ancestress had been
able to force the king to marry her. . . . But that she would
have chanced: they had paid penalty enough for having
broken the rules of the club. She could carry her head high
enough: not obtrusively high, but sufficiently! For, in effect,
they had surrendered Groby in order to live together and had
endured sprays of obloquy that seemed never to cease to
splash over the garden-hedges.

No, she would have faced Mrs. de Bray Pape. But she
would hardly, given Christopher's half-crazed condition, have
kept herself from threatening Mrs. Pape with dreadful legal
consequences if she touched Groby Great Tree. That would
have been to interfere in the silent Northern struggle between
the brothers. That she would never do, even to save Christopher's reason—unless she were jumped into it! . . . That
Mark did not intend to interfere between Mrs. Pape and the
tree she knew—for when she had read Mrs. Pape's letter
to him he had signified as much to her by means of his
eyes. . . . Mark she loved and respected because he was a
dear—and because he had backed her through thick and
thin. Without him . . . There had been a moment on that
dreadful night . . . She prayed God that she would not have
to think again of that dreadful night. . . . If she had to see
Sylvia again she would go mad, and the child within her.
. . . Deep, deep within her the blight would fall on the
little thread of brain!

Mrs. de Bray Pape, God be thanked, provided a diversion
for her mind. She was speaking French with an eccentricity
that could not be ignored.

Valentine could see, without looking out of the window,
Marie Léonie's blank face and the equal blankness with which

she must have indicated that she did not intend to understand. She imagined her standing, motionless, pinafored and unmerciful before the other lady, who beneath the three-cornered hat was stuttering out:

"Lady Tietjens, *mwaw,* Madame de Bray Pape, *desire coopay la arbre. . . .*"

Valentine could hear Marie Léonie's steely tones saying:

"On dit 'l'arbre,' Madame!"

And then the high voice of the little maid:

"Called us 'the pore,' she did, your ladyship. . . . Ast us why we could not take example!"

Then a voice, soft for these people, and with modulations:

"Sir Mark seems to be perspiring a great deal. I was so free as to wipe . . ."

As, above, Valentine said: "Oh, heaven!" Marie Léonie cried out: *"Mon Dieu!"* and there was a rush of skirts and pinafore.

Marie Léonie was rushing past a white, breeched figure, saying:

"'*Vous, une étrangère, avez osé. . . .*'

A shining, red-cheeked boy was stumbling slightly from before her. He said, after her back:

"Mrs. Lowther's handkerchief is the smallest, softest . . ." He added to the young woman in white: "We'd better go away. . . . Please let's go away. . . . It's not sporting . . ." A singularly familiar face; a singularly moving voice. "For God's sake, let us go away. . . ." Who said "For God's sake!" like that—with staring blue eyes?

She was at the door frantically twisting at the great iron key; the lock was of very old hammered ironwork. The doctor ought to be telephoned to. He had said that if Mark had fever or profuse sweats, he should be telephoned to at once. Marie Léonie would be with him; it was her, Valentine's, duty to telephone. The key would not turn; she hurt her hand in the effort. But part of her emotion was due to that bright-cheeked boy. Why should he have said that it was not sporting of them to be there? Why had he exclaimed for God's sake to go away? The key would not turn. It stayed solid, like a piece of the old lock. . . . Who was the boy like? She rammed her shoulder against the unyielding door. She must not do that. She cried out.

From the window—she had gone to the window intending to tell the girl to set up a ladder for her, but it would be more sensible to tell her to telephone!—she could see Mrs. de Bray Pape. She was still haranguing the girl. And then

on the path, beyond the lettuces and the newly sticked peas,
arose a very tall figure. A very tall figure. Portentous. By
some trick of the slope, figures there always appeared very
tall. . . . This appeared leisurely: almost hesitant. Like the
apparition of the statue of the commander in Don Juan,
somehow. It appeared to be preoccupied with its glove: undoing its glove. . . . Very tall, but with too much slight-
ness of the legs. . . . A woman in hunting-breeches! Grey
against the tall ash-stems of the spinney. You could not see
her face because you were above her, in the window, and
her head was bent down! In the name of God! . . .

There wafted over her a sense of the dreadful darkness
in the old house at Gray's Inn on that dreadful night. . . .
She must not think of that dreadful night because of little
Chrissie deep within her. She felt as if she held the child
covered in her arms, as if she were looking upwards, bending down over the child. Actually she was looking downwards. . . . Then she had been looking upwards—up the
dark stairs. At a marble statue: the white figure of a woman:
the Nike . . . the Winged Victory. It is like that on the
stairs of the Louvre. She must think of the Louvre: not
Gray's Inn. There were, in a Pompeian anteroom, Etruscan
tombs, with guardians in uniform, their hands behind their
backs. Strolling about as if they expected you to steal a
tomb! . . .

She had—they had—been staring up the stairs. The house
had seemed unnaturally silent when they had entered. Unnaturally. . . . How can you seem more silent than silent.
But you *can!* They had seemed to tiptoe. She had, at least.
Then light had shone above—coming from an opened door
above. In the light the white figure that said it had cancer!

She must not think about these things!

Such rage and despair had swept over her as she had
never before known. She had cried to Christopher, dark,
beside her: that the woman lied. She had not got cancer. . . .

She must not think about these things.

The woman on the path—in grey riding things—approached slowly. The head still bent down. Undoubtedly she
had silk underthings beneath all that grey cloth. . . . Well,
they—Christopher and Valentine—gave her them.

It was queer how calm she was. That of course was Sylvia
Tietjens. Let it be. She had fought for her man before and
so she could again; the Russians should not have . . . The
old jingle ran in her calm head. . . .

But she was desperately perturbed: trembling. At the

thought of that dreadful night. Christopher had wanted to go with Sylvia after she had fallen downstairs. A good theatre fall, but not good enough. But she had shouted: No! He was never going with Sylvia again. *Finis Sylviae et magna.* . . . In the black night . . . They had gone on firing maroons. They could be heard!

Well, she was calm. The sight of that figure was not going to hurt the tiny brain that worked deep within her womb. Nor the tiny limbs! She was going to slub the warm, soap-transfused flannel onto those little legs in the warm of the great hearth. . . . Nine hams up that chimney! Chrissie looking up and laughing. . . . That woman would never again do that! Not to a child of Christopher's. Not to any man's child, belike!

That had been that woman's son! With a girl in white breeches! . . . Well, who was she, Valentine, to prevent a son's seeing his father. She felt on her arm the weight of her own son. With that there she could confront the world.

It was queer! That woman's face was all blurred. . . . Blubberingly! The features swollen, the eyes red. . . . Ah, she had been thinking, looking at the garden and the stillness: "If I had given Christopher that I should have kept him!" But she would never have kept him. Had she been the one woman in all the world, he would never have looked at her. Not after he had seen her, Valentine Wannop!

Sylvia had looked up, contemplatively—as if into the very window. But she could not see into the window. She must have seen Mrs. de Bray Pape and the girl, for it became apparent why she had taken off her glove. She now had a gold vanity-box in her hand: looking in at the mirror and moving her right hand swiftly before her face. . . . Remember: it was *we* who gave her that gold thing. Remember! Remember it hard!

Sudden anger came over her. That woman must never come into their house-place, before whose hearth she was to bathe the little Chrissie! Never! Never! The place would be polluted. She knew, only by that, how she loathed and recoiled from that woman.

She was at the lock. The key turned. . . . See what emotion at the thought of harm to your unborn child can do for you! Subconsciously her right hand had remembered how you pressed the key upwards when you made it turn. . . . She must not run down the narrow stairs. The telephone was in a niche on the inner side of the great ingle. The room was dim: very long, very low. The Barker cabinet looked very rich, with its green, yellow and scarlet inlays. She was leaning sideways in the nook between the immense fire-place and the room wall, the telephone receiver at her ear. She looked down her long room—it opened into the dining-room, a great beam between. It was dark, gleaming, rich with old beeswaxed woods. . . . *Elle ne demandait pas mieux* . . . the phrase of Marie Léonie occurred constantly to her mind. . . . She did not ask better—if only the things were to be regarded as theirs! She looked into the distant future when things would spread out tranquilly before them. They would have a little money, a little peace. Things would spread out . . . like a plain seen from a hill. In the meantime they had to keep all on going. . . . She did not, in effect, grumble at that . . . as long as strength and health held out.

The doctor—she pictured him, long, sandy and very pleasant, suffering too from an incurable disease and debts, life being like that!—the doctor asked cheerfully how Mark was. She said she did not know. He was said to have been profusely sweating. . . . Yes, it was possible that he might have been having a disagreeable interview. The doctor said: "Tut! Tut! And yourself?" He had a Scotch accent, the sandy man. . . . She suggested that he might bring along a bromide. He said: "They've been bothering you. Don't let them!" She said she had been asleep—but they probably would. She added: "Perhaps you would come quickly! . . ." Sister Anne! Sister Anne! For God's sake, Sister Anne! If she could get a bromide into her it would pass like a dream.

It was passing like a dream. Perhaps the Virgin Mary exists. . . . If she does not we must invent her to look after mothers who could not . . . But she could! She, Valentine Wannop!

The light from the doorway that was open onto the garden was obscured. A highwayman in skirts with panniers stood in the room against the light. It said:

"You're the saleswoman, I guess. This is a most insanitary place, and I hear you have no bath. Show me some things. In the Louie Kaator's style. . . ." It guessed that it was going to refurnish Groby in Louis Quatorze style. Did she, Valentine, as saleswoman, suppose that they—her employers— would meet her in the expense. Mr. Pape had had serious losses in Miami. They must not suppose that the Papes could be bled white. This place ought to be pulled down as unfit for human habitation and a model workman's cottage build in its place. People who sold things to rich Americans in this country were sharks. She herself was descended spiritually from Madame de Maintenon. It would be all different if Marie Antoinette had treated the Maintenon better. She, Mrs. de Bray Pape, would have the authority in the country that she ought to have. She had been told that she would be made to pay an immense sum for having cut down Groby Great Tree. Of course the side-wall of the house had fallen in. These old houses could not stand up to modern inventions. She, Mrs. de Bray Pape, had employed the latest Australian form of tree-stump extractor—the Wee Whizz Bang. . . . But did she, as saleswoman but doubtless more intimate with her employers than was necessary, considering the reputation of that establishment . . . did she consider? . . .

Valentine's heart started. The light from the doorway was again obscured. Marie Léonie ran panting in. Sister Anne, in effect! She said: *"Le téléphone! Vite!"*

Valentine said:

"J'ai déjà téléphoné. . . . Le docteur sera ici dans quelques minutes. . . . Je te prie de rester à côté de moi! . . ." I beg you to remain beside me! Selfish! Selfish! But there was a child to be born. . . . Anyhow Marie Léonie could not have got out of that door. It was blocked. . . . Ah!

Sylvia Tietjens was looking down on Valentine. You could hardly see her face against the light. . . . Well, it did not amount to more than that. . . . She was looking down because she was so tall; you could not see her face against the light. Mrs. de Bray Pape was explaining what spiritual descent from *grands seigneurs* did for you.

She was bending her eyes on Valentine. That was the phrase. She said to Mrs. de Bray Pape:

"For God's sake hold your *damned* tongue. Get out of here!"

Mrs. de Bray Pape had not understood. For the matter of that, neither did Valentine take it in. A thin voice from a distance thrilled:

"Mother! . . . Mo . . . ther!"

She—IT—for it was like a statue . . . Marvellous how she had made her face up. Three minutes before it had been a mush! . . . It was flawless now; dark-shadowed under the eyes! And sorrowful! And tremendously dignified. And kind! . . . Damn! Damn! Damn!

It occurred to Valentine that this was only the second time that she had ever seen that face. . . . Its stillness now was terrible! What was she waiting for before she began the Billingsgate that they were both going to indulge in before all these people? . . . For she, Valentine, had her back against the wall! She heard herself begin to say:

"You have spoilt . . ." She could not continue. You cannot very well tell a person that their loathsomeness is so infectious as to spoil your baby's bathing-place! It is not done!

Marie Léonie said in French to Mrs. de Bray Pape that Mrs. Tietjens did not require her presence. Mrs. de Bray Pape did not understand. It is difficult for a Maintenon to understand that her presence is not required!

The first time that she, Valentine, had seen that face, in Edith Ethel's drawing-room, she had thought how kind . . . how blindingly kind it was. When the lips had approached her mother's cheek the tears had been in Valentine's eyes. It had said—that face of a statue!—that it must kiss Mrs. Wannop for her kindness to Christopher. . . . Damn it, it might as well kiss her, Valentine, now! . . . There would have been no Christopher to-day but for her!

It said—it was so perfectly expressionless that you could continue to call it "it"—it said, coldly and without halt, to Mrs. de Bray Pape:

"You hear! The lady of the house does not require your presence. Please go away!"

Mrs. de Bray Pape was explaining that she had been telling the saleswoman that she intended to refurnish Groby in the Louie Kaator's style.

It occurred to Valentine that this position had its comicalities: Marie Léonie did not know that woman; Mrs. de Bray Pape did not know her, Valentine. They would miss a good deal of the jam! . . . But where was the jam! Jam yesterday, jam to-morrow. . . . That figure had said "Mrs. Tietjens!" In sarcasm, then? In delicacy?

She caught at the telephone shelf; it was dark. The baby had moved within her. . . . It wanted her to be called "Mrs. Tietjens!" Someone was calling "Valentine!" Someone else was calling "Mother!" A softer voice said: "Mrs. Tietjens!" What things they chose to say! The first voice was Edith Ethel's!

Dark! . . . Marie Léonie said in her ear: *"Tiens toi debout, ma chérie!"*

"Dark, dark night; cold, cold snow—Harsh, harsh wind, and lo!—Where shall we shepherds go, God's son to find?"

Edith Ethel was reading to Mrs. de Bray Pape from a letter. She said: "As an American of culture, you will be interested . . . From the great poet! . . ." A gentleman held a top-hat in front of his face, as if he were in church. Thin, with dull eyes and a Jewish beard! Jews kept their hats on in church. . . .

Apparently she, Valentine Wannop, was going to be denounced before the congregation! Did they bring a scarlet letter? . . . They were Puritans enough, she and Christopher. The voice of the man with the Jewish beard—Sylvia Tietjens had removed the letter from the fingers of Edith Ethel. . . . Not much changed, Edith Ethel! Face a *little* lined. And pale. And suddenly reduced to silence—the voice of the man with the beard said:

"After all! It does make a difference. He is virtually Tietjens of . . ." He began to push his way backwards, outwards. A man trying to leave through the crowd at the church-door. He turned to say to her oddly:

"*Madame* . . . eh . . . Tietjens! Par*don!*"

Attempting a French accent.

Edith Ethel remarked:

"I wanted to say to Valentine: 'If I effect the sale personally, I do not see that the commission should be payable.' "

Sylvia Tietjens said they could discuss that outside. Valentine was aware that, some time before, a boy's voice had said: "Mother, is this sporting?" It occurred to Valentine to wonder if it was sporting of people to call her "Mrs. Tietjens" under Sylvia Tietjens' nose. Of course she had to be Mrs. Tietjens before the servants. She heard herself say:

"I am sorry Mr. Ruggles called me Mrs. Tietjens before you!"

The eyes of the statue were, if possible, doubly bent on her!

It said drily:

"An' the King will ha'e my heid, I care na' what ye do wi' my——" It was a saying common to both Mark and Christopher. . . . That was bitter. She was reminding her, Valentine, that she had previously enjoyed Tietjens' intimacies —before her, Valentine!

But the voice went on:

"I wanted to get those people out. . . . And to see . . ." It spoke very slowly. Marmoreally. The flowers in the jug on the fald-stool needed more water. Marigolds. Orange. . . . A woman is upset when her child moves within her. Sometimes more, sometimes less. She must have been very upset: there had been a lot of people in the room; she knew neither how they had come nor how they had gone. She said to Marie Léonie:

"Dr. Span is bringing some bromide. . . . I can't find those . . ."

Marie Léonie was looking at that figure: her eyes stuck out of her head like Christopher's. She said, as still as a cat watching a mouse:

"Qui est elle? C'est bien la femme?"

It looked queerly like a pilgrim in a ballet, now, that figure against the light—the long legs slightly bent gave that effect. Actually this was the third time she had seen it—but in the dark house she had not really seen the face. . . . The features had been contorted and thus not the real features: these were the real features. There was about that figure something timid. And noble. It said:

"Sporting! Michael said: 'Be sporting, mother!' . . . Be sporting. . . ." It raised its hand as if to shake a fist at heaven. The hand struck the beam across the ceiling: that roof was so low. And dear! It said: "It was Father Consett really. . . . They can all, soon, call you Mrs. Tietjens. Before God, I came to drive those people out. . . . But I wanted to see how it was you kept him. . . ."

Sylvia Tietjens was keeping her head turned aside, drooping. Hiding a tendency to tears, no doubt. She said to the floor:

"I say again, as God hears me, I never thought to harm your child. . . . His child. . . . But any woman's . . . Not harm a child . . . I have a fine one, but I wanted another. . . . Their littleness . . . The riding has done it. . . ." Someone sobbed!

She looked loweringly then at Valentine:

"It's Father Consett in heaven that has done this. Saint and martyr: desiring soft things! I can almost see his shadow across these walls now it's growing dark. You hung him: you did not even shoot him, though I *say* you shot him to save my feelings. . . . And it's you who will be going on through all the years. . . ."

She bit into a small handkerchief that she had in her hand, concealed. She said: "Damn it, I'm playing pimp to Tietjens of Groby—leaving my husband to you! . . ."

Someone again sobbed.

It occurred to Valentine that Christopher had left those prints at old Hunt's sale in a jar on the field. They had not wanted the jar. Then Christopher had told a dealer called Hudnut that he could have that jar and some others as against a little carting service. . . . He would be tired when he got back, Christopher. He would have, nevertheless, to go to Hudnut's: Gunning could not be trusted. But they must not disappoint Lady Robinson. . . .

Marie Léonie said:

"C'est lamentable qu'un seul homme puisse inspirer deux telles passions dans deux telles femmes. . . . C'est le martyre de notre vie!"

Yes, it was lamentable that a man could inspire two such passions in two women. Marie Léonie went to look after Mark. There was no Sylvia Tietjens. They say joy never kills. She fell straight down onto the ground, lumpishly!

. . . It was lucky they had the Bussorah rug, otherwise Chrissie . . . They must have some money. . . . Poor . . . poor . . .

4 ~

MARK TIETJENS had lain considering the satisfaction of a great night he had lately passed. Or perhaps not lately: at some time.

Lying out there in the black nights, the sky seemed enormous. You could understand how somewhere heaven could be concealed in it. And tranquil at times. Then you felt the earth wheeling through infinity.

Night-birds cried overhead: herons, duck, swans even: the owls kept closer to the ground, beating along the hedgerows. Beasts became busy in the long grass. They rustled busily, then paused for long. No doubt a rabbit ran till it found an attractive plantain. Then it nibbled for a long time without audible movement. Now and then cattle lowed, or many lambs—frightened by a fox maybe. . . .

But there would be nevertheless long silences. . . . A stoat would get onto the track of the rabbit. They would run, run, run, brushing through the long grass, then out into the short meadow and round and round, the rabbit squealing. Loudly at first.

In the dim illumination of his night-light, dormice would climb up the posts of his shelter. They would remain regarding him with beads of eyes. When the rabbits squealed they would hunch themselves together and shiver. They knew it meant S-t-o-a-t=stoat! Their turn soon!

He despised himself a little for attending to these minutiae —as if one were talking down to a child. . . . On his great night the whole cattle of the county had been struck with panic; you heard them crashing down through the hedges and miles down into the silent valleys.

No! He had never been one to waste his time and mind on small mammals and small birds. . . . The flora and fauna of Blankshire! . . . Not for him. It was big movements interested him: "wherein manifesteth itself the voice of God! . . ." Very likely that was true. Transport. Panic in cattle over whole counties. In people over whole continents.

Once, years—oh, years and years—ago, when he had been aged twelve and on a visit to grandfather, he had taken a gun to Redcar Sands from Groby, over the moors, and with one shot he had brought down two terns, a sandpiper and a herring-gull. Grandfather had been so delighted with his prowess—though naturally the shot had been a fluke—that he had the things stuffed, and there they were in Groby Nursery to this day. The herring-gull stiff on a mossy rock, the sandpiper doing obeisance before it, the terns flying, one on each side. Probably that was the only memorial to him, Mark Tietjens, at Groby. The younger children had been wont to refer with awe to "Mark's bag" for long years afterwards. The painted background had shown Bamborough Castle with lashings of foam and blue sky. It was a far cry from Redcar to Bamborough—but that was the only background the bird-stuffing chap in Middlesbrough could paint for sea-birds. For larks and the like he had a cornfield in the Vale of York; for nightingales, poplar-trees. . . . Never heard that nightingales were particularly partial to poplars!

. . . Nightingales disturbed the majesty of great nights. For two months out of the year, more or less, according to the nature of the season. He wasn't decrying the beauty of their voices. Hearing them, you felt like seeing a good horse win the St. Leger. No other things in the world could do it—just as there was no place in the world like Newmarket Heath on a breezy day. . . . But they limited the night. It was true that nightingales deep down in the spinney near where Gunning's hut must be—say, a quarter of a mile away—could make you think of great distance, echoing up through the deep woods. Woods dripping with dew beneath the moon. . . . And air raids not so long ago! The moon brought air raids and its shining was discouraged. . . . Yes, nightingales made you think of distance, just as the nightjar forever crepitating from twilight to dawn seemed to measure a fragment of eternity. . . . But only fragments!

The great night was itself eternity and the Infinite. . . . The spirit of God walking on the firmament.

Cruel beggars, nightingales: they abused one another with distended throats all through the night. Between the gusts of gales you could hear them shouting on—telling their sitting hens that they—each one—were the devils of fellows, the other chap, down the hill by Gunning's hut, being a bedraggled, louse-eaten braggart. . . . Sex ferocity.

Gunning lived in a bottom, in a squatter's cottage, they said. With a thatch like Robinson Crusoe's bonnet. A wise woman's cottage. He lived with the wise woman, a chalk-white-faced slattern. . . . And a grand-daughter of the wise woman whom, because she had a cleft palate and only half a brain, the parish, half out of commiseration, half for economy, had nominated mistress in the school up the hill. No one knew whether Gunning slept with the wise woman or the grand-daughter; for one or the other he had left his missus and Fittleworth had tanned his hide and taken his cottage from him. He thrashed them both impartially with a hunting-thong every Saturday night—to learn them, and to remind them that for them he had lost his cottage and the ten bob a week Fittleworth allowed such hinds as had been in his service thirty years. . . . Sex ferocity again!

> And how shall I thy true love know from another one?
> Oh, by his cockled hat and staff and by his sandalled shoon!

An undoubted pilgrim had suggested irresistibly the lines to him! . . . It was naturally that bitch Sylvia. Wet eyes she had! . . . Then some psychological crisis was going on inside her. Good for her.

Good for Val and Chris, possibly. There was no real knowing. . . . Oh, but there was. Hear to that: the bitch-pack giving tongue! Heard ye ever the like to that, sirs? She had had Groby Great Tree torn down. . . . But, as God was her maker, she would not tear another woman's child within her. . . .

He felt himself begin to perspire. . . . Well, if Sylvia had come to that, his, Mark's, occupation was gone. He would no longer have to go on willing against her; she would drop into the sea in the wake of their family vessel and be lost to view. . . . But, damn it, she must have suffered to be brought to that pitch. . . . Poor bitch! Poor bitch! The riding had done it. . . . She ran away, a handkerchief to her eyes.

He felt satisfaction and impatience. There was some place to which he desired to get back. But there were also things to be done: to be thought out. . . . If God was beginning to temper the wind to these flayed lambs . . . Then . . . He could not remember what he wanted to think about. . . . It was—no, not exasperating. Numb! He felt himself responsible for their happiness. He wanted them to go rubbing along, smooth with the rough, for many long, unmarked years. . . . He wanted Marie Léonie to stay with Valentine until after her deliverance and then to go to the dower-house at Groby. She was Lady Tietjens. She knew she was Lady Tietjens, and she would like it. Besides, she would be a thorn in the flesh of Mrs. . . . He could not remember the name. . . .

He wished that Christopher would get rid of his Jewish partner so as to addle a little brass. It was their failing as Tietjenses that they liked toadies. . . . He himself had bitched all their lives by having that fellow Ruggles sharing his rooms. Because he could not have borne to share with an equal, and Ruggles was half Jew, half Scotchman. Christopher had had, for toadies, firstly Macmaster, a Scot, and then this American Jew. Otherwise he, Mark, was reconciled with things. Christopher, no doubt, was wise in his choice. He had achieved a position in which he might—with just a little more to it—anticipate jogging away to the end of time, leaving descendants to carry on the country without swank.

Ah. . . . It came to his mind to remember, almost with pain. He had accepted nephew Mark as nephew Mark: a strong slip. A good boy. But there was the point . . . the point! . . . The boy had the right sort of breeches. . . . But if there were incest . . .

Crawling through a hedge after a rabbit was thinkable. Father had been in the churchyard to shoot rabbits to oblige the vicar. There was no doubt of that. He did not want rabbits. . . . But supposing he had mis-hit a bunny and the little beast had been throwing gymnastics on the other side of the quickset? Father would have crawled through, then, rather than go all the way to the lich-gate and round. Decent men put their mis-hits out of their agony as soon as possible. Then there was motive. And as for not putting his gun out of action before crawling through the quickset . . . Many good, plucked men had died like that. . . . *And father had grown absent-minded!* . . . There had been farmer Lowther had so died; and Pease of Lobhall; and Pease of Cullercoats. All good plucked farmers. . . . Crawling through hedges rather than go round, and with their guns at full cock! And not absent-minded men. . . . But he remembered that, just now, he had remembered that father had grown absent-minded. He would put a paper in one of his waistcoat pockets and fumble for it in all his other pockets a moment after: he would push his spectacles up onto his forehead and search all the room for them; he would place his knife and fork in his plate and, whilst talking, take another knife and fork from beside it and begin again to eat. . . . Mark remembered that his father had done that twice during the last meal they had eaten together—whilst he, Mark, had been presenting the fellow Ruggles' account of Christopher's misdeeds. . . .

Then it would not be incumbent on him, Mark, to go up to his father in heaven and say: "Hullo, sir. I understand you had a daughter by the wife of your best friend, she being now with child by your son. . . ." Rather ghostly so to introduce yourself to the awful ghost of your father. . . . Of course you would be a ghost yourself. Still, with your billycock hat, umbrella and racing-glasses, not an awful ghost! . . . And to say to your father: "I understand that you committed suicide!"

Against the rules of the club. . . . For I consider it no grief to be going there where so many great men have preceded me. Sophocles, that, wasn't it? So, on his authority, it was a damn good club. . . .

But he did not have to anticipate that *mauvais quart d'heure!* Dad quite obviously did not commit suicide. He wasn't the man to do so. So Valentine was not his daughter and there was no incest. It is all very well to say that you care little about incest. The Greeks made a hell of a tragic row about it. . . . Certainly it was a weight off the chest if you could think there had been none. He had always been able to look Christopher in the eyes—but he would be able to do it better than ever now. Comfortably! It is uncomfortable to look a man in the eyes and think: "You sleep between incestuous sheets. . . ."

That, then, was over. The worst of it rolled up together. No suicide. No incest. No by-blow at Groby. . . . A papist there. . . . Though how you could be a papist and a Marxian communist passed his, Mark's, comprehension. . . . A papist at Groby and Groby Great Tree down. . . . The curse was perhaps off the family!

That was a superstitious way to look at it—but you must have a pattern to interpret things by. You can't really get your mind to work without it. The blacksmith said: "By hammer and hand all art doth stand! . . ." He, Mark Tietjens, for many years interpreted all life in terms of transport. . . . Transport, be thou my God. . . . A damn good God. . . . And in the end, after a hell of a lot of thought and of work, the epitaph of him, Mark Tietjens, ought by rights to be: "Here lies one whose name was writ in sea-birds!" As good an epitaph as another.

He must get it through to Christopher that Marie Léonie should have that case, with Bamborough and all, in her bedroom at Groby dower-house. It was the last permanent record of her man. . . . But Christopher would know that. . . .

It was coming back. A lot of things were coming back. . . . He could see Redcar Sands running up towards Sunderland, grey, grey. Not so many factory chimneys then, working for him, Mark Tietjens! Not so many! And the sandpipers running in the thin of the tide, bowing as they ran; and the shovellers turning over stones and the terns floating above the viscous sea. . . .

But it was great nights to which he would now turn his attention. Great black nights above the purple moors. . . . Great black nights above the Edgware Road, where Marie Léonie lived . . . because, above the blaze of lights of the old Apollo's front, you had a sense of immense black spaces. . . .

Who said he was perspiring a great deal? Well, he *was* perspiring!

Marie Léonie, young, was bending over him. . . . Young, young, as he had first seen her on the stage of Covent Garden. . . . In white! . . . Doing agreeable things to his face with a perfume like that of heaven itself! . . . And laughing sideways as Marie Léonie had laughed when first he presented himself before her in his billycock hat and umbrella! . . . The fine, fair hair! The soft voice!

But this was silly. . . . That was nephew Mark with his cherry-red face and staring eyes. . . . And this was his light of love! . . . Naturally. Like uncle, like nephew. He would pick up with the same type of woman as his uncle. That made it certain that he was no by-blow! Pretty piece against the apple-boughs!

He wanted great nights, then! Young Mark, though, should not pick up with a woman older than himself. Christopher had done that, and look!

Still: things were takking oop! . . . Do you remember the Yorkshireman who stood with his chin just out of the water on Ararat Top as Noah approached. And: "It's boon to tak opp!" said the Yorkshireman. . . . It's bound to clear up!

A great night, with room enough for heaven to be hidden there from our not too perspicacious eyes. . . . It was said that an earthquake shock imperceptible to our senses set those cattle and sheep and horses and pigs crashing through all the hedges of the county. And it was queer: before they had so started lowing and moving, Mark was now ready to swear that he had heard a rushing sound. He probably had not! One could so easily self-deceive oneself! The cattle had been panicked because they had been sensible of the presence of the Almighty walking upon the firmament. . . .

Damn it all: there were a lot of things coming back. He could have sworn he heard the voice of Ruggles say: "After all, he is virtually Tietjens of Groby!" By no fault of yours, old cock! But now you will be cadging up to him. . . . Now there speaks Edith Ethel Macmaster! A lot of voices passing behind his head. Damn it all, could they all be ghosts drifting before the wind! . . . Or, damn it all, was he himself dead? . . . No, you were probably not profane when you were dead.

He would have given the world to sit up and turn his head round and see. Of course he *could,* but that would give the show away! He credited himself with being too cunning an old fox for that! To have thrown dust in their eyes for all these years! He could have chuckled!

Fittleworth seemed to have come down into the garden and to be remonstrating with these people. What the devil could Fittleworth want? It was like a pantomime. Fittleworth, in effect, was looking at him. He said:

"Hello, old bean. . . ." Marie Léonie was looking beside his elbow. He said: "I've driven all these goats out of your hen-roost." Good-looking fellow, Fittleworth. His Lola Vivaria had been a garden-peach. Died in child-birth. No doubt that was why he had troubled to come. Fittleworth said: Cammie said to give Mark her love for old time's sake. Her dear love! And as soon as he was well to bring her ladyship down. . . .

Damn this sweat. With its beastly tickling he would grimace and give the show away. But he would like Marie Léonie to go to the Fittleworths'. Marie Léonie said something to Fittleworth.

"Yes, yes, me lady!" says Fittleworth. Damn it, he did look like a monkey as some people said. . . . But if the monkeys we were descended from were as good-looking. . . .

Probably he had good-looking legs. . . . How beautiful upon the mountains are the feet of them that bring good tidings to Zion. . . . Fittleworth added earnestly and distinctly that Sylvia—Sylvia Tietjens—*begged* Mark to understand that she had not sent that flock of idiots down here. Sylvia also said that she was going to divorce his, Mark's, brother and dissolve her marriage with the sanction of Rome. . . . So they would all be a happy family down there, soon. . . . Anything Cammie could do . . . Because of Mark's unforgettable services to the nation . . .

Name was written in . . . Lettest thou thy servant . . . divorce in peace!

Marie Léonie begged Fittleworth to go away now. Fittleworth said he would, but joy never kills! So long, old . . . old friend!

The clubs they had been in together . . . But one went to a far better club than . . . His breathing was a little troublesome. . . . It was darkish, then light again.

Christopher was at the foot of his bed. Holding a bicycle and a lump of wood. Aromatic wood: a chunk sawn from a tree. His face was white: his eyes stuck out. Blue pebbles. He gazed at his brother and said:

"Half Groby wall is down. Your bedroom's wrecked. I found your case of sea-birds thrown on a rubble heap."

It was as well that one's services were unforgettable!

Valentine was there, panting as if she had been running. She exclaimed to Christopher:

"You left the prints for Lady Robinson in a jar you gave to Hudnut the dealer. How could you? Oh, how could you? How are we going to feed and clothe a child if you do such things?"

He lifted his bicycle wearily round. You could see he was dreadfully weary, the poor devil. Mark almost said:

"Let him off: the poor devil's worn out!"

Heavily, like a dejected bull-dog, Christopher made for the gate. As he went up the green path beyond the hedge, Valentine began to sob.

"How are we to live? How are we ever to live?"

"Now I must speak," Mark said.

He said:

"Did ye ever hear tell o' t' Yorkshireman . . . On Mount Ara . . . Ara . . ."

He had not spoken for so long. His tongue appeared to fill his mouth, his mouth to be twisted to one side. It was growing dark. He said:

"Put your ear close to my mouth. . . ." She cried out.
He whispered:

> " ' 'Twas the mid o' the night and the barnies grat
> And the mither beneath the mauld heard that. . . .'

An old song. My nurse sang it. . . . Never thou let thy
child weep for thy sharp tongue to thy good man. . . . A
good man! Groby Great Tree is down. . . ." He said: "Hold
my hand!"

She inserted her hand beneath the sheet and his hand
closed on hers. Then it relaxed.

She nearly cried out for Marie Léonie.

The tall, sandy, much-liked doctor came through the gate.
She said:

"He spoke just now. . . . It has been a torturing afternoon.
. . . Now I'm afraid . . . I'm afraid he's . . ."

The doctor reached his hand beneath the sheet, leaning
sideways. He said:

"Go get you to bed. . . . I will come and examine you. . . ."
She said:

"Perhaps it would be best not to tell Lady Tietjens that
he spoke. . . . She would like to have had his last words.
. . . But she did not need them as much as I."

AFTERWORD

I ~

The first half of *Parade's End—Some Do Not . . .* and *No More Parades*—shows us England immediately before the First World War, when the parade of Edwardian society was almost hectically brilliant, and during the war, when the ruling classes of that society lost control in the military conflict in France and the "best" people lost their moral authority in a feverish struggle for status at home.

In *Some Do Not . . .* we see a peacetime England that is apparently stable but actually decaying from within and losing responsibility and discipline. The government is becoming a system suited to the talents of Macmaster rather than those of Christopher Tietjens, and in the realm of private conduct the privileged lives of the upper classes are becoming exercises of irresponsible whims like Sylvia Tietjens', while the responsible lives of Mrs. Wannop and her daughter, Valentine, subject them to starvation and the danger of arrest.

In *No More Parades* we see the collapse of governmental authority; the processional figures of the staff like General Campion and Levin are badly confused, and the authorities in Whitehall are living in a world of vicious fantasy. The real fighting is being done by insignificant, muddy, half-crazed soldiers like O Nine Morgan, McKechnie, and Christopher. We see too the collapse of private discipline; Sylvia leaves her retreat at Birkenhead to pursue Christopher to Rouen in a disintegrating passion to seduce and dominate him. The disciplined moral life is being led by Valentine Wannop in the obscurity of a girls' school.

At the conclusion of these two novels Christopher Tietjens deliberately ends his effort to live, publicly and privately, by the code of his society because his personal experience has forced him to recognize that the actual life of his society, in its management of the war and in the personal conduct of its "best" people, has become a parody of its own professed intentions. He sees it will be suicidal for him to cling to the way of life of a world that is dead. The collapse of the Edwardian world has freed him to live his own life, to work out a standard of conduct that fits his real feelings and to try to live by it. In *A Man Could Stand Up*— we see Christopher transferring his sense of moral obligation to the fighting soldiers of the front lines and determining to start his personal life over again with Valentine Wannop. In *Last Post* we see him—ironically enough, largely through the mind of his brother and double, Mark, who has chosen to die with his world rather than change—painfully reconstructing himself and his life.

This is the general thematic development of the two novels in this volume, but *Parade's End* is not a straightforward narration arranged chronologically or logically. Throughout the four novels Ford uses the time shift, overlapping narration, and other devices to arrange the events in the order they might have for a perceptive mind that is as much concerned with the significance of the events as with their existence. Since the order of Ford's narrative is determined by meaning, not by time, its action must, like the actions of Pound's *Cantos* and Joyce's *Ulysses*, be conceived by the reader as occurring on the timeless stage of the author's mind rather than in a temporally ordered "real" world.

2 ~

Ford's way of ordering his events can be seen most clearly in *A Man Could Stand Up*—, which begins at approximately eleven o'clock in the morning of November 11, 1918, Armistice Day. We are in the mind of Valentine Wannop, who is at the telephone in the girls' school listening to Edith Ethel Duchemin, now Lady Macmaster, who is telling her that Christopher Tietjens is back from France and in London. We stay with Valentine and within her mind until she has finally admitted to herself—and explained to the shocked headmistress, Miss Wanostrocht, an old pupil and lifelong admirer of Valentine's father—that the enlightened late-Victorian standards her professor father had inculcated in her simply do not work in the postwar world and have to be discarded. She has at the same time faced what she has been trying to suppress ever since she and Christopher parted the night before he left for the front in August, 1917, namely, that she is helplessly in love with Christopher. Having thus discarded the high-minded, unworkable character she has so far struggled to live up to and having faced the truth about herself, she determines to seek out Christopher and to commit herself to life with him.

Part Two begins "months and months before," in Christopher's mind. It is, to be precise, six months before, a few minutes before dawn of an April morning in 1918. Part Two covers in time the relatively quiet morning of this day during the great battle in which Ludendorff so nearly defeated the Allies. During this morning we watch Christopher's gradual recognition of the consequences of his decision to cease to live by the standards he had learned as a child at Groby and at school. Slowly he sees how his real feelings unite him with the front-line troops—"gaily rueful and impenitently profane"—rather than with the outwardly still confident and correct rulers of the Edwardian world, the General Campions and the Macmasters.

Then, by a movement of the mind that is logically incomprehensible but perfectly coherent psychologically, his brooding about the war brings him to the discovery that he loves Valentine Wannop. He has been thinking of the Germans across No Man's Land, "confoundedly irritated to think of the mess they had made of his nice clean trenches."

The beastly Huns! They stood between him and Valentine Wannop. If they would go home he could be sitting talking to her for whole afternoons. That was what a young woman was for. You seduced a young woman in order to be able to finish your talks with her. You could not do that without living with her. You could not live with her without seducing her; but that was a by-product. . . . You have to wait together—for a week, for a year, for a lifetime—before the final intimate conversation may be attained . . . and exhausted. So that . . .

That in effect was love. It struck him as astonishing. The word was so little in his vocabulary. . . . Love, ambition, the desire for wealth. They were things he had never known of as existing—as capable of existing within him. He had been the Younger Son. . . .

Now: what the hell was he? A sort of Hamlet of the Trenches! No, by God he was not. . . . He was perfectly ready for action. Ready to command a battalion. He was presumably a lover. They did things like commanding battalions. And worse!

He ought to write her a letter. What in the world would she think of this gentleman who had once made improper proposals to her, balked, said "So long!" or perhaps not even "So long!" And then walked off. With never a letter! Not even a picture postcard! For two years! A sort of Hamlet all right! Or a swine!

Well, then, he ought to write her a letter. He ought to say: "This is to tell you that I propose to live with you as soon as this show is over. You will be prepared immediately on cessation of active hostilities to put yourself at my disposal; please. Signed, " 'Xtopher Tietjens, Acting O.C. 9th Glams.' " A proper military communication (pp. 132–33).

Thus Christopher becomes conscious of his mind's decision to shuck off the character of the Younger Son, "a sort of eternal Second-in-Command" of Edwardian society, the character he had, with such simplicity of idealism and such agony of effort, been trying to live up to in a world where that character no longer made sense. Fused in his mind are the psychologically related decisions about his public role ("He was perfectly ready for action. Ready to command a battalion") and about his private life (" . . . put yourself at my disposal; please"). In wry amusement at the psychologically coherent but logically absurd fusion of these feelings, he imagines his proposal to Valentine in military language: "A proper military communication."

The passage is a characteristic example of Ford's kind of interior monologue, a typical illustration of *Parade's End*'s wonderfully dramatic representation of the way the mind can carry on simultaneously two or three emotionally linked trains of thought without confusion or loss of meaning. It dramatizes in something like interior conversation the complicated, tenuous movements of thought and feeling that constitute the life of the mind. By these means it shows us the way Christopher's conscious mind struggles against the resistance of its own official commitments through a series of ideas connected by underground links of feeling toward an understanding of its own unconscious decision, until it discovers suddenly ("It struck him as astonishing") its own commitment ("That in effect was love"), its determination to act ("He was perfectly ready for action"), and the action it intends to take ("He was presumably a lover. They did things like command battalions. And worse! He ought to write her a letter").

Once Christopher has reached this point, he can see that he must cease to try to carry out what he has heretofore thought his duty, his job in the Imperial Department of Statistics (which wanted him to betray the principles it presumably stood for and fake figures) and his gentlemanly loyalty to Sylvia (who wishes he would beat her). He will resign from this world and start afresh with Valentine in exile.

Part Two of *A Man Could Stand Up—*, then, though it has no visible chronological relation to Part One, parallels it very closely in meaning. Part One had shown us the psychological process of Valentine discovering the irrelevance of her Edwardian character ("It isn't what I *want*—to be a cross between a sergeant in the army and an upper housemaid") and determining to discard it, and simultaneously discovering her love for Christopher and determining to act on it ("Who cares!"). Part Two shows us Christopher discovering the irrelevance of his Younger-Son character and determining to discard it, and simultaneously discovering his love for Valentine and determining to act on it.

Part Three therefore begins as Valentine, carrying out her decision to join Christopher, arrives in the square; it is about noon of Armistice Day. Through the next few hours we are alternately in the minds of Valentine and Christopher as, almost wholly without words—but with assistance from the enlightened Victorian voice of Mrs. Wannop speaking to them from a considerable physical and psychological distance (these remote telephonic voices are heard speaking faintly and with ethical irrelevance by both Valentine and Christopher throughout *A Man Could Stand Up—*)— Christopher and Valentine approach complete understanding. The novel ends with a party at Christopher's house, now stripped by Sylvia of all its beautiful old furniture and decorated with only Christopher's camp-bed. Christopher and Valentine are celebrating the end of both the world war and their more private social war; therefore they celebrate in the company, not of the General Campions and the Macmasters, but of an incongruously mixed group of Christopher's frontline friends. The last words of the book indicate clearly what has happened, as Valentine, in Christopher's arms as they dance together, thinks, "On an elephant. A dear, mealsack elephant. She was setting out on . . ."

Once Ford's characteristic form is clear to us in *A Man*

Could Stand Up—, we can see that it is used, with minor variations, in the other three novels. *No More Parades* is also organized into three acts. The first covers a typical night in Christopher's hut at the base near Rouen as he struggles with the endless problems of his command. The second covers the next night at the hotel in Rouen as Christopher struggles with the equally endless problems of his marriage with Sylvia. The third covers the next morning, again in Christopher's hut, as he struggles even more fiercely with himself during the well-intentioned but uncomprehending cross-examination of General Campion. *Some Do Not . . .* is also divided into three acts, though this design is half concealed by the fact that both the first and third acts are subdivided into scenes. *Last Post,* unlike the other three novels, has no clear act divisions, but is like them strictly limited as to time and place: it takes place entirely in and about Christopher's cottage and lasts one afternoon. It is divided into scenes rather than acts, each of which is governed by the interior monologue of one character—Mark, Marie Léonie, Cramp, young Mark, Mark (the solid center of the novel), Marie Léonie, Sylvia, Valentine, and finally Mark with his magnificent dying meditation.

The structure of the tetralogy as a whole is similar to that of the constituent novels. The main lines of Ford's subject—the breakup of civilization in a world war and the collapse of Christopher's private life in a sexual war with Sylvia—have been laid down by the end of *Some Do Not. . . .* Although the chronological sequence of events that underlies *Parade's End* moves in time in the three succeeding novels, each of them is primarily concerned to go back over the two wars of *Some Do Not . . .* in order to penetrate more deeply into their meanings. Each of the succeeding novels, therefore, overlaps *Some Do Not . . .* and constitutes a parallel to some part of it. In *No More Parades* Christopher's experience of both the public and the private war is given us directly and in detail. In *A Man Could Stand Up*— he becomes fully conscious of the meaning of the war and, as a consequence, commits himself to the decision that was logically indicated but not consciously present in his mind at the end of *Some Do Not . . .* when he confronted Sylvia in the darkened room in Gray's Inn and then, after she had walked out, heard her say to the cab-driver, "Paddington"—that is, the decision to end the intolerable strain of his public pretense of a marriage with Sylvia and of his effort to serve his society, and to begin anew with Valentine in exile. *Last Post* shows us the conscious, almost willed death of the old society embodied in Mark, a death that was implicit in Mark's observation when he discovered in *Some Do Not* . . . that Christopher's check had been dishonored by a maliciously dishonest banker: "By God! this is the last of England." At the same time, *Last Post* is showing us, indirectly, the birth of the new life that Christopher and Valentine are struggling to build for the child Valentine is carrying, the child for whom Mark speaks at last, as he is dying:

> " ' 'Twas the mid o' the night and the barnies grat
> And the mither beneath the mauld heard that. . . .' "

"Perhaps it would be best not to tell Lady Tietjens [Marie Léonie] that he spoke. . . . She would like to have had his last words. . . . But she did not need them as much as I," Valentine says.

3 ⁓

Thus, although the action of *Parade's End* is frequently dramatized in scenes that have the concreteness and immediacy of realistic narration, the relations of the events within each scene and the relations of the scenes within the total structure of *Parade's End* are such that the reader is always more aware of the evaluating connections of the events than he is of their "objective" chronological relations. The form of the novel, that is, is determined by an understanding; it is what Ford called "an impression." Intensely realistic though the representation of the separate events is, they are made, by a process of selection and arrangement, into something that is less like a history than like a poem in which the events are unified by the meaning they have for the perceiving consciousness of the author.

For example, General Campion, driving through a dense fog a new-fangled automobile he has no real idea how to control, comes with reckless confidence out of his driveway and crashes into the old-fashioned, reliable horse Christopher drives with complete understanding. The whole difference between the two men is implicit in that crash, and behind that there is the distinction between conventional rectitude and genuine rectitude that is very close to the center of the novel's meaning. General Campion will show the same self-confident irresponsibility when he is in control of the war machine in France, and Christopher the same frustrated rightness about Schomburg, the coffin-headed bright chestnut he rides regularly. Ford's description of the accident itself is a good example of the characteristic way in which he modified Conrad's trick of describing events, not in their logical order, but in the order they have for the surprised participant. In Ford's description we move in and out of the participant's mind.

> Not ten yards ahead Tietjens saw a tea-tray, the underneath of a black-lacquered tea-tray, gliding towards them: mathematically straight, just rising from the mist. He shouted: mad: the blood in his head. His shout was drowned by the scream of the horse (*Some Do Not. . . .* p. 144).

(The description of the shelling at the front in *No More Parades* begins: "An immense tea-tray, august, its voice filling the black circle of the horizon, thundered to the ground.")

Or, amidst the luxuries of the Duchemin dining room, sits "Breakfast" Duchemin, a sex-obsessed lunatic of the most impeccable antecedents, with an ex-prizefighter behind his chair to control him, muttering, *"Post coitum tristis!* Ha! Ha!" or suddenly shouting, "Chaste you observe! What a world of suggestion in the word . . ." This vividly realistic scene evokes echoes from half a dozen other places in the novel. "I stand," says Christopher firmly to Macmaster, "for monogamy and chastity." "The man with the oily hair [in the golf house] said in a sickly voice that Gertie was hot stuff, but not the one for Budapest with all the Gitana girls. . . ." "Strip the bitch naked! . . . Ugh . . . Strip the bitch stark naked," he shouts as he chases Gertie Wilson across the golf links. "Look here, Edie," Valentine says to the mock-chaste Mrs. Duchemin. "Stop worrying about my mind. If you think anything I hear at your table after nine months as an ash-cat at Ealing, with three men in the house, an invalid wife and a drunken cook, can corrupt my mind, you're simply mistaken. . . . But . . . I'd like you to understand that in spite of it all I'm pure! Chaste, you know. . . . Perfectly virtuous." "There's something beautiful, there's something *thrilling* about chastity," says Mrs. Duchemin in her best false-profound Pre-Raphaelite manner. "You mean like an egg and spoon race," says Valentine. These echoes ultimately reach out through the tetralogy, linking up with the whole complex of dramatized judgments of sexual relations that are at the heart of *Parade's End*'s image of the social and private life of its time.

Behind these impressions made by the scenes are the impressions made by the settings. There is the Duchemins' house with all its sensuous luxury, its paneling, its orange Turners, its Chippendale, its rich food; there is Mrs. Wannop's cottage with its silver picked up at sales, its old cut glass, its "admirable lunch of cold lamb, new potatoes and mint sauce variety"; there is Christopher's house in Gray's Inn with the "eighteenth-century distinction" of its breakfast room, where, on a mindless impulse, Sylvia throws a plateful of cold cutlets in aspic and several leaves of salad at Christopher's head.

Behind these impressions, in turn, are those of the literal action of the novel. There is, for example, the contrast between Macmaster's steady, unscrupulous climb up the social ladder and Christopher's equally steady, scrupulous slide down it. This leads us to the contrast between their sexual lives. On one hand, there is the unspoken, even unconscious, love for Valentine Wannop of the already married Christopher Tietjens, with its sharp, happy arguments over Ovid and Catullus and its strict personal discipline: "Steady, the Buffs!" Christopher exclaims to himself when he is shocked by the discovery of an impulse to kiss Valentine. On the other hand, there is the talkative, consciously posturing love of Macmaster for the already married Mrs. Duchemin, with its easy seduction carried on to the accompaniment of quotations from Rossetti about the thrills of chastity ("Better far though hearts may break,/Since we dare not love,/Part till we once more may meet/In a Heaven above")—and its outbursts of fishwife vulgarity from Mrs. Duchemin when she imagines she is pregnant.

4 ~

Behind all these impressions, their final cause and the meaning toward which they all ultimately point, is Ford's impression of the age as a whole. The living history of this age is in the effects it has on the consciousnesses of the individual characters, and Ford puts them in the foreground. But that history is also present in the temporal sequence of socially significant events, and therefore Ford indicates carefully, in the background of his novel, all the chronological and causal facts of that history. Perhaps these facts were easier to sort out when the period itself was more familiar to readers than it is today. Or perhaps readers, failing to see how radical are the effects of Ford's inversion of the form of the conventional novel, fail to read *Parade's End* with the kind of attention it demands. The very success Ford has in adopting realistic detail to his impressionistic purposes may mislead them into doing so. But *Parade's End* cannot be read as a realistic novel.

The determinant of the formal arrangement of events in a conventional realistic novel is their temporal and causal sequence. The evaluative relations between them can be established—by incidental cross-references, repetitions, and allusions—only after the temporal and causal relations have been formally established. The reader must therefore be specially alert for hints of the evaluative relations and must work them out with some care. But in *Parade's End* the determinant of the formal arrangement of events is a perceiving consciousness with its insistence on giving precedence to the evaluative relations of events. By concentrating the action into acts and scenes that are strictly limited as to place and time, Ford limits the freedom of this consciousness and sets bounds to the otherwise shapeless fluidity of interior monologue. Nevertheless, the scenes are arranged in a meaningful, not a chronological order, and within each scene we are most of the time inside the minds of the characters. In a novel thus ordered, the chronological and logical relations of events can be indicated—by psychologically plausible allusions to significant dates and causally important incidents —only after the evaluative relations have been formally established.

In *Parade's End* what the reader sees immediately is the impression of the events in the minds of the characters and the author; what he must work out with some care is their chronological and causal relations. The critical books about Ford suggest that this kind of explication does not come easily. One of the best of them tells us that Christopher first possessed Sylvia in a French train compartment; it was in fact "in a railway carriage, coming down from the Dukeries" (*Some Do Not* . . . p. 127). (The Dukeries are what remains of Sherwood Forest and are in the western part of Nottinghamshire.) That kind of slip is perhaps minor, but it is indicative; less careful critics go visibly astray about major details, asserting, for example, that *Some Do Not* . . . starts in 1908, which is four years too early, and that Sylvia and Christopher are preparing for bed in Sylvia's hotel room in Rouen, when the point of this crucial scene in *No More Parades* is that Sylvia is trying to seduce Christopher, who will not sleep with her and comes to her room only to discuss their strained relations.

It is important to understand this pattern of chronological and causal relations in the background of *Parade's End,* just as it is important to understand the pattern of evaluative relations in the background of the conventional novel. It may help the reader to do so if the main chronological sequence of *Parade's End* is summarized.

5 ~

The story begins at the end of June, 1912, when Christopher Tietjens (twenty-six years old and the youngest child of an old Yorkshire family of four sons and two daughters) and Vincent Macmaster are traveling down from London to Rye to play golf and to interview a man named Duchemin, who has known Rossetti, about whom Macmaster has been writing a monograph in the hope of gaining promotion in the Imperial Department of Statistics, for which both young men work. Christopher's wife, Sylvia, had run off four months earlier with a man named Perowne. Sylvia, who is four years older than Christopher, had trapped him into marriage when she thought herself—mistakenly as it turns out—pregnant by an earlier lover. She has just written Christopher that she wishes to return to him, having with some difficulty escaped from the violently possessive Perowne at a town called Yssingueux-les-Pervenches and joined her mother, who has been living at a German air resort named Lobscheid pretending for the benefit of London society that Sylvia is with her. Sylvia has just ordered Christopher to come to Lobscheid and get her. It is his worry over this problem, complicated for him by his idealistic Tory conception of the gentlemanly attitude in sexual relations and marriage, that makes him so furiously impatient with Macmaster's laboriously pretentious essay on Rossetti and his later Pre-Raphaelite "gurglings" over Mrs. Duchemin.

On the following Saturday the two young men breakfast at the Duchemins, and that same night Christopher and Valentine take their memorable drive to deliver Gertie Wilson, Valentine's suffragette friend, to Valentine's uncle's house some thirty miles away. On the following Tuesday, at five-fifteen A.M., Christopher leaves to join Sylvia at Lobscheid. His plan is that they shall make an appearance at Wiesbaden to quiet any possible gossip. But when he arrives at Lobscheid, he receives word that his mother has died, apparently of a heart broken by the knowledge that Sylvia is returning to Christopher. Christopher cannot then take Sylvia to Wiesbaden, since they have to go into mourning; he cannot take her to England because he will not have her at his beloved mother's funeral. He therefore takes her on an extended trip to Kiev.

From then until 1915 Christopher and Sylvia, though they do not live together as husband and wife, keep up the appearance of marriage. Just before the outbreak of the war, in July, 1914, they are visiting at Bamborough, in the north of England. Christopher leaves Sylvia at Bamborough to go and stay at a nearby cottage where his sister Effie has been caring for their child since Sylvia's escapade with Perowne in 1912. (Somewhat confusingly, this child is called Tommie in *Some Do Not . . .* , later Michael, and later still, Mark, though in *Last Post* it is explained that he was originally christened Mark and renamed Michael by Sylvia when he was received into the Catholic Church.)

While Christopher is with his sister, Macmaster arrives, much agitated because he and Mrs. Duchemin have been spending what they intended to be a quiet lovers' weekend together and have been discovered by friends who may at any minute realize that they are lovers. To help them out of this difficulty, Christopher escorts Mrs. Duchemin back to London. It is August 3, 1914, the day war was declared, and everyone who is anybody is on the train hurrying back to London; they all see Mrs. Duchemin weeping on Christopher's shoulder and this starts the rumor that Mrs. Duchemin is Christopher's mistress, which Sylvia keeps alive for the rest of *Parade's End*.

Christopher continues to work in the Imperial Department of Statistics for a little more than a year after the war starts, but by the fall of 1915 he cannot any longer bear faking statistics to help the British government blackmail France. In November, 1915, at one of Macmaster's receptions, where Mrs. Duchemin presides with all her Machiavellian skill in assisting Macmaster to climb to the top, Christopher tells Valentine he cannot reconcile it with his conscience not to enlist. He reaches the front early in 1916 and is in the fighting throughout that year. Early in 1917, he is shell-shocked and invalided home. In August, 1917, he is

declared fit again and is returned to France, though his
memory is still gone. When he goes, Sylvia retires to a
nunnery at Birkenhead, where she stays for two and a half
months reading prewar romances.

Shortly after Christopher's arrival in France he is hos-
pitalized with lung trouble, but a month after his return he
is back on duty, in command of a staging base for new
drafts, near Rouen, where Brigadier-General Campion has
his headquarters. With the help of Perowne, who is on
Campion's staff, Sylvia makes her way to Rouen in November in pursuit of Christopher. There she gets Christopher
into such trouble that General Campion relieves him of his
base command and sends him to the front as second in
command of the Ninth Glamorganshires. He goes up February 14, 1918, and fights through the great battle of that
spring. In April, during the crisis of the battle, he is forced
by the collapse of the commanding colonel to take over the
battalion. Three days later General Campion relieves General Perry ("Old Puffles") of command of the whole army
and immediately takes Christopher's battalion away from him
and sends him to command a prisoner-of-war detail.

Early in the autumn Christopher is back in the hospital
with lung trouble, and from there, in October, he is sent to
a depot at Ealing. On October 20 he goes to see his brother
Mark, who is in bed with pneumonia and may die, and per-
suades Mark to marry his longtime mistress, Marie Léonie
Riotor. For the next three weeks Christopher helps nurse
Mark, and Mark, to Christopher's financial distress, uses his
influence to get Christopher demobilized just before Armistice Day.

On Armistice Day Christopher, needing money, starts out
from the house in Gray's Inn with the only piece of furniture
Sylvia has left in it, an eighteenth-century cabinet, to try to
sell it to Sir John Robertson, who had once offered one
hundred pounds for it. He meets Valentine as he comes out
the door and tells her to go upstairs and wait for him. Sir
John—since taught by Sylvia to hate Christopher—now offers five pounds for the cabinet. Christopher then carries it
to Mark's house, where he arrives shortly before noon. Mark
refuses to lend him money on the cabinet, insisting that he
accept his share of the Groby estate, which he will not do.
"Pour le dieu d'amour," Marie Léonie lends him forty pounds.

Christopher then returns to Gray's Inn and he and Valentine, together with Aranjuez, his Nancy, and "the pals," go
out to dinner to celebrate the armistice; as they are driving

home afterwards, Christopher's ex-colonel dies in the cab. Valentine and Christopher finally arrive back at Gray's Inn and are met there by Sylvia, who announces that she is dying of cancer, pretends to faint, and falls down the stairs, putting her ankle out of joint. Valentine fiercely insists that Christopher not assist Sylvia but return with her to Mark's house, where they arrive at two in the morning. When they finally leave for Christopher's house once more, Marie Léonie receives a call from Lord Wolstonmark in Mark's office announcing that the allies are not going to occupy Berlin. When she conveys this information to Mark he has a stroke. Marie Léonie calls Christopher and Valentine and they return. Thus passes their "honeymoon."

Last Post picks the story up six months later, about June, 1920. During the interim Sylvia has first played sick and then started divorce proceedings, not intending to carry them through (she is a Catholic) but wanting her lawyer to have a chance to malign Christopher publicly. During the single afternoon covered by the present time of *Last Post* Sylvia is overwhelmed by the discovery that Valentine is pregnant and by a vision of Father Consett, her confessor, who had been killed with Roger Casement; she decides to give up her war against Christopher and to leave him and Valentine in peace. Mark, no longer having to "will against" her, dies.

Parade's End concludes with Christopher and Valentine struggling to build up the new life for Chrissie to inherit. At the same time, the sustaining will of the old life dies in Mark, and it has no heir, literal or figurative, because Sylvia's son by Christopher refuses Sylvia's name for him (Michael) and dissociates himself from Sylvia's attack on Valentine and Christopher. Even those who cling to the Edwardian way of life have lost faith in it: General Campion, still helplessly charmed by Sylvia, has ceased to believe Sylvia's more and more desperate lies about Christopher; and Sylvia herself, losing all hope of winning her war against Christopher, decides to marry Campion and go with him to India, that last, dying satrapy of Edwardian empire, where what even Sylvia knows now to be the meaningless parade of the old life can be continued for a little while.

ARTHUR MIZENER

A NOTE ON THE TEXT

This Signet Classic edition reprints the first editions of *A Man Could Stand Up—* (1926) and *Last Post* (1928), published by Gerald Duckworth & Co., Ltd., London.

Punctuation and spelling have largely been brought into conformity with current British usage, and obvious typographical errors have been corrected.

SELECTED BIBLIOGRAPHY

OTHER WORKS BY FORD MADOX FORD

The Fifth Queen, 1906 Novel
Privy Seal, 1907 Novel
The Fifth Queen Crowned, 1908 Novel
Ancient Lights and Certain New Reflections, 1910 Memoirs
The Young Lovell: A Romance, 1913
Henry James: A Critical Study, 1913
The Good Soldier, 1915 Novel
Joseph Conrad: A Personal Remembrance, 1924
No Enemy: A Tale of Reconstruction, 1929 Novel
Return to Yesterday, 1931 Memoirs
It was the Nightingale, 1933 Memoirs
Ladies Whose Bright Eyes: A Romance, 1935
Provence: From Minstrels to the Machine, 1935
The Great Trade Route, 1937 Novel
Portraits from Life, 1937 Memoirs

BIOGRAPHY AND CRITICISM

Bowen, Stella. *Drawn from Life*. New York and London: William Collins Sons & Co., Ltd., 1941.

Cassell, R. A. *Ford Madox Ford*. Baltimore: Johns Hopkins Press, 1962.

Goldring, Douglas. *Trained for Genius*. New York: E. P. Dutton & Co., Inc., 1949.

Hunt, Violet. *I Have This to Say: The Story of My Flurried Years*. New York: Boni & Liveright, 1926.

Lid, R. W. *Ford Madox Ford: The Essence of His Art*. In preparation, to be published by the University of California Press, Berkeley.

Meixner, J. A. *Ford Madox Ford's Novels*. Minneapolis: University of Minnesota Press, 1962.

Ohmann, Carol. *Ford Madox Ford: From Apprentice to Craftsman*. Middletown, Conn.: Wesleyan University Press, 1964.

Wiley, P. L. *Novelist of Three Worlds: Ford Ma* Syracuse, N.Y.: Syracuse University Press, 1